THINGS THAT GO DARK IN THE LIGHT

STAN G. DUNCAN

CONTENTS

 1. Borders — 1

 2. The Leaving — 9

 3. Apartment — 13

 4. The Call — 19

 5. Donuts — 25

 6. The Institute — 37

 7. Closing — 45

 8. The First — 49

 9. The Plaza — 57

10. Escalón — 65

11. The Incident — 69

12. Moving Day — 79

13. Pupuseria — 81

14. Bety's — 85

15. Zacamil — 93

16. Universario — 99

17. Embassy — 111

18. Dinner — 121

19. Phone Call — 127

20. Visitor — 131

21. Usaid — 135

22. Leer — 147

23. The Sickness — 157

24. The Morning — 161

25. Tours — 167

26. Clínica De Emergencia Rural — 173

27. Normal — 179

28. Oficina De Identificación De Víctimas — 189

29. Beers — 203

30. Encounter — 211

31. Héctor 215
32. Doug 223
33. Beers II 231
34. Robbie 239
35. Visitor 245
36. Last Night 253
37. Zacamil 259
38. Bus 267
39. Report 275
40. El Campo 281
41. Check Points 285
42. Baby 291
43. Arrival 295
44. Los Morros 301
45. Assignment 317
46. Market 323
47. San Salvador 327
48. School 331
49. Truck 335
50. Tank 341
51. Sara 343
52. David 347
53. Sara 353
54. Tank 357
55. Los Cañones 363
56. Tank 365
57. Sara 367
58. Tank 369
59. David and Sara 371
Epilogue 373

Things That Go Dark in the Light

A Novel by

STAN G. DUNCAN

Paperback ISBN: 979-8-89283-264-9
Ebook ISBN: 979-8-89283-265-6

For any information contact Stan G. Duncan, at standuncan@post.harvard.edu

Published by:

Books to Hook Publishing
bookstohook.com

Printed in the United States of America

My editor, David E. Potts,
my publicists, Charlotte Flair and Tamara Mitchell,
my friend, Susan Peterson,
and my children, who kept me sane.

El Salvador

anales
CA10
CA11A
Comayagua
Jutiapa
Palmerola
CA1
CA7
17
Chalatenango
Santa Ana
°Los Morros
Ahuachapan
7
Sonsonate
San Salvador
El Salvador
3
Acajutla
Santa Tecla
San Miguel
1
CA1
La Libertad
2
Usulutan
La Union
2

CHAPTER ONE

BORDERS

David should never have said yes to any of this, but after coming this far, there wasn't much he could do to get out of it now. He was a thousand miles from home, traveling through sun-warped villages, mountains, forests, and an endless amount of dust for a job he knew almost nothing about. And for a pay that would be an embarrassment to one of his student interns. But what would "home" look like anymore if he tried to go back to it? What did he have to go back to?

Of course, he made it worse by mistakenly taking the domestic bus out of Mexico City instead of the international one, which meant they had wandered off the more direct route and stopped at least five times (maybe ten?) instead of just twice at the borders of Guatemala and El Salvador. Whenever the bus stopped, he had to get off, unload his suitcase and backpack, wait in the station for the next bus, and then check his bags and re-board again. For that mistake, a simple trip from Mexico City to San Salvador, which would normally take about two days, had dragged on for four, and they were only now approaching the final border-crossing at San Cristóbal Frontera. When the bus touched the edge of town and slowly wound its way through the maze of people, animals, and market carts, he should have been relieved, but instead, he was just tired, his long legs were painfully folded up against the seat in front of him, and he was irritable.

He began to realize that they were nearing the final border when, late in the afternoon, with sun still burning down on top of them, people in the seats in front of him started shifting towards the aisle, clutching their possessions as though making ready to exit. Bags, food, boxes, a cage of chickens, and two small children, with eyes wide open, who were staring in amazement at his strange face, light hair, and long legs, which were now stretched into the aisle for relief. The bus had been on the road that day for about six hours, and David was more than ready to stop anywhere, even if it was just for gas and to use the *servicios*. And now, with emotions of both relief and anger, he could finally see the border crossing into El Salvador at San Cristóbal.

Spanning the street in the center of the town was a high, imposing arch that connected the *Aduana* customs offices on both sides. One side for people traveling into El Salvador and the other for people coming out. When the bus stopped, the adults, children, and luggage (and the cage of chickens) were ushered off and into a long, restless line in front of the main entrance. Wearily, David dragged his legs, his overstuffed suit-case, and new black backpack to the line with the others, and there all of them stood and waited. Unfortunately, they had arrived at 3:00 in the afternoon, when the entire staff was still eating their mid-day *almuerzo*, so all the bus passengers had to stand, one by one, in the sun—the afternoon *hot* sun—waiting and waiting and waiting...

Eventually, after what felt like an impossible amount of

time, a door opened, and the exhausted travelers were allowed to enter the migration office and sit down. When David entered, he looked around and blinked to see in the darkened light. It was a plain, dimly lit room, with rows of benches facing two desks at the front. Each was decorated with stacks of papers, an ink blotter, a black rotary phone, and an apparently bored *escribiano* behind it processing papers. Along the walls were the national flag of El Salvador, a map of Central America, various posters of the greatness of the country (including one with US vice president, George H. W. Bush shaking hands with Salvadoran president, Álvaro Magaña), and faded copies of typed instructions listing what documents the applicants had to have with them when their turn in line arrived. The clerks at the desks slowly pored over the passenger papers, stamping and re-stamping each sheet three or four times, attempting to give the illusion of multiple levels of competent oversight to what seemed otherwise to be an intentionally punishing process. When David's time came, they thumbed vacantly through random pages in his notebooks and backpack. None gave any indication that they could read English, so if he happened to have anything they could hold against him, there was little chance they would have known it. Nonetheless, they seemed to want to make sure he knew that they had seen it, with their own eyes, just in case.

Several young men were standing in the entrance. Most looked to be in their early twenties, though some perhaps even younger, dressed in military olive drab and carrying rifles that were nearly as long as they were tall. David recognized them as M16s, that were a recent American gift to the Salvadoran Army. They were somewhat dated by US standards, and he smiled when he thought about it. The US military had never totally accepted the Reagan Administration's obsession with anti-communist wars in Central America, and one way they expressed their displeasure was by sending second-hand weapons to El Salvador and saving the shiny new versions for themselves. Ironically, those rifles were also a popular weapon of the revolutionary guerrilla coalition, the FMLN, because they could be purchased cheaply from corrupt Salvadoran commanders or confiscated when government troops fled an outpost under rebel attack.

Young boys were swarming around the doorways, aged about ten to twelve, offering to help travelers with their bags or papers or any other need, for a small fee. When David came into the room, he was immediately noticed and surrounded by eager young faces competing for his attention. He was taller and whiter than everyone else in the room and looked tired and confused, a perfect match for their services. This was, of course, their way of making a living for families at home who were desperate for any tips or cash that foreigners could bestow upon them. David was sympathetic, but he was weary and didn't need any help, so he waved his hand through the strap of his backpack and said "No, no, no," as firmly as he could. He sat in one of the metal folding chairs and turned it to the wall, hoping to send them a message. Most of them eventually moved away and searched for other customers, but one of them steadfastly refused his signals and wouldn't leave. He was a small boy, very eager, perhaps not quite ten (though it was hard to tell), who wore faded pants and a gray tee shirt that hung to his knees, and he wouldn't leave. He begged and begged for David to let him be of service.

David tried to be firm. "*No es necesario,*" he said, "It's not necessary." But the boy refused to leave and pleaded again. David tried to be kind, but he wasn't carrying too much cash and didn't want to spend it on aid that he didn't need. But the boy kept at it and begged to be allowed to help with David's bags or papers...or even arrange something for his dating life if desired. David legitimately felt sorry for him. He looked beaten and far too fragile for what should have been ~~an~~ a young, exuberant boy. He was dark and sweaty, and his hair was matted with sand and dust. The boy squinted. He needs glasses, David thought. He can barely see me.

"*¿Como se llama?*" David asked, "What is your name?"

"*Guillermo,*" the boy said. Normally, that would be "William" or "Bill" in English, but he shouted out, "*Mi nombre es 'Gil' en Inglés.*" The boy was proud of having a name that could also double for English.

"Gil," David said, now smiling. He didn't know much Spanish yet, but he pointed to his bag and made a lifting gesture with his hands. "*¿Cuánto cobran?*" "How much do you charge?" He didn't think that was exactly right, but it would do.

"*Dos colones,*" Gil said. It was an almost criminally small amount. The dollar value of two Salvadoran *colones* in 1989 was about seventy-five cents, but a cheap exchange for David would be a windfall for little Gil.

In his halting Spanish, he asked Gil if he would take four *colones* as payment to *not* carry his bags. Gil's eyes opened wide, yes, of course he would!

David took out his wallet, peeled off four *colones,* and gave them to the boy. Thank God he had changed a little money at an earlier stop so that he didn't have to negotiate with this kid over the relative prices of Guatemalan *quetzales* to Salvadoran *colones.* That would be an endless—and probably nationalistic—debate that could go on and on and have little to do with bags and little boys who carried them.

Gil took the money and ran from the room (to stash it in a hiding place?) but then returned minutes later offering to carry David's bags as though nothing had happened between them. "*¡No!*" David said to him, this time growing angry. "It isn't necessary! I don't need you." David didn't know enough Spanish to get into a shouting match with a little boy, and soon he'd run out of ways to say "no." But it didn't matter anyway, because Gil seemed oblivious to any words David might have used in either language.

"Please, Gil, no," he yelled, pulling back on his backpack. "I really don't need you. I'm sorry, I just want to sit here. I can't help you!"

But instead of backing off, Gil lunged for the strap of David's backpack and tried to sling it over his shoulder. It was almost as big as he was, so he couldn't have been much help, even if David had gone along. Then he reached for the handle of the suitcase, knocking it over and David heard a loud snapping sound coming from under it. One of the wheels on its bottom had broken off.

"Gil!" he screamed, "*¡Detente!*" "Stop it. Just stop it. I don't want you to help me, and I can't help you. Do you get it? I *can't* help you. Leave me alone. *I can't help you.*"

He felt something swell inside of him that felt more like grief than anger at his inability to help this little boy and stop his onslaught of eagerness. His eyes were tearing as he yelled. He grabbed the handle of his suitcase and pulled it back, pulling Gil and the bag nearly on top of him; they both fell awkwardly to the ground. As he attempted to roll to his knees and lift his suitcase back upright, a deafening sound like a clap of thunder roared through the room. He didn't realize what it was at first because he was still pulling on his suitcase. But then he sensed that Gil had stopped pulling back. In fact, he was limp and barely moving at all. He looked up at David with a questioning, puzzled look on his face and then fell back onto the bag. There was another explosion and Gil's body jerked a second time in response. Blood beaded through new holes in his frayed tee shirt. David dropped the bag and lifted Gil's head and looked closely at his eyes. They kept their puzzled look, but there was no life in them. "Gil," David shouted. "Can you hear me? Gil!" He lifted Gil's small body and held it tightly in his arms, crying, Gil's blood now shared between them. He looked around the room. People looked uncomfortable, but not at him. "Somebody help us," he shouted, "*¡Ayúdamos!*" "Is there someone here who is a doctor?" Stupid question, he thought, in the entire town, there was probably only one doctor, and he wouldn't be in a bus station. He looked frantically for someone in authority to look up, but everyone seemed intent on being overly involved with paperwork, passports, and visas, and not with him. "Can someone help us?"

Then he saw someone. Standing directly across from him, several yards behind where Gil had been, standing against a wall, holding a vintage M16, was a smiling face. But it wasn't a face of help or sympathy, it was a face of pride. There, standing proudly in front of them, was a young man, not many years older than Gil, smiling, and with an earnest look on his face, as though expecting a reward or a word of praise. This was the creature who had just murdered a little boy, David thought. The young soldier continued to smile at him, even while David was screaming in horror and begging for help. The young man was waiting to be thanked. He thought he had done something good. He thought he was helping out the tall gringo who needed the removal of a source of irritation. He had murdered a little boy to help David in an argument over whether to carry a bag.

The young man against the wall nodded, as though speaking. He seemed to be saying, *Yes, did I do good? Are you pleased?*

David felt a sickness swell in his stomach. A sickness of memories of death that were larger than Gil, larger than the room, and made his vision swirl and break. He held Gil in his arms, leaning against the wall, and slid down to the floor. He closed the boy's eyes and wailed in horror. After a long moment, he looked around the room again and noticed for the first time a banner hanging on the wall behind the desks at the front. It said, *"Bienvenido a El Salvador."* "Welcome to El Salvador."

CHAPTER TWO

THE LEAVING

David, you've got to quit this, and you know it." Bernard was not smiling. He was pacing and he was breathing heavily, and he was late for a faculty meeting that he was supposed to chair. His office had dark wood paneling all around it and his desk, chair and overstuffed sofa were all dark. And today it all matched because Bernard's mood was also dark.

"You're miserable here and your students know it, and you know it, and everyone knows it." In fact, David did know it, but he didn't know how to change it. "You've got to pull yourself together, take a break, see a therapist, move up your sabbatical—we can swing that—or quit altogether, or...or do *something*." He waved his hands in the air, attempting to demonstrate the feeling of exasperation. "But this can't go on. You're going to ruin your career and ruin your life."

Bernard stopped pacing and stood facing David. He was not as tall as David but had a thick chest and heavy, unplumbed voice that gave off an aura of size and conviction. David refused to look at him and remained deep in the stuffed sofa, unable to move. He wanted to speak up and deny the reality that he had been missing his classes, showing up unprepared, and receiving complaints, but he couldn't do it because it was true. *Ruin my life?* he thought. *That's wrong. I don't have a life.*

Bernard stepped back to his desk, slid aside a pile of student essays, and sat down on it. "David, I care about you, and I want to support you. But my God, man, it's been over a year, and you have to start at least acting like you are alive again. I don't mean 'get over it,' that'll never happen. But at least get through it...somehow. You've got to. If you don't—or you can't—then eventually we won't be able to keep you, and if you have to leave under crappy circumstances, you probably won't be able to get another position. Anywhere. You understand? This is critical. Let someone help you. Can we get you a therapist or a priest? Or...Anything?"

David wanted to say something. He wanted to defend himself. He wanted to say it was going to be okay, that he'd gotten the message, and he would finally start preparing better for his classes again. But he couldn't. He couldn't ever see himself back teaching like he had before, and he couldn't lie and say he would. In fact, right now he wasn't sure that he could even say anything at all...to anyone. Bernard was right, it had been more than a year since Kathryn died, and he still wasn't "over" it. Kathryn was still all over their house. She was inside their car. Inside their bedroom. Inside his life. Half of his life had stopped living when she stopped living and he couldn't think or move or breathe with only half a lung, half a heart, half a mind.

Finally, he pulled some energy out of God-knows-where and raised his body into an upright position. "I'm sorry," he forced his mouth to say, "but I can't talk now. I've got to go."

He looked for the door. Bernard didn't expect that and rose like he was going to stop him.

"Where are you going?" he asked. "What are you going to do?"

David stopped with his hand on the door, but he was shaking. He couldn't think of anything more to say. "I don't know. I don't know what I am going to do."

Bernard put his hand on David's shoulder. "Son, you're going to be fine. You're strong inside. You're just going to have to get back on your feet again."

David pulled away from Bernard's hand and looked at the floor. "I don't know how to get back on my feet again. Kathryn should be alive now and she's not. I don't deserve to be back on my feet again." He turned back to Bernard with a look filled with wounds and hopelessness. As it happened it was the last look they'd ever share together for the rest of their lives. "I'm sorry, Bernard. I'm sorry. I'm sorry." He managed to close the door behind him and then wearily pulled his body down the hall and down the steps, then down the next hall and pushed open the outer doors to the front of the building and stopped. He sat down on a metal bench in front of the doors and took a deep breath. He put his face in his hands and cried.

CHAPTER THREE
APARTMENT

When David's bus finally pulled into the terminal in San Salvador, he looked out his window at the shadows of the city around him and wondered again if all of this had not been a terrible idea. His life had been a mess when Alf called him, so it was easy to say yes to anything that would take him away from that. But coming here was also crazy. And dangerous. Moving from a quiet suburban, south shore town in Massachusetts—even with his own miseries—to an unfamiliar, hard-to-find, poor country in the middle of a bloody civil war, could kill him. Or, he thought after standing, stretching, and getting in line with a dozen others slowly moving to get off the bus, on the other hand, if he survived this experience, it might possibly save him.

He retrieved his suitcase, with its broken wheel, and looked around the parking lot and the city landscape of San Salvador. At the terminal, he saw the hub of a modern transportation center. Rows of buses waiting or arriving, offices, lobbies, police guards, and lines of people at windows buying tickets.

But across the street from the high fence and gate into the terminal, were sounds and sights of a very Latin city, thick with walkers and shoppers. He saw multi-colored carts under canopies selling fruit, food, clothes, Tee shirts and pirated cassettes. The air was filled with smells of spit-roasted chicken, ground coffee, corn flour baking into tacos, and an occasional fragrance that might be urine. He stood there for some time watching the people and taking in the emotional textures of the scene. But he was exhausted from the trip and needed to move on. In addition, he was still shaken by the senseless killing of little Gil at the border, and how it pushed him back into memories of the death of Kathryn. Everything looked darker and more hopeless when seen from the lens of losing her. And it would be a long time before he got over, or around, or through all of that. He held out his hand at some passing taxis and immediately a stained and battered yellow car with the words "Taxi, Alessandra Lopez de Barillas" painted on the side swung towards him at the curb. A thin young woman, probably no more than 20, wearing a bright yellow tee-shirt and a Yankees ball cap, leaned over to the passenger window, and yelled up at him. She had a name tag on her shirt that said, "Lessi," over a hand-drawn smiley face. David smiled. She didn't look like a "Lessi." But then, she didn't look like an "Alessandra" either. "*¿A dónde vas?*" she said. "Where are you going?"

David dug down into his pocket and pulled out the letter Alf had sent him with directions. "*Momentito,*" he called back. He looked at the scrawled notes on the page. "Apartamentos Los Cañones," he called out to her. "*El número es...*" but he stopped. He couldn't remember how to say "one hundred twenty-one" in Spanish. So, he slowly counted out the single numbers, "*Uno...dos...uno,*" holding up one finger, then two, then one again, as he counted. Then, "Also it says, 'in back of the school.'"

"Back of school? I know this place," Lessi the young driver yelled back in English. "Maybe yes, I take you there?"

"You speak English?"

"No much, but a little. I speak to many *norteamericanos*. Get in please."

David pushed his bags across the back seat and slid in beside them. "What is the school it is in back of?"

Lessi darted back into the moving traffic, barely missing another taxi that was already in her lane. "I do not know, but it is *escuela privada*."

"Private school?"

"*Sí*, and with many *apartamentos* in its back. You will teach in the school?"

David thought for a moment about his answer, and then said slowly, "No I'm not...I'm *probably* not. No, I'll just be staying near it." It felt odd saying that he wouldn't be doing something that he actually had been doing for over six years since graduate school.

"There are maybe very many teachers who live there," said Lessi. "And there are many schools also in Zacamil. And you will maybe teach in one of them?"

David wanted to ask where, or what, was "Zacamil," but Lessi seemed more focused on outrunning the other cars around them. She weaved, swerved and lunged for several blocks, through thick and chaotic traffic, nearly missing one car and swearing at another. Eventually she turned down a smaller side street lined with a tall white wall bearing a larger-than-life painting of assassinated Archbishop Oscar Romero on it. The wall stood thirty feet high, with barbed wire coiled along the top and wrapped around the corner down into what appeared to be a long parking lot or wide alley. *"La escuela!"* she said and pulled the taxi into it looking for apartments. On the left side was the continuing wall, and on the right were trees, apartments, and houses. When they reached the end of the lot, Lessi slowed the taxi to a stop and leaned forward to look out of her front window. There before them were seven rows of long four-story apartment buildings, each separated by a walkway of sidewalks, trees, and shrubs and closed off at each end by tall chain-link fences and gates.

"Is this it?" asked David.

"Sí, Está allí," she said, pointing to the building directly in front of them. In large letters across the front were the words, *"Apartamentos Los Cañones."* She pointed again. "You see now the name, Los Cañones?" She had a big smile as though making a joke, but David didn't get it. "See," she said, "the tall rows, long like 'Cañones.'" She twisted her face, trying to remember a word. "They are ...Cañones. *No?"*

"Oh, *'Canyons'*! I get it."

"Sí, muy bueno," and she laughed again, as though they both had just heard the joke together. She got out of the taxi and opened the back door for David. "And you are here *'Uno dos, uno.'"* She pointed a few doors down beyond the gate in the first row.

David carefully backed out of the door, pulling his suitcase and backpack behind him. "Are you sure?"

"I am maybe sure," she said. *"Veinte colones."*

"Thanks for the ride," he said, taking a twenty-*colon* bill from his wallet and three ones for a tip. But as he took it, she began bowing before him, as though David had done her a great favor.

"Thank you more!" she said. "You are my first passenger."

"I was your *first?"* David wasn't sure he'd heard right, but she seemed very certain and very grateful.

Her eyes went wide open, as though just remembering

something. "*¡Se me olvidó!*" She reached back into the open car window and took out a small wooden box and held it up. "You must have one of this." She opened it, took out a small piece of paper, and offered it to David.

On it was a phone number, a tiny hand-drawn picture of a taxi, and the words typed,

"Alessandra Garcia Lopez, Mejor Taxi en El Salvador"

"This is us," she said holding up the paper proudly. "I am now starting, and these are our..." She paused, searching for a word. "*¡Tarjetas de visita! Sí?*"

David frowned. "You mean your 'business card'"?

"*¡Sí, sí, sí! ¿Es eso?*" "These are our first and you must have one. You will call me, it has my number, and I will drive you. I am careful driver, I have insurance, and I am best Taxi in San Salvador."

David smiled. She was thin and small and looked like a child, and yet she was launching her own business.

"I will be pleased to take your card, Lessi. And I promise I will call you some time for your help."

"Thank you, thank you, thank you. I will serve you many times. I know that you are a good man and are here to do good. And I will help you."

David didn't feel all that good at the moment, but he smiled again and put the card in his pocket.

She bowed a second time. "*¡Claro, Señor!* And it will be many times. I am safe for you, and I have insurance for you for my taxi." She turned and ran back to the car as quickly as she had jumped out of it and restarted the motor. David raised his hand to wave goodbye, but the small taxi had already burst back into the parking lot, nearly missing a larger car that was in its way. Then she was gone, leaving David standing alone with his backpack and suitcase staring at the big gate in front of him and the long line of doorways, sidewalks, and lawn. He looked at the paper in his hand again and up at the row of doors on the right. Four doors down, one had a small metal plate over its header that read simply, "121." Well, he thought, I guess I'm here. Now what?

CHAPTER FOUR
THE CALL

Just north of Bridgewater State College is a town called Abington. Founded in 1711, it's one of the old towns of Massachusetts. And the church in its center is even older, since towns in those days couldn't be founded unless there was first a church that could anchor it to the divine. Down the hill and around the corner was a long straight street named "Lincoln," supposedly named following a visit by the president in another age, but no one knew for sure. The street today was filled with sturdy, modest, middle-class homes, built in the 1950s and 60s during the first burst of growth after the war.

The very first in that row of houses was a two-story raised ranch with blue trim, a two-car garage, and shingle siding. In the driveway sat a black Mazda 323 Sedan, one that Kathryn had once dubbed "Molly Mazda," and David was sitting in it.

He wasn't sure, but he thought that he had been there for at least an hour, maybe more. And so far as he could see, there was little point in getting out after the next hour had passed either. There wasn't much to do once he went inside. He would just sit inside as he was now sitting outside and probably be less comfortable. He probably needed to take the trash out sometime because the next day was trash day, but that wasn't really very important. He also needed to do some laundry, but that wasn't important either. The lawn and the flowers and plants needed to be watered, but he was too tired and didn't really care what they looked like. If he left them alone long enough the flowers would eventually die, and he wouldn't have to worry about them again. And then the plants would die, and then the grass would die. And eventually, he would die, and eventually Kathryn would...no, Kathryn already...no, Kathryn was—and he began—for the four thousandth time in the past year—to cry.

There was a time in recent weeks when he felt like he had finally come close to conquering the wailing screaming crying that he had done too often in the beginning, and he prided himself on doing that. But he hadn't yet conquered the crying itself. It still came, and he didn't know how to stop it, because Kathryn's death had started it, and he didn't know how to stop her death. It wasn't just Kathryn that had died, as though she was a storyline in a movie or a person in history. Kathryn's whole life and presence had died. Her daily interaction with him died. Their conversations died. Their touching died. Dreaming died. Their trips, their talks, their shopping, their sleeping, even their arguing, had all died. Everything was gone. It wasn't a person—or *just* a person. It was also a way of being, a way of acting, thinking, feeling. All that had died and now— yes, he reminded himself, it had been almost two years—but still, *now*, none of those pieces of life managed to work or function by themselves, on their own without her life inside them.

What he was feeling, sitting in his car in front of his empty house, was something close to boredom, but it wasn't exactly that. Terror maybe, or fear or anger. But with the same numbness of boredom. The feeling of not feeling, and it clung to him like wet clothing, and it wouldn't go away.

As he sat there, watching the sun go down and a neighborhood deer, from the nearby town forest, calmly eating at his grass, he thought he could easily stay there for another hour, maybe two. Maybe three. He wasn't hungry so there was no point in going inside. Maybe he'd eventually nap until it was morning when he had to go to work again. He had done that once before. Did anyone notice? Then he remembered that yes, they did notice and that if he didn't change his moods soon, there was a chance he might not be employed at the university, by the end of the semester, for doing things just like that.

He heard a noise and for a moment didn't know what it was, but then he realized that it was the phone ringing.

The phone was just inside the door, and he could hear it from outside. Someone will answer it, he thought at first, but of course that wouldn't happen. The machine will pick it up, he thought, but somehow that didn't happen either. It kept ringing, probably because he seldom checked it, and its tape was full. It stopped for a moment, and he was pleased. He didn't want to have to go inside for it. That house was haunted, and he didn't like being there anymore. But the phone rang again. *Damn!* he thought. He hated people who did that. He hated people who kept trying to call him, who kept bothering him. But it still rang.

Finally, more out of disgust than curiosity, he pushed open the door and forced his body out of the car and down the long and difficult ten-foot path to the door. The garage door was still broken. It still had boards over it. He probably should fix it one of these days, he thought, but he hated that garage door. He would never fix that door. That garage door hated him too. He put down his briefcase and fought with his keys. Maybe by the time he got inside the ringing would stop. And it did, for about thirty seconds, but then rang again. He pushed open the door, took off his coat, picked up the receiver, and said hello. "David," said a voice. David thought he recognized it, but it sounded distant and scratchy. It wasn't unpleasant, but David wasn't in the mood to talk even if it was with someone pleasant. "This is Alphonso," the voice said.

"Alf?" David said back with a voice full of gravel. He noticed it when he spoke but hoped it hadn't sounded too weary or disembodied. "It's good to hear from you. Are you back in the States?"

"No, still in El Salvador," Alphonso said. "So, I should talk fast." Alphonso Rodriguez Hernandez had been a visiting scholar at David's university some years earlier, and the two of them had been friends. Alf came to the States because civil war had broken out in his country and his wife thought it wasn't safe to raise a family there. Later, when the fighting seemed to diminish, Alf and his family moved back home again, and he and David had seldom spoken since.

Alf took a long pause before starting. "David, are you okay?" he said. "Do you have someplace to go? I've got a reason for asking."

David wanted to say he was fine, just in a low spot, and that he'd be back to normal soon, but he couldn't remember any of those words, so he couldn't speak them. All he could remember how to say that might sound appropriate was, "I've been better."

"No, I mean after you're gone. After you leave the school. Do you have any plans?"

David was a little puzzled, but it may have just been his weariness. "I'm not leaving. It's been hard but..." He tried to add, "but I'm getting better," but those words felt too hard for his mouth to pronounce so he stopped.

Alphonso paused again. "David, you do know that the

review committee met today, and you didn't get a good notice. You knew that didn't you?"

No, he did not know that. He knew that the committee was going to meet sometime soon. Bernard had told him that it might happen this week, but he didn't really, *really*, think anything would come of it. At least not now. At least not this soon. And how could Alf know about it, but he didn't? Could that have been what some of those phone calls he hadn't answered last week were about? "What'd they say?"

"Oh, David. I'm sorry. I didn't think I would be telling you this; I thought you already knew. I've been talking to the Dean about a program down here for a while, and this week he told me what you had been going through, and what they did. And I'm really sorry to hear about Kathryn. I didn't realize I'd been away that long."

"Thanks." That was all that David could say back. He didn't want to start crying again.

"And he told me that your contract was up at the end of this semester and that the committee voted to not renew it for next year. You didn't hear that?"

"No," he said. "I hadn't...I *haven't* heard that. I... I didn't know that." He hadn't had much world around him to live in since she died, but now he suddenly felt like even that was beginning to fall away.

"Yes, I am sorry. I thought they had called you."

"No. I mean, if they'd tried, they didn't make it. I haven't heard yet. Did they say it was absolute and non-negotiable?"

"Well, I don't know, but I think so. You might want to ask Bernard that. He said he'd given you a couple of options and warnings, and it sounded like you had decided not to take any of them."

"Well, no, but, I mean, I thought they were just ideas or things. I didn't really think it was like this."

David didn't go on, and Alf stopped talking for several seconds. Finally, he said, "You must have thought I was crazy asking that."

"Asking what?"

"Asking what you were planning, if you had any plans."

"I thought you were just asking how I was doing."

"Well, that too, sure, but I had another reason too."

"What's that?"

"I need some help with something. And after talking with Bernard, I thought you might be interested in it."

"You mean down there? Aren't you in a war zone?"

Alf laughed. "Well, yes, sort of, but it's not that bad. Most of the fighting is over. And you'd be in San Salvador, the capital, most of the time it's fairly safe."

Now, David had to smile. "'*Most* of the time?' When you first moved up here, there were bombs and Death Squad murders every night."

"Well, that's true, but it's not like that now. There are plans for peace talks coming up. And it's much safer in the cities."

"So, what are you needing? You didn't catch me at a good time."

"I realize that now and I'm really sorry. But here's the story. Some of us in the university here, and some other activists in the community, have started a pilot program, working with nonprofit organizations to see if we can help them enhance their work and do more good. And God knows the country needs it. And they need someone to start up the initial research for the project for us. So, I'm sorry to bring it up this way, David, but...would you like a job?"

CHAPTER FIVE
DONUTS

He finished his first full day. He had unpacked, put things away, and gone shopping, at least for a few basic supplies to make his kitchen look less abandoned. And now, the next morning, he was attempting his first breakfast. These actions didn't yet rise to the level of feeling like an actual life, but they at least they were beginning to look like one, at least they were better than the multiple levels of hell he had been living in back in the States. Keeping busy and putting a "normal" cloak over his real feelings sometimes paused the attacks temporarily. Down the sidewalk past *Los Cañones*, was a small side street that led into a major thoroughfare named "Zacamil," the same name as the *colonia*, "neighborhood," where he was now living. And along that street was a chaotic collection of small *tiendas* selling anything from indigenous tapestries and wood carvings to aspirins and Kellogg's Cornflakes. He looked inside some of them but managed to narrow his shopping list to ingredients for a few simple meals and a 16-ounce bag of locally grown and ground coffee to help it go down. And now, exhausted and still groggy from only four hours of uneasy sleep, he was unsuccessfully studying the tiny two-cup coffee maker in his tiny one-person kitchen, and trying to decide how many scoops of Latin American coffee should go in the filter to create one cup of North American- tasting coffee. Then someone knocked on his door.

Jesus, he thought. I'm not in the mood for visitors. Is it the manager? Someone selling Bibles? (Did they do that here?). At least he wasn't naked. He pulled open the door, expecting to be angry at whoever would be intruding this early on his first and most confusing day, but in the doorway was a tall man with a wide smile and wide mustache, and holding two Dunkin' Donuts bags and a cardboard tray of coffees. "Alf!" said David.

"Amigo!" Alf said, rushing past David and into the kitchen. "Sorry, I brought breakfast and one of the coffee cups spilled on my pants." He sat the cup container on the counter, and a puddle began forming around its edges. "I bought five," he said. "Two for you and three for me. But one tipped over when I was getting out of the car and poured all over the seat and my leg." He saw a roll of paper towels at the end of the cabinet, pulled off several squares and began dabbing at the wet counter and his pants. "Well, it looks like it's two for you and two and a half for me."

"Aside from the accident," said David, "it's good to see you. And you're just in time. I was just trying to figure out what I would be doing for breakfast."

"Good to see you too, Amigo," and he gave David a big hug. "I was hoping I would get here before you had eaten. Do you have any plates in here? When we rented this place for you, they said it was furnished, but that doesn't mean they have everything. Oh, and get that other sack and bring it over. It has the donuts."

"Sounds good," said David. "What kind of donuts and why?"

Alf sat down in one of the small chairs around the table and began prying the tops off the coffee cups. "First, they're jelly donuts, which are my favorites, and 'why' is that they're *muy sabroso,* very tasty, and they're perfect for your first lesson in our Salvadoran reality."

David laid out two plates on the small two-person table. He pulled off two more squares of paper towels and laid them by the plates for napkins. "So, for my first day here, you're going to teach me how to bake donuts?"

"No, I'm going to teach you why our country is poor and why we are at war. And donuts are a good start on doing that. I use this illustration with my students, and they love it."

"Love the illustration or love the donuts?"

"Both—though maybe the donuts more. Now *sientese,* sit." He gestured with his now-half-full coffee cup for David to sit across from him. "I want to talk about two things this morning and we need to be fast about it because I know you're going to be visiting with our colleague, Héctor Castañeda, later today and he will try to keep you there all day long. And if he did that and I waited to see you afterwards, Beatriz would change our locks on our doors, and I'd have to live in the streets."

"That's an appealing image, but assuming she keeps you, how is Beatriz doing? It's been, what, five, maybe six years since you all were in the States?"

"Four for me, five for Beatriz and the little *niños*—who are not so little anymore. In the beginning, she didn't want to come back because she wasn't sure that the violence had died down."

"Did it?"

"Well, that's one of the things I want us to talk about. But before we get into that, I want to talk about you." He pushed the bag of donuts over to David's side of the table. "I want to know how you are doing. Having you come here was just a staffing idea for us, but for you I think it's a—what do they call it in the states? An 'existential crisis'? I don't want us to get lost in all the work and background and lose sight of the fact that you came down here before you ever got over grieving about Kathryn. You were going through hell that day I called about this job, and I've wondered a hundred times since then whether or not maybe I should have called the whole thing off and let you work through your grief on your own back in Massachusetts."

"I don't know either," David said. This was not a topic he enjoyed discussing. "And I thought the same thing a hundred times on the way down here. Did I tell you that just as we entered El Salvador I had a little boy get shot in the customs office while I was holding him?"

Alf put down his coffee cup and leaned forward. "No," he said, "*¡Qué horrible!*"

"It broke me in half," David said. "A cute little boy who had done nothing wrong. He was wanting to carry my bags, and I was trying to tell him I didn't need it. And a guard shot him in front of a room full of people and the killer just walked away, smiling."

"That doesn't speak well for our *sistema judicial*, but..."

"I almost grabbed my suitcase and walked to the other side of the crossing and bought a ticket back to the States."

"We're glad you're here, David, but given what you had already been going through, I wouldn't have held it against you."

"Well, I wasn't doing much of a stellar job working through my own life before you called. And maybe a pilgrimage through a war zone will be good for me."

"If it doesn't kill you."

"Well, the jury's still out on that. I just got here."

"So how are you doing right now?"

David thought for a moment. "Here's a good image. Overall, I'm feeling a little bit like someone pulled a live hot poker out of the fireplace and then drove it up through my chest."

"*¡Demonio!*" Alf said, jerking his head back so quickly he nearly spilled more of his coffee. "That is a picture. You caught me off guard with that because you look like you're doing fairly well."

"Well, I'm glad, because I'm trying to look better. Back in the States, I let grief and pain, and a lot of guilt, take complete control of my body and my face and it ruined me. It nearly drained what little life I had left out of me. After that day when you called me, and then Bernard told me the department was going to suspend me, I promised myself that I would never again allow myself to look and act so raw and obsessed like that."

"How successful do you think you are doing on that?"

"Well, I'd say I'm there about forty percent of the time. Maybe fifty on a good day. And maybe ten when I'm alone by myself. But even ten percent is better than the time of your infamous phone call in my driveway."

"Well, right now you do look good, and I hope that's a good sign. Beatriz and I both liked you and Kathryn and felt awful when we heard what happened, and what you went through afterwards."

"Thanks. I appreciate that. But...." His voice trailed off and he turned his head away.

"But what?"

"I dreamed about Kathryn again last night. And the hurt came back again as though she died last week. I may look better, but I just wish I could make the constant pain go away. I want it to go away."

Alf put his cup down. "No, you don't. Not altogether, anyway. I think that pain you have is a gift."

"Prove it."

"I think it's there to remind you that you once loved someone and that someone loved you back. It can change, it can go down, it can be covered up. But it can't totally go away, and it shouldn't. If you stop feeling the pain, then you stop feeling the face, the touch, and the eyes of Kathryn, who you loved. And you don't ever want that. It would be a bigger loss."

David put on a weak smile. "Thanks, Alf, I appreciate that. I don't know if I understand it, but I appreciate it. For now, though, I think I'd rather talk about something else. I feel a little stronger when my brain is moving and not my stomach. If I let myself go, I can still spiral down pretty quick into a hole that's deep and dark and hard to get out of."

"*Entiendo, mi amigo.*" He slapped his hand on the table with a look of relief. "That's fine with me and probably good for both of us. And we have much to cover about the country itself."

"Thanks," said David.

"*Bueno*, let's start." Alf lifted the jelly donuts bags and waved them at David. "When you finish with the sandwich, which is good for your body, take one of these. They're good for your soul." He paused for a moment and looked up. "No *en realidad*, actually, neither one is good for your body, they're "Dunkin'" after all, but the sandwich will at least do less damage."

David laughed and took one of the bags.

"What I'd like for us to do is to meet up and talk every now and then, just like this—though next time I'll let you pay for the breakfast. Héctor can guide you in the program we've started, and what we want to accomplish, but you and I will talk politics, economics, and the terrible insane leadership that made us such a broken country and is keeping us from finally becoming a democracy."

"That's fine, but how's your democracy coming. I tried to read up on El Salvador before I came, and the press covers your elections and candidates fairly positively."

"They're being generous. We've dabbled in establishing a real democracy here a couple of times over the last two decades, but each time we get close, the oligarchy pulls the rug, and we swing back towards an authoritarian dictatorship. Right now, we are at a big swing point again. If the next couple of elections go well, and the new ruler decides to follow the basic laws and constitution, then we might finally take our place in the democratic pantheon of the world. But if they don't and if the new ruler starts shutting down newspapers and news programs and starts sending in the military again to stop protests, and uses the war as a pretext for arresting protesters and political opponents, then we may slide back into another fifty years of authoritarian rule. Adolf Hitler is very popular with the people at the top, so who knows?"

"That sounds terrifying. So, is that what you're going to talk about today?"

"Yes, but let's start with donuts. They're very good, *muy sabroso*, but the reason I use them is to illustrate one of the reasons why the Salvadoran economy is so bad off."

David lifted one eyebrow. "Um, donuts? An indigenous Salvadoran food, right? I suspect there's an interesting story behind them."

"Actually, two stories. The first is the economy and the second is military. And I'll try to be quick."

"I know you and know that won't be easy."

"Watch it, Amigo, I know you're feeling bad, but that won't stop me from eating one of your donuts if you get out of line."

"I'll be good," David said smiling.

"Okay." Alf picked up one of the jelly donuts and took a bite. "There are a thousand mistakes that we have made to keep our country poor. But there are also policies and blunders from the outside that seemed to have conspired with ours to do the same thing. The story of donuts is a good way to illustrate some of those outside forces, and they're also tasty, so I'll start with them, but also, talking about the military is harder and darker so I'll save that for last. And since you're the econ prof, you'll probably recognize some of the donut story already.

"Well," said David, pulling some of the soggy wrapping off of his sandwich, "I'm guessing that the issue is something about how US trade policies up there have an impact on donut prices down here."

"Close, but more than that. El Salvador has always been poor, but about ten years ago, your president, Mr. Reagan, decided he wanted to destroy our neighbor, Nicaragua, for its socialist leanings, so it started sending us tons, *increíblemente grande* tons, of free wheat, which they usually send to countries for famine relief, but here to create the political mirage that capitalism was making El Salvador richer than Nicaragua and becoming a free market paradise. We didn't know what to do with it all."

David wiped a bacon crumb from his face. "But as I recall, El Salvador grows mainly corn, not wheat. So, what did that do to the corn growers here?"

"Ran them into the ground," said Alf. "That free US wheat destroyed about half of our corn farmers."

"I'm not surprised."

"And while the farms were being destroyed, Dunkin' and others like them, moved in and made a fortune creating pastries and donut shops everywhere because their raw materials were almost free. Today there's a 'Dunkin'' in nearly every city and town in the country, and most of the proceeds go back to the home office in the States. Meanwhile, when the US newspapers and news shows come down to look around, they see these shiny new stores selling US sweet rolls and Dunkin' Donuts and they think, 'Damn, this little country is doing just fine.'"

"Sounds pretty clever."

"Right, but what the US didn't plan on, because they didn't understand economics, was that after that, thousands of broke farmers and their sons—and some daughters—ran off to the mountains to join the rebels, guaranteeing the revolution will be longer and bloodier than it should have been on its own. Good work, USA!" He pumped his fist in the air celebrating the win. "That's the quick and easy economic story. We can talk about more of that at another time."

"What was the second thing, about military aid?"

"It's similar, but more complicated. Over the past ten years the US has also been pouring in thousands, and millions, and billions, and gazillions, and quadrillions, in military aid to our country, and it has turned us into the military state that our fascist ancestors could only have dreamed of. Everywhere you go there are guns and uniforms and armored cars and a huge increase in the number of people 'disappeared' into some prison that nobody has ever heard of, never to be heard from again. This sweet little community of Zacamil, where you now live, is one of the worst areas. This *colonia* has been known for its support for the rebels, and so in return, today it's becoming also known for the number of 'disappeared' husbands, raped wives, and burned houses. You'll be safe here because you are tall, white, and North American, but your neighbors aren't so lucky. In the old days, if a president or governor did not like the way a newspaper covered his graft, it would just be threatened. But today they blow up the paper's offices. We're that far along on the authoritarian path. 'Watch for it coming to a country near you.' Or before, if some politician pulled his head out and complained about our funding private right-wing schools and cutting money for public education, he'd just be threatened. Today we'd find his body the next morning at the bottom of *La Puerta del Diablo*, the "Devil's Door," a steep, sharp, cliff right outside of the city. And up in the mountains, if a little *pueblo* complains today that the army wouldn't let them vote in the last election, they'd be bombed and burned to the ground just in time to open the polls. The guardrails are gone. It's not totally the US's fault, but bankrolling the tripling of our military size was clearly a big contributor."

"That sounds scary."

"It is very scary. We had a politician here about twenty years ago, named Duarte, who ran for president. A good man, a moderate. He probably won, but we'll never know because the far right shut down the elections and declared someone else the winner. Then a few years later there was a progressive junta that took over, and they brought him back as a provisional president. But after a couple of years the old elites and new military shut him down. Then about five years ago Duarte ran again and this time he won, and we thought the Kingdom of God had arrived."

"Did it?"

"No, he was well intentioned, but by then not strong enough to stop the repression or make some of the basic changes that we needed. So, now, this year, his term is up, he's dying of cancer, and we're about to have another election."

"Yeah, I saw some of the campaign signs when I came in."

"Right. This could be our most important election in decades. We've now had a short experiment with a democratic vote. It didn't turn out great, but we got a taste. If we can elect someone now from at least the middle or center-right, this might go down in history as the time we turned the corner. But if we don't, if we elect someone from the new far-right ARENA party—which is new and modeled after your US Republican Party—we'll go down as a failed state, and more and more people will die.

David put his cup down and leaned back in his chair. "That's not just scary, that sounds dark and deadly."

"Most likely the first thing is that the war will continue, the economy will collapse, and then the government will fall. Depending on how well our next elections go, we'll probably try to act like a democracy for a while, electing rich landowners with European last names, but with high unemployment, more bodies in the streets, and violent street gangs, and eventually the whole country will get scared and beg for a 'strong man' to come in and clean up the crime and take over. You know, the kind of leader who isn't very fond of constitutions or term limits? And we'll be back to where we started. Fear is a magical elixir to dictators. They love it. The more we are afraid, the more we will vote for them. And *that* is why I wanted your first meal here to be a donut."

"Thanks, so now I'll never eat another one.

CHAPTER SIX

THE INSTITUTE

David was glad that Alf had come by that morning and offered to get together again if David needed some support or companionship. But it wasn't the "job," or a task, or the condition of the country that he often still felt crushing down on his shoulders, it was life itself. It was good that he was managing to look better in front of others more often, but inside there was still a lot of the same lifeless life that kept him feeling weary, frightened, and ashamed and he was never quite free of that. He took a deep breath and forced himself to walk from his apartment to *Calle Zacamil* and hailed a taxi to take him to see Héctor Castañeda, the director of the institute sponsoring his project. A taxi swerved in at him almost as soon as he put his hand out and he got in. It then lunged back into traffic almost before David had shut the door. He sat back in the seat and looked out of the window and told himself to look strong and confident. Today will be a fifty percent day, he thought, but as he was about to take a second big breath, the car jerked suddenly to a stop and the driver began waving his arms wildly and shouting.

"*Dime la dirección de nuevo,*" he said. "*¡Rápido!*" David couldn't understand exactly what he was saying, but he knew that *dirección* meant "address" and *¡Rápido!* sounded like "rapid." So, he folded the welcome letter from the Institute so that the address showed on top and reached over the seat to give it to the driver, who immediately waved it away. "*No, no, no,*" he screamed. "*¡Léelo, léelo!*" "*Read it, read it.*"

"Okay. Let me check." David looked from the address to his map and back to the road. "I *think* we turn right, right over there." He pointed to a street. "*¡Derecha,* right!" The driver wrenched the car forward ahead of a bus and then turned left sharply. The bus honked a long deep belching noise at them. "Okay, now," leaning into the front seat and holding up the letter. "*A la próxima Esquina.*" "The next corner!" The driver made a sudden swerve back to the left again to miss a small car with Yugoslavian plates, and David nearly fell onto the car floor. "*No, Derecha,*" he said. The driver pulled back from the close encounter with the Yugoslavians, and then turned abruptly, just in time to make the sharp turn to the right.

"Good job," David told him. "So, now I think it is right here. He looked at the address and then the numbers on the buildings before them. "Right there! Right there on the left. *¡Ala izquierda!*" He pointed to a small unassuming house fitting tightly between two larger, more imposing structures on either side. "I think that's it."

The driver stopped sharply, still in the street. *¿Aquí?* he said, looking at it unconvinced. "*Es esto?*" He seemed surprised that an "*Instituto*" would be so small.

"*Sí, sí,* I think that's it." David was a bit surprised himself. It was related to the university, but evidently that connection did not merit it a more distinguished building. "Could you pull over a little closer to the curb? *La acera?*" He pointed to the left, but the driver had already left his seat and was running to

David's door. "*¿Tus bolsa?*" he said, reaching in for David's backpack.

"No, no, I've got it," David said, pulling it close to him. He reached into his wallet and without asking the amount, drew out several Salvadoran *colones* and hoped that it was somewhere close to what was needed.

The young man took the money but then fell suddenly against David and the car door to avoid getting hit by a rushing Volvo. The car honked, and the driver yelled something back at them that David assumed was unpleasant. They pulled back to get their balance. "*¡Lo siento, ¡Lo siento!*" he said. "I'm sorry." He gathered up a handful of bills that he had dropped during the incident and gave another one to the driver for a tip. He hoped again that it was enough. "*Gracias,*" the driver said, and seconds later he was gone.

And there he was. David looked around at the building and its surroundings, tangled with people and cars on both sidewalks and street, and thought, well, my first day. My second orientation conversation. He leaned down and picked up the backpack and began winding himself through the crowd from traffic to curb and through a gate in front of the small plain building. Above the door were the words, "*Instituto de Educación y Apoyo no Gubernamental,*" and then below it, in English, "The Institute for non-Governmental Support and Education (IEAG)." He rang the bell, wiped a circle of sweat from his forehead with the back of his thumb, and waited for a response.

A speaker on the door buzzed for a moment and then a light cheerful voice came out. "*Buenos días. ¿Podemos ayudarte?*"

David thought for a moment. "*Mi nombre es David Patterson,*" he said slowly, trying hard to pronounce the unfamiliar words correctly. "*Tengo una cita con...*"

"Oh, Dr. Patterson!" the voice said back brightly. "You're

here to see Dr. Héctor. Just a sec." The door buzzed one more time and then made the sound of a latch being released, and a young, thin, woman with light brown hair, opened the door for him. She spoke with a clear North American accent. "Come in please and have a seat. We're all looking forward to meeting you."

David hadn't expected such an expansive welcome. "Thanks," he said. "Am I late?"

"No, no, no." She said, waving him in. "We're just glad to see you."

The door opened to a nondescript office with gray walls, two desks, two chairs, one file cabinet, a door to another room, and what appeared to be a nineteen-sixties glass water cooler. David hadn't seen one of those in years. Behind the desk, covered with papers, folders, and a steel black Royal typewriter, stood a round, balding man with thick-rimmed glasses and a black bow tie, smiling broadly and with arms out wide in a welcoming gesture. "Yes, yes!" he shouted. "Come in, come in! You must be our new research advisor. 'David...David...?' He frowned and looked down at the papers on his desk. He looked up. "Is it 'Richardson'?"

Alf had described Héctor Castañeda by using the very American expression, "a piece of work," and meeting him now, David suspected that description was apt. He set his backpack down and extended his hand, "No, it's *Patterson*."

"Of course, it is, of course," said the man, shaking David's hand energetically. "So sorry, so sorry. Please sit down. And I am Doctor Héctor Castañeda. I am the director here at the Institute." He waved his arms around the room expansively as though presenting a magnificent edifice. "I am certain that they have told you much that is about me. I think I am to be your new boss—your *jefe*." He smiled a wide smile, as though he had just told a very funny story. "And this is young Marsha

Whitman, our wonderful intern this year from one of your US universities in...in..." He gave Marsha a frightened look.

"Tennessee," she said.

"Yes, yes, and she is from an important university in your state of Tennessee, and she is studying economics, which is, I think, the subject you teach."

"Yes, I did teach economics, but I'm not..."

"You will have much in common, and we will miss her when she is gone. Sit, sit, you must be tired."

Héctor gestured to one of the two chairs in the office. "Marsha, get Doctor Patterson some water. We have clean water. He looks dry from travel, and we have water." Marsha took two cone-shaped paper cups from a container behind the water cooler and began filling them. Héctor looked back at David and said, "Or would you like a beer? Or some Coca-Cola? We do not have them here, but if you want something I can send Marsha down to a *tienda* and get them for you."

"No, thank you," he said. "I'm fine, I'm just very glad to finally be here and meet you." He turned to Marsha. "Both of you."

"Yes, yes, I am sure that you are exhausted, and we are glad that you are here too. Drink the water. It is *agua pura*, it is pure, so you can drink it. We will not want to keep you here long this morning, but there are many things that we do need to speak to you this morning, things we will talk about." He sat down again and leaned forward on the desk clapping his hands together. "We have been looking for this day for some time. We think you are going to be a blessing to our work here. We have much to do, there is much need in our country, and we have been told that you are very, very qualified to help us. We are honored to have a scholar of your stature to come and be with us in these difficult days." David wondered if an accurate translation of that gushing praise would be that they had trouble finding someone who was stupid enough to come to a third-world country for an undefined job in the middle of a civil war, but he didn't say it. "We at the Institute have much to talk about and much to share. I hope you are ready."

"Well, I think I am," David said, smiling but feeling hesitant. He suspected that Alf had been doing a little overselling of his skill level. His economics background was more along the lines of taxation, international trade, exchange rates, and monetary policy. Not how to help struggling nonprofits raise money and help clients. He opened his backpack and looked for his notebook and pen. "Well, we might as well start. Alf has told me a few things already but tell me more."

For the next hour, Héctor described to David some of the tasks of his new job. He would travel around the city and the safer "departments" of the country, interviewing nonprofit aid agencies to see how they worked and who they served, and how they were funded, and then he would compile the data so that the next researchers could use it to help the agencies network together for skill-sharing and support. Héctor gave David a notebook containing the names of organizations that they already had information on, ten pages, single-spaced. Looking through it, David realized that he had underestimated the enormity of the project. He was aware that in any poor country, there would be many organizations offering food, shelter, education, or health care for the poor and that many of them received funding from individuals and groups in the US, or the US government itself, but the number of them here in El Salvador surprised him.

"How many organizations are we talking about?" he asked Héctor.

"Oh, Doctor Patterson, not too many. So far, maybe just three hundred. Maybe just four. Maybe no more than five. Maybe we do not know the total. Marsha is still adding names... She is still doing research...she is very good...maybe no more than five. But as you will see, we have already contacted some of them, so your task will be smaller."

David looked at the pages, he counted two or three names on each that had been checked off. "Are some of them close together?" he asked. "I mean are they all one area of the city? Or scattered around?"

"Oh, many are here in the city, but some are out in the *Campo,* or up in the mountain villages and by the ocean or in the other cities of our vast country."

"Does the institute supply a car for this position?"

"Oh, my! No, Doctor." He laughed. "We do not have that kind of resources. But do not worry. Our wonderful country has within it one of the finest networks of buses and outstanding taxi drivers in the world, so you will have no problem whatsoever getting to your destinations."

David smiled, remembering Lessi a day earlier, who was among those "outstanding" drivers, but he held back his thoughts. "So, where is my office and when do I start?"

"My goodness Doctor, you are magnificently eager. We are so pleased. You can start as soon as tomorrow morning if you would like, and your office is right here. Look, we have cleaned off our desk for your work." He gestured to the second desk in the room which was, in fact, clean on top, except for a note-book, a container for pens, and a dark green desk pad. "And with it, you will have our telephone, and a chair, and drawers, and free fresh water for you every day. And look," he pointed down at his desk. "We have a typewriter just for us. It is a very good one. I used it often when I was in university. You can use it whenever you wish. You will love it too, I am sure."

CHAPTER SEVEN

CLOSING

David's office at the University was a mess, and he had little energy to clean it out. He'd picked up a few boxes from Frank over at Harmony Liquors but hadn't given him much warning, so the store didn't have many to offer him. However, it was just his office, so this may be enough.

Some of the things on the bookshelf were easy. Just grab a handful of books and drop them into a box. Try to fit them in together so they don't fall out in transport, but other than that, just get them in. That filled up most of his boxes. He tried to keep them organized by topic: statistics, trade, debt, and globalization.... It took a while, but it had to be done. Tired as he was, he kept at it. In fact, there was something about the finality of the act that gave him a burst of energy he hadn't felt in some weeks.

Next were the walls. Not much there, but some of it was meaningful. He had a narrow space, on the wall next to his window, filled with diplomas and certificates. It was kind of vain to put them all on the walls, but he'd once thought (probably wrongly) that it might impress his students or colleagues that he'd won some awards years ago (when he was younger and smarter). Actually, few people ever noticed or cared about that, and today neither did he. One of these glassed-in and framed pieces of paper, plus about two dollars, could buy me a cup of coffee, he thought. Better yet, three of them would get him a cheap scotch.

His desk was harder. He wished he'd had some "Bankers' Boxes" for his files, but the liquor boxes were about the same size, so he took batches of them and dropped them together into the boxes. However, they couldn't hold the hanging files, and they fell over into an unorganized pile. But hey, he thought, I'm never going to look at them again. So, who cares?

The top of the desk should have been easy, but it wasn't. All it had on it was a big (and badly stained) desk pad, a pen case with a cheesy name plaque on the side of it, a plastic box for paper clips and "Post It" notes, and then the photos. He threw away the desk pad and slid the other things into the boxes and then picked up the photos. They burned to the touch. There were three of them and he had a hard time holding them in his hands. One was of Kathryn and him about ten years earlier on the Playa Bonita beach near Limón, Costa Rica. They were far too young and far too poor to have done that, but they did it anyway, and the picture today was almost charming in its sweetness and naïveté. Another was at their wedding reception, up in Boston, two years later. It wasn't their official picture. It was taken by one of their friends at the reception, but he loved it. It was a casual picture of the two of them dancing to Louis Armstrong's "What a Wonderful World," in their wedding clothes, and they looked very much in love. The third was in their empty new home, two months after he had accepted the position at the university and the morning of the day the moving vans were coming to put everything in it. They had the real estate agent take a picture of them, arm in arm, in front of the fireplace wearing ratty, wrinkled, work clothes, but to David, it said something deep and spiritual about what it felt like to move into a new place with a person he loved and planned to live with forever. He held the pictures and looked at them for a long time. He didn't know which one he hated most.

"STAND STILL," she said. "You'll look jiggly in the photo, and it'll ruin it."

He laughed, "But I'm a kind of 'Jiggly' guy. It's what makes me so charming."

"There are a lot of things that make you charming, sweetheart." She was giving him that sly accusing look she had. "But 'jiggly' is not one of them."

Terrell, the agent, said, "Okay, now, hold steady for just one minute more, and I think I've got it." He clicked and there was a flash. "I think that one worked. I can't guarantee anything, but at least we've got you. Now I need to get back."

"I'm sure it's fine," she said. "We weren't looking for great art. Just wanted to chronicle the occasion."

"Well, I think we've at least done that." Terrell handed the camera back to her. "Listen, while you are setting up and settling in, if you need anything else, anything at all, please give me a call. I want you to know that our help doesn't stop at the sale."

"So, how about a Big Mac and an order of fries, with a medium Coke," said David. Terrell looked blank for a moment.

"He's just being silly," she said. She pushed David. "Quit that. He doesn't know how you are."

David feigned innocence. "Well, he did say 'anything.'"

Terrell looked relieved and laughed. "Well, I'll look into the Big Mac and see what I can do."

"You do that," said David, and Terrell picked up his briefcase and coat.

"We'll walk you to the door," she said. "It'll be our first time saying goodbye to our first guest."

"It's a milestone," he laughed.

When they got to the door he turned back and, without warning, gave them both a hug. "You are good people," he said. "And I loved working with you. You'll love this house. And I hope you live here happily for a long, long time."

"I know we will," Kathryn said. They held hands and watched him as he left their new home and walked down their new sidewalk to his car.

David stood over his desk for some time looking at the last photo. He held it in his hand and watched them as they posed for it, holding hands and hugging. They looked good together and he missed them like they were dear friends from decades earlier. Then the bell rang in the hallway, signaling the beginning of a class that he would never be teaching again.

CHAPTER EIGHT
THE FIRST

David was facing the front of the building of his first appointment in his new job. It was a small square adobe building with the word, "Ayuda" over the door. He stood in front of it for a minute feeling very anxious about how it would go. Anxious about the interview, anxious about his inadequate Spanish, and anxious about even being here at all and doing this. He wanted it to go well, but his fears about it came out clearly in his voice. "Okay," he said taking a deep breath and stepped forward.

The name of the organization was *Ayuda*, which roughly meant, "help" or "relief," and it set up schools for children and basic vocational training for parents, especially those whose lives had been disrupted by the fighting.

He was going to be joined by Héctor, who had volunteered to come and help him get started. So, this visit would be both for information-gathering and also training. Some of the organizations, Héctor told him while they were waiting in the Ayuda office, were wonderful and did good work, and David would feel like he could fall in love with them for life. David wasn't sure if that would happen, but Héctor used expressions like that a lot, so he didn't pursue it. Others, however—and here Héctor paused for a moment with a wry smile—"With others, I think you should, as you Americans say, 'count your spoons' when you are ready to leave," and he laughed out loud as though it was the best joke he had told in years.

"What does that mean?" David asked.

"It means in truth that not all 'Christian' organizations," he paused again, "are very good about being, you know, '*Christian.*'" And then laughed again.

Just then the door opened and a large woman with bright red hair burst through it with her arms open wide and rushed straight towards them. "Héctor!" She screeched and gave him a long, joyful hug, and kissed him on each cheek, twice. Then she turned to David and said something loud and incomprehensible in Spanish and hugged him just as strongly. David was startled but tried not to pull away. Héctor seemed pleased. He took her hand and said, "Dr. Patterson, I would like for you to meet my sister, Señora Ximena Guadalupe Perroni."

"Sister?" he said, surprised, but trying not to sound awkward. "I didn't know we were meeting your sister here."

"She is the director of *Ayuda,* and I kept that from you for a secret until now." He smiled at David. "Do not be surprised with her. She is a little...*Demasiado expresiva,* we say, 'over expressive,' in her emotions."

David started to say something about pots calling kettles black but held back. *Mucho gusto,* he said to her.

"*Igualmente,*" she responded and hugged him one more time.

"She has been wanting to meet you ever since I told her that you were going to be working with us. She is honored that we have such an esteemed scholar working now at the Institute."

David laughed. "Well, don't tell her the truth now, I'd hate to disappoint her before we got acquainted."

"Why don't we sit? You can ask your questions of Ximena about the work of *Ayuda*, and I will translate for you, and we will have a nice conversation. You sit here in the big chair, and she and I will sit on the couch before you."

The two snuggled together on the couch and after a few moments and considerable effort, Ximena was able to lower her enthusiasm level and talk solidly about *Ayuda* and its work —with only an occasional burst of exuberance. It was an organization that she had been with for many years, and she was *muy emocionada* about it. It had been founded decades earlier by a missionary couple, Ralph and Maude Perkins from Texas in the United States. They had been sent originally by the American Missionary Association, to establish schools for poor children in Central America that would teach basic education and the Christian Gospel. But they soon found that many of the children were so poor and so hungry that they were unable to concentrate and unable to learn. "If they can't eat, they can't learn," she said through Héctor and smiled broadly as though this discovery was not only important but humorous.

Ximina explained that after a few years, the Perkins couple left the Missionary Association and set up their own food program that supplied free breakfasts and free lunches to schools throughout San Salvador, paid for by many of the same donors that had supported them when they were doing their missionary work. It was a success and educators in the region lauded it because they were able to see a marked improvement in the learning skills of their students. In the beginning, the Perkins' asked their donors to send canned goods to an Ayuda Center in Waco, Texas, which would then ship them down to El Salvador for the schools. But eventually, they realized that the cans themselves added extra weight and cost to the shipping, and they were expensive to dispose of in the city.

Plus, bringing down huge amounts of free food from the US harmed the incomes of local grocers who often sold the same foods that the donors were sending and giving away for free. By giving free food to local poor people, they were hurting local grocers. So, they changed course again and asked their donors to just send checks which would be used by the local *Ayuda* organization to purchase a much wider variety of foods locally.

"Did all of the donors go along with the change?" asked David.

"Many did, yes," she said, through Héctor. "But others wanted just the teaching of the Gospel, so they left us." She frowned, clearly disapproving. "I believe in the Gospel," she said, "It is very important to me. But I believe that helping the poor, teaching the farmers, educating the women, *is* the Gospel. It is not just words; it is also actions." Her voice and eyebrows rose with the pronouncement. "And now many more have joined from other churches and religions and organizations—those who believe in helping both 'body and soul.' And that is when it became the magnificent program that it is now."

Ximena was clearly excited about this part of the story. She said that eventually, Maude Perkins learned that many families in the region were preparing meals that were filling, but not nutritious, so she experimented with holding simple cooking classes for young mothers. And after a few months of that, she began organizing the young women in her classes to teach similar cooking techniques to other gatherings of mothers. *¡Cada uno, enseña uno!* she yelled, her face bursting in a smile.

Both of them sat up straight, looking at David expectantly, but he was blank. "It is your American expression," said Héctor, leaning forward, urging David to understand it.

"Sorry?" said David.

"It is 'Each one teach one.'" He looked a little disappointed that David didn't get it. "It is what you Americans tell us is a good development program. And we—I mean *Ayuda*—has been doing it here for years."

Once again David felt a little embarrassed and again wondered if he was up to this job. "I'm sorry, it's my, you know...my Spanish. It's still not very...."

Héctor fell back onto the couch. "It is okay. You will do better. Let us now go on."

They went on for the rest of the morning, describing how the program grew and evolved. How Maude Perkins eventually began to feel resistance from some in the community that classes in cooking were being led by a middle- aged, North American *Gringa*, who knew nothing about traditional Salvadoran cooking. So, with their limited funds, they hired a health and nutrition instructor from the University to lead the classes, and the attendance rose measurably. They now had dozens of classes and teachers and students all throughout the city and as far as Soyapango in the west and Apopa in the north, and it was still growing. Now hundreds of people were eating more and eating better and learning more. "It was a great success," said Héctor. "It was a tremendous success." He bounced up and down and clapped his hands in gleeful celebration.

"Sounds wonderful," said David, honestly impressed.

"*Muy fenomenal,*" said Ximena.

"You have a project here that is growing and growing, but that also means that the costs to support it are growing. You can't be still depending on those original donors from the old days. Most of them have probably passed on by now."

"*Es muy difícil,*" said Ximena, growing quiet and looking down.

"This is where they need the most help," said Héctor. "They have grown their donor base some over the years, but the base is getting older and smaller, and the needs here have been getting larger. They need to do better. I have been of some help to them. I have applied for a used, donated computer from Apple for the office and it can do magic things, but it is just one, and many people—including me—do not know totally how to use it."

"Did it come with any bookkeeping and accounting software?"

Héctor shook his head. "No, I am sorry, but it does not."

"No need to apologize. Does it come with a lot of memory for storage? And do you have a printer for it yet?"

Both Héctor and Ximena shook their heads together. "It has very small memory," Héctor said. "But for her we have these discs that we use in the university." He formed a square with his fingers about five inches. "And more than a very large megabite can be held in them. And yes, we also wish for a printer to go with it, but they cost over fifty dollars in our local computer store, so we are saving our money to buy it. For now, I can sometimes print for Ximena at the university."

They continued talking for over an hour with David asking as many questions as he could think of and Héctor translating them to Ximena and then reporting her responses back. Often her words to Héctor would cause him to burst with laughter. But then when he translated it to David it would be a simple "yes we do that," or "no, we don't" answer. They were having a good time, David thought, playing with this non- bilingual gringo. But he didn't mind, and he did wind up the meeting with lots of information he didn't have before.

When they finally quit for the evening, he let them both give him big hugs and Héctor gave him very detailed instructions on how to get home. David felt good about the meeting.

Of course, his first interview was easier than most because it was more like a training interview with Héctor and his sister, but still, he felt like he had picked up tips and ideas on how to proceed with the next ones. And with those, he would learn even more, and when he had completed all of these interviews, he might even be interested in staying longer to help some of these small nonprofits that were struggling to get by in this war-ravaged country. He waved goodbye to them as he walked to the corner, and just as he got there the number 32 bus was pulling up and it stopped in front of him. This has been good, he thought. This might work out. The doors opened, he got on, gave the driver a guess at the fare, and it continued north towards Calle Zacamil.

CHAPTER NINE

THE PLAZA

Buenos Diaz, big boy. Wanna go for a ride?" David had his face in the refrigerator looking for lunch when the phone rang but was not surprised. It had been over a week since Alf's "donut" visit, and he'd been expecting a call.

"No, but if you ply me with Salvadoran junk food again, I might reconsider. That'll be my bribe for having to look at your ugly face for an hour."

"Good, I'll be over in about five minutes, we're going for a picnic. And by the way, Beatriz thinks I'm lovely."

Fifteen minutes later, David was waiting at the gate to his apartment complex and a battered, black Pinto turned down into the parking lot. Alf's left arm was waving from the driver's side window. When it came to a stop, David put his backpack in first and got in, but before he could speak, Alf said, "So, we haven't talked much in a while, how did your visit go with Héctor?"

David laughed, "Well, he seems to be a very dedicated guy, but your expression, 'a piece of work,' seems appropriate."

"*Si, Señor.* It is a good one for poor Héctor. He's a little odd, but he's a good person, and we love him. He works for nearly nothing, and he keeps the office open for those of us on the planning team and he has known the project from the very beginning." He made a quick right turn onto the street and then merged sharp left to avoid a garbage truck that was in the same lane. David reached for his seat belt. There wasn't one. "Alf, would you like for me to drive?"

"No, no, no," he said, steadying the car and honking at the truck. "You'd kill us both. You need practice to get good at this."

"Good" wasn't the description that David would have given the performance. He pushed his feet into the floorboard and held the door handle. "Where are we going?"

"Over to a Plaza on the university campus. It's only a few blocks from here and it's one of my favorite places to eat outside."

The "Plaza" that Alf referred to, was a circle of grass and benches and walkways in the center of the campus. At one edge was a large and ancient Maquilishuat tree in full bloom. The national tree of El Salvador and beautiful when its flowers burst open to show off their colors and smells. The ground around it was a carpet of discarded pink and red petals. They were thick and soft, and a light, sweet smell rose from within them. Just under the tree was a cement picnic table, barely recognizable under its cover of flowers. Alf stood for a moment, lunch bags in his hands, and stared at it. "She's beautiful this time of year," he said. "*¿Verdad?*" He gestured up at the tree with one of his bags then used one of them to wipe pink petals off the table below it. "I'll give you a better tour sometime, but now we're in a little bit of a hurry."

"So, what's on the menu this time?" David asked, frowning at the two bags. Is this going to be another donut object lesson?"

"No, my friend, this is an authentic Central American delicacy." He reached into a large bag and brought out two smaller ones. "One for you and one for me. Though mine has more spices and is *poquito* larger."

"What is it?"

"Fried chicken." He smiled broadly. "*Pollo Campero,* the best chicken in the entire Americas and it was invented right here." He pulled a drumstick out of his bag smelled it while smiling. The people of Guatemala claim that they invented it, but I do not believe that. I believe that we had it here first. And I will always believe that."

David took a bite of one of the oddly shaped fried pieces in his own bag. It was good, he thought, but a little spicy. In the bag he also found a more familiar-looking cup of coleslaw and a big Coca-Cola. Except for the spices, he felt like he could have been eating Colonel Sanders from the States.

"Just don't think of Colonel Sanders," Alf said, interrupting David's thoughts. And you will love it until you die. This is much better."

David did like it, but Alf's praise was something he would have to think about. For now, it was just good chicken. "So, how much time do we have to talk?" he asked. "Should we get into it?"

Alf finished a drumstick and wiped a gathering of crumbs from his mustache. "Yes. I didn't think we had much of a chance last time for 'Q&A.' So, let's start with that. Was there anything you wanted to know more about?"

"Okay, here's a general question. I would just like to hear more, from your perspective, about this mysterious job that you've talked me into against my will. Héctor gave me a general picture, but on occasion he got so wordy that I got lost and couldn't follow him. I think I understand it, but I want to get your version of it too."

"Talked you into? You mean the job that you said yes to without any encouragement because you had just gotten fired and had no place to go and nothing to do? Do you mean *that* one?"

"Well, if you put it that way."

Alf wiped his mustache again. "Okay, so if you got the general picture from Héctor, let me tell you a little about *why* we started this project. This is an idea that we've had for some time now. In fact, a few people from different departments in the University were discussing it back in the seventies before the war. The idea is simply that El Salvador is a very poor country. The government does not help much, but there is an army of organizations here, and all-over Central America, trying to do something to lift the average *campesino* or *migrante* out of poverty. Some of them do good work and some are terrible. Some are well-intentioned, and some are not—at least not in my opinion. But many of them—good and bad—don't know much about each other and what each of the others are doing. They work in isolation. Some of their projects are very narrow, like, say, a feeding program for hungry children—and my God, we have thousands of those—but they are very good at fundraising in the States. And others are broader and do solid long-term development, like teaching agronomy or farming or how to start up a marketable weaving business for women, but they do not know a thing about fundraising. Those are the problems. So, we thought, why can't we put together a network of these groups and have them talk to one another, and share ideas and, you know, like 'best practices' as they call it in the States?"

"So that they could interact and learn from each other?"

"Yes. Too often in the past, someone like you—well, not exactly like you, but someone from the States —would come down here and say, 'Hey, let me do it for you,' or 'Let me show you how we farm up in the plains of Kansas.' But that did very little good in the mountains of El Salvador. One time one of those well-intentioned, but stupid, guys raised a bunch of money in the States and bought a John Deere tractor and sent it up into the mountains, the *altiplano,* of Guatemala, and the first time they tried to show it off, it slid down the mountain into a ravine, and they never got it out. It was useless. It was stupid. And it cost them thousands of dollars. On the other hand, some of our people really know what they're doing, and they could be the best teachers for others—that is *if* they all could get together. That's the big picture of what we're trying to do." He waved his hands, one holding a chicken leg, widely around in a circle. "And we have to do all of that while at the same time fighting a civil war that is a defining event of our existence as a country."

He pointed to David's backpack. "Did Héctor give you our list?"

"Yes." David unzipped the side of his backpack and took out the binder that Héctor had given him and opened it up on the table.

Alf pulled it over to him and ran his finger down the rows of names of organizations, each with location and leader and type of service listed under them. "Here's what we are working with. Here in the city alone, there are probably more than a hundred of these. Out in the *campo,* there are hundreds more. Some are close to one another and know something about each other. But there are others who do similar work, and are just across the town, or in the same department, but know hardly anything about each other. They just labor in the vineyard and squeak by. Maybe they are helping, maybe they aren't, but *nadie sabe*, nobody knows—not even themselves in many cases."

"By the way," David said. "I hate to sound stupid so early in the game, but I've been practicing up on my Spanish and am embarrassed to realize how much of it I've forgotten."

Alf laughed. "I thought you said you took Spanish in college."

"I did, but I didn't major in it or anything, and it was a hundred years ago."

"Well, keep studying. Eventually, you're going to have to be fairly fluent. You will be fine most of the time here in the capital because many people you will work with will know a little English, and they'll like the chance to practice it on you. But when you go out into the *departments* you'll need to know more. Keep practicing, and we'll work it out."

For the next hour, Alf led David through the names that he already knew something about, what they did, and who they were sponsored by. David was overwhelmed by the number and variety. He had heard of some of them because they were reasonably well known in the States, like "Project Hope" or "CARE." Others were recognizable because they were related to a church or religious organization, like the "Mennonite Central Committee," or "Catholic Relief." But there were others that sounded—at least in Alf's opinion—like vanity projects named after their wealthy founders or big evangelists, programs like the "Peterson Family Foundation Orphanages," or the "James Lucas' Help the Children" program.

"James Lucas?" said David, puzzled. "The basketball player from Arkansas a few years ago?"

"That's him," said Alf. "And now he's wealthy, an evangel-ical—not that there's anything wrong with that—but he runs one of the worst direct-feeding programs in the country. It's one of those child sponsorship things. Some of them are fine, but a lot of them I do not like. He gets families back in the States to pay out twenty dollars a month to feed a hungry child, but then two dollars goes to the child, eight goes to overhead, and ten goes to our friend, Jim. It's not quite a scam, but it is also not much benefit to the child. Also, it tends to put the little *niño* you've sponsored in an upper-class status to all his friends. You know, like 'I'm having to quit school and work because my *papá* doesn't have a job, but you're doing fine because you have some rich family in Arkansas paying all your bills.' That sort of thing. And not very good for community and childhood trust."

"I've heard of that. It sounds messy and hard on the child." David closed the notebook and sat back on his concrete bench. "This is quite a list. And I'm supposed to visit with all of them and make some sense out of the chaos?"

"Of course, my friend. And you like chaos. I've seen you in the classroom."

"That was when I was young and happy. Today I'm old and tired."

"Well, you're not old, but you do look tired. You've been through hell. I promised to not talk about it much, but I want you to know that I feel for you. I don't know if I could have gone through what you did with Kathryn, and still somehow find a way to be up and walking around and breathing air today. So, maybe taking on a challenge like this will give you a little energy again."

David managed a humorless smile. "Yeah, well, maybe. But it could also age me faster."

Alf smiled back. "Well, if this kills you, let me know. I'll have my wife's priest do the Mass. He does a world class funeral and the whole campus will show up to watch."

CHAPTER TEN
ESCALÓN

Not in David's neighborhood, but somewhere else, in a beautiful home, on a beautiful street in a beautiful Colonia named Escalón, San Salvador, where there are groomed trees and high walls and well-manicured lawns, several men—only men—are meeting. There is one woman in the house, she is the *niñera* who normally takes care of the children, but the other helpers have been sent away for the weekend, so on this night, she is a waitress. When a small bell is rung, she comes into the room bringing coffee, bowls of sugar cubes, individual milk pitchers, and snacks—cheese, crackers, salami, nuts—the kind that would appeal to a North American palate. Later she returns to clear plates. There are six men altogether, and others, mainly in uniforms, come and go during the evening bringing papers, information, or questions. The room is large with high ceiling, deep carpet, and dark paneled walls. On one wall is a Spanish coat of arms. On another, above the heavy stone fireplace that is seldom used, is a large, distinguished painting of General Manuel José Arce y Fagoaga, a leader in the independence movement of El

Salvador from the Spanish Empire. The owner of the house does not know this history. The decorator chose the painting because it portrayed dignity and importance, not lineage or heritage. In the beginning, all the men are standing around a large table. They are all speaking in English, three with Spanish accents and three without. The three without wear long white *Guayabera* shirts with expensive embroidery on the edges, a frequent uniform for North Americans hoping to blend in by wearing expensive local clothing. Two of the three with Spanish accents wear dark suits, the third is in uniform. Only two speak.

The host for the evening has a full head of smooth black hair, combed straight back, and parted in the middle, he is wearing thick silver, artisanal sunglasses. He has a large, pocked nose and watery eyes. On his little finger there is a bright gold ring. When he enters the room, he speaks to none of them, but nods at the three in *Guayabera* shirts, then gestures to all of them that they may sit.

He is taller than the two in suits and does most of the speaking. It is a deep voice, a guttural voice, with an intensity that he believes projects gravity and authority. He reads to them from a copy of a document each of them has in front of them titled, "Regional Force Strength and Funding."

The document he reads asserts that the war situation has become grave and that it has the potential to become worse. "The FMLN terrorists," he says, referring to the main rebel coalition, "are well funded and they are not tied down by the normal rules of combat." He taps a gold pen on the document in front of him and looks up. "But this assessment is incorrect. We have the best, most capable fighting force in the world today. Gifted men, skilled men. We will have certain victory over the Communists."

One of the men with an American accent and Guayabera

shirt, is concerned about how long it should take. "We have been at this for a very long time, now," he says. "I have read the peace proposal that the FMLN released and parts of it seem reasonable—allowing absentee ballots, putting both parties on the election council, banning partisan poll watchers from surrounding the polls. In a free and fair election, these ideas are not extreme."

"These proposals were made solely because the terrorists are weakening," says the man with the gold ring. "They are proposing elections because they know they are militarily weak and that we will win the war soon."

"How soon?"

"Two years more, maybe three."

"Three years? I don't think you can expect the US Congress to continue funding at these levels that far into the future."

"It is not a long time. We are winning now, but the enemy is entrenched, and they have created many allies in the cities and communities. But..."

Another white-shirt participant interrupts. "Tell me how Ilopango is going," he said. "Is that cleared up?"

"Yes, the insurgents have been driven out. There is absolutely no resistance in Ilopango or Suchitoto today."

The questioner seems doubtful. "Where did they go? Did you push them into the river? Did you put them on boats? Where did they go?" He shows his teeth, but he is not smiling.

"No," says the suit. "The insurgents and those who aided them are...no longer alive." He pauses for a moment, and then adds with emphasis, "By *legal* and *just* procedures within the terms of our constitution."

The man in white does not appear to agree. "The reports we have received indicate that there were quite a few incidents of what appeared to be torture and that perhaps most of the casualties were civilians."

"And I assure you that that is incorrect. There were very few civilians. Many *appeared* to be civilians but were secretly working with the insurgents and had to be dealt with, but very few were civilians. One family, for example, was reported to have been hiding insurgents under their house. When they refused to allow the army soldiers to search the house, they were dealt with. Nothing more. We had no choice."

"How did they die?"

The man in the suit pauses again. Like the American, he is smiling, but with the face of one who has been insulted. "Fire," he says at last. "During the fighting an unfortunate fire broke out. They refused to leave, and the house was surrounded. They died in the fire. It was unfortunate, but also good. Had the house survived, they would have protected even more communists and that would have made an even greater threat to our democracy. It was regrettable, but unavoidable."

"So, how are the two towns now?"

"Beautiful," he says, smiling again. They are calm and...." He searched for a pleasant-sounding word. "Breathtaking!" He twirls his gold pen in his fingers. "You must go there sometime."

"I'll do that," says the shirt.

CHAPTER ELEVEN

THE INCIDENT

After weeks in Colonia Zacamil, David's life was beginning to be a balance of good days and bad ones. Today had been both. Most Monday mornings he would call Héctor to check in and see if there had been any additions or feedback from the organizations he had visited. Then he would make calls to as many of them as he could to set up new appointments during the week—or for the following week if the groups were busy. Then Tuesdays, Wednesdays, and Thursdays, he would pay them a visit and ask them a growing number of questions about their history, goals, work, structure, and philosophy of development. Friday was the day he tried to spend time compiling notes and unwinding, and today was Friday. Usually, he might have a quick interview or run errands, and after that he would come home early and relax in a lawn chair he had set out in front of his apartment window, drinking a rapidly warming beer, and going over his notes from the week. Today the Salvadoran heat was especially oppressive, so he was looking forward to the break.

He actually had two interviews that day, one good and one bad. In the morning, he met with an organization from Arkansas whose mission was not to give away food or medicine, but to supply poor families with young farm animals for breeding and then sharing. When the animals grew, the families were to share eggs, calves, and goat kids with their neighbors, and the neighbors would raise and share them too so that eventually the whole village would benefit. He liked those people a lot. But then in the afternoon, he met with some doctors from Texas who came down once a year to a clinic in San Vicente for a week and gave away leftover medications and glasses, and when they ran out, they flew up to the beaches of Belize to scuba dive and drink for two weeks. When they got back to the States, they would write off the entire trip as a charity donation. David was not impressed and barely managed to make it through the interview.

But now it was late afternoon, he was back at his apartment, and glad to be there. He had his beer, files, and clipboard and was sitting out in front of his apartment on his lawn chair and feeling relaxed. He smiled, realizing that he was beginning to like living here in Apartamentos Los Cañones and its surroundings. The apartment was small, at least compared to the previous two-story, four-bedroom home that he and Kathryn had shared in the States, but it was more than adequate for one person, and the neighborhood was perfect for his needs. It was off the major streets, lined by trees on one side and a tall wall enclosing a private school on the other, and within walking distance to shops, markets, and accessible buses. On top of all of that, one of the apartments at the end of his row had been turned into an ice cream shop, which he had already managed to visit a few times, even though he had only been settled in for little more than two months.

He even prided himself for almost stopping talking to

Kathryn every day. Well, that wasn't quite true. He greeted her just yesterday morning when he woke up and said goodnight to her twice the night before. But at least he wasn't seeing her every day on the bus or in the market or walking through his kitchen. At least he wasn't waking up in the middle of the night screaming at her to move or jump or just not be back there and then seeing her not move in spite of his yelling, and then seeing it happening all over again. At least he wasn't doing that, at least not as much, at least not as often.

Los Cañones was a typical Salvadoran apartment complex. It was made up of seven long rows of four-story high-rise apartments that were plain and almost ugly from a distance, but in between those rows were trees and walkways and occasional small playgrounds that gave it a pleasant, neighborly look. It also came with certain amenities that he appreciated, such as free water and electricity and, best of all, a free maid that came in once a week to sweep and pick up—and bring him a sealed pitcher of fresh water! Her name was Camilia, and she spoke about as much English as David did Spanish (though he kept telling himself that he was getting better at it). She came with the apartment, which seemed generous, but David suspected that the landlord had probably had a few unsavory tenants in the past and somewhere along the line decided to build the service into the rent. David had only spoken to her a handful of times because she was usually there during the day when he was gone. But occasionally he would come home early and greet her as she worked the apartments on his row.

"*Buenos*," she would say, nodding matter-of-factly when he found her doing his dishes or vacuuming his carpet. "*Buenos*," he would say back, nodding also at the formal informality of the ritual. And that was the extent of their conversation, at least for the first few times they met. Eventually, he started attempting full sentences, like, "*¿Dónde vive usted?*" "Where do you live?" Or "*¿Cómo está usted?*" "How are you?" Or "*¿Tiene usted hijos?*" "Do you have Children?" When he first started doing that, she responded with long cheerful descriptions of her health and home and family, and the many trials of raising girls without a present father but soon realized that the deep blank looks he gave her in return showed that he understood little of what she was saying. Then she started matching his looks with blank stares of her own that said, silently, *"I'm going to be patient with you, but you must learn Spanish if you're going to live here."* It was his fault, she was right, and he knew it.

Carlos, the apartment manager, was also interesting. He lived in the complex himself, a few doors down from David, where there were apartments for the staff, and they passed each other going or coming several times a week. Carlos was single with two teen boys who lived with their mother somewhere else in the city. Carlos and the mother were evidently estranged because David never saw her anywhere in the complex. The boys came to visit now and then, and David tried to greet them, but they didn't seem interested in conversation, so he never learned their names. They just walked to and from Carlos's doorway looking glum as though it was a required visit, and never spoke, even to each other, until they entered. Carlos, however, was very friendly and spoke lovingly of them and somewhat longingly when they were away for too long. He seemed to be convinced that the family would one day be together again. Though David didn't know the mother, from what he could tell in Carlos's stories and the boys' dour demeanor, he didn't see much hope that a reconciliation would ever come to pass.

Occasionally he saw Carlos and Camilia standing together on the balcony, talking. They looked very comfortable together, and in the beginning, David wondered if they might be a couple, but he never saw any other evidence of a deeper connection. Perhaps just a good working relationship. Perhaps the strained hopes for a reconciliation with his ex-wife and sons prevented him from being open to feeling close to another person.

Directly across from his ground floor row were four interesting apartments, two on the first floor and two just above them on the second, and they seemed related. They had no visible names or markings, but each had two folding chairs in front and there were almost always one or two young women sitting in them, dressed in lingerie or short skirts, high heels, and revealing tops. Occasionally he would see a man come down the sidewalk, walking from the gate that was supposed to be locked, greet one of the sitting women, chat for a moment, and then accompany her inside one of the apartments. The visit was seldom for more than an hour, and when it was over, the woman would come out first and the man would follow. The two would nod, usually silently, exchange something that appeared to be money, and he would leave. And the woman would return to her chair. Twice a man in a police uniform came to visit. He didn't go inside but instead stood formally in front of the women in their chairs speaking loudly, almost like giving orders or addressing staff. David was curious about what he was saying, but the man never turned around and when he had finished, he left as sharply as he had arrived.

When the women were not engaged inside the apartment, they usually sat quietly outside, smoking, and looking at the sidewalk and grass with blank, non-focused eyes. Most of the time they didn't seem to notice David when he came through the gate (always unlocked when they were in their chairs) and crossed the narrow grassy lane to his side and to his own apartment. But now and then one would look up expectantly when he passed. Not a friendly, welcoming look, but a hesitant, expectant look. He felt stupid that it took him so long to understand who they were and what they were cautiously waiting for, sitting silently by their doorways. After that, he began to almost fear them. Not because of physical harm, but because in their presence he was treading into a foreign territory where he didn't have a solid land mass of experience to hold onto. The idea of someone having to make a living by selling her body, in the middle of the radical disintegration of the country around her and doing so with the constant possibility of disease or violence, created a horrifying image for him. There wasn't much in his suburban childhood or academic adulthood that prepared him for the reality that, for many of these women, this huge risk was better than other alternative livelihoods.

Occasionally, women would come through the gate and cross over to his side and go down to one of the empty apartments, beyond Carlos'. They dressed more professionally, as though they could have been a clerk at a bank (if he had ever gone into a bank to look, which he never did).

One of them, and someone he later learned was named "Isabel," was older and taller than most of the others. On almost every Friday, towards the end of the day, she would enter the gate between the apartment rows, speak to the others on the chairs across from him, and then cross over to his side and down to the room where she could take the appointment. Usually, she was alone when she arrived, but not long after, a gentleman would appear coming down the sidewalk on his side and join her in the apartment.

After a few visits, Isabel started nodding politely at David as she passed and sometimes smiling. At first, her friendliness startled him. He thought that perhaps she was trying to offer her services. But it was clear that she wasn't doing that, so eventually he began nodding back, then smiling back, and in time he looked forward to her passing and neighborly nods. He knew almost no one in the area, so a woman (nice looking and well dressed) walking by and smiling, had a feeling of normalcy about it, even given what for him was her somewhat other-worldly vocation. It gave him the feeling— false though it was—that he had acquired a friend in the neighborhood.

One time, late at night, in the middle of the week, he was roused from sleep by loud talking and flashing lights. He went to his window and saw an ambulance in the parking lot to his left and several people gathered in front of the apartments across from him. Two were police, others, wearing white jackets, were apparently medical personnel, and the rest appeared to be onlookers from neighboring apartments. He couldn't make out much of what they were saying, but they were energetically discussing something among themselves. The policemen were talking to a tall slender woman standing off to the side. Several young women were crying and screaming and hugging each other. Someone's been hurt, he thought, so he dressed quickly and made his way across the grass to the other side and stood silently at the edge of the growing crowd. He got there just as three men in white rolled a gurney out of the doorway with a small woman on it bleeding badly around her face and neck. She moaned painfully and writhed left and right on the gurney. The woman who had been talking to the police went over to her and spoke to her quietly for a moment. She leaned down and kissed the injured woman gently on the forehead, and then the men rolled the gurney away. When she stood up and turned back to the others, he recognized her. It was Isabel, his sometime neighbor and acquaintance.

One officer arrived late and passed the others to go straight into the apartment. He stayed there for a while and when he came out, he called to one of the other officers to go in and clean up something. He seemed to be in charge of the investigation and also knew the women. David looked hard at him from his perch at the edge of the crowd and thought he recognized him. Was that the same officer he had seen earlier visiting and yelling at the women in the doorways? When the man ushered the other officer into the apartment, he turned to Isabel, and they talked actively for some time about what had happened. David couldn't understand the words, but he could tell there was anger in his voice. Once again he seemed to be addressing Isabel and the others as though they were employees, not victims of a crime. After a few moments, the officer turned and walked out to the street as abruptly as he had first come in.

David did not know the young woman who had been beaten so badly, or any of the others who were gathered around her, but there was something personal in her pain and disfigurement that made him choke and grieve with the rest. He'd never seen her before, but he knew agony, and blood, and suffering, and their memories fought him and wouldn't let him go.

There had been a great deal of blood in the incident, and it was not even immediately clear that the young woman would live. Isabel evidently had been called by the others when it happened, and she had dressed and wrapped some of the injuries herself before the paramedics arrived. Was it an accident? A beating by a client? He couldn't tell, but Isabel calmly talked through it all with the police and seemed to be the one in control of the situation. He was surprised to see her there because, though he knew that she also lived somewhere in the complex, he never saw her here at night. Perhaps she was something like the godmother for the younger women who worked here. Perhaps she had received some kind of medical training in her past and was called upon to use it when situations like this arose. Or maybe she had just lived through these kinds of incidents too often and had become skilled at dressing wounds. He didn't know.

Suddenly two more officers came out dragging a tall blond-haired man in handcuffs who spoke English. "Let go of me," he yelled, jerking wildly, trying to pull away from them. "She's okay...she started it...I didn't do anything..." The evidence against him seemed pretty strong, but that didn't seem to dissuade him from claiming otherwise. "She's lying...She tricked me...I didn't know we were coming here," and more.

The two officers holding him smiled almost tauntingly as they pulled him down the sidewalk to the street. That guy, David thought, is going to be in trouble for a very long time. But then, when they got to the parking lot, and away from the apartments, the officers stopped for a moment, talked to him, laughed loudly, and then undid his handcuffs and let him go. He stood for a moment, looking somewhat bewildered, but thanked them, and then ran straight north to Calle Zacamil and was gone. My god, thought David. What allowed a white guy from the States to get off so easily?

After he was taken away, Isabel, the police and EMTs all finished up and left the apartment, so he went back to his own apartment and back to bed. What an ordeal, he thought, and fitfully tried to forget it all and go back to sleep.

The following Friday, when he was again sitting outside of his own apartment, again drinking his beer and studying his notes, he saw Isabel coming through the gate and walking down his sidewalk for her weekly appointment. She greeted him again quietly and silently as she so often did and he nodded back, but this time he spoke to her. He asked her in Spanish what had happened that night.

She paused for a moment and responded, also in Spanish,

"A man beat her," and then continued walking past him. But after a few steps she paused and turned back. "I was able to stop the bleeding, but she needed surgery."

"Is she alright?" he asked.

"No," she said. "She will never be 'alright' again. He beat her in the face and head. He broke her shoulder."

"I am so sorry."

She stood looking at him without moving. It was not a friendly look. It was a look that pondered whether she should blame all rich gringos for the actions of this evil one. "Her face will always be scarred, always damaged," she said. "*Y morirá de hambre.*" "And she will then not be able to work again and will die of hunger." Isabel turned away from him on the sidewalk and continued walking.

CHAPTER TWELVE

MOVING DAY

Along Lincoln Street there wasn't always a lot of activity. Especially down at the end where David and Kathryn would soon be living. But today was different. In the street was a long moving van. In the driveway were two cars, and across the street there were three young boys and two dogs who stood silently staring at the noisy, rapid movers and their dollies, hand trucks, blankets, and many, many boxes. There were five of them, four looked right out of college and one—who did most of the pointing and talking—was closer to middle age.

Both garage doors were open, and David was in and out carrying boxes with the more fragile items from the cars in the driveway. This was his third trip today from their condo in Boston, and he was exhausted and ready to stop. It was late in the afternoon, and the movers were about to wrap up, and when they did, he and Kathryn would be ready for a much-needed break and glass of wine.

Kathryn was mainly standing guard just inside the front door like an aggressive traffic cop, directing that this chest should go upstairs, and that couch should go down. She had thought it all out in advance and knew where everything would go and how it would fit. Only occasionally did she call out to David for advice, and that was for items belonging to his side of the family and did he want it in his office or in the guest room to be decided upon later. Usually, it was the guest room, where they both suspected the items might stay for months because they would be slow to make final decisions on them.

"David," she called out at last, "I think the sofa and end tables are the last things. Do you want to say something to the boys?" By "boys" she meant the young movers. David slammed down the trunk of his car and looked around at them. Three were in the yard and two others were coming out of the front door after they had placed the sofa in the perfect place in the living room, just as Kathryn had directed them.

"Is that it?" he yelled up at them.

"Think so," said one. "You didn't have much, so I think we're done."

David stayed outside with them for a while signing papers and thanking them, and he added a small tip for each of them from his pocket. Kathryn went inside to pour the wine and set it out in their newly furnished living room. She had a grocery bag and liquor box set aside for just this occasion, and she put it all out, gouda, brie, crackers, hummus, olives, and red wine. Just as she finished putting it all in place, his head appeared at the door, and he looked around at the new surroundings he believed would be their perfect home for many years. It still looked rough, especially with nothing on the walls and small boxes scattered around filled with kitchen and bathroom supplies that needed to be unpacked. But their new living room, with a fireplace, piano, couch, coffee table, and the recent addition of a "Happy Hour" wine spread, looked just perfect. Kathryn was sitting straight up on the edge of the couch with her hands folded properly in her lap and looked at him somewhat triumphantly, and a little seductively. She was beautiful, and he was in love. I am so damn lucky, he thought. This is perfect. Just perfect.

CHAPTER THIRTEEN
PUPUSERIA

The sun was just beginning to dip below the tops of buildings along Calle Zacamil when Alf turned his Pinto pickup down the wide alley in front of Los Cañones. He was bringing David home from a meeting that afternoon with Héctor and two others from the university about the progress of David's work. David carefully pulled his backpack and legs out of the cab and stepped to the ground. His thighs hurt from the amount of walking he had done that day.

"You going to be okay?" Alf asked.

"Yeah," he said. "I think I'll be fine. I just pulled something walking so much this morning. Thanks for the lift."

Alf shifted the car into reverse but stopped. "Did I tell you about the party next Friday before semester Break?"

David leaned against the car door frame rubbing the sore in his calf. Stretching it helped a bit. "I don't think so," he said, not looking up.

"I should have. It's an informal gathering at the university. You are considered faculty there—officially anyway—so you should come. Nothing special, but we like to get together before we all take off for the break, and you'd get a chance to meet a few people."

David was feeling a little better but still rubbing his leg. "If they're all like you, I should probably pass."

"You're such a nice guy. *Mira*, when all of this is over, you'll thank me for saving your *pompis*, and you know it."

David knew it was true. "I know," he said more soberly, "and trust me, I do appreciate it. So, what's the occasion and where is it?"

"It's in our Engineering building. They have a big room in the basement with a kitchen. It's kind of our faculty hacienda and we have a lot of parties there. And *Salvadoreños* do party a lot. If you want, I can pick you up."

"No, if it's just there at the university, I can get there by myself. And that way if you want to party until three, I can get myself home, because *Salvadoreños* do party a lot."

Bueno! said Alf. "The meal starts at about 7:30, with some great Salvadoran beers and awful Nicaraguan rum before then." He frowned. "How have you been doing with food and groceries. The last time we met you sounded like you were just eating at the little ice-cream shop down from your apartment. Have you branched out from that?"

"Yeah, sure, and I've tried some of the other local places too. But for tonight, I don't know. Maybe I'll just fry up some fish I found in the market and hang out here."

"I think I remember when you bought that fish, and when you should have eaten it. And if you eat it now, call me and I will give you directions to the *farmacia* where you can also find medicines for your stomach." He gestured with his thumb at the row of shops in back of them. David frowned, so Alf pointed a long finger past Los Cañones and into the trees beyond it. "Okay, so I think there's a little Pupusería in one of the apartments down that street in back of you. I think it's on the right after you go a couple of blocks. It's before you get to the Mercado. *Mi tia* used to work there years ago. And it's within walking distance." He smiled. "Even for you."

David smiled too and ignored the comment. "I'll give it a try sometime." He swung his backpack over his shoulder and waved. "But for tomorrow, I'll call you if I need you for anything."

"You will always need me." Alf put the truck in reverse again and began backing out into the street.

David stood on the sidewalk for a long time thinking what he might do. He looked at his watch. It was nearly 6:00, so he'd start feeling hungry fairly soon. He did have the fish in the refrigerator, but Alf was correct in insinuating that it had been there a while, and he'd hate to eat it and get sick and then have Alf laugh about it later. Then there was the little ice cream shop. It was nice, but the actual food they served was made elsewhere and often crusty by the time they offered it for sale. It was evening now, so it had definitely reached its crusty vintage. He looked down past Los Cañones at what appeared to be a small park and a street beyond it. He'd not gone through there so far, and Alf did recommend a *Pupusaría* in that direction. Why not? he thought and started towards it. From a distance, he had originally thought it would be just an alley, but it opened into a wide street and a separate neighborhood with more rows of apartments like his. Lined side by side, with trees, sidewalks, an occasional car, and even a tricycle. The architecture looked Hispanic but otherwise reminded David of any number of streets in the US.

He walked past one long row of apartments and then another, and then another, and after the third, he began to wonder if he had in fact come out on the right street or perhaps had gotten turned around. There was nothing around here that looked like a *Pupusería*. To his right was a basketball court, straight ahead was Avenida Norte, a major thoroughfare, and to his left was another long row of apartments. Here we go again, he thought. I'm lost. He carefully turned towards them and almost immediately saw it. He had been walking and looking through the apartments and couldn't see anything, but at a corner to his right there it was. It was so ordinary that at first he didn't realize what it was. It was the first apartment at the beginning of one of the long rows of apartments. It had a plain front with a small patch of lawn that blended in with the rest of the neighborhood, except this one had a small sign, a very small sign, on the front door that said, "Pupusería Bety." He smiled. At least they don't spend a lot of their profits on advertising, he thought. He walked up the steps and knocked.

CHAPTER FOURTEEN
BETY'S

When the door opened, he saw what appeared to be a family living room but tightly filled with tables and chairs on the left, a small bar on the right, and an elderly, immaculately dressed, woman in front, greeting him. "*Beinvenido,*" she said, waving broadly into the room. *Pase adelante.* He smiled and walked in slowly, looking cautiously left and right. This is very nice, he thought. Tiny, but also charming. This could become a regular place for him. The woman, who looked very much like an owner or manager (perhaps Bety herself?) ushered him into the small dining room and made gestures indicating he could have either a table by himself or a seat at the bar. He thought the bar would be fine and would save space for later patrons. "*Bueno,*" she said, and took him by the hand and led him to the last stool, next to a door to the kitchen and just inches from a table where two young boys and a mother were eating. The mother was looking embarrassed, and the boys were burping and giggling. They were cute, he thought. He and Kathryn had not had any children, and he always wondered how their lives would have been different if they had. For a brief, painful moment the older boy looked up at him, and he saw the face of little Gil at the border who had tried so hard to carry David's bags and paid for it brutally in the end. He shook his head and turned back to the bar. Let it go, he told himself. In front of him, behind the bar, a silver-haired man with a distinguished, tight, thin mustache was drying and stacking glasses and looked up at him. "*¿Qué te gustaría?*" he asked.

David fumbled for a moment. He wasn't sure what to ask for. "*Pupusas?*" he asked.

The man slid a laminated one-page menu across the bar to him. "*¿Que tipo Pupusas?*" He asked. "*Tenemos muchos tipos diferentes.*"

David stared intently at the menu but was overwhelmed. He knew that Pupusas were a delicacy and said to be delicious, but none of them were familiar to him. *Pupusa revuelta, Pupusa de quesillo, Pupusa de chicharrón, Pupusa con loroco...*He knew, for example, that *Loroco* was some kind of flower indigenous to Central America, but he didn't know what it looked like and couldn't imagine putting a flower in a dinner pastry. The man with the mustache came back after a moment with a pad in his hand and looked at David impatiently. David was still deliberating. "I'll have...." He scoured the list looking for familiar words and saw *chicharrón* which he knew to mean pork. "*Este,*" he said, pointing to the name.

"*Bueno,*" said his host, "*cuanto?*"

"Um, *dos...no tres.*"

"*Bueno, y, para tomar?*"

"*Una Cerveza,*" David said, "A beer." Then remembering his manners, he added, "*por favor,*" and slapped the menu down decisively. That hadn't been so hard.

Then the man looked up and said in a rapid monotone, "*¿Quieres algo con eso? ¿Una ensalada? Quizás frijoles y arroz?*

Nuestras pupusas son muy pequeñas. Es posible que quieras algo más para ir con ellos."

David stopped. He had been in El Salvador for some time by then but recognized nearly nothing in the man's fast string of words. The man began to smile, but just slightly. David was sure he was enjoying the confusion but didn't know how to defend himself. Behind him David heard sounds of giggling coming from the two little boys. He turned around and saw the mother tapping gently on the table. *"Niños, Niños!"* she said. *"Ser cortés, cortés,"* but as soon as he looked at them, they laughed even louder. He looked back at the waiter. *"Lo siento,"* he said, "I'm sorry," and added a phrase he used often when he got into language trouble. *"No hablo muy bien el español."* "I don't speak the Spanish very well." His fallback self-effacing phrase.

The man's smile grew larger. "Yes, I could tell that," he said in very precise, but accented, English. "Would you like for me to say it again in English?" The boy chorus behind him exploded with more laughter. Even though they didn't understand David's English, they were enjoying his confusion. *"Niños, Niños,"* the mother was saying, tapping her hand again, but she was clearly enjoying the joke on David as much as they were. David wanted to be angry, but it was hard to show anger at little boys laughing. He held up a finger to the man in front of him. *"Un momento,"* he said. He turned around to face the table. They were delighted at the show. "So, do either of you guys speak any English, better than my Spanish?"

The younger of the two, perhaps eight, understood the question and immediately burst out, *"Eiens, Zwei, Drei, Vier, Fünf."*

The older boy, who looked about ten, hit him on the arm. *"¡Estúpido!"* he said. *"Eso es alemán,"*

Immediately the smaller boy realized he had the wrong

language and started again. "One, two, three, four, six, seven, ten." His face was bright with pride.

"Good for you," David said. "You know about as much English as I know Spanish."

"They are taking English in School," said the mother, speaking to David for the first time.

David jumped. "You speak English very well," he said. "Yes," she said, "some." She looked almost embarrassed. "Where did you learn English?" he asked.

En la Escuela, she said, reverting, and then caught herself. "And also, I was in the United States for four years when I was in school." She pulled back almost shyly. "Now I sometimes translate at the University and help the *niños* practice their lessons."

The boys were staring at her in what looked like amazement at her strange language noises. David started to say something back to her when he felt a tapping on his shoulder. He turned and saw the elderly gentleman holding up a pencil. "May I help you with your decision?" he asked. He had evidently been entertained enough.

"Yes," David said, "I'm sorry. Can you suggest anything?"

He leaned over the menu and pointed the eraser at one of the items. "If you want the *Pupusas de chicharrón,* a salad could go with that, and beans with cheese. It is very good here." He raised one eyebrow, waiting.

"Yes, that would be nice," David said and pushed the menu back at him. "Thank you. I'll do that."

The mother then spoke again. "Are you here with business?"

"No," he said. "I work here. I have a job."

"What is the job?" She paused for a moment and then said very slowly, frowning, "*El Agencia...de los Estados Unidos...par...*"

She paused again and then *"el Desarrollo Internacional..."*? He recognized that she was trying to say the name of the US "Agency for International Development," but struggling to remember it.

He laughed. "No, but that's a good guess. I work for a non-governmental organization. Not USAID. Do you know of the 'Instituto de Educación y Apoyo no Gubernamental,' the IEAG?"

She shook her head.

"I'm supposed to be an advisor to development organizations. To help them balance their books, raise money, publicize themselves. That sort of thing."

"Do you mean like, Accion Catolica, or Servicio Mundial de la Iglesia?"

"Yes!" He said, surprised that she knew the names, "though there are many others like those. They all want to do more work together and I've been asked to help them."

"So, you are a good man?" she asked.

"Ha, well, I hope I can help at least some of them. There is much that the organizations do that I don't know anything about."

The boys were pushing at her and wanting to talk, but she was still curious. "But why are you here now? It is dangerous here."

"That's true, but I'll...I'll watch out." He had no way of explaining why he went to one of the most dangerous countries in the world for what amounted to little more than a glorified accounting job. He changed the subject . "I'm an economist," he said. "Normally I teach in a university. But I'm here now trying to—*hopefully* trying to—help some of these organizations learn how to do better at their work and not lose money. I've only been here a few months, but that's what I'm going to try to do.

She looked pleased but still puzzled. "But why here? There are poor people in *los Estados Unidos, tambien.*"

"That's true," he said. He didn't know how to answer that. Should he try to talk philosophically about what would bring first-world people to third-world countries to try to do work like this? Should he say he was a man whose wife died tragically, and he had run away on some kind of irrational spiritual pilgrimage? Or should he just say it was a job that paid a salary and that's why he was there? He couldn't say the last one, not after she had just called him a good man for what he did, but he was stuck and couldn't answer.

Just then the two boys began pushing their mother again for information about who he was and what the two were talking about. She spoke to them quietly and then smiled at David. "They want to know who you are and why am I talking to you."

He laughed again. "Well, my name is David, and I don't have a clue as to why you are talking to me."

"'Clue?'" she said looking puzzled. "Do you mean in a mystery story?"

"Oh, sort of, I mean I don't know why you are talking to me. You are just being nice to a stranger, I guess. I think that means that you are the nice person here."

She sat back, her face looking embarrassed, then she turned and spoke softly to the boys again. There was more laughter and chatter that he didn't understand.

Then in almost an instant, the youngest looked like he remembered something and ran for the door. "I think we must go home now," she said to David. "Daniel wants to watch the *televisión.* And that one," she pointed to the older boy. "That one is Tomas. He has his work for his studies."

"Do you mean 'homework'"?

"Yes," she said energetically. "*Homework.* Thank you."

"Did you say, '*Daniel*'?" He said, his eyebrows rising.

"Yes," she said. "It was his father's name."

"Mine too. I mean, it was my father's name too." He felt vaguely embarrassed for stumbling with his words.

"It is the same name. Maybe we are related?"

For a moment, he didn't realize that she was joking, and he didn't know how to answer. Then her smile turned up and gave it away and he smiled back. "No, that would be unlikely. Your Daniel is much better looking than I am."

Then it was her turn to laugh. "They are my two trouble-makers." David smiled and raised his hand to wave at them, but both had reached the door by then. She began wrapping up the remaining pupusas from the boys' plates, but looked at him and said, "My name is Sara, Sara De León." She held out her free hand to shake.

He paused for a moment not knowing what the protocol was about shaking hands with a woman. "We shake hands in El Salvador too," she said, enjoying his discomfort. He took it awkwardly and said, "*Mucho Gusto,* Miss De León."

"And also to you." Then more quietly she added, "*Dahveed.*" She drew the name out as though it was a long and unfamiliar word, "we are here on almost all of the Fridays. If you are here also next Friday too, we can...we can talk again?"

David didn't know how to answer her. It was an invitation, from an attractive woman, to meet in a restaurant and talk. It felt warm and sincere and very kind, and he would love to have a friend in this strange place. But to say yes also felt like a betrayal. In fact, he still had his wedding ring on. And he felt an even stronger sense of betrayal when he noticed himself noticing that she did *not* have one on.

"I might be gone next week," he said, not sounding convincing. "I don't know when I will be around again."

She looked disappointed but nodded. He suspected that she didn't believe him. "Well, we will be here."

"Sure," he said, trying to sound encouraging. "Yes, and if I'm here next week, I'll come to Bety's again on Friday." He felt like his face said he was lying and that she could tell. But he knew that he couldn't *allow* himself to mean it, and then she left.

CHAPTER FIFTEEN
ZACAMIL

Several blocks away from David's apartment, closer to the university, though still in Colonia Zacamil, set back from the street, is a house. Not a grand house like those in the wealthy neighborhoods of Colonia Escalón, but large enough for gatherings, meetings, and families, and on this day for hosting revolutionaries who come from all parts of El Salvador, and all parts of the capital, to assess the revolution.

There was a man in that community who has held meetings at his house many times in the past to discuss strategies moving forward. The man was a leader, a benefactor, an organizer, and a fighter, and when he spoke, the others who attended that evening listened. There were eight men around a large table in the room, no servants, and two women. In the pre-revolutionary days of conservative El Salvador, there would have been no women in such a gathering, but this night there were two. They were welcomed and encouraged by most of the men present, but some, who were still drawn to the rules of older times, were unhappy with their presence in the discussions. It was not that they thought the women were inferior, they were saying, but simply that God had given them different roles in the world, and it was not the men's place to experiment dangerously with what God has chosen. Women should be honored and revered for their childbearing and home keeping and not be asked to endure the trials of the jungle with weapons and dangers. It would be demeaning to women to have them do work that was made for men.

There were also others who were present, who were younger than the others and less attracted to the older customs, and possibly more attracted to the women in attendance, and they made a case for the opposite. The women are strong, they said, they are smart, and they are committed. There is nothing but adherence to the old rules of the old ways that should keep them from our meetings.

In the beginning, the meeting's host, who stood at the head of the table, with a long beard, sullen eyes, and dark skin, ignored this discussion and instead read solemnly through documents and folders that were laid out before him. There were many papers, photos, notes, and files, on the table and he looked through all of them, and he looked tired. But eventually he was finished and looked up at the others in the room. He waved the back of his hand across the table, which told them all to be silent. "¡*Silencio!*" he said in a low strong voice. "We have much before us with which to contend. But the presence of women fighters will not be one of them." He paused to look around the room and into each man's eyes. "We all know our *Companera*, Febe Elizabeth, a fearsome fighter and leader at FENASTRAS union. And can any of you say that she is not as worthy as some of you?" No one spoke. "It is *1989*, my friends, not 1889, our mission is in danger, and the women will stay." The supporters were pleased, the detractors were angry, the women were silent and looked straight ahead, and the discussion ended. The two women were sisters. They both wore tan khakis, brown work vests, green shirts, and bandanas with the initials FMLN around their necks. They didn't speak. But they were here, they were not leaving, and the meeting went on.

"So far we have been successful at keeping the enemy out of the *departamentos* that we occupy." He spoke with an impatient tone. "We have been able to fight with small units to penetrate their rear and strike as soon as they approach the zone in their big trucks and fight until they withdraw. We have been agile, and we have been strong."

"And we also have not advanced," said one of the others around the table.

"Yes, but we *have* held our zones," said one of the women. "We have just not expanded."

"And now," said the other, "we have a new peace proposal. Even some of the Americans say it has parts that are worth supporting."

"But the fascist army will never support peace," said one of the older men who had been unhappy with the presence of women. "The only thing that they support is more killings. They will negotiate and negotiate, and in the end, we will still hold the same lands that we have held for many years. And more of our people will be murdered."

"But in those lands, an experiment in a new democracy is happening," said the host at the head of the table. "We are creating a new reality in those zones. A reality in which all are equal, women will vote, children will not work in the fields, and men will receive wages that can sustain their families...we are winning. This will remain. It will be the new reality of El Salvador."

A young man at the other end of the table raised his voice. "But when? We have been in the struggle for too long. We need to bring all of our fighters together at once, and all the people who support us, and surround the cities, and surprise them with a force that the enemy could never have expected. We know that the poor in the cities will rise up and fight with us. And when we win, we will have an entire country in which to experiment with this new democracy." As he spoke, his voice grew louder. The others looked at him, some were nervous at his rising emotion. "And do not speak to us of peace talks," he said. "We have had peace talks for four years and everyone here knows that they are frauds. The enemy wants only to hold charade talks to continue their oppression and keep us from winning against them. And we all know this."

"But we cannot win," said the one who had spoken first. "They have the strength of American weapons and training that we cannot match. We cannot win without more money, more weapons, and more fighters."

"Yes, we can win," the man who had spoken last said. "We have the strength of the people. We know that. If we attack the cities, the people will come together with us. They will support us. They want change. There would not be a force strong enough to withstand the will of the people."

"Calm," said the leader at the head. "Yes, it is true that we have not grown in strength or land in some time. And yes, most of the people do support us. But still, we must wait. If we attempt a new 'Final Offensive' on the cities now, the casualties would be heavy—on our side and on theirs—and many of our international supporters will oppose us because of the deaths. We want justice and liberation, not more morgues and graves. For now, we must wait for this new round of talks. If they fail, we will reconsider, but for now, we wait. We will have good men" —he looked nervously at the two women sitting at his side— "and *women,* at those talks, and if a pathway to peace can be found, they will find it."

"You always say 'wait,'" the first speaker said again. "We have been waiting for many years, and our people are still dying. When do we do more than just create small attacks around the edges? When do we show the enemy that this is still a war?"

"What you are saying is true," said the leader at the front, with his voice slow and rumbling. "But for now, we will still wait."

CHAPTER SIXTEEN
UNIVERSARIO

Two weeks later, on Friday, and on his way home, David had the taxi drop him off at the university so he could use the copy machine in the department office. He had written a new form letter to send out to some of the organizations he wanted to talk to, introducing himself and requesting a visit, and he needed to make copies to send around.

He got there at about 6:00, and just as he was going in the front door, Alf was coming out and gave a shout. "Hey gringo, aren't you here a little early?"

David gave him a puzzled look. "I just arrived," he said. "And I'm needing to do a little work tonight, so I wanted to steal some of your whiteout and paper."

Alf raised his hands in a look of mock outrage. "Well, just don't drink it down like you used to do in the States. It took us days to pump it out of your stomach when you did that."

"Well, some like beer and some like whiteout. What can I say?"

"How long will you be here?"

"Not long, why? Will I be in the way?"

"No," said Alf. "But tonight is that Semester Break party I told you about. Just a little get-together before we take off. In fact, I thought you were here now because you had come early for it. You should come. Some of these people are not nearly as terrible as I am." He smiled broadly, forcing his mustache to cover most of his face.

David thought for a moment. For some time now, he had thought little of parties and socializing. But Alf was sincere about the invitation, and he didn't have any good excuse not to, so he answered, "Sure. *¿A qué hora?*"

"I think they're setting up the downstairs for it right now, so probably in about an hour or so."

David looked at his watch. "I could do that, but I won't have time to go home to change clothes or anything."

Alf laughed again. "Don't worry, man. Most of us won't either, so your smell will be to us, *muy similar*. We just go down when we get free up here, and just chip in where we are needed. When you get there, look for a giant gorilla named Emilio Bhutto. He teaches mathematics but likes to tend bar whenever we have a function. He's huge and looks scary but is a lot nicer than he looks."

"If I'm real nice to him, will he give me a discount on the beer?"

Alf laughed. "Unlikely. I said he was nicer than he looks. I didn't say he was actually nice. Bhutto is a loner and doesn't get along with any of us very well, so he'll appreciate your talking with him."

Less than an hour later David finished his work in the copy room. He filled his backpack with the letters he'd been copying and made his way down the staircase to a large conference room. There were only a handful there when he walked in, but it was early. The group reminded him of any faculty party he had been to in the States—professional-looking people, many wearing glasses, dressed neatly but inexpensively. He saw what appeared to be a makeshift bar set up next to the wall, so he made his way over to it. He walked quickly, not wanting to be forced to make conversation with strangers, something he was not always good at, even during his best days. The bar looked immediately familiar. An eight-by-four-foot white Formica-topped table on wheels. Every campus he had ever been on in his entire life had a dozen or so of these. In fact, every college, church, and union hall had a few stashed away for dinners, receptions, and conferences. They never went out of date and always served the purpose.

The food, he discovered, was free, but the drinks he had to pay for. A bad set of options, he thought, because what he really wanted was a drink, and some of the free food looked like leftover school cafeteria options and slightly intimidating. A very large man with a large square face, a stiff brush of mustache, and a dour demeanor, looked at him from behind the table. He knew at once that it must be the giant, Emilio Buhto. The size and attitude fit Alf's description. He was taller and wider than anyone else in the room and had a sneer seemingly engraved in his face, and he seemed to bask in the intimidation that it offered him around others. He looked at David unsmiling and impatiently waiting for him to decide.

There were three beers on tap and three more displayed on the table. "*¿Cuál es el mejor?*" "Which is best?" David asked.

Bhutto frowned and gave David a look that he interpreted to mean, *if you have to ask, you should stick with water.* He pointed at the third of the tap handles and said, "*Ese.* That one," then in very slow and deliberate English, "It is from Havana; it is our radical political beer." He withdrew his hand and leaned across the table glancing around as though fearful of being heard, "It is not better, but it will give you credibility from the many socialists on the faculty if they think you drink it."

David laughed, "Well, I'll just have to have it then. I guess I need to build up my credibility."

"Yes, you might eventually have to do that," he said, pulling down the weathered wooden handle. "There are some here who do not know who you are or why you are here. There is talk that you might be with the CIA."

David let out an incredulous laugh. "Now that has got to be a joke. I have a lot of places I need to visit in and around San Salvador, but the CIA offices are not one of them. I don't even know where they are."

Bhutto did not smile and lowered his voice. "That is not true. You will be there next Thursday. I know this."

David shook his head. "No, that's not right. Next Thursday I am supposed to be at the US Agency for Economic Development."

Bhutto leaned back from the table and looked smug. "They are the same," he said. "I work there too, and I know this thing."

"I didn't know that..."

"They are the same," he repeated.

David couldn't tell if what the man was saying was true or that all American agencies were the same. "What do you do at AID, or CIA, or whatever...?"

"I teach math to children of the Americans. Americans do not want their children to be poisoned by our schools, so they have people from the universities teach them. Americans are bigots." He paused for a moment for effect. "And they cannot add or subtract."

"I didn't know that," David said.

"Many of us are there, we teach American children in a classroom at the building. We teach them what they should have learned in the US but didn't. Did you know that they only want us to teach math and science and engineering? But nothing about the country they now live in? They will not hire us to teach history or literature or religion or political science."

"Is that because they don't trust you because you are from a liberal university?"

"Perhaps. But they also use professors from UCA, the Jesuit University, which is more conservative. And they say also to them, 'Only teach us science and math. No history. No geography. No theology.' I think it is because they do not care about our country. They do not care about our poets or writers or artists or theologians. They only know that we have a war, and they are only here to 'fix' it for us. They have much money and many ideas on how to build a military and kill communists, but they do not have any interest in the lives and culture, and history of the place they are living in...and that their aid is *destroying*. This is why they do not want their children to learn." His voice was rising. He clearly was exercised about the issue.

He paused and looked at David intently. "I don't know you, but Alphonso says you mean well. Just be careful. You can be used here, and not always for the good."

David didn't know how to answer. "I'll watch out," he said cautiously. For a brief moment, the man looked at him with a look that was almost sympathetic.

"You should, because your friend, Alfonso, he will not always be able to take care of you."

David decided to change the subject. "How much is the beer?"

"Five dollars."

"In dollars?"

The man smiled for the first time. "Just wanted to make you feel at home. The beer is actually *cincuenta colones*, which is fifty *colones*, and close to five dollars. Take four of those rectangular pieces of paper out of your pocket, with the number 'ten' on them. It will be enough."

David knew that the price was inflated and was insulted at the condescending tone but decided not to get into an argument with an angry professor who outweighed him by a hundred pounds. Instead, he quietly took out his wallet and produced the five "pieces of paper," handed them over, and then turned away to avoid any further conversation. But as he turned, his hand holding the beer swung into the arm of a small woman standing behind him, whom he hadn't noticed, and slops of it spilled on her shirt sleeve.

"Disculpe," she said, "I did not mean to stand so close to you."

David jerked back. "Oh, I'm so sorry. I didn't see you." He turned back to set his beer on the table and saw Bhutto behind it holding out a roll of paper towels and rolling his eyes. David tore off a sheet and began rubbing it on the woman's sleeve. *"Lo seinto,"* he said apologizing again.

"No," she said, "it is me. I stood too close. I was trying to see if it was you."

David looked at her for the first time. She looked familiar. "Me?"

She laughed. "Do you not remember us?

Slowly, he did recognize her. "Are you the woman, the mother, of those boys at the uh...*Pupusa* place?"

She laughed again, "Yes, at 'Bety's.' Did we make such a small impression on you?"

"No, no, I just, I've had a lot going on. Yes, I remember you...with the little boys, right?"

"Yes, and one of them has your father's name, *Daniel.* Do you remember now?"

"I'm sorry." He stepped back, feeling self-conscious about

continuing to rub a paper towel on a woman's arm when there actually hadn't been too much spilled on it.

"And you did not come back the next week to Bety's. We looked for you."

He felt embarrassed, but she was right. "I'm sorry. I was…" he couldn't think of a non-embarrassing way to finish, so he didn't. Instead, he said, "Do you work at the university?"

She took the towels and handed them back to Bhutto who smiled at her from behind the table. "I am one of the translators for the university," she said, pulling her sleeve back down over her wrist. "They have many students and guests here who do not know Spanish. So sometimes I translate. Sometimes a new American student needs tutoring. It helps them and it helps me. I am actually a *costurera*. Do you know that word?"

He shook his head.

"It means 'seamstress.' I take up pants and let out waistbands and sometimes make dresses for wealthy families who live in Colonia Escalón. It is nice, but it is part-time. And so, I do this too. It helps. It is very difficult to live in El Salvador without more than one job."

"Where are the kids tonight?" he asked.

"They are with their *Abuelos*, their grandparents."

"Do they live close by?"

"Yes, in Colonia Regalado, in the east of Zacamil, near us."

"I live in Zacamil," he said. "It is not far from here."

She laughed again. He remembered her doing that a number of times at the pupuseria also. Was he that awkward and odd?

But her laugh was pleasant and didn't sound disapproving. "You are in Zacamil now," she said. "The University is also in a part of Colonia Zacamil."

He was embarrassed. Of course he should know that, but

since he usually took a bus to get around, he was often disoriented about where he was in the city.

"Zacamil is like a...a *suburbio*," she said, frowning. "Is that it? A small town at the side of a bigger town? It is a 'suburb,' yes?"

"Yes," he said, "that would be called a 'suburb,' at least in the US, it could. We had a lot of those where I came from in Boston."

"Boston?" she said with eyes wide. "And you were a teacher there, yes? You teach at Harvard?"

"No," he said, and for the first time in a long time, he wished that he had. "No, a state college south of there." For a moment he thought he saw her enthusiasm drop just a bit, but it didn't last.

She lowered her voice. "How long will you be visiting our country?"

"Maybe a few months more. I've been here working on a job for the last few months, and it will take a while longer to complete."

"Good, so you have time to learn about our country and our troubles. El Salvador is the most beautiful country in the world, but right now it has also the most sorrow. You will learn of this and probably will fall in love with it and not want to go home."

He laughed. "That may be true. Actually, I think I'm looking for something to fall in love with right now." He stopped. That sounded wrong. "I mean the beauty and history and culture. That's what I meant. I've loved everything I've seen so far."

"Good. I can take you to the Plaza and the *Catedral* and museum sometime, and you will learn much about all of this."

David smiled, but her offer felt vaguely uncomfortable, like their conversation at the pupuseria. He responded to her very slowly, taking great care with each potentially loaded word. "I'm...not...sure," he said. "First...let me ask you a question. Is there...a *Mr.* De León, in your family, a *Señor* De León?"

She frowned and her face grew very serious, and when she spoke it was with a low, solemn voice. "Yes," she said, "I am sorry if you misunderstood me. There *is* a Mr. De León in my life. He is a very good man, and I love him very much...and he is married..." she smiled and looked up at him, "to my mother!" And as soon as she said that she burst into laughter, and he realized that she had been leading him on. And he laughed too. They both laughed.

And it turned out they both laughed many times that night, on that topic and on many others, while standing together in the basement of the Engineering School of the University of El Salvador, talking like old friends, drinking *cincuenta-colon* Cuban beer, and finding out who they were and why they were there, and what they liked and loved and did and believed in. David told Sara that he was from a small city in western Massachusetts called Pittsfield. She said she was from a small city in western El Salvador called Santa Ana. He said he had been the first in his family to go to college. She said that she had been the first in hers as well. He told her that he had gotten a scholarship to go to college at a private university in New Hampshire. She told him that she had gotten a scholarship to go to a state university in Oklahoma. He said he had gotten a doctorate in economics and then worked for a senator, and then taught economics in Massachusetts, and then got married, and then...

"Married?"

He stopped. His face began to feel warm. Yes, he had said "married." But was he *still* married? Did he *feel* married? Maybe this conversation had gotten too personal. Maybe he really did still feel married. Maybe he shouldn't be talking like this with a woman. But it had been more than *two* years! And he knew that if there really was a heaven, Kathryn was probably in it now screaming down at him to keep talking and move on. After all, she was the one who...

"Are you married?"

Her voice was calm but persistent. He wouldn't be able to avoid the question. He closed his eyes and slowly squeezed out words that he never ever wanted to say out loud. "No... I mean no I'm not divorced, but I'm *not* married. I mean, my wife, my wife...died. About two years ago." He opened his eyes to see if Sara was still there. She was looking up at him with heavy sadness in her face. She had dark brown hair and wide brown eyes. She reached up and touched the side of his face with the tips of her fingers.

"I am sorry," she said.

"It's okay," he lied, eyes burning. "I'm much better about it these days." Her hand made them burn even more.

"I know," she said. "I mean, I think I know too. My Daniel has been gone for almost four years."

David looked up startled, feeling stupid. Of course, he thought. She had children. Of course, there had to have been a man in her life somewhere and one of her children was named for him. "It was the time of my deepest sadness," she said. "If I did not have Dani and Tomás, I would have tried to die. I loved him and I still miss him."

"I'm sorry to hear that too," he said. "How long were you married?"

"It was maybe six years. Little Tomás was just two, just a baby. And Daniel was five."

"Oh my." David's eyes widened at the news.

"It was for us a time of much fear," she said. "I did not know where he was or how he died, and I was alone with a baby." She looked down for a moment.

"Oh my," David said again. "I am so, so sorry."

She leaned close to him and said quietly, "Is it maybe possible that we not talk here about this? There are people here who did not like my Daniel."

"Of course," he said. "In fact, we don't ever have to ever talk about it again, if you don't want to."

Her mouth turned up again. "So, there will be an 'again' when we will talk about this and maybe other things also?"

He was still feeling embarrassed but returned her smile. "Yes, I think that is possible."

"I would like that. But, if maybe you will call me, we will meet and we will be friends and talk."

"I don't know your phone number."

She took a pen from the side pocket of her jeans and began writing on one of the paper towels they had been using. "Next week is their school break, and we will be in Santa Ana with their cousins, but if you call, we will maybe meet soon after?" She handed the piece of paper towel to him. "Now. It is official."

He looked at the number. He tore the paper into half one more time and took her pen and started writing his number. "Now it's my turn," he said and handed it to her. For a moment she looked startled but smiled and took the paper and pen and put them in her pocket. "Does this mean we are now officially friends?" he asked.

"No, not yet." She reached up with both hands and pulled his face down to her level and kissed him lightly on the cheek.

"Now we are friends."

CHAPTER SEVENTEEN

EMBASSY

There were two key US institutions that Alf had insisted would be important for David to check in with, the US Embassy and the US Agency for International Development (USAID). He wasn't looking forward to spending time with either, but he put them on his list and eventually scheduled appointments.

The building that housed them both was an imposing structure. During the expansion of Salvador's civil war, it had grown to be the most heavily fortified US Embassy in the world. Behind high concrete walls that stretched around an entire block was a small city of offices, conference halls, garages, cafeterias, a gym, and even residences for some of the live-in aides and guards.

When David arrived at the great stone entrance, a line of well over a hundred people had already gathered along the sidewalk in its front. Most appeared to be Salvadorans applying for visas to take their families out of the country and into the US for safety. Fortunately for David, he had a letter from a Mr. Robert Sweeney, Special Temporary Assistant to the

Director of Public Diplomacy, whom he had contacted in advance, and who had left word with the armed servicemen at the gate to keep watch for him. Just go to the front of the line, Sweeney had said, show them my letter and they'll let you in, and he did that. After he made his way through the metal check, the body check, and papers check, he turned to the very serious, official-looking guard, who had just patted him down, and asked where he might find Mr. Robert Sweeney, and at first he received a somewhat impatient look. The guard then looked at the others. "Guys," he yelled, "any of you know where that kid, Sweeney, is supposed to be today?" "Kid?" David thought. What did that mean?

Without looking up, one of the others shouted back, "Check in Walker's office. He's gone for the day, and Sweeney sometimes sits in there when he's away."

The guard turned back and said, "Hallway to lobby, elevator, third floor, double doors on your left."

"Right," said David and started off.

"No, left."

"No, I meant 'right,' I meant, '*correct*,' I'll do that."

"Turn left."

"Yes, I get it. Left. I'm... "

The guard had already turned away while David was speaking, so he didn't finish, but he hurried through the opening and down the hallway following the directions. When he reached the Embassy lobby, he was surprised that the surroundings looked so "American." Other than random wall photos of Salvadoran tourist sites, it could have been a government office building anywhere in Washington or Boston or Denver, he thought. The lobby was full of people, mainly men, mainly young, mainly white, and mainly wearing North American-looking business clothing, walking hurriedly up and down the halls, carrying briefcases, notebooks, and papers, and looking very important, or, at least, looking like they *thought* they should look, to be very important. Acting as though the resolution of all the conflicts in the country was resting on their shoulders and would be affected by what they accomplished on this day.

Lobby, elevator, third floor, turn left. He got out of the elevator and was at a crossroads of hallways. Left at the center? Or left from the corner? Or ...

"Then he heard, "May I help you?" The voice seemed to come from nowhere until he saw a small black box, centered just over two official-looking doors just before him.

"Yes," he said to the box. "I'm here to see Mr. Sweeney, Mr. Robert Sweeney? Do I have the right office?"

"Yes," the box said. "Just a moment." Seconds passed. Then, "The Ambassador is gone for the day, so Mr. Sweeney is using his office while he is away."

"Is he expecting me?"

"The voice in the box boomed out, *Robbie! Is someone expecting to see you?*"

Behind him, David heard the sound of water flushing and a door slamming. He turned to see a tall, thin, red-haired young man, in what David judged to be his early twenties, rushing towards him. One hand was extended out to shake, and the other was pushing his shirt tail under his belt. David held back while he studied the hand to see if it was still wet. "Doctor Patterson!" the young man said. "So good to see you." Seeing David's hesitancy, he awkwardly pulled his hand back and pulled a white cloth from his pocket to dry his hand and then thrust it out again. "Yes, yes. we've been looking forward to this."

He stood smiling broadly in the hallway pumping David's hand up and down and then said, "Come, come, let me show you our office," and he pushed open the doors into the Ambassador's suite. Inside, the voice from the box outside was sitting behind a large desk in front of them looking poised and irritated, with her hands folded formally on the desktop. "Wanda," Sweeney said to her, "this is Dr. David Patterson, he's from that Institute of Studies—or whatever—I told you about."

"You didn't tell me you were going to have any visitors."

"We're going to be in a meeting for a while in my office, while I introduce him to life and culture in El Salvador. Could you bring us some coffee for the two of us while we chat?"

"You didn't say you were going to have any visitors."

He turned to David and said, "You take anything in that?"

"No, I usually just take..."

"Tell you what, Wanda, bring us a little pitcher of cream and some of those little sugar cubes that everyone uses here. He needs to learn how to drink like the natives do." He looked at David and let out a huge laugh. "So, come, come into my office so we can get started. Sounds like we have a lot to talk about. We're going to be here a while."

He opened the doors to the Ambassador's inner office and expansively waved David into it, while Wanda, still at her desk and still not moving, said, "Ambassador Walker will be back by four, and you need to be out of there by then." And the door closed.

"Sit, sit," Sweeney said, directing him to a thick black sofa, while he went to the chair behind the Ambassador's desk. He leaned forward onto it clasping his hands and said, "So, what can we do you for? What do you need to know?"

Sweeney, himself, was relatively new to El Salvador. As he explained it to David, he had recently graduated from college in Lawrence, Kansas, and had been looking for something interesting to do, so his mother suggested that he might talk to her brother, the Section Chief for Public Diplomacy in San Salvador and that he might be able to find something for

Sweeney. After some initial resistance, her brother eventually agreed and eventually young Robbie Sweeney became the "Special Temporary Assistant to the Director of Public Diplomacy in the U.S. Embassy of El Salvador."

"So, what brings you here?" Robbie was saying. "I understand you're doing interviews around town and need our help in figuring things out here. I don't know everything yet, but I'm good at figuring things out and I can help you find things." He waved his hands around the room as though sharing his realm with a petitioner. "But start with you, I don't know much about the Institute that you are with."

David had been nervous about this conversation from the beginning, and now he found that the only person the Embassy could find for him to talk to was nearly half his age, family connected, and clearly not qualified for the job. It made him wonder if it had been a mistake to be here at all. He didn't really have too much to say or ask, but both Alf and Héctor had advised him to make the effort in case people in the field began to ask why this *Norte Americano* was wandering the country asking questions. At the very least, he'd expected someone with a little more information in him who could discuss things like the political situation, the US plans for developing the country, and ending the war. Instead, he got someone who looked like a kid on a high school field trip and who thought he was Inspector Gadget.

"The institute I work with..." David started.

"Wanda, could you hurry up with those coffees?" Robbie yelled at the door.

"I don't get coffee for guests in the Ambassador's office," the door answered back.

Robbie laughed. "My secretary. She's like that, but we love her."

"...was established to help bring together some of the aid

and development organizations here in the country, to help them do their work better."

"I think I know just what you're talking about. You mean like some of those people we fund over at AID, right?"

"Yes, but some are also funded by people in the States and..."

"You mean like those child sponsorship people? I know those. I think they do good work."

So far, David had not been impressed by some of the sponsorship programs, and what they did in the name of "development," but he didn't think now was the time to debate the issue. "Yes," he said, "It's kind of like some of those. There are a lot more organizations that do other things, but some of them do that."

"Well, that's great, so we'll have a lot in common on that. I gave some money to one of those groups back when I was in college one time. The 'James Lucas' Help the Children' program. I saw an ad on TV, on a Saturday, with someone like Marla Maples or someone talking—I forgot her name—saying how easy it was and how much good they do, and I called in and, just like that, I gave them twenty dollars. And they do very good work."

David was feeling uncomfortable with the direction the conversation was going. "I'm sure they do," he said.

"And I'm sure that you know by now that we in the US are the biggest development organization in all of El Salvador. USAID funds more of those organizations than anyone else in the world and it's really beginning to make an impact."

"I'm sure it is, but I was wanting to ask you about..."

"When we first started up here, this country was really in the toilet, I mean really going downhill. But now it's turned around and we're going to have a big impact on the overall economy very soon."

David was curious. "Like how?"

He laughed and slapped his hand down on the desk. "Well, here's a great story. They told us this at our orientation, and it's great." Robbie's eyes grew wide with excitement. "They really are doing much better, economically, since the Americans have been down here putting in money where it can do the most good. I know that sounds like propaganda or something, but it's also true."

"I'm sure."

"And here's the example. It's kinda funny, but it makes the point. Here, nine or ten years ago, if one of those 'Death Squad' guys wanted to have you murdered it would cost about fifty dollars."

"Oh."

"And today it would still only cost you about fifty-five dollars."

David frowned, "Sorry, I don't...?"

Sweeney waved his hands, looking disappointed that David didn't get it. "What it means is that the prices have not been going up by much. They're stabilizing!" he said. "The prices on things are going up slower in these last few years and they used to go up sky high every year. They had inflation here something terrible. It means that the value of their money, the *colon*, has almost stabilized. The country is just simply doing a lot better."

"So, have the killings gone down?"

"Oh, I don't know. Who knows, maybe a little, but that's not the point. The point is that the economy is going up, that's all I was trying to show. I just thought that that was a funny way to illustrate it. And at the same the economy of Nicaragua is in the toilet. So, that shows you something, you know?"

"Has the price of killings gone up in Nicaragua"?

Robbie looked annoyed. "Well, I don't know. I don't think

so. Nicaragua never had that many killings. But that's not the point. Listen, I don't want to talk about politics. My point is that the economy of El Salvador is stabilizing with the help of the US aid down here. And the socialist economy in Nicaragua is not. I just used that example to show you some real clear evidence if anybody ever tells you that it was a bad thing for the US to get involved down here." He wrinkled his nose. "I should have thought of a better example, but I thought that one was funny, so I told it. That's all."

"Sure, I understand."

He looked around the room for a moment, searching for something else. His eyes seemed to find it, and he turned back to David. "Okay, here's another example they gave us, and it doesn't have anything to do with death squads and all that. It's that another way you can tell that the country is better off today is that the price of some of the food is going down.

"Like what?"

"Well, remember that Title One and Title Two program? The 'Food for Peace' wheat? Well, we send millions of tons of our excess wheat down here to these people and they've used it to feed their people. That's a very good thing. Without our wheat, a whole lot of people wouldn't have gotten fed. I'm proud that our country did that."

"That's true, though people down here don't eat much wheat."

"Yes, I know that. But they have it now and it's practically free and they're beginning to start eating it. And I'm proud that we're the country that'll be giving it to them. It's all good. Just look around at all the bread stuff in the stores now that *we* started with *our* money. And look at the bakery shops going up in the bigger towns. Dunkin' Donuts stores going in everywhere. They never had any of that before we started helping.

Jeez, General Mills just opened a '*Wheaties*' factory, for Chrisake!"

David was feeling uncomfortable. He didn't doubt that wheat-based products were expanding here now that the US was supplying it almost free, but he wasn't sure that it was doing the good that Robbie believed it was. Thoughts of Alf's breakfast donuts conversation came to mind. "Mr. Sweeney, I don't know much about El Salvador yet, but with the thousands and thousands of tons of free wheat coming into the country now, is that good for the local corn farmers and all the corn-based merchants here?"

"Not sure what you mean."

"I mean that if, say, you made a living selling groceries, and suddenly someone down the street started giving away free groceries, the people would all stop paying money for your food and go get the free stuff, and you'd go bankrupt. Isn't that right?"

Robbie's face looked tense. "That wheat there was a gift from the president of the United States of America. And he did it because he was wanting to help these people. I know that."

"I don't doubt that at all," David said, though he actually wondered if it was always true. "But you can see what I mean about free food not always being good for the country. It may help the thirty or forty people in that Wheaties factory, but at the same time, it could be putting hundreds—maybe thousands—of corn farmers out of business."

"I don't know all about that, and I don't know if what you're saying is right." He swung his chair around and began to stand. "Mr. Patterson, I think you're a nice man and I wish you well. But it doesn't look like we have much in common after all and I don't think I can help you anymore." He walked towards the door. "Why don't we just say goodbye as friends for now and if there's anything else that you might need, you just give the embassy a call, and I'm sure we can help you out with it." He stuck his hand out for a shake one last time.

David rose to his feet. "I didn't mean to speak out of turn."

"No, no," he said, shaking his head. "No, but I just think we've said about as much as we're gonna say here. You just go on now and take care of yourself and keep in touch." He opened the door and gestured to David to go through it. Inside Wanda was still sitting up straight at her desk typing. As David opened the outer door to leave, he heard Robbie say to her, "Wanda, you don't need to worry about that coffee and all, we're all done now."

"You have to be out of here by four," she said, without lifting her eyes from her typing.

CHAPTER EIGHTEEN

DINNER

L ooking back on it now, it actually had not been all that long since Daniel died—four years maybe, maybe five? Sara wasn't sure. She had, in fact, tried not to remember because much of the times since then had been hard. Her life and the boys' lives had been upended so dramatically by his death that it felt longer, and she was pleased with that because she wanted to move on. She had felt safe, trusted and protected with Daniel. When he died, when that awful time came, she and her children lost everything, not just the companionship of a good man, but also security, income, and social position. She eventually was able to supplement her sewing jobs with intermittent translating at the university, but in the beginning, it had been very difficult.

Daniel was someone who worked too much and was not always attentive to the boys, but he was also mature, older, and trustworthy. She was not sure she could say she had been deeply in love with him, but he made her feel safe and that was important. He also did not mind that she had not come from a good family. And he seemed to be proud of her that she was born poor but won a scholarship to study in the States and he could introduce her as an equal.

Sara still missed him, especially on days like this, when she was home for most of the day and the boys were still in school, and he would have been working from home. They would have had coffee in the morning or lunch in the afternoon and would talk and laugh and make plans for their lives for a time when this cloud of war had passed, and they could be freer to move around the country. Daniel was the mayor of San Antonio de La Cruz, a small town up north and east of Guazapa Mountain, but worked from home much of the time because of the dangers of the fighting in that region. His dream for the future was that when those he considered to be communist rebels were finally defeated and punished, he would then help in the rebuilding of the new democratic government. Sara personally felt much closer to the goals of the rebels and feared the army, but they seldom spoke of it because it was a difficult subject upon which they disagreed. Instead, they would laugh at the silly telenovelas on TV, or swap gossip about the infidelity of the couple next door, or whether the music of Álvaro Torres got better or worse after he left El Salvador for Guatemala and then the US, (they both agreed it got worse). Those were good memories, and she smiled when they came back to her.

She looked at the clock and saw that the boys would be coming home soon, and she should start thinking about dinner for the evening. She thought through what was in the refrigerator and what she might prepare. She remembered lots of leftovers: rice, beans, fruit, cabbage, chicken...Those could work, but she had already served that combination twice this week. The boys would love it, but Sara wanted to move on. She also had most of the ingredients to make pupusas, but they took a lot of time, and the boys liked Bety's better anyway. Earlier in the morning, she had planned to make a light dish of ceviche.

She liked it and had the ingredients for it too—lime, avocados, tomatoes, and some unknown white fish she bought at the market—but the boys thought it was a fancy party dish and often played with it when she served it. She got up from the sofa where she had been sitting and walked to the kitchen doorway and stood for a while assessing what else might be possible. They had some very plain rolls in the cabinet that could be cut in half to look like buns. And some tomatoes and onions that could be sliced. And she still had some nice goat cheese from the woman who made dairy deliveries to the neighborhood every Monday. She also had some potatoes that could be cut into small strips and deep fried and salted. Absently, she put her hand on the telephone on the wall and held it there thinking, would David enjoy an American meal of hamburgers and French fries, something he doesn't see too often in El Salvador, aside from the McDonald's in El Centro? Would he find the offer too forward? Would he be offended? She reached down to one of the drawers under the phone and pushed a few things around for a moment and found a torn quarter of a paper towel. It had the remains of a days-old beer stain on one edge and a number written just beside it. She lifted the receiver and dialed the number on the towel. It rang for a long time. Maybe it's too early and he's not home, she thought. Maybe he had a phone machine. Maybe he doesn't like to use his phone. Maybe...then someone answered.

"*Hola?*" said a voice.

"Congratulations," she said, in what she hoped would be a self-assured voice. "You are learning Spanish!"

She heard laughter coming from the other end and felt better. "Okay," he said. "So, how about if I say, '*Buenas noches, ¿cómo estás? ¿Bien?*' Would that be better?"

"Even better. And you used the 'familiar' tense, so that means we are friends." She wished she hadn't said that. It might have sounded pushy. "But don't feel bad. I'm only making fun of you because I think it will be better for you in your work when you learn more Spanish."

"Me too," he said, laughing again, "and I'm working on that."

"*Daveed*, I am going to make an American dinner tonight. I am going to make hamburgers for the boys. Even French fries and Coca-Cola. You will feel right at home. And the boys, they like you. So, you will have a good time."

The boys barely knew him, and she realized he must know she was lying, but it felt mysteriously pleasant to suggest that the boys wanted to know him better. It was a way of saying that their acquaintance might last a while. And it also felt good to sense that he didn't really mind that.

"I'm sure I will," he said. Then after a pause, "Is this a date? Are you asking me out?"

"Yes!" she said, with her voice sounding indignant. "Maybe it is. It is the eighties, and I am a liberated woman. I lived in America, and I know that women can ask men out."

He laughed. "Well, I guess it's fine, I'm just not used to this."

"It is not for me used to it either. But it will be fun."

"Okay, what time? And where do you live? Will I need to take a taxi?"

"Oh, you do not know? We are neighbors. I live here, at the seventh row of Los Cañones. You are in row one and I am in row seven."

"No! I didn't know that at all."

"Yes, we are in the corner of the fourth floor, and I have seen you walk by our row many times. Did you know this?"

"No, I had no idea."

She hoped that he wasn't angry about that. "I am not spying on you," she said. "I just look out of my window in the morning, and sometimes you are walking there to the *callejón,* the small street, to *calle* Zacamil."

"Well, I'm going to have to start looking up at your apartment and waving when I do that from now on."

"And I will wave at you also." His comment made her feel more relaxed, and she was pleased that the invitation was going well. "What time can you be here? Come soon and I will put rum and *limón* in your Coca-Cola, and make it a Cuba Libre, and then maybe after dinner we can talk again."

"Well, that's a good selling point. I just walked in the door. So, give me a chance to put things away and clean up and I'll be there."

"*¡Maravilloso!* And I'll let you help by cooking the hamburger in the pan. You will have a good time."

"Of course."

CHAPTER NINETEEN

PHONE CALL

Exactly one week from when Sara invited him over to experience her Salvadoran hamburgers, David got another call. This time it came at the end of the day just after the bus he was riding turned off of Zacamil Calle and onto the corner that opened into the long, wide parking lot that led to his apartment.

David enjoyed that spot. Here, instead of the weariness he often felt during a day of long and tense interviews, he always had a sense of release. Zacamil, even with its reputation for violence and retribution, was in fact beginning to feel like a real neighborhood. In spite of the obvious horror of war inflaming the countryside, and periodic explosions in the city, this little piece of the colonia felt safe. In this location, in this community, it didn't feel so hard to just live.

El Salvador was a beautiful country, and he was meeting some beautiful people, even though many of them had lives that were hard to manage and were often painful. When he was meeting them, he felt a strong empathy for their lives and their work, under incredibly difficult conditions. One church he interviewed that morning sponsored a very helpful, and non-controversial, ministry of collecting food and clothing for the growing homeless population of the city. More grimly, another group organized a trip to Lago Ilopango to help trawl for and identify bodies tossed in the water after a mysterious mass killing two weeks earlier. He knew it was an illusion, but when he got to this street, even while standing beneath a huge wall mural of assassinated Archbishop, Oscar Romero, in front of these rows of apartments, he felt safe from some of that. Here in notorious Zacamil, he felt hidden and secure.

He smiled at himself for these thoughts and started down the hill to Los Cañones. On the left was the wall that marked the edge of the private school. On the right were trees and houses and smaller apartments. In front of many of the houses were campaign posters because it was an election year, and the presidency was up for a vote. Green signs for a middle-right party, and red, white, and blue for the far-right ARENA party. Many thought that the center-right would win again this year because the national popular mood seemed to be shifting more towards democracy, but a powerful, wealthy, minority in the far-right was certain that the old oligarchy would again prevail. Soon, everyone would find out.

When he reached the gate that led into his row of apartments, he put down his backpack and began fumbling to get his keys from his pocket. But as he was searching, he heard a phone ring in the distance. He wasn't certain, but it sounded like it was coming from one of the apartments on his side, maybe his. He seldom received phone calls here, so every one of them could be important. He rattled his pocket for the keys. Maybe Camilia was working today and, if so, she would pick it up. But she wasn't. He found the key, put it in the lock, grabbed his backpack, and rushed through the gate towards his door. The phone continued to ring, and he could tell now that it was, in fact, his. It rang again. He ran across the grass to his door and nearly hit someone coming the other way. It was Isabel, evidently returning home early after an afternoon appointment. Startled, she jumped back to let him pass. "Oh, sorry," he said. He turned back to her, trying to apologize and run at the same time, but then backed hard into his apartment door. "*Yo tenía mucha prisa*," he said. "I'm in a hurry."

She laughed. "*No hay problema.*"

He got to the door, turned the key, pushed it open, and ran to the kitchen and picked up the phone. He coughed and cleared his throat and tried to sound composed. "Hola?" he said, but no one answered back. "Hello?" he said again, this time in English, but still no response. David waited for a moment longer and was about to speak again when he heard a "click" on the other end and then a dial tone. Very strange, he thought. Actually, this had been the second time that someone had done that. The first time, he thought it was just an accident. But after two times, he wondered if it was something more.

Surely it doesn't mean anything he thought. Almost nobody around here even knows who I am. He put his backpack on the sofa and looked around his living room and noticed that some of the things seemed out of place. For one, the sofa was pulled out a few inches from the wall. Had I done that, he wondered? And the lamp that usually sat on the side table was now on the floor. When did that happen? He walked into his bedroom and there, too, things were moved. The chest of drawers on his left had drawers opened. The papers on his desk, which he recalled being in several separate piles were now drawn together into one. The file cabinet to the right was open and several open files were lying below it on the floor. Were some of them missing? He couldn't tell. What the hell happened here?

He went back into the living room and immediately saw something else he hadn't seen before. On the floor, under the front window and to the left of the front door, was a small scattering of glass. He went to the window and pulled the drapes out of the way showing a break in the window, about a foot wide, large enough for a hand and arm to go through, and just inches away from the front doorknob.

CHAPTER TWENTY
VISITOR

Bam, Bam, Bam. The door shook with the repeated pounding of David's fists. "Carlos, Carlos, are you home?" he yelled in Spanish. "Carlos!" The door jerked open revealing an angry, shirtless Carlos Empanada holding a pair of shoes and looking impatient. "I'm here, I'm here," he said. "Just knock on the door and I will come."

"I'm sorry," David said to him, still nearly screaming, "but I have an emergency. I need your help."

"What is it? Is it a fire? Have you had a gas fire in your kitchen? The propane is dangerous and can start fires in our kitchens."

"No, no, it isn't that. Someone has broken into my room."

"Wait, please." Carlos went back into his bedroom and for a few moments, muffled voices could be heard coming from behind the door. Then he returned to the living room wearing his shoes and buttoning a shirt in front. He closed the door behind him. "I was napping," he said with a guilty look.

"That's fine," said David. "I don't care, just come to my room. Something has happened and I'm not sure what to do."

He led Carlos down to his apartment and the two of them stood in the doorway looking silently at the jumble of furniture and lamps and broken glass in David's living room.

Carlos stepped in and looked around. "This is odd, Mr. David. Do you know if anything was taken?"

"I can't tell. I need to look more closely, but so far it doesn't look like anything is missing."

"That is good, and you may not want to inform *la Policía*."

"Why?" That didn't make any sense to David.

"I am ashamed to say it, but in my country, sometimes if nothing is missing before the police come, some things will be found missing after they have left. And you never see them again."

David shook his head. "Okay, so, what else can we do? Have you seen anyone around here who could have been looking in at my apartment? Maybe we should ask the neighbors to find out if anyone of them has seen anyone."

"I have not seen anyone near your apartment since this morning at eight-thirty when the man you were having breakfast with was leaving."

"Carlos, there was no one here this morning."

"He was your friend. I saw him this morning when I was coming back from fixing the fire in Sr. Lopez's stove. We spoke when I saw him coming out of your apartment."

David was horrified. "No, I left early this morning," he said. "I wasn't having breakfast with anyone."

Now it was Carlos' turn to look surprised. "He lied to me?"

"Who lied to you? Who did you see at my apartment?"

"He said that you had been sharing coffee, and that you did not make it well, and that he was on his way now to go to work."

"No, no, no. I don't know who this man was. He lied to you. Did you recognize him?"

"No, I did not know him, but I thought he was your friend, so I did not study his face. I thought you two had been meeting or talking together. I didn't know. I am sorry." Carlos was looking distressed and almost tearful.

"It's okay, Carlos, just tell me everything that you know. What did he look like?"

"He was a very big man. And he wore a black suit as some men in business do. But no tie. He was so wide in the neck that his buttons would not touch. And he had a deep voice. He was coming out of your apartment. He was closing your door, and it looked like he was saying goodbye. I greeted him and he said he was your friend. But he was not very friendly."

"Did he look like an American or Salvadoran?"

"Salvadoran, because he had no accent, but was very big... and wide." Carlos rubbed his forehead and looked around the room, as though searching for a helpful memory. "He also had a mustache," he said, "but there are many men with mustaches, so I do not know."

"Anything else?"

"No, but I will ask others on your row to see if anybody saw him too, perhaps as he was going in. It is also possible that he was watching you from the other side so that he would know when you left and then came in after that. The gate is sometimes left open by careless tenants. I will ask people on both sides to see if they saw him."

"Thank you, Carlos. I appreciate it. And are you certain it wouldn't help to go to the police?"

"Let me investigate first, and then we will try the police. Sometimes they can be very good and sometimes no. Do you have any money?"

"A little, why?"

"Because the police are paid badly and if you have money

to add to their salaries, they can become more helpful to your cause."

David smiled. "I get it. Maybe I can do that. But meanwhile, could you ask around and see what you can find out? I'll go back in and start cleaning things up."

"Yes, Sr. David. And one more thing."

"What?"

Carlos looked slowly around the living room one more time and let out a long whistle. "Señor David, do you have any enemies?"

CHAPTER TWENTY-ONE

USAID

"You look like a man who has gotten himself lost." David was in fact lost in a long hallway in an unfamiliar building, but the thick Spanish accented voice was more irritating than helpful. He turned and saw a massive body and a scowling face standing several feet behind him. His eyes grew wide. Was that the guy, he wondered, Emilio Bhutto, who sold him the overpriced beer at the faculty party, now smiling a sneering, unfriendly smile in this hallway? "The person you are looking for is Mr. Douglas Grantham, and his office is the one at the end of the hallway, the one that you undoubtedly thought was a storage closet. Most people would have recognized it immediately."

David didn't want to revisit their uncomfortable previous conversation. "Hello," he said. "I didn't recognize you. Are you sure that door's the one?"

"Yes, of course. Unlike Americans, I never lie."

"Were you following me?" David asked. "Do you work here too?"

"Of course, you do not know the answer to that question

because at the party you were more interested in our *muy lindo* young translator than in listening when I told you that I did." His tone was dismissive. "I do not have an office here, but I do have a classroom. My office is back at the University."

"So, why were you here at Grantham's office? Did you know that I was coming here?"

"No, I am in charge of the classrooms. On the first floor past the reception desk, there are two of them. They are small but sufficient. There are not many Americans in San Salvador who believe our country can educate children, so the size does not need to be large to hold them all."

"But why were you here, at *this* office? Normally he wouldn't ask so many questions, but Bhutto had been insulting in his comments, and it made him angry.

"I have education business to discuss in that office. Our friend, Mr. Grantham, oversees the education program, and I needed to discuss the new lists of teachers and students. But you go in now." Bhutto gestured toward the door. "It is there. He is waiting for an American who wants to wander through our streets playing detective, and I knew it was you. I told him that you were harmless, but not to trust you." And then with a quick, but formal, nod he turned and walked stiffly to the elevator, ducking when he entered it. That guy is dangerous, David thought.

He stood for a moment in front of the door that Bhutto had been referring to. It was ajar, and he could see a slice of an office with two desks inside it. But he didn't move. He was still thinking about their conversation. Large, tall, man, black suit, mustache...that sounded uncomfortably similar to the description Carlos had given him of the man he saw coming out of David's apartment the day it had been rummaged.

"May I help you?"

His mind pulled back to the office in front of him. Through

the crack in the door a woman was standing looking at him. He pushed it open. "I'm sorry," he said. "I was just trying to make sure I was at the right office." It was a lie, but it was a plausible one.

A tall middle-aged man stood on the left, looking intently down at some papers, and a more-than-middle-aged woman stood patiently in front of him. He could also just see on the far left a file cabinet with a television on it, and the edge of a couch next to it.

"May I help you?" she said again.

David pushed the door open further and looked at his note card. "Sorry, is this Douglas Grantham's office?"

"It is," both voices said at the same time, one masculine. "Are you Dr. Patterson?" the woman asked.

"Yes," he said, "I am."

The tall man walked towards hm and reached out his hand. "Good, I'm Doug Grantham, and we're glad to meet you, come in. Professor Bhutto from the University was just here, and he says he knows you."

"A little. We know each other briefly at the University." David put down his backpack and shook Grantham's hand. "What kind of business was he here on?"

"He teaches a class here, so we discuss that occasionally. He also has a lot of fingers in a lot of other activities and knows some of the people we are trying to get better acquainted with. So, his information can sometimes be helpful to both of us. So, he drops by now and then. But he seemed also interested in what I knew about you."

David looked amazed. "And did you have much to tell him?"

"Not much. Aside from what you passed on to Priscilla when you called. You haven't done anything to tick him off, have you? He didn't say it, but he sounded angry at you for something."

"I have no idea about what. Our only conversation was at a party at the University, and he was playing bartender." David was feeling uncomfortable. He told himself he should call Carlos soon to see if his other neighbors had told him anything new.

Grantham shook his head. "I wouldn't worry about him. He's a whole lot less important than he thinks he is." He waved his hand at the couch and a chair next to it. "Please sit. We don't have a lot of space here, but we're good about sharing. And if you promise not to say anything dangerous or criminal in front of Priscilla, here, we can allow her to stay around and take notes, while we talk.

"Sure," David laughed," I'll do my best to keep it G-Rated."

Grantham pulled the padded chair around to face the couch and reached up and turned off the TV. "Coffee?"

"Sure, black."

He stepped behind his desk and pulled out a coffee pot and two cups. "That's good because we don't allow any cream in this office. It's a sin against God."

"A sin?"

He placed the two cups on the coffee table in front of the couch. "I believe that if God had wanted coffee to be white, God would have created white coffee beans." He dropped into the chair, enjoying his joke.

David had already heard the joke several times, but he laughed politely.

Grantham took a long drink of his non-white coffee and set the mug down. "So, let's talk. I've heard a little about your project, so we can start further in. Part of what we do here is to give aid and support for the kinds of nonprofits that you are talking to, so maybe we can help you too."

"Thanks," he said. "I'll try to be as brief as I can." David was actually relieved since he only had a few questions. He was mainly there following Alf's suggestion that he meet someone at AID in case something came up later and he needed a reference. "For one, I may be traveling out in some of the conflicted zones on occasion, and I've heard that on special occasions, you might be able to supply special identification papers to keep people from being stopped by either the FMLN or government troops."

"That one's easy. The answer is we don't do that anymore. Too many people asked us for some kind of free pass to go risk their lives out there, so now we officially say no to all requests. Have you asked that question with the people at the Embassy? If you get the right person, in the right mood, one of them might get you something. What's next? What's number two?"

David was startled at the abruptness of Grantham's response, but went on, trying to look calm. "Well, number two is that Dr. Gutiérrez, over at the institute..."

"Yes, I know Héctor."

"...has said that AID used to put out a handbook of all the relief and development organizations in the country. We have a pretty good list, but we could use some help compiling a more complete one."

"Okay, that one's easy too. We do have some of those, but they're getting out of date. Congress cut that project out of our budget a couple of years ago and we didn't have the resources to keep it up on our own. But I can get you a copy of one of our older ones. Most of the same organizations are still around, and some of the same people are still with them, so they may be good enough for your needs. What next?"

David really didn't have much to say after that. He'd hoped the first two questions would take a little longer. "Okay," he said, "here's a general background question. I'd like your take on the economic situation here from the US standpoint. My background is in economics, but I'm not as familiar with Latin America as I should be."

"Don't worry about it. Most people who think they know Latin America, tend to make bad assumptions about El Salvador." David suspected that until recently, he might have been one of those with the bad assumptions, so he ignored the comment.

"But from what I've read, there seems to be more poverty in this country than in others of about the same size and natural resources, and I'm sure the civil war has caused the poverty to be worse.

"And also, poverty is the main cause for them being at war."

"Right." David was surprised at the bluntness of his response. "So, first, what made it such a poor country in the past, and second, how are you guys in AID attempting to address it today? Those two things. The US is the largest donor to the country, so, aside from military spending and funding for humanitarian aid agencies, talk to me about the plans, projects, and philosophy of development...that sort of thing?" David had actually been reading a lot recently about the economic history of El Salvador, but he hoped that tossing out an open-ended question would use up more of their time.

Doug thought for a moment. "Okay, both of those are long subjects, and we don't have much time, but let me first say that El Salvador does have a lot of natural resources and, if they could just stop having earthquakes and volcanoes go off every couple of generations, they'd be a lot better off."

"I can still see a lot of the rubble and damage down in the city from that one a few years ago."

"Right. over a thousand died, ten thousand injured...It was the worst earthquake in their history. And those things are of course part of the reason for the poverty. But on top of that, they also have had a very, very long history of brutal rule by an oligarchy. They call them the 'Fourteen Families,' have you heard of them?"

David was about to nod yes, but Doug moved on. "There are actually more of them than fourteen today, but those families still run everything today."

"But there are a lot of developing countries that have a ruling class, and not all of them are as poor as El Salvador."

Doug lifted his glasses and rubbed a sore spot on the bridge of his nose. "Yes, but the Conquistadors ruled here as though the indigenous people were just beasts of burden and not human beings. Maybe not quite like slaves in the US, but close, and they never had an emancipation proclamation that officially set them free. That attitude was deep and cruel, and it still has a powerful impact on attitudes and economic structures today. Things are not quite that bad now, but it's still the general mindset behind a lot of the political decisions the leaders make. Did you know that the vast majority of school children today are not even taught the history of the European near-slavery of their indigenous ancestors? Or that in 1932 the army put down a revolt by killing more than forty thousand people?"

David unzipped his backpack and took out his notebook. "But didn't the wealthy oligarchy turn most of the ruling over to the military?"

"Well, yes. That was pretty much true until recently. Historically the wealthy elites had a pact with the military that if they kept the peace and kept the populace from rising up against them, then the army could do whatever it wanted with the peasants—the *campesinos*."

"But that's not true any longer, is it?"

"Right, it's changed a little in recent years, partly at the urging of the US, and partly because some of the wealthy civilians wanted to start getting involved in politics. And that's a good thing. The elites aren't saints when it comes to their attitudes towards poor people, but at least they aren't like the army that would collect the ears of campesinos as prizes of battle. It's a small inch forward," he smiled, but with an unhappy look on his face, "but we'll take it."

He stopped for a moment and bit into the left stem of his glasses. "Look, Dave, we all realize that this country is a mess, and there's not a lot that we can do about it. People here are very poor. Your heart goes out to them. Short life expectancy, disease, malnutrition...children dying. That's why we help them get better trade deals and do more local manufacturing and exporting. That's also why we build schools, help small businesses, and fund those groups, like 'Save the Children' or 'Feed the Children.' That's why the USAID is here."

"And conditions are worse out in the countryside."

"Right, but the sad truth is that a portion of the people here —and other countries like it—will always be like that. It can't it change totally. The world is just like that. There will always be places where people are poor and babies are hungry. It's painful to watch, but the hard reality is that it can't be cured— at least not altogether. There will always be some number of people like that."

David looked skeptical. "So, what are you saying, that there's nothing you can do to fix it?"

"What I'm saying is that we can't fix *everything*, but we can do more to at least help people stay alive and get by. What we can do is create more ways to help people feed their families, keep the country stable and the military strong, so that will not be disrupted by wars and revolutions every other decade. So that the poor people don't start joining revolutionaries— sometimes coming in from other countries like Cuba and

Nicaragua—who promise the world but make things worse. We can't do everything, but at least we can give them that. We're wanting to at least help them have a stable country and not one torn apart by some Marxist, Leninist, utopian— whatever you want to call them—rebels who are only here out of greed."

"How are you doing that?"

"That goes back to your question. Militarily, a lot of what Congress has been doing has been to give them a strong military and police force to protect them from the violence of the Death Squads on the right and revolutionaries on the left. And then that gives us some space, here at USAID, to work with solid, good organizations, fund some, sponsor others, and meanwhile negotiate IMF loans and grants to the national government so that they can at least function, pay the bills, and make the trains run on time. You know what I mean?"

David finished writing a note to himself and looked up. "But from what I've seen, even given what you've said, the bulk of the non-military money you spend here winds up going to the elites and not to the poor. I looked at the numbers for their tax reform package, and it seems like it mainly helped rich people. And the value added tax and the consumption tax they passed mainly hurt the poor...And I can cite a lot of economic studies that show that giving money to the poor is the best thing to jump start an economy because they spend every dime of it and that moves the economy forward. But if you give it to the rich, they bank it or send it overseas."

Doug took a deep breath. "Yes, that's partly right. But truly we can't change that. If we don't give a bundle of money to the rich, they'll turn on us and throw us out and then where would anybody be? Where would the country be? Trouble is, the oligarchy doesn't care if the country survives. They don't care if democracy survives. That's why they don't fund public education like they should. That's why they threaten (and sometimes destroy) the newspapers that don't follow their official line. That's why they don't teach the nasty history of how their ancestors treated the Pipil and Lenca peoples they found here. Poor campesinos who can read newspapers and understand the issues are a real threat to the reigning oligarchy." He paused and removed his glasses again, turning the stem in his fingers. He frowned and looked around the room uncomfortably, as though thinking he had said too much. "Look, Dave, everybody knows this, but almost nobody can do much about it. They don't care what happens to the country. They can afford bodyguards; they can move to France. It's a nasty trade-off, but it's what we've got."

He raised his hand, evidently to add more to that thought, but the phone rang, and he stopped and looked at his secretary. She picked it up and talked quietly for a few seconds. She then put her hand over the mouthpiece and glanced at him. "Will you be much longer? Wade wants to talk to you about the interviews this afternoon."

Doug looked at his watch and with a pained expression, said, "Tell him to hold on. I can be with him in just a minute. We're wrapping up." He stood and turned back to David. "I'm sorry," he said, "but I need to go. A lot of people from the US media are here this week and they're wanting to do something like a group interview with an AID division head, and I've been elected to be the sacrificial lamb thrown to the lions...or however that metaphor goes."

David laughed, "I think you got it a little off, but I get the point."

"Listen, I really do appreciate the work that you and the Institute are doing. And if you or Héctor, or anyone else have more questions or need any help with anything, please call us again. Maybe we can handle it on the phone, but if it's something big, let me know and we can get together again."

"Thanks, I appreciate that."

Doug picked up his phone but looked back at David. "Oh, and give your address to Priscilla and she'll send you a copy of our listing of non-governmental organizations in Salvador."

"Great. I'll do that, and thanks again." Doug went back to the phone and Priscilla slid a pen and note pad across the desk to him. David wrote down his address and left.

CHAPTER TWENTY-TWO
LEER

The next morning, David was trying to force himself to concentrate on the lists of addresses for his next interview, but he was still shaken by the break-in at his apartment. The event had made him feel vulnerable and frightened, just as he was beginning to feel alive and strong again. Just as he was beginning to feel more at home and safe. And it was affecting his ability to focus on the list and remember the name and address of the program he was needing to visit next. And his time was running out on when to be there. The appointment was at one o'clock, and it was twelve now and he had completely forgotten who it was with. Héctor had arranged the interview and told David about it by phone, and usually David had a pretty good memory for details. But today he felt scattered and unfocussed and couldn't remember what Héctor had said. He ran his finger up and down the names on the new list that Héctor had compiled using Doug Grantham's additions, but nothing he saw jogged his memory. Some were well-known, like "Americas Watch,"

"Oxfam," and "World Vision." But most were small and obscure, and he couldn't recognize any of them.

It had something to do with vision or seeing or reading or... and then he saw it. Running his finger rapidly down the list he saw "LEER," Spanish for "To Read." Following it was the description, "Basic literacy training for adults and children in low-income communities." That was it! he thought. It came back to him.

Ordinarily, if he wasn't in a hurry, he would go out to Calle Zacamil, wait for the half-hour bus (which came every forty-five minutes) and then, depending on the number of stops and slowdowns, arrive about an hour or two later. Today he couldn't do that. He snapped his notebook closed, turned to the wall phone in the kitchen and started dialing a number that, by now, he knew by heart. After a few moments a voice said, "*¡Taxi más rápido en El Salvador!*"

"Lessi? Is that you?"

"*¡Hablando!*"

"Lessi, I need to get to somewhere in Escalon again, and very, very fast. Can you help me?"

"*Si, Senior Patterson,* I will be there in very fast, very fast. We are best fast taxi service in entire nation. I will be there in almost right now."

HÉCTOR HAD ASKED if he could join him on this visit, and sure enough, when David arrived, just before one, Héctor was already inside and patiently waiting. That wasn't surprising because Héctor was seldom just on time, but usually quite a bit early. He stood up and greeted David with his wide arms and wide smile and gave him a big hug, as though they were lovers reuniting after years of being apart.

The office, however, was considerably less friendly. It was small and simple, with only one window and nothing on the walls. There was a small couch for two on a side wall and a simple table that may have been a receptionist's desk at the front but with no chair behind it, and a scattered pile of papers in the middle. A cigar that appeared to have been out for several hours was in an ashtray next to them. After standing uncomfortably in the office for several minutes, they moved to the couch to sit uncomfortably for several more.

Finally, the door to an inner office opened and a thin, middle-aged man with bright red hair and a blue tight-fitting suit came out, at first not seeing them. He rustled through papers in what looked to be an overflowing "outbox" on the desk and frowned. Whatever document he was looking for was evidently not there, and at last he looked up at them and said, "I'm sorry. Are you the people about the telephone?" He spoke in English with an American accent.

"No," said Héctor, standing. "We are here for the interview. Are you Señor Jeminez?"

The man looked puzzled. "I don't understand."

"We're from the institute, the *Instituto de Educación y Apoyo no Gubernamental?*" said Héctor. "We are to interview the director, his name is Señor Ramon Jimenez."

The man took off his glasses and seemed impatient with the interruption. "He's no longer here. I'm sorry. And I think they said you would be here later, at 1:00?"

"*Sí, Señor*, and it is more than one o'clock now," said Héctor.

He looked startled and glanced at his watch. "I'm sorry, I lost track of the time."

"It is for us no problem. Do you want for us to come back at another time?"

"No, no, no," he said, still looking at his watch. "You are

here now, so we should talk. I'm sorry I forgot the time but stay. We'll talk." He waved at the couch with the papers in his hands and leaned back uncomfortably against the desk. "Now, who did you say you were?"

Héctor bounced in his seat and put on his "best friend" smile. "We are from the Institute, as we mentioned. Do you know of us?"

"No, I'm afraid not. I just took over here a couple of weeks ago."

Héctor nodded and then patiently gave his lengthy, standard description of what the Institute did and how it was started, and what this new project was, and why David was there, and at the end the man looked more relaxed and sat back further onto the desk. "Okay," he said, "but, how can we help? There aren't many organizations in the country that do what we do."

"Actually," said Héctor, "this is not totally true, and that is why we are here, to help them help each other. There is one that is only a small distance from you and is mostly similar. It is named '*Alfabetización Mundial*,' which means, 'World Literacy.' Do you know of this group?"

"Yes," the man took a long breath. "They are one of the few we know of and we are talking with them about merging together soon."

Héctor's eyes widened. "Why is that? You do good work here. I have heard much good about you."

"Thank you, but we have hit some very hard times."

"Why?'

"Well, there are a couple of reasons. The first is fundraising. For one, there are some wellp-intentioned liberals in the states who hear we have a religious background and they don't want to fund anything that smacks of religion. And there are also many would-be donors who just don't understand what we do. They like organizations that feed cute little children but not those who teach them to read and function in the society. And that's what we do. What we do is important and something that could change the whole future of a country. There are a lot of organizations that do good for poor people, but if your people can't read, the state can't survive. Your democracy can't survive. This country is on the brink of losing its last chance to create a democracy because many of its people can't read and don't know enough about what is being decided about them from above. Imagine what the US would be like if its people stopped reading and learning about the important issues of the day and started voting for people who were loud and powerful and who claimed they could fix all their problems without being a democracy. That's why we have hundreds of US-funded feeding programs in El Salvador, but only two or three, like Alfabetización and ourselves, that teach them how to read and how to be a democracy."

"It is a problem for my sister's teaching program also," said Héctor. "Perhaps we can be of some help to you. My friend, Dr. Patterson, is a renowned professor of economics in Boston, USA, and he is here to help us do this research."

The man stuck out his hand to David. "And I'm Larry Dennison, and I'm a teacher too. At least I used to be until I got involved here."

David shook his hand sensing a kinship, "Why did you change?"

"I taught English for a few years after college. It was fine. I enjoyed teaching rich kids how to read Dickens, but I eventually became acquainted with this group, which was teaching poor people how to read at all, and how to open a bank account, and how to cast a vote. That vision became more of a draw for me, so I quit."

"I think I'm beginning to understand that draw," David

said. "I came here after a tragedy back at home, but I'm really beginning to feel pulled by the struggle in this place."

"I get that," said Larry. "Welcome to the family."

"Was there a second problem?" asked Héctor.

"Yes, the second reason is simply that it's hard to keep our doors open in a country where the government overtly does not want people who can read, and it's hard to recruit new teachers when they know their lives will be in danger. The government here thinks that keeping its people illiterate is just fine and shouldn't change. Uneducated people tend to vote for loud voices on the right, and authoritarian governments like that. Then, when organizations like ours come along—ones that try to educate people—they are called socialist or communist or whatever. The government does everything it can to defund public education and make it just for the rich, and that puts organizations like ours out of business. And I think they may soon be successful."

"Has that caused some actual conflicts?" asked David.

"Did you hear about three weeks ago that some of our people here were captured and tortured, and one of them was murdered?"

"I'd heard that something like that happened," said David, "but I didn't know that it happened to you."

"The one who died was our in-country director, and that's why I'm sitting here now. We thought that if we sent someone down from the US office for a while, he might be less likely to get shot. No one, especially the Salvadoran military, wants to see their name in the *New York Times,* being accused of killing someone from the US, the country that gives them a million and half dollars a day in aid."

"Sorry," said David. "That's an awful reason to bring you down." The pit of grief that still lived in his stomach began to stir again at the thought and reached up for his throat. He coughed and turned away while he pushed the memories down again. "Did you know any of them?" he asked.

"Only one. A good man named Juan de la Cruz, and he was one of our best. He was one of our regional teachers. He traveled to the States a couple of times to give fundraising talks, and I met him then. A good, honest, and dedicated guy. That's probably why he was on their hit list."

"Why did they do it?"

"Well, the general answer is, again, that authoritarian governments—not just here, but everywhere—don't want too many people walking around who are literate and well-read. If you shrink down public education and close public schools, then you have fewer people who know who their real enemy is. They start looking to the side for their enemies instead of up, where the strings are being pulled. You have fewer people who can read a contract or a property lease or know that they are being cheated by their boss. The "Fourteen Families" who run the country don't want any of that. It's not good for business."

"And that's why they attack your people."

"Yes, and they'll continue doing it as long as we're small and vulnerable. And that's why we may have to shut down or try to merge with another organization with higher visibility and a wealthier donor base in the States."

David closed his notebook and slid his pen in the spiral wire at the top. "Look, Larry, I know that this has been difficult for you, and we appreciate this, but you've got a whole lot more important things to deal with right now than talking to us. We've got a pretty good idea of the kind of work you're doing here, and it's important work. So, why don't we just wrap it up and let you get back to it?"

"And we will read your brochures and call you on the telephone if there are other small questions," added Héctor.

Larry had a look of weary sadness in his eyes. "Thanks, and you're right, I do need to get back."

OUTSIDE, on the crowded sidewalk, Héctor took a big breath and said, "That was *muy difícil,* very difficult. You looked like you took some of that personally. Are you okay?"

"Yes," said David, "Thank you for noticing, but I'll be fine if I don't talk about it."

"Would you like to accompany me back to the Institute to talk for a while? Marsha is there but she would not bother us. We now have cold Coca-Cola that we can serve to our guests who come visit us."

David smiled, grateful for the offer. "No, I think I'll just walk back to my apartment from here. It's not that far. It would give me a chance to gather my thoughts, and besides, I could use the exercise."

"*Bueno.* You must do that then. It will be good for you. But if you do need anything..."

"I'm fine, really, you go on ahead. I'll call you tomorrow. But for now, I think I need to be alone."

Héctor stood for a moment with what David interpreted as a look of doubt on his face. But then he smiled and turned to the street and hailed an oncoming cab. As it approached, he turned to David and gave him a big hug. "You are a good man, my friend. We will speak again soon." He stepped into the cab, spoke to the driver, and it drove away. David waved at him as the taxi plunged into the sea of competition drivers and then stepped back into the crowd gathering for an approaching bus. He took a deep breath and looked down the street before him, trying to assess how long it would take him to get back to Los Cañones by walking. But before he could decide, he saw a large man, dressed in black, wearing a black fedora, come quickly out of a dark alleyway beside the LEER building, looking anxiously down the street in the direction of Héctor's taxi. He raised his hand at another one moving in the same direction and stopped it at the curb. He leaned down to the window, spoke to the driver, and got in. But before he closed the door, he glanced back at the LEER building and saw David still there watching him from the sidewalk. They both looked at each other and David stepped backward realizing who it was. The man turned to the driver and pounded on the headrest yelling something. He got out, threw some money into the window at the driver, and began walking away. David raised his hand to say something, but as quickly as the man had appeared, he disappeared again into the maze of people on the sidewalk and was gone. I think I know him, David thought to himself standing alone in the crowd. It was Emilio Bhutto.

CHAPTER TWENTY-THREE
THE SICKNESS

When David got home, he was tired, very tired. It had been a good thing for him emotionally, he thought, to walk the two or three miles from the LEER offices to his apartment, but it also wore him out. Everything had been tumbling around inside of him lately—his work, the country, Sara, his past—and tonight that strange encounter with Emilio Bhutto on the street. All of it needed to be sorted through, so a good long walk to think and remember was a good thing. David occasionally got home tired but tonight seemed different. So tired that when he approached his door, looking down and searching for his keys, he didn't even notice Camilia standing in his doorway, opening it for him to come in. *¿Buenos?* she said, puzzled and stepping back.

"I'm sorry," he said to her in Spanish. I didn't see you."

"*¿Está usted bien?*" she asked.

"*No, no. Quiero decir, sí. No, estoy bien, estoy bien*" he said, "No, no. I mean, yes, of course. No, I'm fine, I'm fine." The words blurred out of him in an awkward jumble of English and Spanish. "I'm just very tired."

As he made his way in, Camilia stepped out, pulling a vacuum behind her. But then she looked back at him with a concerned look and pointed over to his couch. She put her hands together next to her cheek, closed her eyes and made a gesture of sleeping.

He laughed. "Yes, of course, I probably need to do that."

She then pointed to the refrigerator and moved her hand to her mouth as though eating. He smiled again. "And, yes, I promise I'll do that too."

When she left, he closed the door, put down his backpack, and collapsed on the couch, feeling more sleepy than tired. Camilia was probably right about his needing to nap. He was supposed to go over to Sara's that evening for dinner, and it would be bad if he was dragging when he got there. But it wasn't just sleepiness. He was also feeling groggy and unsteady. He looked warily around the room a little frightened. He hoped that he wasn't coming down with something.

The week had been unusually emotional for him. In addition to the conversation at LEER, and the mysterious sighting of Bhutto afterwards, the week in general had been stressful. One day he visited with a very sweet group of people who gathered up clothes from local churches and distributed them to the kids at the city dump who were so poor that they collected salvage from the piles to sell in the downtown market. The next day he interviewed an organization made up mainly of people from a religious broadcasting network and funded mainly by viewers. They brought canned goods from the US and gave them away (along with Bibles written in English) to poor children around the capital. That's all they did. Nothing long-term, no development, no sustainability, no local participation. Nothing. Plus, it also hurt the neighboring stores who were trying to sell many of the same canned goods. When David finished the interview and left their building, he noticed an enormous pile of empty cans with remnants of food inside them, rotting in the tropical heat. I'm not coming back here, he thought.

And then today, he had had that painful conversation at LEER, about people who risked their lives trying to do something as simple and important as teaching reading to kids and also adults. It broke his heart to remember it.

Today, though, he felt more than his usual tired. More, also, than he would have expected from a difficult interview and a three-mile walk to get home. And the longer he lay there on his couch, the more his body was beginning to hurt. His first thought was that he wanted a beer, but then, after staring into his kitchen for several minutes, he realized that what he really wanted was just some cold water—and a lot of it. He was feeling unusually dehydrated. He got up to go to the sink, but by the time he got there, his tiredness had become more queasy. He had to steady himself at the counter to get a glass down and wasn't sure what was happening. Jeez, he wondered, what had he eaten today? That morning, waiting for Lessi to pick him up, he bought some very nice, shaved ice and mango syrup out on the street. He knew that it was a risk, but he'd been in the country for several months now and hadn't gotten sick with anything yet. He thought for a minute. Yes, but it was ice after all...made from water...and sold, not in a clean *cantina*, but *on the street*. O my God, he thought. I'm going to die. He put the glass back quickly and then crumpled to his knees. What have I done, he thought, and then fell over. His chest and stomach swelled and heaved again and again, until his throat and mouth exploded with eggs and rice and tacos and mango juice all over his clothes and floor.

After that, he became still. Occasionally twitching with chills, occasionally ejecting more food. And then quiet. Quiet and still, for a long time, a very long time.

CHAPTER TWENTY-FOUR
THE MORNING

David looked up. Actually, he opened his eyes first and then looked up. They had been closed for some time; he didn't know how long. He did remember consciously closing them because they hurt, and he hurt, and he was afraid if he kept them open, he would throw up again. So, he closed them but then threw up anyway, and after that, his memories seem to run out. He hadn't been sleeping, but something deeper, not caused by a long day and a need for rest but of a long hurt and a need for healing. He hoped that this time had been only a few minutes long, but he knew it probably wasn't. Probably hours ago, maybe more, maybe days. He wasn't sure. He also wasn't sure where he was now and who was touching him. Two hands were lifting his shoulder, and they straightened something, maybe a pillow, under his head. The hands pulled a sheet up around him and then tucked it around his neck and shoulders. It wasn't necessary. He wasn't cold. Then the hands patted him. It felt good. It felt affectionate. They then ran their fingers through his hair. Then touched his cheek, almost like a caress. This is not a nurse, he thought. And that's when he opened his eyes, and then he looked up.

It wasn't Kathryn. For a moment he hoped it might have been Kathryn because he missed her and over the last three years, he had occasionally missed her so much that he wished he could die also so that he could be with her. But it wasn't Kathryn. He had to blink a few times to clear his eyes. It was Sara.

Kathryn was a lot taller than Sara. Kathryn's father was from Norway and her mother's family was British, so Kathryn was tall. She had sharp angular features and had what he used to call a "fierce beauty." She would laugh at that. "I'll accept the 'beauty' part," she once said, "but not the 'fierce.'" Sara didn't look at all like Kathryn. She was much smaller, perhaps five-one, maybe two. And with dark, non-European, colors. She was thin at the top and round at the bottom with brown, kind, eyes. Gentle and forgiving eyes. David needed forgiveness in his life, though whenever he allowed himself to think those words, he followed them by thinking that he also didn't deserve any.

Sara was talking. She had been saying words that he couldn't quite hear for a few moments and then, while she was still touching his cheek, he smelled the warmth in her hand and recognized a question, "Are you better?" She likes doing this, he thought, she likes touching his cheek, and he liked her doing it.

"I'm not sure," he said. "Was I in a coma, or dead, or...?

She laughed. "No, *mi novio,* just sick. Very, very sick. You have been asleep for several hours. Do you remember anything?"

He blinked and pulled his eyes together. "I remember feeling sick to my stomach. Then I got dizzy and threw up. I didn't make it to the toilet. After that, I'm not sure. I don't remember."

She smiled, "Yes, it was very bad, very bad."

He looked embarrassed. "Did you see it?"

"No, but I heard. Do you remember that you were coming to my house, and I was going to cook you dinner?"

"Yes, I do. Did I miss it? I'm so sorry."

"Yes, it was last night." She smiled. "And now it is the morning. You missed it by a lot."

"How did I get here, then?"

"When you didn't come, I sent Dani to your room, and he found Carlos and Camilia to open your door. Then, actually" (David liked the way she pronounced "act-u-al-ly," slowly with four very precise syllables) "Carlos wouldn't let Dani follow them in because he was afraid that something had happened to you. Then Camilia cleaned up your kitchen a little and he cleaned up you a little and then they let Dani in."

David grimaced. "I'm glad," he said.

"Me too. You must have made the vomit several times before they found you. And I think you had the diarrhea too. Carlos told me most of the room smelled very bad." David's grimace deepened. "And then they brought you here. I showered you. I hope that is okay. You were not awake."

For the first time, David realized that he was nearly naked, and the sheet was all that was covering him. It wasn't the first time that someone had seen him naked, but clearly the most embarrassing. "I am so sorry," he said.

"It is nothing," she said. "But what would have happened to you if we had not been here?"

David didn't know. And the thought frightened him. If something like this had happened to him in Massachusetts, no one would have found him. Even if Kathryn had still been alive, she would have left him by now and not there to help. "I guess I would have just laid there until I finally woke up and then…"

He was silent for a moment. He sensed that he could see an invitation on her lips for him to do something, and he considered what it might be, but at the end of the pause, Sara changed the subject. "Act-u-al-ly," she said, "you did almost see a doctor or an 'almost' doctor."

"How?"

"You know her, Isabel Marroquín, she is your neighbor."

David frowned. "I don't think so."

"Well, not exactly your neighbor, she is a *paramédico* and she lives just here in my row. But she says that she visits your row frequently and she recognizes you." She turned her head and said, "*Isabel, ¿reconoces a esta pobrecita?*" "Do you recognize this poor boy?"

He heard a woman's laugh from somewhere else in the room. "Yes, of course," she said in Spanish. "We are good friends. He just does not remember me."

With great effort, he lifted his head and saw the tall woman who frequently passed his window on Friday afternoons, often accompanied by a male friend. She was standing by the door with a bag in her hand, as though preparing to leave but had paused when he woke up. "Hi," he said weakly. "I'm sorry, I *do* know you. But I never knew your name."

She smiled, "And until now I never knew yours. I didn't know that you and Sara were… *románticos?*" He felt uncomfortable about the description, but he didn't deny it either.

"You should stay in bed today. At least until tonight, perhaps even tomorrow. Sara knows what would be best to help you if you will let her. She has bananas, rice, and potatoes which you should eat. And water—Sara, remember to make him drink plenty of water, even when he does not want to." She opened the door but before she left, she paused and said,

"And don't worry, you are not the first man I have helped undress." She laughed and closed the door behind her.

He shifted his weight to get more comfortable in the bed, and Sara responded by snuggling her hips closer to his. That felt very pleasant, he thought. His body still hurt in many places, but gratefully the queasy stomach, dizzy head, and urge to vomit again seemed to have passed, at least for the moment. He was not just embarrassed about what had happened, but also humiliated and ashamed. But also grateful to Sara and Carlos, and the mysterious Isabel, who had all conspired to take care of him. He dropped his head back down on the pillow and sighed deeply. "Thank you," he said to her. She looked down at him and smiled. Lovely eyes, brown eyes, caring eyes. "I mean *really* thank you. I don't know what I would have done if you had not been here." He reached up and touched her cheek like she had just done to him moments ago.

"But I like you," she said, as though her actions needed justification. "And I was worried about you. And I liked taking care of you." She paused for a moment and then spoke quickly, "And...and I would like it too for you to stay." She pulled her head back, looking anxious at how her offer might have sounded.

"Well, it looks like I'll have to for a while," he said, smiling weakly, avoiding the deeper suggestion in her words. "If you don't really mind. Maybe for today, maybe tomorrow. But I think I'll be fine soon, and I don't want to be a bother."

"Noooo, it is not for me a bother. I mean I would like it if you want to stay. I mean, if you *want* it, I would want you to stay here with us. The boys like you too."

He felt a small tremor shake through him. The thought was both appealing and frightening. He was not even yet sure how much he felt for Sara, let alone thinking of living with her. He gathered his thoughts and took her hand in his. "That's incredibly kind of you," he said. "But for right now, no. I mean, maybe some time, but I don't think I *can* do that right now." The look of expectancy in her face dropped. "But I'll tell you what. Let's continue to spend time together. Let's continue seeing each other. Let me get used to this. And then in a while, maybe not long, can we talk about it again?" Her eyes opened wide again, and she looked as though she was about to say something but stopped. He hoped that he had said the right thing, making the right decision. "I like you too," he said, "and maybe sometime I will be ready for that, but not right now. Not right now. I don't think I can. Is that okay?"

She held his hand up to her face and kissed it. "You stay here for today and I will take care of you. Maybe by tomorrow you will be well enough to leave." She tilted her head and smiled. "And tonight, I will tell the boys to let you watch the terrible American TV shows."

He shook his head feigning being insulted. "But they like them too."

"No," she said. "They are just being polite. I have taught them well." He started to protest, but she put her finger on his lips. "And then, before you leave tomorrow, we will make a plan for when we will meet again. And again, after that. And then again. And then someday, when you want to do it, we will talk of this again." She leaned forward and kissed him on the forehead. "I want you to be here and be in our home with my family, but I also want you to want to. When you are ready, we will talk."

CHAPTER TWENTY-FIVE
TOURS

After he recovered from his awful ordeal with the sickness, David began spending more time with Sara and the boys. And he enjoyed it a lot. He began going to her apartment several days a week and she would show him the "correct" ways to cook Salvadoran meals. Then, after dinner and the boys were in bed, he and Sara would stay up talking and laughing and telling stories about their pasts and the work they were involved with now. He told her about the wide range of organizations he was talking to—from competent to incompetent, and some that were just creepy. For her, it was stories of the odd American students she worked with who thought they could come down here, have one or two Spanish lessons, and then be able to keep up with lectures and write papers. They had no idea how lost they were. A few times, in the mornings, when he had not scheduled interviews and the kids had gone to school, Sara would take him with her around San Salvador, and show off some of the beautiful archi-tecture, galleries, museums, and monuments of fallen leaders, in a city that she loved. There is so much that is beautiful here, she would tell him at almost every stop, but most of the world only knows about the poverty and war. And she wanted him to love her country as much as she did. Twice they all went back to Pupuseria Bety, the place that Tomás called *"el escenario del crimen,"* "the scene of the crime," and laughed every time he said it.

Occasionally, when there was a pause in the conversation, or when he was alone walking back to his apartment, he thought that he just possibly was falling in love. Certainly, he was in love with the idea of falling in love. And that was something he had not come close to feeling in several years. And when they walked the streets together, and she would point to a statue or a two-hundred-year-old building, and he would follow her gaze and make a comment about what they were seeing, he would casually reach down and hold her hand and they would walk that way together. It felt very good, and it felt almost normal.

After several of these adventures, Sara told him she had an evening translating job at the university, so he went home early. He volunteered to stay with the boys while she was gone, but she said no. She had already made arrangements with the grandparents and the boys hadn't seen them in a few weeks and missed them. When he told them all goodbye and gave the boys hugs, and walked down her balcony to the stairs, he took a long and satisfied breath. Who would have thought that he would ever be capable of enjoying himself like this again?

He loved the little colonia, Zacamil, where he lived. It had a reputation of violent repression by the police because of its history of sympathy for the rebels, but he seldom saw any of that. Instead, he saw ordinary people working hard, struggling to get by when their country was fragile and shaking. And he liked the fact that, in a small way, his whole purpose in being here was to help it move forward.

He walked through the gate at the end of Sara's row of apartments and down towards his own and smiled enjoying this new life. For a while, even after coming to El Salvador, he had still felt a haunted and burning abscess in his stomach at the loss of Kathryn and his shame at how she died. But recently, he was feeling a new sense of not just being alive but purposeful. This was still a beleaguered country, but somehow, strangely, he felt indebted to it. El Salvador was being good to him, and he felt safe there. I'm feeling better, he thought, and I think this country has hope. It has its struggles, but it is overall a good place. There was talk of possible peace negotiations happening, and there are good people here like Sara and Alf and Héctor, and the others, who were personally involved with fixing lives and healing the country.

As he approached his row of apartments, he saw that the gate was open, and a garbage truck was parked in front of it. Two young men were rapidly moving down the row, stopping at each door to pick up bags and boxes of trash. It was a scene that could happen in almost any town in the US, he thought. Campaign signs from the recent election were still up in some of the lawns and nailed to trees. The moderate Christian Democrats had lost, and the right-wing ARENA had won, contrary to polls and projections, and accusations of voter suppression were in the air. When he went through the gate a car stopped, pausing to pick up two young girls who had evidently been visiting friends or family. He looked down his row with sidewalks on either side and lawn and trees between them. The little ice cream shop at one end, and apartments for Carlos and Camilia at the other. It felt peaceful and safe.

When he reached his door, the garbage workers had nearly

made their way to the end of his row and were each hauling bags back to the truck in the parking lot. They were ordinary workers doing ordinary work, and probably glad to even have a job. He unlocked and opened his door and went inside. Soon a light on the inside flickered on. And music from his radio drifted into the street.

The men tossed their bags onto the truck and hurried back to the last two doors on the opposite side of the lawn from David's. The third was back at the truck, operating the hydraulic cylinders crushing trash deep into the truck's bowels to compress it to rubble. It was a routine that happened the same way at each residence, at each block, each week, in each neighborhood.

From inside his apartment, with the door still ajar, David heard a sound. It was small at first, and he thought it might have been from the truck. But then it grew and became a scream. He put down his keys and stepped back to his open door and at first, he couldn't see anything. The noise had come from one of the two workers, just out of his sight, down to the far end. One of them was shrieking and backing away from something he had seen. The other ran to him, to see what had happened, but stopped suddenly when he arrived, looking at a large receptacle by a fence at the end of the row. The first worker had been pulling boxes and bags and loose trash out of it and was dragging them down to the truck to throw inside. But as he pulled at hands full of trash and bottles and other unpleasant items, two thick plastic garbage bags had tumbled out onto him. They were heavy and lumpy and damp, and one of them roughly resembled the shape of a human bent in a crouching position. The other was the same, but smaller and more compact. A dark thick liquid formed around the opening of one and poured down onto the hands and chest of the worker.

He screamed and backed away pointing at the bags. The other man approached him slowly as though standing at the edge of an enormous evil abyss. One more step and he would fall into something endless and dark. The first was screeching and waving his bloody hands. "*¡Son cuerpos!*" he yelled. "*¡Son cuerpos! ¡Son cuerpos!*" "It's bodies! It's bodies! It's bodies!"

CHAPTER TWENTY-SIX

CLÍNICA DE EMERGENCIA RURAL

Just north of San Salvador there is another city, smaller than San Salvador and not as well known, but protruding northward to some of the main regions at war, and its name is, "Apopa." When there is fighting in the villages of the north, and the casualties are soldiers or people in sympathy with them, they are taken to one of the many larger state clinics in other parts of the country, where they receive excellent care. When the casualties are rebels or people who are in sympathy with them, they are taken to smaller, privately funded clinics, like those in Apopa. One of them is called *La Clínica de Emergencia Rural.*

"I'm sorry, but you should not to visit with us today."

David was peering into a small space in the door held nearly closed by a man inside wearing rimless glasses and a white lab coat. "I had an appointment with Dr. Edina Morales," he said. "Are you not allowing visitors in today?"

"Yes, but we have a problem," the man said, opening the door just slightly. "We have had a large number of patients today and we very much will not be able to talk to you and to answer your questions."

"But since I'm here anyway, is it possible that I could at least stand somewhere out of the way and observe? I could wear a mask and not touch anything, and it would still be helpful to me because I'd like to just see your work. And then we could set up a better time for a conversation later. Would that be okay?" He knew that this would not normally be appropriate, but he thought he'd ask, just in case. "I could wash and clean up and wear a mask and everything."

In the small opening in the door, David could see portions of several beds arranged in rows over the man's shoulder, and people moving between them. A woman's voice from inside said something in Spanish and for several seconds she and the man at the door spoke intently. Then suddenly the door opened and a large, round woman, also wearing a lab coat and glasses, stepped outside where David was standing. "Mr. Patterson," she said, "can you tell me why you are here and who you represent?"

David had become accustomed to that question. "Well, I work at the University of El Salvador," he said. "I'm a part of a project studying nonprofits in El Salvador. I travel around and..."

"Who do you work for in the States?"

"Well, no one. The University of El Salvador, here, has set up a small institute to study the work of nonprofit humanitarian aid agencies like yours. It's the *Instituto de Educación y Apoyo no Gubernamental.*' Have you heard of them?"

"Yes. Will you excuse me?" She abruptly stepped back through the door and pulled it to its nearly closed position again. He could hear her speaking to the man who had first opened it. He heard them say the name of the institute and the word *telefono*, and then suddenly she opened the door. "We are calling them," she said. "Wait here." And the door closed again.

After several minutes passed, the woman appeared at the door again, this time still imposing, but smiling. "So, you are a good friend of Professor Castañeda?"

David smiled. He could easily imagine Héctor praising their friendship if asked about it. "Yes, he is my boss. Like my *jefe*," he said.

"He speaks well of you, and of your work. I apologize for being hesitant, but we must be very careful today. I hope you understand."

"Yes, of course. No need to apologize."

"I am Doctor Edina Morales, and yes come in." She stepped back and gestured for him to come through the door. "But be *very* respectful of our patients and our *paramédicos*. Stay here up against this wall and do not talk or bother them unless they choose to speak to you." She handed him a pair of surgical latex gloves. "Wear these." Then she folded a face cloth cut to resemble a medical procedure mask. "And wear this. We are in a big crisis today."

He fumbled trying to juggle his notebook and mask and gloves. "Thank you. What happened?"

"We do not ask the patients when they have military wounds. But it looks like crossfire."

"Crossfire?"

"Yes, maybe. We know that there was a time of conflict near the little *aldea* of Guazapa two days ago and yesterday arrived many *no combatientes*." She struggled to find a word. Finally, she said, "People who are not combatants. *Civilians?* Those who were wounded in the fighting."

"Are they all people who were just civilians in the area?"

"Most yes, but we do not think all. There were two this morning who looked like the *Muchachos*. Young men, green shirts, camouflage pants, bandanas around their necks. But we do not ask. If someone is shot, we will treat them."

Six beds were against the walls on both sides of the room. In between them were a number of cots and floor mats for the overflow. Some of the patients appeared to be resting, with an arm or leg or chest wrapped in bandages, others had open wounds being treated by the staff.

"Mr. Patterson, we do not have much time. What can I tell you?"

"Of course, Dr. Morales, I am so sorry that it turned out that I came on such a hard day for you."

"We have always days like this. So, it possibly won't ever be better for you to come. If we did not have wounded people here, we would possibly have people who were dying from malaria or dysentery or diarrhea. There is much suffering in this country, even without the war, and there are not many places that have medicines or *paramédicos* for the poor."

David looked around the room and its solemn gathering of tragedies and losses. It was nearly silent as the attendants worked patiently, almost prayerfully, with their damaged sufferers. One young woman, quietly and in tears, kneeled down and kissed the forehead of a man who had evidently stopped breathing. Others around him seemed destined to soon do the same or perhaps survive but be crippled for life. David watched them all with horror and respect. This small group of dedicated helpers was given the grim and crucial task of blessing the dead or pulling those who could make it back into something like a manageable life.

"Forgive me, Dr. Morales, I appreciate your offer to talk, even if for a small amount of time, but you need to get back to your patients. And I don't need to be here in the middle of your work taking up your time."

"You are very kind, Doctor Patterson, and it is very right

that I should get back to my people. Thank you for trying to help and I hope your research goes better with the others."

He reached out and took her hand in both of his and held it for a moment. "Thank you. I'll do my best and thank you too for what you and your clinic are doing here. The world needs more of you."

Later, outside on the sidewalk, he stopped for a moment and closed his eyes. They filled with tears and visions of suffering and dying. Kathryn, Gil, the trash men, the morgue, Sara's husband, people in a crossfire. "God, how I hate death," he said out loud to cars and pedestrians around him. "I hate it."

CHAPTER TWENTY-SEVEN

NORMAL

"How do you manage to look so...so 'normal'?"

Sara laughed. She often laughed and David enjoyed seeing her laugh. But this was also a nervous laugh. Maybe a self-conscious laugh. "I'm not sure what you mean," she said.

He wasn't sure either. "When I talk to some of the people in these organizations or read a story in the paper, *El Mundo,* I get the feeling that the nation is on fire. There are bodies found in the streets, or mysteriously disappearing, or even in the trash of an apartment down the sidewalk from me. A non-profit clinic I visited today had to break their appointment with me because they just had a 'shipment' of wounded people come in from the *campo.* And she said that I probably couldn't reschedule my visit because every day they have more "shipments." Alf says that here in the city the killing has gone down, but my God, look at the number of funeral homes here! They're everywhere. Every corner has one on it. And you've lived under all this for years. I mean...how do you do it? When I come over to see you, you look so sweet and so calm as though everything around us is doing well and fine, while everything around you is clearly not."

She put her hand over her mouth and laughed again. "I am embarrassed at 'sweet.' In Spanish we use that word for 'candy' or 'ice cream' but thank you."

"But I think you know what I mean. You go to work and raise your boys like anyone I would meet in any other country that was not going through a very tough, very hard civil war. How do you do that?"

She put down the glass she had been drying at the sink and turned to face him. She breathed deeply and then took his hands and held them tightly. She did that often when she wanted to say something serious, and David liked it. They had a slight, sweet scent to them, and he enjoyed that too. "There are two—no maybe three—reasons." She looked away for a moment trying out different words. "First, I need to say that I like you. I like you very much."

"Well, thank you for that. I...I like you too." He tried not to think too hard about how much.

"I mean, I like you very much, and therefore I try to act like an American girl."

"What does that mean?"

"I mean I lived in America for a while, for four years. I know how boys and girls act. I know how they talk to one another. And when I am around you, I try to act like that."

He pulled his head back and smiled mischievously. "You were in a college in Oklahoma. Are you sure you know how college girls and boys talked in, say Boston, or St. Augustine, Florida?"

"Well..." She stretched out the word. "Maybe not *exactly*, but I think I have a good idea. And my point is that when I am with you, I try to be like the girls you are used to back in the US.

"You are not the girl I'm used to back in the US." He felt his voice grow tense.

"No," she said, pulling her head back. "I just mean girls in general. I try to look like the people you are familiar with."

"How?"

She looked away again and frowned. "For one thing, I have some clothes that look more 'American.' And I try to always wear them when you come."

"I didn't know that," he said.

"And usually, we don't go to movies here. The boys and I hadn't been to a movie since Daniel died. And now, since you have been here, we have been to two."

"Three," he corrected her.

"Okay, three. But that's the point. And each time it has been to one of your American movies." She caught herself and added, "I don't mean that's a bad thing. The boys loved them."

"They really like the action movies with lots of running and shooting."

She laughed. "Yes, and the one about the man who was a weapon, the..."

"'Lethal Weapon'"?

"Yes, that one. They thought it was funny."

"Yes, and it also has a lot of running around and shooting people. At least they're consistent."

"But my meaning," she said, holding his hands more firmly, "was that for a long time, I was depressed and frightened and we didn't go see movies at all. We didn't go to the park. I didn't go out with them and just play as often as we have since you have been..." she closed her eyes and spoke slowly and deliberately, "since you have been a part of our lives."

David was surprised. "I didn't know that."

"I did not want you to know that. I wanted you to know

that we liked you, but I didn't want you to know how recent it has been that I was *able* to like you. For a long time after Daniel died, I wasn't *able* to like someone." She shook her head. "And did you notice that I cut my hair?"

He actually had noticed. She had near-black, beautiful hair, smooth and straight and it was now shorter than when they first met. And he had told her when she first did it that he liked it.

"I think it is more common for professional women in America to have shorter hair. So, after I met you, I cut my hair." She tossed her head from side to side, smiling broadly. "I told Sra. Ramirez to cut it to look like in the American magazines. We looked at pictures."

He hadn't thought about it, but yes, it probably did look more American than Salvadoran. "Sara, you didn't need to do that."

"Perhaps," she said, breaking her gaze and looking down at their hands. "But I maybe don't know that." She corrected herself, "No, I *didn't* know that. In the beginning, I didn't know what you liked. Maybe now I know better. Now I know that I love you, and I think very much that you love me too. So, today I wouldn't do that." David pulled back. The logical, appropriate thing would be to make an affirming, caring pronouncement, to say she didn't need to put on a show because he *did* in fact love her and loved her for who she was. But he didn't know—he wasn't *certain*— if that was true, and if he did, he still couldn't make those words come from his throat. They probably were there, and if he said them, he would probably mean them, but he somehow couldn't say them. He finally pulled his hands back from hers and stood up. "Sara," he started. "I...I'm not...I'm not. I think..." There was something that he truly wanted to say, but he didn't know what it was, and he couldn't say it. He shook his head to try to erase some of the confusion he was feeling and looked toward the door.

"Are you leaving?" she asked. "I'm sorry if I presumed something that wasn't true."

"No, it's just that..." He grimaced and waved her back with his hand. "I've got to go," he said and looked around for his jacket.

"On the chair," she said, without looking up.

He grabbed it and tried to put it on, but he was shaking badly and couldn't find the arm holes. It seemed to be backward or inside out, or something, and he couldn't make it work. So, he quit fighting it and walked to the door. He stopped there for a moment with his hand on the handle and turned around to look at her. She stood still. "It's not your fault," he said. "I'll call you."

"No, you won't," she said, in a angry tone. "I do know American men that much, and I think you will walk away and never call again."

"I don't know what I'll do," he said. "I don't know anything right now. But I'm sorry. I didn't mean for this to happen. I'm very sorry."

He opened the door and stepped onto the balcony where it was a warm and clear night and started walking towards the stairs. He heard the door close quietly behind him.

At the end of her row, he sat down at the top of the steps and didn't move, not wanting to go home and not being brave enough to go back. He sat there wiping tears from his face and listening to conversations inside him with ghosts.

"*Why are you doing this?*"

"I'm so sorry."

"Please tell me."

"I'm just so sorry."

"Why are you doing this? Why are you leaving?"

"I didn't mean for it to happen."

"How long?"

"I'm sorry, it just happened."

"HOW LONG?" He was shouting now.

"A year, maybe a little longer."

"A year?"

"Yes, and please don't yell at me."

He was shaking and also shouting. "I love you; I love you," he said. She turned her head away with a look of shame drawn into her features.

"I don't know how not to yell at you right now. Why did you do it?"

"I'm sorry," Kathryn said, "I don't think I've loved you for a longtime. I just couldn't find a way to leave."

"So, you waited until you found someone else to help you do it?" He was shouting again. "You're leaving me for that asshole, and I can't yell? Kathryn don't do this. Please don't do it."

"It's too late. I have to. I have to get away. I would have left eventually, even without Michael. I'm sorry, it hurts me so much to tell you this, but I haven't loved you in a long time and I have to be away from you."

"Hurts you? Hurts YOU?"

"I've got to go. Michael is waiting for me. You are a good person, but I just don't love you anymore."

He put his hands over his ears. "Don't say I'm a good person, but you're still leaving me. I can't. I can't let this happen. If you go now, then everything...everything will just end. Please don't go."

She put the box into the trunk and closed the lid. "I have to," she said. She turned and walked back to the door. "I'm so sorry. I didn't want this to happen, but it just did."

"No, no, no, that's the way they talk in movies. This is…this is, not a movie. This is…this is crazy, this is real life. And I don't want you to go. Can we talk about it?"

"No," she said, her voice impatient. "You know we haven't been getting along well." She walked back into the kitchen, looking around to see if she had forgotten something. David ached with a pain beyond anything he had ever known before. Tears were in his eyes, and he could no longer think in real words. He saw that she was now in the front room looking for her keys. She was ready to leave. And after that, everything would be over. Everything. He saw her looking around and he realized that he had the set that she was looking for. He had picked it up when she first came in. While she looked, he ran back into the garage and got in her car. His eyes burned and he could barely see. He didn't want to act like the crazy blind husband who was being jilted for another man and then did stupid things, but he did feel crazy and blind and couldn't think of doing anything else. He actually was the jilted husband, and it tore at his stomach and mind and it was impossible for him to think clearly. He turned on the motor and thought to himself that he had to get the car away from the house so she couldn't use it. Part of him knew that was senseless, but another part wanted to do something, anything, to keep her from being able to leave for just a little while longer. Maybe if she got delayed, they would have time to talk. He heard Kathryn's voice calling his name from somewhere far away, but he didn't answer. It was getting louder, he could tell that, but he wasn't sure where she was. He knew what he was doing was stupid, but he couldn't think and couldn't see, and he wanted to get the car away from her. He lifted his sleeve and tried to wipe tears from his eyes. They were tears as much from fear as sorrow. He pushed the button for the garage door opener, but he accidentally hit it twice, and after it jerked once upward it stopped and jammed at half open.

Damn that door, he thought, screaming the words in his head. It's stuck again. He pounded his fists on the steering wheel. Hurry, he thought, staring hard at it in the mirror. In a moment she might come into the garage, and she could stop him with just a word, and he knew that, and he didn't want it. So, he put it in reverse, shoved his foot on the accelerator, and jerked the car backward, straight into the door, as fast as he could make it go, and with a terrifying crack, the door flew up in the air in back of him, pieces of wood and iron flying like an explosion in all directions, and he saw in the mirror that Kathryn was not in the kitchen as he had thought, or in the hallway, or in the house at all, but there, standing in the driveway, right in back of him, yelling at him, screaming to him, as he drove the car fast and hard and crazed, right into her.

Sara looked around the room. She took the two unfinished beers from the coffee table into the kitchen and poured them out and threw away the cans. She dried her hands and put the towel into the handle on the stove and turned out the light. She went into the bedroom to check on the boys who had been asleep for over an hour by then. She looked in for a moment and watched them sleep, and then kissed each one, lightly, on his cheek. She closed their door and started toward her own room when she heard a knocking sound from the front of the apartment. She went back into the living room and opened the door and there was David.

"I'm sorry," he said.

"That's okay," she said, not very warmly.

"May I stay?" he asked.

"Stay?" She was puzzled. "Stay the night?"

"Maybe," he said. He reached his hand out to hers and pulled it up to his cheek as she so often did to him. "At least tonight. Maybe more if you'll have me. I think...if you'll have me."

She stepped back pulling his hand in with her. The outside door closed, and for a few moments, only unrecognizable words could be heard inside. Then the lights went out, and the speaking stopped and there was darkness and silence for the rest of the night.

CHAPTER TWENTY-EIGHT
OFICINA DE IDENTIFICACIÓN DE VÍCTIMAS

"Sr. Patterson?" David didn't look up. He was lost in memories— painful, wonderful, revealing memories —of last night with Sara, their conversation, their embrace, their touch, and he didn't see that a young woman had entered the reception room and was standing right in front of him. He was far away in stories that they had shared together of past lives—his with Kathryn and hers with Daniel —and possibilities now of creating future stories together.

"*Sr. Patterson?*"

"I'm sorry." He jerked forward awkwardly and dropped his pen.

"*Puede entrar ahora. La Sra. Martínez se está reuniendo con alguien ahora mismo, pero estará con usted en un momento.*" David gave her a blank look. By now, his Spanish had gotten better, but his mind was on other things and he missed much of it. She smiled with a look of recognition. "Sorry," she said, this time in English and much more slowly. "I said, Sra. Martínez is with someone right now, but she wishes that you will wait for her in here." She gestured to the room behind her.

"Thank you," he said, reaching down for his pen. Not a good way to make a first impression, he thought. "Is that her office?"

"No," she said, "it is our...our..." She paused. "It is called our 'library.' It is where we help the people find their families" She opened the door and gestured for him to go in.

When he went in, he expected to see a room filled with noise and active people looking through family records. But instead, it was very quiet, very much like a library as the woman had labeled it. It was about the size of a college class-room and was surrounded on three sides by tall, plain wooden bookcases fastened to the walls. As he waited for Sra. Martínez, he studied the shelves. Most were lined with what looked to be thick scrapbooks, the kind found in any office supply store. Some were labeled with dates and some with letters, alphabet-ized, "A- B," "C - D," etc. Were these the reports on missing people, he wondered? Some chronological, some alphabetical? Probably, but if they were, he was struck by the number of them, that there would be enough names and notebooks to fill nearly all the shelves around the "library." In the center of the room were three plain tables surrounded by metal folding chairs. A small group of people had gathered around one of the tables looking silently through the binders before them. Family members, he thought grimly, or researchers, or the press, or maybe all three. He couldn't tell. To the right of the tables and left of a second door, was a scarred, worn, wooden desk, piled with books, scrapbooks, papers, a powder blue Smith Corona manual typewriter, and an oscillating fan that labored to swing back and forth noisily, causing papers on the desk to flutter every few seconds when it passed. Someone had obvi-ously been there recently because everything seemed laid out for work, with weights on the papers for protection from the fan. He began looking through the bookcases and had just reached up for one of the scrapbooks when he heard a voice from behind him. "Mr. Patterson?" it said. He turned to see a small attractive woman, perhaps in her late forties, dressed in formal, but not expensive, business wear. She had on a black jacket and dress that one would wear to an office. She reached out her hand and in near-perfect English said, "So good to meet you."

"Thank you," he said. "Happy to meet you as well." "Please sit down. May I get you some coffee?"

"No, thank you," he said. "I just had some."

"We were informed by a man from some kind of 'institute' at the university that you might want to speak to us. I understand that you are a journalist."

David pulled out one of the chairs next to the desk. "That's not exactly correct. Did they say I was a journalist?"

She frowned but retained a patient formal smile. "Not exactly, but they said that you were here interviewing people and organizations for a publication in the States. And we just assumed...Is that not correct?"

"Well, that's close to correct." She looked disappointed. "It's true that I'm going around interviewing people like you in various nonprofit organizations, but it's to get a sense of the number and kind of humanitarian aid agencies are in El Salvador. There are hundreds of them, and many don't seem to have much integration with others.

Sra. Martínez sat down at the desk and took out a notepad and pen from her purse. "I think I understand," she said.

He smiled, "And also, I wanted to talk to you in particular because I thought your organization might help me get a sense of the political or social climate around El Salvador."

She wrote something in her notebook but was still smiling. "I will try to help you." She put the pencil behind her ear and closed the notebook. "But first let me tell you that there are some things I can talk about and some I cannot. I hope you understand. And when possible, I would like to ask you to not use my name or even the name of our organization in any of your publications. The work we do is very different from what you will find with a simple clinic or feeding program."

"Yes, I'm aware of that."

"Our work is often political, and the government is often suspicious of us and what we do, even when we try hard not to make it so."

David nodded. "I understand that too, and I'll try very hard to be respectful of that and not use your name or push you for information that you don't feel comfortable sharing. Just start where you want to. Tell me a little about your funding and your relationship to the government, what exactly you do...and whatever else."

She folded her hands on the desk and leaned forward. "Well, let me begin with our name, which explains a lot about what we do. We are the '*Oficina de Identificación de Víctimas*,' the 'Office of Identification of Victims,' or 'OIV.' So, our main task is to identify people who have died in mysterious, or 'extra-judicial,' killings and to connect them to their loved ones. We were established by the archdiocesan office some years ago, in partnership with another organization called 'The Mothers' Committee,' *CoMadres,* do you know of them?" He nodded that he had, though he hadn't visited with them yet. "It is good that you know of them because we are similar," she said. "I will only add, then, that they are made up of mothers— or *mainly* mothers— of those who have been murdered or 'Disappeared' during this war. Our work is broader, and we are independent of them, but similar. We also are independent from the Government except through an agreement with the diocese to work with the state coroner to share our information. So, we do work with the government in that way."

"How does that work?"

"Our arrangement is that when the morgue receives bodies of those who have been 'disappeared' we will try to identify who they are. It is a task that should be quite ordinary for a normal city morgue. But in the last, maybe, ten or twelve years, they have become increasingly overwhelmed by bodies with no names, and often no family willing to come forward and identify them. So, we try, in a very non-political way, to help families identify their loved ones without having to go to the authorities, some of whom were probably responsible for the death."

She lifted the edge of one of the scrapbooks on her desk and played absently with its cover. "We go there to take pictures of all the unnamed bodies that they have received, or sometimes they will do it first and send the pictures to us, and then we do research to find out who it is. On paper, we work closely together to help each other."

"On paper?"

She closed the scrapbook. "I will only say that even though we work with them, the authorities often do not like us, so we must be careful. In practice, in addition to our identifying the bodies who they take pictures of, we also have mothers and wives come to us for help in *finding* the bodies, and that is what the police and National Guard often do not like. The people in the coroner's office try to believe that the number of deaths in the city is going down because it makes the city look safer, but then we produce data that shows that forty, fifty, sixty people have been killed in the streets in a single day, and that is not good for their public face."

David shook his head in disbelief. "I've heard numbers like that a few times," he said, "but they still amaze me."

"Somedays it is even higher. Of course, we do have people dying in accidents and natural causes, but in August last year, five hundred people died sudden deaths in one month. Some of those were clearly accidents, but can five hundred people die in one month by falling from windows or being hit by trains? In April we had four hundred."

"And you mean that talking about that, or looking into that, makes your work political."

"Yes, very political. They want the deaths to be caused by common crime, gang violence, or natural causes."

"And I'm assuming that can't be true."

"No, and in addition to what information they send us, family and friends also bring us photos—hundreds of photos —of Salvadorans who had their faces beaten in or cut open or dismembered. The people in the morgue will say publicly that we work closely with them and officially we agree, but in truth, they are often slow to give us access to the bodies and slow to share information about the ones that they do have, and very fast to say that a man with his arms cut off died of kidney failure."

"Why?"

"To be fair to them, they are under great pressure from the government and the military, who do not want the world to think that things are this bad here. They want the US to believe that we have rounded the corner, and the deaths are going down, and it is safe here now. Bring back the tourists. Bring back the conventions, open the beaches. But we count the faces, we interview the families. We know the truth, and they do not want us telling it."

She looked down and rubbed her hands together. "We used to have a doctor from the Morgue, a—I don't know the name you say in English, *Patóloga forense*?"

"Forensic Pathologist"?

"Yes, we had a *Forensic Pathologist* from the coroner's office, who worked with us once a week. He went with us when we found bodies buried or drowned and helped us identify causes of death and age and gender of some of them."

"That sounds like a terrible job."

"It was an official position, paid for by diocesan money, but twice when he was coming here, he was beaten and robbed. That alone did not stop him, but once a group of men surrounded his taxi and took him out of it and threatened to kill his family. That made him quit because he did not want anything to happen to them. The government did not want him to do his job. And it does not want us to identify people and help the families find their loved ones and arrange for them to have a personal burial mass. The government does not want any of that because it will contradict their smiling message that everything is fine here and just needs more parties and marimbas."

She looked at him somberly. "You are not taking notes."

He looked down at his hands and his pencil. He'd become so engrossed with her story that he'd forgotten. "Sorry," he said.

"You look like a nice man. So, I will tell you again that if you are stopped sometime soon by someone from the government and they ask you who you have talked to and where you have been, please do not tell them that you have been here. It might not be safe for us, and it might not be safe for you."

"Thank you, I'll do my best."

"An organization like ours that contradicts the official reality of our country, is a threat. We have had many of our volunteers followed on their way home. Interrogated, threatened, and sometimes jailed. Fortunately, no one of ours has so far been hurt because the killers know that if they do, the archbishop will denounce them in his homily the next Sunday, and it will be broadcast across the nation. And probably reported in the *New York Times*. Our high international visibility helps us in that."

"Is it just as bad out in the countryside?"

"Worse. In the cities we have killings, in the campo they have massacres." She tapped her pencil nervously on the desk. "Mr. Patterson, I do not recommend this, but if you actually want to know what our country's reality is, you should also go up to the northern departments: Cuscatlán, to Guazapa Mountain, or Chalatenango. You should see the reality of oppression and war in our country from there as well as from here. It is not safe, but if you could do it, you would learn things. We are about to lose our fragile democracy, and we need people to tell our stories to the world to keep that from happening."

"I can't promise anything, but I'll try to do that. What things should I look for if I go up into those areas?"

"Things like the so-called 'Repopulation Villages,' those little communities that were driven out of the country and into Honduras years ago. The people there learned to support one another in refugee camps and are now returning and attempting to create new self-supporting communities, governed by a real democracy, and based on radical ideas of equality and justice. This is very new, and it is very threatening to the white minority nationalist authoritarians who rule our government."

"But the far-right just won the last election."

"That is because the far-left rebels boycotted the election because they knew it would be a fraud and the near-left voters were blocked from voting, in many places. That is why the ARENA, the "Nationalist Republican Alliance," party is now in power. But imagine what could happen if the FMLN would win the war. The model of the Repopulation Villages could become the model for how to run a new El Salvador. And maybe the model for all of Latin America. But the oligarchy in our country won, and they will never allow that to happen. They will never allow a real democracy to happen. They have to have an authoritarian leader who knows how to control the people and doesn't mind violating our own constitution to do it."

"Thank you for the suggestion. I may try to get up there to look around."

"But remember, I did not tell you to do that."

"Okay. I'll remember that. I promise.

He put down his pen and closed his notebook. "But I do have one more thing..."

"Yes?"

"What made you get involved in all of this? What brought you here?"

She frowned for a moment as she turned and reached behind her chair for one of the scrapbooks on the shelf and laid it on the desk. "Look on page two hundred thirty-six."

He slid the thick heavy volume over closer to him and started thumbing through the pages. "Two hundred thirty and...?"

"Six."

When he finally turned to it, he saw a black and white photo of a man's face. Someone in perhaps his mid-thirties. A man with a high forehead and smooth black hair combed straight back over his head and a tight black mustache, lying on his back with his eyes wide open, looking absently upward at the camera. His face was torn open with a wide, dark, gash extending from his chin, up through his nose and across his right eye and forehead. His mouth looked swollen and bloody. David briefly pulled back and looked away. He looked up at Sra. Martínez.

"My husband," she said firmly, almost defiantly. "Enrique."

"My God, I'm so sorry."

"Thank you," she said. "He was a good man," she said. "He

was a *Protestante*. He went to church. He gave food to the poor. He volunteered in the shelter for women..." Her voice trailed off.

David fell back into his chair and took a breath. "I am so sorry. I didn't realize..."

"So, I work here now."

David turned through the next few pages, and each one had photos of people like Enrique, brutally maimed, scarred, and with distorted faces. Sometimes they were on their backs lying on a metal slab in the morgue. Sometimes they appeared to be in a field or by a river where, evidently, bodies had been dumped by killers. Sometimes the facial features were distinct, and sometimes they were missing altogether. He wanted to turn away, but he felt he shouldn't. "Why do they do this?"

"It is not always the same reason. For some, there is a message. They believe that by killing those who do not conform, it will teach others how to behave. Perhaps they will obey out of fear. My Enrique was targeted because he was a journalist, and he published articles that the government thought were controversial. In the 1970s we had just had an election. It was an important election because we thought it would finally decide if we could become a democracy. We had José Napoleón Duarte, a popular mayor of San Salvador..."

"Didn't his party just lose the election this year?"

"Yes, the same man years ago. But that time he was running against Arturo Molina, a very unpopular colonel."

"And, as I recall, the unpopular colonel won?"

"Yes, of course. My husband had been looking at polling in the Colonia Mexicana, near your university. He found that Col. Molina polled at about forty percent, and Duarte polled at about fifty-five percent. But when the election came, Duarte lost by twenty percent."

"I'm not surprised."

"Yes. The party for democracy, and was the most popular, *lost*. And the party of the elites, which was the most repressive, *won*. His numbers were clear and objective, and my Enrique wrote about them, several times in several articles. And after several days, his paper was visited by the police. The papers wrote retractions of his articles and apologized for their 'errors,' but within days a mysterious militia, a 'Death Squad,' took him from our home." She closed her eyes before continuing. "They actually had the nerve to come to him first to see if he would personally denounce his articles. He said no, so they 'denounced' his life. When we found him, he looked like this, and the coroner said he died of kidney failure."

She opened her eyes. Her face was resolute. "So, sometimes they kill like this—to make a point, to send a message. But sometimes they kill more random. Someone is taken from a bus, or picked up at night, or a family's house is broken into. And then they are mysteriously murdered. Stop me if you've heard of this already."

David had in fact heard stories like this, but he didn't stop her.

"At least it *appears* random. The point of the randomness of the killings or torture is to create a low level of fear *all the time*. They believe that if people are constantly fearful, they will not question the 'truth' of this charade of a democratic government."

"Has that ever worked?"

"Never. Look at the fighters out in the campo now. Repression is the best recruiting program for the rebels. The larger it gets, the stronger the opposition. Kill an innocent father in front of his teenage children and you've suddenly created new teenage rebels moving to the mountains to join the movement."

She looked away for a moment and cleared her throat.

"And depending on the message, the killings are sometimes done in different ways."

"How different?"

"Sometimes—no, many times—they will intentionally mutilate the face of a victim to keep him from being recognized at all. They know of our work—and other groups like ours—and they want to block us from investigating them. So, if it is just another anonymous, campesino they will disfigure the face so that even his wife cannot identify him. But, at other times, if the person is well known in the larger community, like my Enrique, or a unionist, or a teacher, or a priest, they will leave the face intact to make him an example for the others." She took a breath and looked up at the ceiling. "How much more do you need to hear?"

It occurred to David that, though it was her job to tell these stories to outsiders, it was nonetheless difficult for her to do so. His own memories of a brutally disfigured Kathryn lying in his driveway were never far from his consciousness, and the more Sra. Martínez talked, the closer those feelings felt. He reached for her hands that were clasped tightly on the desk in front of her and held them. The story of loved ones dying in nightmarish ways created a personal hurt inside him that was different from hers, but probably just as painful. "This is enough," he said. "I don't need to know anymore."

"I am sorry," she said. "I knew some of these people well. And after a while, I have come to feel like I know all of them a little bit." She looked up at him, smiling and her eyes were wet.

He was silent for a moment, pushing his own pain back down his chest. "Listen," he said at last, "you have been wonderful. I've learned far more than I need for my project." He reached for his notebook and pen on the desk. "I think it's time for me to let you get back to doing things that are more important than talking to me."

He started to stand, but she took his hand again and said, "Do me one favor, Mr. David. Would you do something for me?"

"Yes, of course. If I can."

She looked at him intently for a moment and said, "When you go back to your home, back in the United States..."

"Yes?"

"Would you tell our story?"

"Yes, of course, but I can't..."

"I don't want Enrique to have died in vain. I don't want these tens of thousands of my people to have died in vain. I want people in your country to know that, and to remember us. I know there is little you can do to fix it, but I want people to know about it. Our people are suffering, and if the world does not hear that and know that, the suffering will continue. The rich are not able to—do not *want* to—care. But if you and others can speak and can tell our story, we may survive. Otherwise, we will lose our chance at democracy and have decades of chaos and rule by dictators. I want you to tell them that."

"Of course," he said. "Of course, I will."

"In El Salvador, some things grow darker the more light you shine on them," she said. "Sometimes that makes us want to look away and not see the evil that lives near us and within us. But you can't heal a wound that you can't see. Your words can help us see."

"I don't know how...but I will try."

WHEN HE WAS OUTSIDE, he stood for a moment in the tropical heat and felt a chill that he couldn't quite understand. He didn't want to go home alone, and Sara wouldn't be home that early. He looked back at the doorway and thought for a moment. His head was a tangle of thoughts and emotions. He put his hand on the door and pushed it open and went back in. "*Con permiso*," he said to the receptionist, and asked if he could use the phone.

"*Sí, por supuesto*," she said and handed him the receiver.

He dialed a number and then waited until he heard a voice. "*Hola*," it said.

"Alf?" he said to the voice.

"*Hablando*."

"Alf, this is David."

"David, *amigo*. *¿Qué ocurre?* Everything okay?"

"I'm fine, but, Alf, what are you doing right now? Could you get away for a while?"

"I suppose I could leave a little early. Why?"

"Nothing, I just think I need a drink. And I think I need a friend."

CHAPTER TWENTY-NINE
BEERS

So, what is it that we're talking about today?" Alf placed two beers on the table and sat down across from David who was slumped in his chair. It was the middle of the day, and the bar was empty except for David and Alf and a bright gold and red Seeburg Jukebox that flashed lights across the room but made no noise.

"Well, it's no one thing," David said. "Just that there've been so many things piling on recently and I've been feeling a little overwhelmed —and I thought I needed to talk to someone about them. How much time do you have?"

Alf made an exaggerated gesture of looking at his watch. "Well, I've got about an hour. But we can take less than that if you talk faster than you drink."

"Okay, here's one thing—and surprisingly not the biggest —this week my apartment was broken into and a lot of my papers and files were rifled through."

"*¡Puta madre!*" said Alf. "That just added an hour to my listening time. When did it happen? What did they take? Did you call the police?"

David laughed. "It may not be that bad. It happened last Monday. In addition to looking through my files, they also moved some furniture around and opened drawers in my dresser. But so far as I can tell, they didn't take anything. And no, we didn't call the police. My landlord said that might be dangerous and that he would get some of his other tenants in the complex to ask around about it and see if they could find out anything."

"That's good advice. I know Carlos and he looks dumb but is very *sabio*, 'savvy' about these kinds of things. He's seen many break-ins, so trust him if he says it may not mean anything. His friends probably won't find anything, but it will at least let the thieves, or the government if they're in the neighborhood, all know that you're looking for them. Do you have any enemies who could have been looking for something?"

"No, and that was the same question that Carlos asked. I told him that, aside from you, I think most people here like me."

"Okay, that comment just took twenty minutes off my listening time. Were there any witnesses?"

"Surprisingly, Carlos himself says that he might have seen someone by my door that morning, and he's going to share his description with the others to see if anyone else saw the same guy."

"That neighborhood is supposedly thick with FMLN supporters, and a lot of them are used to having their apartments searched, but I wouldn't have expected anyone to suspect you of anything. But you never can tell."

David shifted his weight forward and leaned on the table. "But that's just number one on my list. On top of that—and much bigger—is that I think the weight of all that is going on around here is beginning to beat me down."

"I think I know what you're going to say but tell me anyway."

"Well, it's everything. For example, a couple were murdered in our complex last week. One row over from me. From what I've heard about it he was teaching a class about the slaughter of indigenous Pipil and Lenca people and someone in the city government thought it was too controversial. He refused to censure his class and suddenly he and his wife were shot and killed in their bedrooms at night. Carlos says the official report said random burglars shot them because they were afraid the family might wake up and turn them in.

Then there was a bombing of a church down in the city just a few days before that. The priest had been housing families displaced by the fighting up north and somebody—probably a government paramilitary group, but I don't know—didn't like it. So, they bombed his church to stop him. And just today I interviewed a woman whose job it is to catalogue the ghastly political murders and torture of dissidents or protestors or journalists—including one of them who was her husband! And yesterday, at an education nonprofit, they told us stories about one of their teachers getting killed just for campaigning to save public education. In fact, almost every office I visit has a story of someone getting arrested or dying. Story after a story of torture, beatings, brutality, and corruption. And then there are all these good people in these organizations working against the odds, trying to create a democracy. It's getting to me and I'm feeling exhausted." He took a deep breath, then a deep drink, and set the bottle down. "Alf, listen. You know better than anybody how deep of a funk I was in when I got here. I don't think I show it as much as I used to, but my insides are like my grandmother's China cabinet—thin, fragile, breakable—and sometimes I feel awfully close to breaking."

"You mean, like when people tell you a story about the sudden death of a loved one?"

"Yes, you know what I'm talking about, and I've heard several of those stories in just the last few days."

Alf was silent for a long moment. "I get it," he said finally. "This is a lot to handle for a guy who was pretty eaten up emotionally himself just a few months ago. Those of us who live here sometimes forget how mind-numbing the Salvadoran reality can be to someone coming in from the outside. We're like a cook who handles sizzling pans all day and forgets how hot they are until he passes one to the new guy who screams his face off. Personally, I love it here, but I'm not so stupid as to not know how terrifying it can feel to an outsider."

"Alf, I did a lot of background reading on the country before I came—history, human rights, economy... But honestly, that was all 'big picture' stuff. You know, the wealthy far right wants to steal democracy from the middle and left and the FMLN rebels are fighting to stop them. That sounds so simple. But on the ground, there are ordinary people, day after day, who are bleeding. There's a morgue on every corner. Body-bags in trash cans, schools shut down, newspapers attacked, clinics bombed. Whole villages bombed. This is a beautiful country, I love it here, but it's breaking apart, and sometimes I feel like I'm breaking with it. Listen, my relationship with Sara is getting to be very important to me. But I don't know if I want to stay here and raise her kids in an environment where we could get shot just by standing next to the wrong person on a bus stop."

"Dave, I don't know what to say. No one totally gets it. Like I said, this is my home, but even I still get shocked on occasion."

"But I had heard—in fact from you when we first talked about this—that the violence had died down, that the FMLN and the government were talking about peace talks. That the US press had moved on to other hot spots..."

"All true," Alf said. "But recently the violence has been creeping back up again."

"Why?"

"Well, I think it's because in 1984 we had a president named Duarte, who actually believed in democracy, but was weak and dying of cancer. The military started thinking he was so bad that they could replace him bring back the killings and torture and not have to pay for it. Duarte's whole party was rejected in this year's elections."

"For that Alfredo Cristiani guy? I've seen his posters up everywhere, but I don't know anything about him."

"*Claro que sí.* A smiling, pleasant oligarch who was educated in the States and looks good on camera. With him in power now, the army and paramilitary groups have sensed that they had nothing stopping them from burning down villages out in the conflicted areas to get to the rebels. The people up there support the rebels, and they are creating a tiny new kingdom based on a radical sort of democracy. And democracy terrifies the far right. You should see what they're doing up there—something I don't recommend, by the way. But it would be good to learn about it because there are a lot of very fine clinics, schools, and economic support happening up there."

"So, where's the FMLN with all this?"

"Interestingly, right now the FMLN is...how do you say *aguantando el fuego*, 'holding their fire'?"

David laughed. Alf spoke almost perfect English, and David always loved it when Alf was unsure about a word or phrase. "Yeah, that's the right expression. Why are they doing that?"

"It may not work, but they may be holding back for a while to see what might happen to this last round of peace talks.

Those talks have produced several worthless proposals so far, but the one from this past summer, even the US Embassy said had things they would support."

"If peace talks actually produce something, the FMLN could declare victory, but if it becomes clear that the government is just...just...what's a good word in English for when you try to trick someone?"

This time David laughed so hard he had to put down his beer. "Oh, in the US we have so many words for that, I couldn't begin to list them. We're good at that."

"Well, it's one of those words. And if the FMLN thinks they're being tricked, they might risk another "Final Offensive" like they did back in 1981, and all hell will break loose.

"I understand that was really bad."

"Awful. The rebels took over eighty towns and nearly toppled the capital. They took the government by surprise and probably would have won except that the military started carpet bombing the working-class neighborhoods and killing civilians at a terrible rate, and the rebels pulled back because they thought there might not be a country left to rule if they kept it up."

"Well," David looked at his near-empty bottle. "All of that goes back to my feelings about the weight of all of this, and the thought of maybe staying here, moving in with Sara, maybe getting a job at the university or one of these nonprofits."

Alf leaned forward in his chair. "David, you should go for it. You two look good together. And you're probably a lot more safe here than you think. You're white, male, tall and you speak English. Most of the time, they'll think you're a rich American and let you get by."

David smiled. "Thanks, but I'm also worried about being married to a woman who looks very Salvadoran and who has two young boys. How safe could they be?"

"For one, if they're with you and you have an upper class-looking job—even though we don't pay you like one—that will give you a lot of protection. And by the way did you know that we're talking about bringing Sara into the university too, to teach English classes? That would give her some of the same cover as for you and it would mean she finally has a regular income. And also, if the peace plan goes through, we may have an end to the war in the next couple of years. And that would be a real plus."

"That sounds a little better. And in spite of the grim politics in El Salvador, I think just living here in general has been the best thing to happen to me in years. This little job has been a blessing, Sara is wonderful, her kids seem to like me, and—when I'm not being broken into—I like my neighborhood. So, if I could get past some of these other things, I think I'd be ready to start living some kind of life that isn't filled with grief and misery."

Alf picked up his empty beer bottle and clinked its bottom against David's. "I'll drink to that. For the first few months after you arrived, your face looked like a colorized 1950s Morgue photo. At least you've moved beyond that. And for the last few months, whenever we saw you smile like you remembered what being alive looked like, it was when you were saying something about Sara and her family."

"You're probably right. In fact, I know you're right. But a new life, a new country, a new relationship, and trying to act like a father to two little boys, when I've never been a father myself before…It's still a lot more than I expected and in the middle of all of this turmoil, and occasionally more than I can handle."

"Listen Amigo. You've been through hell; there's no denying it. But you can't put off living again forever. Remember, sometimes death is just death. But sometimes it's also an opening for a new life."

David managed a weak smile. "Thanks, I think I get that."

Alf looked at his watch again. "But I really am needing to get home. This has been a good conversation all around and we need to do it again. I do want this project to go forward and I'm really glad that you are a part of it. But I don't want to lie to you about how safe El Salvador is right now. To be honest, if we had known a couple of years ago what we know now there is a chance we would have put it off. And I probably never would have called you and you would probably still be sitting in your car in your driveway, pining your life away in Abington, Massachusetts."

"Don't think I haven't still done some pining now and then. But the country, the work, Sara...have also been good for me. And I'm grateful to you for that."

"I'm glad. But it's still dangerous, and you should watch yourself." Alf reached around the back of his chair for his coat. "Now, speaking of doing one's best to stay safe, I probably should go home. If I stay out too late, Beatriz will think I'm with a woman." He swung the jacket around his shoulder and put an arm through a sleeve. "Fortunately, you're ugly enough that I don't think she'll be jealous."

David laughed. "Glad I could contribute to your family harmony."

CHAPTER THIRTY
ENCOUNTER

When they left the bar together, Alf started to walk to the curb but suddenly turned to David and gave him a big hug. "Be careful," He said. "Both inside and outside. I want that rawness in your heart to continue healing, and I also want your body to stay alive a little longer too. Just don't do anything stupid."

David laughed. "Little too late for that," he said. After all, I'm already here, drinking beer, and walking home at night in the middle of one of the most dangerous spots on the planet."

Alf raised his hand to hail a taxi coming his direction and then turned back to David. "Do you want to share a ride?"

David looked at his watch. "No, I don't think so. The bus comes by here every twenty minutes or so and stops on Zacamil, by that little *callejón* that goes down to my apartment. So, I'm fine."

Alf opened the door but before getting in, he turned back to David. "*Mira*, Beatriz and I should have both of you over for a meal sometime, *próximamente*, like we did a few times back in the States. It'll be fun and probably do you some good. And if I can convince Beatriz to do the cooking instead of me, you might even survive the evening without another of your vomiting and passing out spells."

"I would like that. It has an old-fashioned feeling of normalcy about it, and my life needs a lot of 'normal' right now."

"*Bien. Hagámoslo.* I will call you." Alf got in and the taxi pulled away.

David looked around for a moment, wondering if he should take the city bus home, but instead he turned back to the sidewalk and started walking. He had a lot on his mind —the day, Alf's conversation, Sara—and perhaps walking would help him clear his thoughts.

The walk was longer than he had expected but the weather was cool, and the streets were filled with more of the "normalcy" that he was wanting, so he didn't mind. He enjoyed studying the sights and smells along the streets. People were walking to and from jobs. Carts under umbrellas selling every item imaginable. Marimba music flowing from an open window, chickens roasting on spits, and dogs barking at passersby. Many of the stores along the way had bars on their windows but were also open for business—friendly, but careful. A small cafe had a very proper *Mozo*, attendant, sitting outside inviting people to come in. One block had a long unbroken wall painted with political slogans supporting the rebels—*Viva la Ofensiva FMLN,* one said—surrounded by cartoon graffiti. The only opening was the backside of a church that evidently stretched to the opposite street. Two young *niños* were playing on the sidewalk knocking a metal ball back and forth to each other with sticks. One would roar with laughter every time the other missed the ball and it rolled to the side.

One time it flew past both of them and into the foot of their mother who was intently flattening tortillas on a grill just over their heads. She frowned down at them but with a smile and nudged the ball back at the players with her foot. Screams of laughter erupted again, and they returned to the game.

And then he turned onto Calle Zacamil, and down the narrow *callejón* to his apartments. Looking down at them, he could see Sara's window up at the end of the fourth floor. He smiled, hoping there might be a light, but it was dark, so he kept walking. Further down, a number of young people were gathered at one of the gates between the apartments, talking and laughing. A car was backing out of one of the parking slots. A dog snarled with some kind of meat. At the near end of the apartments was a man dressed all in black, standing in front of the gate into Sara's row. He was leaning against the fence and looking up at what might have been the fourth floor. Who was that, David wondered? Was he looking up to see Sara's window? The man was large, with a square body and square head and wore a black suit. And then David recognized him.

"Bhutto!" he yelled. "*¿Qué haces aquí?*" "What are you doing?"

Bhutto looked at him, but instead of answering he turned and pulled at the gate, but it was locked. He ran to the next gate, but it was also locked. David started running towards him down the pathway. The man reached the third row, where the young people were standing. He pushed at them and tried to open their gate, but they pushed back, yelling at him and hitting him, and they shoved him away. So, he ran to the next one, and the next, until he finally came to the last gate, which was David's, and it was open. Damn, thought David, running down the apartment rows. The man pulled the gate open and ran towards the opposite end of the row. When David reached the opening, the man was halfway to the end. "*¡Alto! ¡Alto!*" he yelled, but Bhutto wouldn't stop. Just then one of the last doors on the row opened, and Carlos came out of it, unaware of what was happening. David saw him and called to him, "Carlos, *Ese es el hombre que irrumpió en mi apartamento.*" "That's the man who broke into my apartment." Carlos looked up, but before he could speak, Bhutto ran into him and knocked him hard against the open end of his front door. "*Deténganlo,*" said David. "Stop him." When Carlos realized what was happening, he ran, not after Bhutto, but across the grassy area between the rows to the sidewalk on the other side, to block the man when he realized that the gate at the back end was also locked. David came up in back of him and Carlos stood in front of him, and he stopped, trapped between them. Carlos yelled at him to give up, because he'd been caught, but instead of quitting, he pushed back at Carlos and shoved him hard against the wall of one of the apartments. Then he spun around at David, swinging his arms wildly like windmills. David started to yell at him too, but before he had a chance one of Bhutto's heavy fists hit him in the face, knocking him against the fence and then to his knees. He rushed at David screeching high pitched, like an animal, and stomped on his chest, knocking him further down, leaving him coughing for air and barely conscious. When David pulled himself up, he saw Carlos in front of him on his back, gasping and bleeding around his face. Bhutto was already at the other end of the row of apartments, running out through the open gate in the fence.

CHAPTER THIRTY-ONE

HÉCTOR

"I am so happy that you again have come here to see me." Héctor was smiling and sitting behind his desk, his hands wide out from his body and a look somewhere between pain and fear on his face. "Sr. Alphonso has informed me of your terrible ordeal with a man at your apartment, and I have been looking forward to seeing you."

David couldn't help but smile back at Héctor's enthusiasm. "Thanks, I was wanting to see you too, but I'm fine. A little bruised, but nothing broken. We're fine."

"But it was such an ordeal for you. Nothing should be happening to someone we have come down here to help us. We are supposed to protect you from these events."

David laughed. "Well, in this case, I don't know what you could have done. We ran across him in the middle of the night. He roughed us up a bit and then ran away. It was pretty scary for a minute, but then it was over."

"Scary? *Oh Dios mío, oh Dios mío.*" Héctor dropped his hands and clasped them together as though praying. "I will help you," he said. "I will pledge to help you in anything you want, to keep you safe. Anything you want."

"Well, as a matter of fact, I do want your help on something..."

"Anything."

"Actually, I was wanting to see you for some advice.

"Anything."

"And it's logistical advice."

Héctor smiled but tightened his hands. "Of course, and I will help you. And if I cannot, I will know also who to send you to."

"My issue is simple. I want to take a trip up to where so much fighting is going on in Cuscatlán or Morazán or Chalatenango. And I need your help." Héctor's smile began to fade. "I feel like what I'm doing now is just eating around the edges of what's really happening in the country, and I want to talk to more people who are working on the front lines of the war. Part of it is, of course, so that perhaps we can pair some of their work with others like you are doing here in the city. But part of it, frankly, is just so that I can understand more about what is going on in the rest of the country. From what I can tell, it's a bloody mess up there and my heart goes out to them. And I was hoping that you could suggest places to visit and people to see. I think you know a lot of them."

Héctor unclasped his hands and put them palms down on the desk. "Doctor Patterson, that is dangerous."

"I know that, but I want to do it. There's something about being in the middle of this *Lucha* but not really being able to see it at its center."

"What do you mean?"

"It sounds to me like this war is for the soul of the country, about what kind of democracy or autocracy it will become. But down here, with most of the violence either tamped down or killed off, I don't see much of that. I feel a lot of tension, but no heartbeat."

"Doctor Patterson, you just had an encounter that nearly killed you. If you meet the violence up in Chalatenango, you may not have a heartbeat in the end."

"Yes, I know that's a risk."

"Where would you want to go?"

"That's where I need your advice. I've heard from several people about the 'repopulation villages' up in Chalatenango, close to the Honduran border. I think they would be a good place to start."

"Yes, they would be good places to see, they would be most important to see. But they would also be most dangerous. Do you know that the government army bombed those villages less than a decade ago and killed many of their citizens and drove them into refugee camps in Honduras? And that they are coming back now to 'repopulate' their old villages again? And are defying the government to do it?" David nodded and started to speak, but Héctor went on, "And that the government still does not like them and might again drop bombs on them just as you are arriving and are walking around? Mr. David, our authoritarian oligarchy believes the people are their enemy, and the army is very, very faithful to them. They will destroy anybody, they will destroy anything. They will destroy the entire country if the oligarchy tells them to. Do you know all of this?"

David took a deep breath and tried to keep his eyes from seeing images of death. "Yes, I understand all of that and I do understand the risk, but I think I still want to do it. They are, in fact, what I want most to see up there. I want to see their life and activities in action. They sound vibrant. Maybe I could help them communicate better with each other like we're planning for nonprofit groups down here. Maybe I could help connect them with some larger international development organizations for better funding…I don't feel like what I'm doing here has done much yet. I see so many people here who are doing great work with the poor, the sick, and the suffering, and aside from what we *might* get to do for them once my survey work is done, I'm doing hardly anything now. I want to get into it somehow and see if I can help. If Democracy can work on the ground, maybe, eventually it can work higher up."

Héctor leaned forward over his desk, tapping the desk with his clasped hands, punctuating his words. "Doctor Patterson, I do not want to sound personal with you, but do I recall correctly that your wife has passed away recently?"

"Well, not *real* recently, but yes, not long ago. Why?"

"And is it correct that it was an accident and that you were unable to help her?"

This was David's most uncomfortable topic. He looked away and spoke to the bookshelf on the wall. "Yes, that's true, but I would prefer not talking about it."

"Yes, but is it at least a little tiny bit possible that your desire to save people has at least a little tiny bit of connection to the fact that you were not able to keep your wife from dying? I understand from our Mister Alfonzo that you were so terribly distressed over what happened that you were not able to function in your university capacity for some time. Is that true?"

"Yes, that's probably true." David's voice was growing tense. "Look, Héctor, if you can't help me, just say so and I'll leave. I just wanted some advice on how to get around up there. If I've got some kind of deep psychological God-knows-what grief or guilt or whatever, it doesn't really matter. I want to go see if I can find ways to help people stay alive, and I'm going to do it with or without your help."

"No, no, no." Héctor fell back into his chair. "I surely and completely will help you. There are many organizations already at work with the people there, and they may be able to benefit with our networking plans even more than down here in the capital. It is a beautiful place with many beautiful people, and they are attempting to create a model of governing based on acceptance, tolerance, and support that could be a model for how the whole country could be run. The government says it is from communism, but they say it is from the New Testament."

David smiled. "Yes, I've heard that. And I want to learn all about that."

"I am sure that you will learn much and come back with many ideas on how to help them." He smiled again. "I just want to understand better why you wanted to do it. Sometimes knowing that helps me to help you. And even sometimes it helps you help yourself. And if you no longer want to talk about it, I will end with that now."

"Okay, so it's true that I suffered through some fairly serious remorse and shame for my own loss, and today I probably have more feelings for people suffering than I used to, and all that. But what difference does it make if I'm trying to help these people because of a deep mysterious desire to atone for my own failures, or if I just had a good Sunday School teacher as a kid who taught me to love my neighbor? I feel like my whole experience here has been a sort of bridge from the darkness I was living in back in the states to a life that is much brighter and healthier. There is a lot of hurt up there and you and the whole Institute team have resources that could maybe help some of them and help them with their experiment in democracy that's so important and so fragile. You and I both know of people here in the city who can probably teach a good class in how to create a functioning democracy. Or agronomy, or marketing, or capital raising..."

David stood up and turned to one of the windows in the

small office. "I'm kind of thinking this through as I go along, but if their experiment succeeds, then maybe the future of El Salvador succeeds. And if it fails, then the country probably fails and becomes just one more authoritarian neofascist dictatorship. They're kind of on a bridge right now too, between both options and could go either way. Maybe I—or *we*—could also help them get there, at least economically. This is a subject we used to cover in my marketing classes in the States, though mainly in first-world countries. If we could put some projects and startup funding together out in the embattled provinces that could create a growing local economy and do so within the guidance of their new experiments in democracy and collective decision-making, something huge and beneficial for everyone might happen."

"Mr. David, you are very right in all that you are saying, but I must say two things."

"What are they?"

"First, sit down...please." He waved his hand at the chair and David, nervously, sat back in it. "On the one hand I must say to you, that for your safety, you should not go. It is too dangerous, and I do not recommend it."

"And on the other hand...?"

"Yes, and on the other hand, you are also correct in your assessment of the importance of their democratic goals and economic needs, and the potential they have for the future of our great country if they succeed. If the war ends and this experiment in democracy survives—both in the campo and in the cities—then this tiny country might become a democratic model for the rest of the world."

David leaned forward to speak, but Héctor went on, speaking faster. "And I should also tell you that we already have been speaking of sending others into those areas to do these things. The sharing of resources and ideas for economic development and governance that we have started here in the city should be done also in the rest of the country. And you are correct: if their model succeeds, then maybe El Salvador succeeds. Maybe a *new* El Salvador succeeds. And you are a good person to want to help us start that. And, so, yes, I will help you."

David took a deep breath and relaxed. "Thank you, Héctor. I really do appreciate it. Have you been there yourself?"

"Yes, of course, many times, but mainly before our recent difficulties. Only once since the people have started their returns from Honduras. And today, I must tell you, the region is even more dangerous because the government does not approve of their reestablishing their villages, or of their attempting the many fine experiments in consensus democracy that you have evidently been hearing about."

"Yes."

"But if you are very careful, you will probably be fine. You will learn much and I also hope that you will be able to write about it as well. You can help share their story."

"Thank you. This feels important to me. Something I really need to do."

"So, this is what you must do. I recommend first that you go by bus because you will be accompanied by other people. It will take longer because there will be many stops along the way, but it will also be safer." His voice grew more serious. "You must take the national bus at the *Terminal Oriente*, which travels up through northern Chalatenango. On the way, you will stop first at military checkpoints and then at rebel checkpoints—and make sure you have your identification and passage documents. It will take you up and around the lovely *Lago Suchitlán* and then to little Los Morros. It is one of our very finest *pueblos de repoblación.*

"After that, how do we get to some of the other towns?"

"From there you can walk to many of the other communities, or perhaps my good friend, Father Raul from the parish in Las Flores, can take you. I will tell him that you are coming, and he will help you. They are all very close."

"And are all of them about the same?"

"Yes...maybe no. They are all the same lovely people who have been through much suffering and are trying to rebuild their village and lives...but..." He frowned and his face took on a pained anxious look.

"But what?"

"Some of them are more troubled than others. Los Morros is a lovely village, a lovely village, but some of the early *muchachos* who are now in the mountains to fight, have come from this place. And the village has supported them because they believed in the freedom and justice and democracy that the rebels were fighting for. David, they even have a *female* mayor! They are remarkable. And for each of these things, the government of my country does not like them, and possibly wishes to do them harm."

"Yes, I've heard of towns like Los Morros. It's one of the reasons why I wanted to go."

"You may not see any of this when you are there, because they will love you and will welcome you, and feed you, and you will love them, but their lives there are more...more *dificil,* more difficult, than many of the others."

"Well, I'd like to see at least some of that, because I want to get a sense of what a lot of the countryside is going through. And I don't want to be a tourist."

CHAPTER THIRTY-TWO

DOUG

Doug Grantham wasn't in a good mood when David called. He'd already had a pretty miserable day, and it wasn't even noon yet. Congress had just voted to cut a portion of his funding because they thought cutting economic development aid would somehow stop hungry, frightened people from fleeing their countries seeking asylum in the States. Congress is full of buffoons, he thought. Then, one of his staffers called from *La Cárcel Municipal*, the city jail, because he'd gotten in a bar fight at a gringo hangout called the King Kong Klub the night before and was now needing him to send one of their Salvadoran attorneys to come down and talk to the judge. *Dumbass!* Doug thought. And then his wife called saying that their daughter, Karla, had an abscessed tooth that hurt so bad she was sent home from school, and she was asking if Doug would meet them at *La Dentista* to help comfort her. And now this guy, David, whom he barely knew, was calling again asking about setting up a meeting for a favor. He winced when he heard the request and then asked, "Does it have to be soon?"

"Well, there's no deadline, but I'd prefer to speak to you sooner rather than later."

"Then how about right now?"

"Well, I guess so," David said. "I guess I could do it now. I could take a taxi and be there in about half an hour."

"No, not here. I'm just leaving. Do you know where the *Clínica Dental de Morales* is, over in Escalón? My daughter wants me there for a tooth-pulling. And if we both leave now, we could maybe have a few minutes to talk before she and her mother arrive. Do you know where it is?"

"No, but I know a taxi driver who claims to know everything in the city and is the fastest driver in the country."

"Just tell him it's on Calle Mirador, in between the British Embassy and a little hotel I can't think of the name of. He'll find it."

"The driver's a 'she' but I'll tell her."

Doug left immediately after the call because he'd hoped he might have a little time in the waiting room before his wife, daughter and David arrived, to look at the files of some of the projects that were going to be hurt by the budget cuts and perhaps find places where each might slim down and manage to get by. He opened his briefcase and began looking through the folders.

Visiting dentists had become a more frequent occurrence for him these days. Each of his three girls had teeth problems and this seemed to be the year they all required special treatment, and he was beginning to feel oddly at home in the clinic. It was a small room and, since *Escalón* was a wealthy neighborhood, it looked a lot like a clinic in the States. The walls were filled with displays of dental hygiene tips and encouragements to floss, and photos of Salvadoran mountain scenery. At one end was a booth with a glass window and a receptionist behind it answering calls, and at the other was a large, bright orange Naugahyde couch behind a low plastic coffee table where Doug spread out his files and notepad. His new office-away-from-the-office, he called it.

He hadn't been there ten minutes when he saw David standing in the doorway, pausing to get used to the dim light. "You're on time," Doug said, not looking up from his papers. "I was hoping you'd be a little late."

"I'm sorry," David said. "Should we try this another day?"

"All of my days are like this, these days. So, let's just do what we can now. If you talk fast, we may be able to do your questions before I need to go. If not, then we can talk about trying it another day."

David pulled a metal folding chair to the other side of the coffee table. It felt damp with humidity. "Okay, here's the deal." He took a notepad out of his backpack. "I think I need some traveling help or advice and you're someone who I think could help me with that."

"Do you mean travel around the city or around the country?"

"Well, it's around the country, but more complicated than that."

"Tell me."

"I want to go north. Up to Chalatenango or Morazán, that area."

Doug put down his pen and took off his glasses. "That'll be tricky. That's a pretty dangerous neighborhood. What are you looking for up there?"

"It's mainly the 'repopulation' villages. I'm hearing that there is a serious experiment in development and democracy going on in those communities, and I want to learn more about them. I have a feeling that they may be a model that could be used in some other areas, maybe even other countries."

Doug frowned. "I'm aware of all that, but you do know,

don't you, that those people are also mainly strong supporters of the rebels? They fled when the fighting got tough and hid out in Honduras for the past decade and are just now coming home. That doesn't look like a model that could be imitated too easily anywhere else."

"Maybe not that, but I've also heard that they are self-governed, they give women the right to vote and speak at town meetings, they won't let little children under the age of twelve work in the fields. They share workloads, they share incomes, and they even share church. Catholics and Protestants both worship together and share a pastor. I even heard one of them had Muslims in the community and they participated in worship too. I haven't seen that anywhere else in Salvador. In fact, I haven't seen all that too much anywhere. In any country."

Doug continued to stare at him. "You could do that," he said. "In fact, you probably should do it, though don't tell anybody I said that. It's hard to get real facts about the region unless you go there yourself." He lowered his voice. "The people up there didn't just leave the country because of the fighting in general. They left because they supported the leftist guerrillas and the government—the army, actually—was killing them to punish them for doing that. I think supporting the rebels was a mistake, but the army's response was barbaric, and they could do it again at any moment. The government doesn't hate them any less now that they've started coming back home."

"I have some contacts up there who could help me out," David said.

"Maybe, but you know, don't you, that trying to build a true democracy is not something the old-line oligarchs down here in the city are too fond of, and sometimes their unhappiness can get pretty violent. We'd be more helpful to those little villages if they weren't so aligned with the rebels and didn't get donations from liberal groups up in the States. I don't think that was a wise idea. They don't really know what they're doing. We frankly wish they'd just back off and let us do our job. In fact, we've helped the government resettle a few villages ourselves, and we think ours are run a lot better. But if you do this, when you're finished seeing the older ones, I'd really like you to look at some of the villages that we—I mean we with the Salvadoran government—have set up. I could get you some locations and contacts. But remember," he stopped for a moment and considered his words, "that's still considered enemy-held territory and it's pretty dangerous, and we can't really protect you if something happens to you." David nodded, attempting a confident look.

"A lot of that region has been held by the rebels for almost a decade like it was their own little fiefdom, and we're just now beginning to make inroads back into it. It's better, but still fragile. But if you looked in the right places, you could learn a lot about our own plans for the development of the region and the whole country. We could get you some interviews. It could be good for that book you're working on."

David smiled. "Does it show?" He actually had been thinking about writing sometime about his experiences, but he hadn't shared that with anyone.

"You look like a writer, Dave."

David smiled, "I'll take that. So, what would I need to know? Like you said, it's a dangerous neighborhood."

"Well, it certainly is that," Doug said, laughing coldly. "But if you can get into that 'neighborhood,' I could get you connected with people who could tell you stories, let you know what the US is actually doing to help those people, other than just paying for bombs and helicopters—that's what people think of when they think of US involvement in El Salvador. But

I can't do just 'anything.' I can't officially authorize your going all the way up into the northern *departamentos* where so much of the fighting is going on, but I can do things like get you some connections and some USAID identification. I said earlier that I wouldn't be able to get you one of those, but I'm now thinking you might be worth it. And the more papers you have with you, with our name on them, the more you might at least *look* official. After we talk, you might want to go over to the Embassy again and check with them too. They might give you a more official-looking pass, but I'd use it sparingly. The embassy guys are hated by both sides. Get some ID from both of us but use theirs at the army checkpoints. Then, after you've visited one or two of the older re-pop villages and can find your way into to some of ours, our ID will be better for you and get you an interview with some of the mayors or town leaders."

"Will it get me through all the checkpoints?"

"There aren't that many, maybe half a dozen throughout both *Departamentos* and you're not going to be traveling around the entire territory. If any troops stop you, just flash the Embassy badge and some of our AID papers I'm going to give you and tell them you're working for us. The stops are mainly on the southern side of Chalate, where it's safer. After that, you're on your own. Your good looks and charm will have to get you the rest of the way."

Just then the door to the clinic opened and a woman in her mid-thirties came in leading a small girl with eyes red and wet.

Doug started gathering up his folders and putting them back in his briefcase. "So, listen," he said, talking rapidly. "Here's what you do. And pay attention to this, because I don't want you to be the first American killed up there. First, go early in the morning. The rebels don't tend to attack early in the morning. I don't know why, maybe they sleep late or something, but anyway it's true. Also, take the number 39 bus at the

Terminal Oriente, because it's national and only has a couple of stops, and the more places you stop, the more opportunities you'll have for running into trouble. You got that?"

David nodded, wishing he had taken out his notebook and pen.

"It's only about fifty miles all the way up to the Honduran border, though it will feel longer because the roads are terrible. On the way, you'll probably only see two Army checkpoints. One, when you leave the city and one when you reach the Colima Bridge over the Rio Lempa. It's kind of a gateway into the area controlled by the rebels, just before you get to Lake Suchitoto. It's like a bridge between two worlds, or two countries, in El Salvador. Then your next stop or two will be by their guys. You'll probably be safe at both of them. They're still technically in peace talks right now, so neither side wants to kill a Yankee and read about it the next day in the papers. But just in case, our IDs will make you look more official. Sometime soon, maybe Tuesday, after I've had a chance to talk to them, call my office and tell them who you are, and that they should give you one of our ID badges and a copy of our most recent Salvador 'Country Reports.' It'll give you a lot of good information about the area, plus it's in a binder that has the words "USAID" in big letters all over the front of it. Hold that casually, but very visibly in front of you, when you get to the guerrilla checkpoint. You got all of that?"

"I think so."

"So, I've got to go now. If you need anything else, give me a call. And I've got your number, so if I think of anything, I'll call you."

"Thanks, I really appreciate your help."

"Just be careful up there." Doug stood and smiled at his wife and daughter at the door into the inner part of the clinic but paused and turned back. "I mean it, be very careful".

CHAPTER THIRTY-THREE
BEERS II

So, it's your party and it looks like you're a little late." Alf was sitting at a table at their favorite bar, waving a bottle at David and motioning him to take a seat.

David took off his jacket and set his own bottle on the table. Alf was already working on his second.

"I'm sorry," David said. "I wish I could blame it on the Salvadoran bus system..."

"Which is, in fact, awful," said Alf.

"Yes, but unfortunately, it's partially my fault because I tried to squeeze in one last interview for the day, over in Soyapango, and the bus took too long to get there..."

"Which is maybe partially the bus's fault."

"Right, but when I got there, I realized it was almost time that I should be leaving to get over here."

"Which is a lot your fault."

"Wait, it gets better."

"Prove it."

"So, we waited and waited for the bus to show up, and it never did, and finally a car came by from the Western Terminal, and they said that a raid of terrorists had run through the terminal and slashed all the tires of all of the buses."

"Which is El Salvador's fault. Welcome to El Salvador."

"Yeah, I know, it's that 'War of Attrition' thing the rebels are doing to wear the government down, but it does seem a little counterproductive."

"They did the same thing about three-or four-times last year. It's all to try and slow the country down and make the government want to negotiate a peace treaty." He took a sip of his second beer. "*Mira*," he said, "The far-right are some very bad people, but the left also makes some very bad decisions, and that leaves the rest of the country in a very bad mess. We salvadorenos are the best in the world at living in a mangled country and managing to smile and look like life is good. It's what we do."

"Yeah, and you're right about the people here being some of the best in the world. I'm really beginning to love it here."

Alf slid back in his chair, taking his bottle with him. "That's always good to hear. It means that we won't have to give you a raise if you stay on past the project. Okay, so let's talk. When you called, it sounded like something more important than the merits of the Salvadoran bus system. Is there something else?"

"Yes. Remember that suggestion you made a few weeks ago about my going up north to get a larger picture of how the war is going and what life is really like nation-wide?"

"I think I had too much to drink when I said that."

"But you did say it, and I think I want to do it."

"Now I'm sure I had too much to drink."

"I guess I feel for those people—especially the ones in the new villages who are working so hard to put together a new life for themselves. I want to see that first-hand, and then when I get back, maybe the institute and the university would help by sharing some of their people and resources."

"You know, of course, that that's crazy and they'll probably kill you, and then Héctor will blame me, and I'll lose my job, and Beatriz will leave me, and I'll be on the streets dealing drugs and selling T-shirts before my sixtieth birthday?"

"I'll admit that's an appealing image, but I'm actually expecting I'll come back alive."

"You might, but the fact still is that it's very dangerous and you also might not. *Mira*, do you have anyone who could go with you? Someone who is six foot ten, with a bullet-proof chest, and knuckles that drag the floor? Do you know anyone who could protect you?"

David laughed. "To tell you the truth, I was hoping that you might want to go with me, and not because of your chest."

Alf jerked forward in his chair and almost dropped his bottle. "No!" he shouted, then looked around the room to see if anyone had heard him. "I'm too old, I've got bad knees, and a mortgage, and a wife and family to think about. And if you ever tell Beatriz that I mentioned her last on that list by accident, I'll cut your tongue out."

"It was just a thought. I don't know many people here and it would take someone who knew the area and its make-up and could navigate in case things went bad. But don't feel pressured. I think I can get in and out quietly on my own, make a few visits, get a few interviews, take some notes, and get back to report in a week or so without making too much of a stir."

"Are you, *crazy?* You're six-foot-one. You've got blond hair, and you don't think you'd stand out? *Mira*, I'm five-ten and people here think I'm tall. But they'll think you are that giant, Fezzik, in *Princess Bride*." Alf took a last sip from his second beer and set it down. "Ok, tell me, *amigo*, when are you planning this suicide run into the middle of a hail of bullets? And what do you need from me?"

"Perhaps as soon as next week. I still have a couple of interviews scheduled and a couple of reports to get to Héctor, but after that, I can arrange to be free for a while. And what do I need from you? I was hoping I could talk you into going with me, but it looks like that's off the table. Beyond that, I thought maybe you could give me some names of people and places to visit. Perhaps some tips on how to get through the checkpoints."

"I can do some of that for you. But first, let's talk."

"About why you decided to go with me?"

"I thought we already covered that."

"Okay, so what else do we need to talk about?"

"Here's a start. Have I ever told you about my brother?"

"No, I don't think you ever did."

"And that he was a journalist here, back during the first Duarte campaign, the guy whose party just lost the election last month? Duarte also ran back in the seventies, and my brother got caught up in the mess."

"That woman, Señora Martínez, in the Office for Victim Investigation, said she lost her husband in that election."

"And that was my brother."

"God, I am so sorry. I didn't know that."

"Yes. That was back in the days when we were really thinking that we had turned the corner on becoming a democracy. There were democracy protests all over Latin America and nearly everyone thought it was finally going to happen here. But the far-right did everything they could to make sure that no one from the center or left could get elected."

"Like what?"

"Like shutting down voting places out in the *campo*, sending monitors to the polls to terrify voters out of voting, not allowing Salvadoran citizens out of the country to cast their legal vote, and—my favorite—giving the Constituent

Assembly the power to throw out ballots it claimed were fraudulent."

"But how was your brother involved with all of that?"

"Nothing complicated. He just kept reporting on it in *Noticias de El Salvador*. He knew some of the people who faked the numbers and kept writing about it and calling for an investigation."

"And what did they do"

"Well, if you've talked to Sra. Martínez, you probably know most of this. First they called all of the newspapers, 'enemies of the people.' And they threatened all of their editors to get them to stop covering the elections and stop editorializing about the government. Then they came for my brother, Enrique, and they killed him. They just found a bunch of 'Death Squads,'— usually off-duty police or military guys, or out of work young men, who they can pay a little money to beat up dissidents and protestors claiming they are socialists or rebels. And they shot him one night when he was walking from his office to his car. And they didn't just shoot him, they also cut his face off so he couldn't be recognized and dropped him off the rocks at *Puerta del Diablo*, south of the city. Beautiful view, great hiking, and popular spot for tossing bodies."

"Oh, my God."

"And I loved him. He was my older brother and a very good man. A decent man with a good family. He's the brother who got all the religion in the family and he didn't deserve to have that happen to him."

"I'm so sorry."

"It was terrible. I never got over it. I managed to get *through* it, but never *over* it."

"I didn't know that."

Alf paused for a moment, then leaned across the table. "And David, you'll never get over Kathryn."

David took a long drink from his bottle and put it down on the table. "I thought you might go there with this story. I shouldn't even have brought it up."

"Dave, you never get over something like this. My brother... your wife... Sara's husband...you don't get over those things. You just go on living life, and eventually you collect so many new experiences that the worst ones back there begin to feel smaller because they're outnumbered. But they aren't smaller, and they never go away. You can't make it happen. You can't will them away, and you'll live in hell from now on trying."

"Yeah, well that's not happened to me yet." He raised his hand at a waitress across the room.

Alf reached up and pulled David's hand down. "David, I'm sorry, and I won't bring that up again."

"You know I don't like talking about Kathryn."

"But you do like talking about her, you just want to do it on your own terms. All I want—and this is probably stupid of me —is for you to admit that some part of this trip is about saving lives of people who are truly in need of help, but another part is an interior desire of yours to atone for what you think you did to Kathryn. And if you die in the process, it will be some kind of divine justice for your crimes."

"Héctor said the same thing, and I didn't like it then either. So, Alf, okay. Kathryn died because of my 'sin,' if you want to put it that way. I did it. And I'll never get over it. If I do something now that will help others stay alive, maybe that will help. And if I die, maybe it will be a judgement that I deserve. I don't know. I feel like I've been living for some time on a gigantic bridge, with Kathryn, hurt, shame and meaninglessness on one side and a chance to finally do something redemptive to be free of them on the other. Some way that I can pay for my crimes and sins and start being alive again. I know it's crazy, I'm not proud of it, but it's where I am. I'm better about all this today, but it's still here and it hasn't gone away. And, also yes, it's probably at least a part of why I want to do this. One way of another, I need to get to the other side of this bridge—and I have to go to Chalate and do something that would make my little wasted life have more meaning. Are you happy now? Are we done?"

"Yes. Done—except for one thing." "What's that?"

"I want to go with you."

"What?"

"I said I want to go with you. I've decided that I'm going with you."

"But you just said you wouldn't do it."

"Yes, I did, but I changed my mind. You drove a hard bargain. Excitement, adventure, helping poor people...and the possibility of being captured and tortured and tossed off the bridge at Rio Lempa. Who could say 'no' to that? And with any luck the lovely Sra. Martínez at the OIV might recognize our faces in the next morgue photos and we'll be famous. Sounds like an opportunity I can't pass up."

David was stunned. "Alf, thank you. Really. I know you think it's all an emotional Don Quixote thing for me—and maybe it is—so, I really appreciate your doing this."

"You're welcome. But listen, if we do it, we'll need to line up some safe people to see and some safe villages to visit. It's going to take some planning and phone calling. So, maybe late next week sometime? Thursday or Friday. And you should probably contact that Grantham guy you met at USAID and the kid Robbie at the Embassy."

"I called them both. Grantham hated the idea, but agreed to send me some ID and things, and Robbie hasn't gotten back to me yet."

"Good. Meanwhile, I've got to go home and explain to Beatriz that I'm about to prove that I am exactly as dumb as her brother always told her I was. And you're probably going to have a very similar conversation with Sara."

David laughed. "Yes, I'm planning on doing that tonight, except for the part about the brother-in-law." He raised his hand again at the waitress across the room. "Check, please." She stared back at him blankly.

"In Spanish, Dave, you should know that by now."

"Oh, sorry." He raised his hand again. "*Camarera. ¿La cuenta por favor?*" The waitress nodded and started to their table.

CHAPTER THIRTY-FOUR
ROBBIE

When David got to his apartment, he was shaking with excitement. Parts of his conversation with Alf had been tense but it ended well, and he was feeling better about the trip. He was especially grateful that Alf had agreed to come along because his help would be invaluable. He unlocked his door, stepped inside, and leaned back against the door breathing heavily. He stood there for a while, imagining what might happen to them up in Chalatenango. He wanted to be realistic but also hoped that the dangers he'd heard about so often were exaggerated. He knew there was intense fighting in many areas, but it was hard to know how serious it was when local newspapers focused almost entirely on the evil rebels, the noble soldiers, and how bad it was that another cow got stuck in the mud on the highway. He didn't want to make light of the dangers, but he also thought it would be smart to not over- exaggerate them.

He poured a glass of water, went to the living room and fell onto the sofa. This had been a long and stressful day, and he felt good. He was increasingly aware of the enormity of his new life since he had been living in El Salvador. After months of watching boys sing for money on the bus, girls searching for scrap metal in the landfill, and young prostitutes across from him risking their lives to make money for the family's food, who would have thought that he would feel grateful that this was the place he had landed in? In the middle of a small, underdeveloped country, struggling through poverty, corruption, and war, he had feelings of hope and even gratitude. The bridge between a pit of self-hatred where he had been in not long ago, and a new life that could possibly be positive and meaningful, seemed more real than ever.

He laughed when he thought about it. He could never have imagined a transition from that world to this one, with a strange new job, new friends, new experiences, and now a wonderful new woman in his life. He was happy. Things were going well.

Then the phone rang. *Damn!*, he thought. Slowly, he pulled himself up and limped back to the kitchen and took the handset off the wall.

¿Aló?, he said.

"Mr. Patterson?"

"Yes?"

"Mr. Patterson, this is Robert Sweeney. We met at the US Embassy."

"Oh of course. I just wrote you a letter."

"Yes, and I just got it. And I'm calling you back to talk about it."

"That's good, I guess. Will you be able to help us out with the trip?"

"Yes, of course. You don't really need too many things from us, but I can get you some badges and documents, and a letter of passage to help you in case you get delayed at one of the checkpoints. I also talked to Mr. Grantham, at USAID, and he said he was getting some contact names for you too. So, between the two of us, you'll probably be all set."

"That's great Robert. I really appreciate it."

"There is one more thing."

"What's that?"

"The truth is that I'm really only here temporarily."

"Yes, I think I knew that."

"And after this, I don't have anywhere to go. I'll probably go back to Topeka. My parents live there, and I had started college there before I dropped out and my uncle found me this job."

"Okay." David wasn't sure where this was going.

"And I've been here a year and I've never done anything. I mean I've never traveled around anywhere. I've never seen the country. I've never visited anything like the repopulation villages you'll be visiting, and I've never really felt like I've done anything important."

"O-kay..." David said again, this time drawing out the word. "I used to think that God sent me down here to do some good for the world, you know, and now I'm thinking that if that's so, I've done a really bad job of it."

"Well, Robert, I don't know much about—"

"So, I want to go with you."

David was startled. "Listen, I don't know if I could...."

"If you guys will just let me go with you, I will do every-thing I can to help you when you get up there and help you again when you get back. I don't have a big important office here, but I know people, and if we get into any trouble up in Chalate, I can probably make a phone call and get us out. I really want to be involved with something that will make a difference in the world, and you really want to go up into the mountains and see those villages. So, maybe we can help each other. What do you say?"

David was silent for several seconds. "Well," he said, "I guess...I guess... are you sure? This could be a very..."

"Yes! I'm sure. And it would be very important to me, and I think I could even be helpful to you, and I promise I wouldn't get in the way, I promise."

David took a deep breath and put his forehead on his palm to hold his head up. "Okay, let me talk this over with my traveling companion. He may go along with it, but I'm sure he won't like it. Also, we're leaving in just a few days, that's not a long time. Are you sure you can get away that soon?"

"Yes, I've already told my uncle that I will probably be doing this, and he said he was sure that anyone could take my place—I don't think he likes me. So, just say when and where and I'll be there."

"Okay, so, if you're really sure..."

"I am."

David thought for a moment. The head in his hand didn't feel good about this. The growing excitement he had had about the trip was beginning to feel more complicated. "Okay, we're planning on next Thursday morning, at six o'clock. That's when the bus leaves. I'll be meeting Mr. Alphonso Rodriguez Hernandez...."

"I know him, he teaches something at the University."

"Right. That's the guy. And we'll meet up at the *Terminal de Oriente,* the one a few blocks east of the Cathedral in *El Centro.* And, though the bus leaves very early in the morning, we'll need to be there and ready to leave even earlier than that because those bus guys don't wait for anyone."

Robbie laughed. "Yeah, I've had some bad experiences with that too."

"And pack very lightly for only about three days."

"And Mr. Patterson?"

"Yes?"

"One more thing."

"Sure. What?"

"Would you mind letting me call you 'David,' and you call me 'Robbie'? It would make me feel a lot better about this. Kind of like we're friends and not just business partners."

"Of course, Robbie. And I have a feeling that after this is over, we'll feel like close friends. For a long, long time."

"Right. I think so too."

CHAPTER THIRTY-FIVE

VISITOR

David couldn't sleep. He had a lot of things left to do before their trip to Chalate. The bed wasn't comfortable. The night was hot. A neighbor outside was playing loud music. And two mosquitos seemed intent on exploring the inside of his left ear. And he was missing Sara. She had taken the boys to visit their grandparents that evening, and he wasn't invited. She'd said that her parents would surely want to meet him eventually, but for now she wanted to go alone and tell them the news of a new turn in their relationship. That was fine, he'd told her, and they'd be having dinner the day before the trip anyway, but tonight he missed her, and he still couldn't sleep. And the mosquitoes were still making meal plans in his ears.

He rolled over and looked at the clock. It was only four o'clock, far too early to get up, but he was wide awake, and the bed was beginning to hurt. Maybe he should go for a walk, he thought. Maybe write thank-you notes to the people he'd visited last week. Maybe think through (again) the list of people they would visit in Chalate. He sat up and pulled on his jeans, turned on the light and walked into the kitchen. There, he opened the refrigerator looking for the pitcher of *agua pura* he kept there, but before he could take it out, he heard a knock on the door. It was four o'clock, he remembered again. From the kitchen, he could see through the small window at the top of the door and saw the hairline of a head and a black hat, it looked like a Fedora. Whoever it is, he thought, he is not small. He walked quietly and carefully to the window next to the door and looked through a slit in the blinds of the newly replaced window to see who was there. The enormous body of a man dressed in black filled the opening. As he stared up at him, the man's large scowling face turned and looked down at him. It was Bhutto. David jerked his head back. He stood up quickly.

He didn't want to open the door, but if he did, he should protect himself. But with what? He looked around the dining room and saw a broken wooden curtain rod still waiting to be replaced from when his apartment had been ransacked weeks earlier. It was about an inch thick and could probably make a few painful bruises on someone without breaking any bones. He picked it up and as he did, the knocking on the door grew louder and a deep, hoarse voice said, "Patterson, let me in."

David stepped back to the door. He drew a deep breath, holding the rod in one hand and the doorknob in the other. He looked at the clock in the kitchen. This could be bad, he thought. He pulled open the door and before him stood a tall, heavy, and very serious-looking Emilio Bhutto, wearing his now-familiar black suit, black tie, and black hat.

Bhutto spoke with a low, grating voice. "Sr. Patterson, let me in." He moved forward as though intending to come in but paused. "I will not hurt you," he said.

David stood still blocking the door. "But you did hurt me once, and my friend, Carlos. Why should I believe you now?"

"You were chasing me, and I wished you no harm."

"No harm? How could we know that? I've seen you following me for weeks, you broke into my apartment scattering everything around, and that night you were staring into my friend's window."

Bhutto stepped into the room and, with a sweep of his hand, brushed David aside. Then he pointed at the rod in David's hand. "Put that down. If you hit me with it, I will take it from you and I will hurt you."

David looked at his curtain rod that suddenly looked small against the giant Emilio Bhutto and set it down on his kitchen table. "Alright, but you have a lot to explain before I trust you."

Bhutto looked around at David's small living room. Against the window was a small loveseat sofa, a coffee table in front of it, and two small wooden chairs on either side. He pointed a large, beefy hand into the room. "Sit first."

David pulled out one of the chairs and sat in it. Bhutto lowered his immense body onto the sofa. He sat there for several seconds completely silent, looking intently at the blank wall ahead of him. Finally, he said, "I was wrong to do that to you." His mouth twisted as though swallowing an unpleasant taste. "And I was wrong to follow you. And I have come here today to..." His voice trailed off, and his gaze moved from the wall to David's face. "To ask you for your forgiveness."

That wasn't what David expected. "I'm not sure how good I am at granting forgiveness," he said. "Maybe you should talk about that to someone else, like a priest." He said it almost as a joke because he still wasn't convinced the man wasn't there to hurt him.

"I have done that. And it is my priest who sent me here, to you...for your forgiveness."

"I don't think I can do that. Why did you do all those things? Why do you hate me?"

Bhutto voice rose. "I did not hate you." He shook a fist at

David's face, appearing ready to say more, but then he fell back into the sofa. "At least not in the beginning."

"That's interesting, because in the very beginning, at the university party, you seemed to dislike me just because I didn't know Salvadoran beers." David smiled hoping to lighten the tone.

"I hate the ignorance of all Americans. They come into our country and think they know everything and can fix everything. But they know nothing and fix nothing."

"So, what started it? I saw you following me several times after that, you broke into my apartment, and you could have killed Carlos and me when we caught you looking into the apartment gates. And here you are at this insane time in the morning banging on my door. What's going on? Why did you do all that?"

"It wasn't you," said Bhutto, rubbing his thick hands together in his lap. "At least not at the beginning. It was Señorita de León."

"Sara?" David's eyes grew wide. "Why? What has she got to do with all this?"

Bhutto dropped his hands and looked up at the ceiling, silently, as though praying, and then spoke very slowly, squeezing out every word. "It is because I am in love with her."

"Sara?" David said again.

"*Sí*, and I have loved her for many long times. I loved her when her husband was still alive. He taught at the university. He was a good professor, but he was too *vanidoso*, too vain, and he was not as intelligent as Srta. Sara. And I felt bad for her. And also, she was good to me. She would smile and talk and act friendly to me when we were in the faculty rooms."

David was about to ask why that was unusual, but Bhutto spoke first.

"Not many people want to talk to a giant. They want to

point at him and make the jokes of him, or act like they are afraid of him, but Srta. Sara spoke to me. She would ask me questions. She would listen to me. And she told me I was her friend."

David was feeling uncomfortable. He sensed where this was going. "So, you fell in love with her?"

"Yes. I should not have, but yes. I did. Then when Professor Daniel died, I thought our friendship grew stronger. She needed help. I helped her with her inheritance from Daniel. I helped her become working at the university. I helped her find her apartment. I have an aunt who was living there and needed to move."

"Did you ever tell her about your feelings?"

"*Sí*, and I should not have."

"And it went badly?"

"She invited me to her apartment to cook for me. She said it was to thank me for my help, but in my heart, I hoped too much that it was for something more. And in the evening, I told her that I loved her and always had and always will."

"How did she respond?"

"She was not unkind, but she said that she did not have the same feelings for me. She said it was too soon for her to love anybody, and she also wanted for us to be just friends. I knew in my heart that that was true, but I did not want to hear it. I reached out and touched her."

"You mean like on her arm or hand?"

"At first, yes, but when she did not pull away, I took her into my arms and held her, and I kissed her many times. She fought me, not hitting but pushing. But I held her—it was wrong, it made me crazy—hoping that if I held her, she would understand my love for her and she would love me back. But of course, she did not. We struggled in the room until we fell backwards on top of her table in the kitchen, and it broke and both of us fell to the floor. That was when she was able to get away. And she got up and went to the door. She opened it and told me that I needed to leave. 'But I love you,' I said to her. It was *un fallo tonto*, a stupid thing to say, but still I said it. Then she said that I was her good friend but that was all. She said I had hurt her, and she told me to leave. I heard her words in my ears for many months after that. It was an injury, on my inside, I had never felt before."

David reached across the coffee table and put his hand on Bhutto's knee. "I'm sorry, Emilio. That must have felt awful."

"But then you came here."

David sat back in his chair. "I thought that might be coming."

"After a time, we began to speak again. We began to be friends again. She smiled friendly again in the hallways. One time we shared lunch at the cafeteria. I began to think that maybe enough of the time she wanted had passed. Maybe now there was a chance our friendship could grow into something bigger if I waited and did not push her fast. But then you came. At almost the same week that I was preparing to speak to her again, very gently, of my love for her, she mentioned an American she had met at a *pupusaria*. And she liked him very much and wanted me to congratulate her. And when I saw you at the university party, I knew it was you. It was a very hurting thing. You took her from me."

"I'm sorry Emilio, I had no idea. I didn't 'take' her from you. I just met her by accident, and it grew."

"But it drove me crazy," he said, his voice rising again. His face hardened. "That was the first time I had felt happy in many months, maybe years, and you took it away from me."

"I sincerely did not know that..."

Bhutto rose from the sofa and walked across the living room. "I went crazy, I did evil things. I wanted to stop you, to hurt you, to kill you. I thought we could have been happy together, but that you had stopped it. I know it was wrong and now I am sorry, but that's what I thought, and for a while it was all I could think of." He turned his head quickly looking back and forth around the room as though looking for a way to get away, or someplace to hide. David stood up and backed away, but Bhutto turned and faced him. "I'm sorry," he said so loud and so close that David felt the vibration in his voice. "I'm sorry I did those things. I am not here to hurt you. I am here to say I'm sorry I frightened you. I'm sorry I hated you." He put his hands on both of David's shoulders and shook him. "You now must accept my apology. You must say you forgive me. I don't want to hurt you."

David was frightened but he calmly took Bhutto's hands from his shoulders and backed away. "Emilio," he said, speaking carefully. "You are a good man. In spite of all the things you did, I think you have a good heart. And I am very sorry for what you have gone through." He thought for a moment. "And of course I will forgive you, but I still think the biggest forgiveness has to come from you. I think that if you can do that to yourself, you will be better."

"I know that, and I want to do that. But now that I also have your forgiveness, it will help me do it." He smiled for the first time.

An amber light of morning was touching the edges of the window, and the items in the living room were beginning to glow. Bhutto looked at his watch. "Thank you," he said. "And I am sorry also for this loud visit and for my loud emotions. You did not deserve that either."

"It's alright," David said, trying to look relieved. "It was good for both of us. And I'm glad we finally met, though I wish it had been under different circumstances. But I'm glad it happened."

When he left, David stood in the doorway for some time watching the giant wounded man make his way down the sidewalk to the apartment gate. A complicated, lonely person, trying—and sometimes failing—to understand and live in a world that seldom loved him. After Bhutto disappeared from view, David stayed there for several minutes, wondering what he should do next. Daylight would soon be filling the apartment, his adrenalin level had been raging, and he still had a lot to do. On the other hand, he had curtains in the bedroom, and he had lost a lot of sleep, and who's keeping score? So, he went back to his bedroom, closed the curtains, and turned off the light.

CHAPTER THIRTY-SIX
LAST NIGHT

"Why didn't you tell me?" David was pacing in a circle in Sara's living room. He was shaking with emotion. They had just come out of the boys' bedroom where together they said goodnight to them, and he kissed them on their foreheads. But, in the living room, now that they were alone, he raised the subject of his visit with Emilio Bhutto.

"There was nothing to tell you. I didn't think he would do anything."

"Do anything? That guy could have killed either Carlos or me. He's huge. And he has been following me for months." David stopped pacing and turned to look at her. This was their last time to be together before he left, and it was supposed to have been a quiet evening and a chance to say goodbye.

"But maybe he would not have done that to you if you had not yelled at him."

"Well, maybe that's right, but here was a giant guy, who I recognized had been following me for several months, staring up at your window at night. What was I supposed to do, ask him for a cigarette? He may not have meant to hurt anyone just then, but how would I know that? I don't think it's crazy to think that he might have had some kind of violence on his mind. How was I to know he was just someone with an insane misplaced love for a woman who hasn't returned his feelings? I had to at least yell at him. How could we know what he was about to do."

"I'm sorry. Yes, he looks scary, but I know him, and he is a very sweet man. He is lonely and awkward, and I felt sorry for him. We were just friends. *De verdad*. Really."

"Alright, I believe that. To you he was just a friend. But you should have told me about him, because he wanted you to be more than that."

"That is true. I am sorry."

David sat on the sofa and pulled Sara down next to him and put his arm around her. "I know you didn't mean anything by it and Carlos and I made it out fairly well, but it scared me, and I didn't know what to do. If you have any other secrets, dangerous or not, would you promise to share them with me, or at least warn me about them? I don't want to discover some-time that you are an international spy from Sweden, and you've been arrested for stealing Salvadoran Taco recipes."

She laughed and they both felt better. "Trust me," she said, "if I am arrested for stealing recipes, I will call you first." David was glad they were laughing because he wanted the night to be relaxed. He was leaving the next morning, and he didn't want them to fight just before he left, and he had something else he wanted to ask her about that was also difficult. "Sara, he said, holding her hand and looking at her next to him, "I noticed that a few days ago when I mentioned a possible trip up to Chalatenango, you didn't say much."

"I do not want you to go. I have said that before."

It was true. In earlier conversations, she had spoken out

against the whole region, even before David talked about going. "I remember one time," he said, "when I just brought it up as an interesting place, not as somewhere that I might visit, and you said immediately that I shouldn't ever go there. Why is that?"

She lifted his hand up to her face and held it there. "I am worried about you. You don't know the area and it's dangerous."

"I understand that, but there are other regions that are also dangerous. But this one, it seemed like you didn't like it at all, not just for my traveling through it. You looked like you had a negative reaction to the name when I just mentioned it."

"I just...I just..." She turned her head away. "*No me gusta hablar de eso.*" She caught herself falling into Spanish. "I mean, I do not like Chalatenango. I do not like to talk about the place."

David did know something about her hesitancy. She had told him that her husband had had some kind of difficulty up in Chalatenango but had not given him any details. And until now he had made a point of not asking her, because he assumed it was a difficult subject for her.

"But I am going up there in a couple of days, and—if you can—I would like for you to be supportive of the trip."

Sara turned to face him. "David," she said, "I will support you in whatever you do, because I know that you are trying hard to do good. But my husband, Daniel, he was killed there. The rebels murdered him." Her voice began to shake. "They did not even know him, and they killed him. And I never was able to even see his body."

He put his arm around her and held her. "I thought that might be it. You don't have to say any more if you don't want to."

"I never told you this. I did not want to tell you. For many years he was a mayor of La Palma, a small *aldea* up in north Chalate.

"Did you live up there?"

"No. Since the war, most of the mayors in the zones of *la lucha* live here in the city and just go up when needed."

"Because of the violence?"

"Yes, because the rebels kill mayors. They do it to weaken the government."

"But why Daniel?"

"They sometimes kill local politicians to break down the government, to stop it, so that more people will rise up against it. David, I do believe in their cause. I do not speak of it often, but I do. I have gone to demonstrations to support them and to support democracy. But some things they do are wrong, *muy malvado.*'"

David kissed her on her forehead. "David," she said, "my country needs to be a democracy. Our rich leaders only care about the welfare of their rich friends. They do not care about the people. But not all the rebels are smart in what they do to bring it. They say their goal is to create a new society, but sometimes what they do destroys what is already good in the old society, and my Daniel was a good man. He was a supporter of this conservative government, but he believed he was helping to make things better."

"And the guerrillas assassinated him?"

"People in masks just walked into his office and shot him and walked away. No one stopped them and the *Policía* did not arrive for over an hour. It is a very small town, but it took them that long to get to him. And they did not tell me until two days. All I know for certain is that it was the worst, darkest time of my life and it happened up where you are wanting to go walking around and interviewing people for your report." As she spoke, there was a sound of anger in her voice, and it took David by surprise.

He pulled her in closer and for a few moments they both sat in silence. "Sara," he said finally, "I can't promise you anything, but I will try very hard to be safe. I want to come home, and I want to come home to you."

"I know, but I just..."

"And if I hear about any fighting going on anywhere, we can just leave and come back early. Alf and I have talked about this. We can move on to a different location or just come back. I promise I won't do anything risky. I want to come home *alive*." He leaned down to kissed her on the forehead again, she turned her head up to his and gave him a longer, more intimate, kiss.

Later, after they had talked and held each other for a long time, he told her he needed to leave. He still needed to pack his bag and call Robbie and Alf, and it was getting late. They stood in the doorway for some time talking again about the dangers of the trip and the importance of coming "home." They kissed one last time.

When he got to his apartment, David was struck by how tired he should be but wasn't. The adventure before him, as dangerous and threatening as it was, gave him energy and even enthusiasm. It was funny, he thought to himself, how having a goal, or a purpose could do that for him.

He made the last-minute calls to Robbie and Alf, he packed the one bag he was taking, he wrote in his journal, set an alarm, and then turned out the light. And then the phone rang. It was Sara—he knew it would be her. She began by apologizing for calling, but he stopped her. It was fine, he said, and he appreciated that she was worrying about him, because it made him feel loved. And right now, he really enjoyed feeling loved.

"I did not want you to go," she said, "because it scared me to think that Chalate might be taking away from me the only two men I have ever loved. I don't want to imagine the hurt I would have in my heart if it happened twice. But please, go there if you feel like you must. I think it will help you, and it might help our people. You need to do this thing. I respect you, and I will not try to stop you. And I love you."

"Thank you, and I love you too."

When she hung up, he stood in the kitchen for a few moments looking absently into his living room and realizing with some pleasure that, for the first time in a very long time, not only had he said that word, but that he had also meant it.

CHAPTER THIRTY-SEVEN
ZACAMIL

It is November 2, 1989, the traditional *Día de Los Muertos,* "Day of the Dead," and in every village and city in El Salvador and most others in Latin America, families are gathering at the graves of their loved ones with flowers and prayers. It is a time of remembrance, food, and singing. But also on this day there is once again a meeting in Zacamil, in the home the leader of some of the many groups involved in the fighting, and here there will be no songs. Today is a meeting to discuss important steps in in their struggle for justice, and it will also be the last time that some of these people will meet for many years, though at this meeting, they do not yet know that. What they do know is that *La Lucha,* "the struggle," is at an impasse. It is the belief of those gathered, that most of the people of El Salvador are in support of the revolution and the goals of democracy and economic equality, but they also believe that, as the army continues in losing battles, it will increase the use of savagery as a tool of war: more killings, more tortures, more massacres. There are those in the military and the oligarchy who believe that the slaughter is a necessity, that to rule over a destroyed country is better than not ruling at all. This dark prospect broods over the fighters and leaders in this room in Zacamil, and many argue that a new path forward needs to be chosen before the country itself is destroyed. And they have been encouraging a discussion on what that path should be.

There are eight people in the room, including now a third woman who has joined them from one of the fighting zones, and they represent all geographical *departamentos* in which the rebels have a strong presence. The one at the center of the table, the one they most often call "*Comandante*," though occasionally by another name, though that is also not his real name, has hardly spoken this evening. Tonight, they have been disputing goals, decisions, and procedures for resolving the conflict. Some say that the war has lasted too long, and the losses are too high. And now it must come to an end. Others say no, the revolution must continue and be won because their cause is just. "We are strong now," says one, "and have never been stronger, and the people are with us. We can take the cities with a nationwide final offensive, and the state will fall, and we will win, and justice will prevail."

The new woman, dressed in black, as though in mourning, and sitting next to the one they call *Comandante*, says, "Yes, but there are also now peace talks. And the enemy—the new Salvadoran government—is participating in them. And some of their US benefactors have voiced approval of some of our proposals and have forced the enemy to make at least one concession so far and they might make another." She is referring to the Salvadoran government's offer to allow the revolutionary FMLN combatants to enter civilian life after the war and run for office as a political party.

"This is madness," says the one who supported a new 'final' offensive. "We had peace talks in Mexico. We had peace talks in Honduras. And we have peace talks now in Costa Rica. But they are all a charade. They only continue with these 'talks' so that their stupid American friends will continue sending them money and weapons. What time have they ever kept a promise? What year, what day?"

"Listen to what she is saying," the Comandante finally says. "It is true that we could win a national attack, but it will be bloody, and the cities could lose many lives, and we could lose the moral imperative behind our cause."

"But the enemy has never had a 'moral imperative.' All they want is to spill our blood and the blood of our people. They will talk and talk while continuing to bomb our people and slaughter our children."

The woman says, "But it is true that for these last several days, they have stayed faithful to the truce that we have just signed. It does show that there is at least someone in the government who is standing by its word."

"How long has it stood?" asks the Comandante.

"About two weeks," she says.

"It is more like ten days," says the offense promoter. "And as soon as they can, they will return to massacres and slaughter and killing."

"Do we have evidence of breaches of the truce?"

"Yes, two weeks ago the national police raided the homes of members of FENASTRAS, the union federation. They captured and tortured many of them. And last week when they walked into an all-night music and fireworks vigil, they murdered seven people and walked away. They're not interested in peace. They are only interested in shedding blood."

"But right now," says the woman, "we do have a truce in our fighting forces, and we do have a commitment from the enemy to continue talks through next month." Her voice begins to rise. "That is surely something." She brings her hand down on the table with a defiant, angry sound.

As if timed by magic, a phone on a small table by the door rings. One of the men who has been standing near it answers. He speaks quietly into the receiver with a growl that all present could hear. There is a pause in the debate and the people turn to him. He nods and talks into the phone for some minutes. Eventually, he puts his hand over the receiver and addresses the group. "It is my colleague," he says. "There has been an incident." The room grows quiet. "One day ago."

The Comandante asks, "What kind of incident?"

"A bomb. Someone, or some people, hid a bomb—a big one, they are thinking a fifteen-pound bomb—in the offices of our supporters, FENASTRAS, the Trade Union Federation."

The Comandante's eyes close. He sits down at the table where most had been standing. "How many hurt?"

The man on the phone turns back for a moment and then looks up. "Not just hurt but died. Forty were hurt and eleven were killed. It is a great loss."

"Do they have evidence of who planted the weapon?"

"No, but some of the survivors testify to seeing military Jeeps—the black ones the US gives to the Army— parking in front of the offices earlier this week and taking pictures. And after the explosion, a witness saw a large lorry, large enough to carry several men and a bomb of this size, drive away."

"Do they have names for the dead?" The Comandante places his elbows on the table and clasps his hands.

"Yes, they have some. Radio *Venceremos* will be announcing a full list sometime tomorrow. There are some in the hospital who may not survive, so they want to wait."

"Do they know yet about Febe? Was Febe there? Was she harmed?" Febe Elizabeth Velásquez, the General Secretary of the Union, and a good friend of the Comandante, and who had been attacked and kidnapped by death squads two times before this.

The man on the phone asks about Febe. A moment later he turns to the others and says, "I'm sorry...but yes, she was there...and she was among those who died."

The Comandante takes a deep breath and closes his eyes.

"I am sorry, my Comandante. It is indeed awful news, and I am sorry to tell it to you."

The Comandante slams his fist down on the table with a loud explosive sound. He opens his eyes and looks around the room. He turns to the one who had argued for a final offensive and speaks in a slow whisper. "Miguel, we have been together in this struggle for many, many years, haven't we?"

"Yes, Comandante, we have."

"We have won many victories and won many hearts."

"Yes, we have."

"But with every success, with every battle won, the evil empire in the north gives the evil generals in our country even more money, more weapons, more tools."

"Yes."

"Anything. They will do anything and pay anything to support authoritarian regimes and keep our small country from becoming a democracy." The Comandante removes his glasses and rubs a sting of moisture from his eyes. "So, no matter how many hearts, how many victories, how many successes, we will never be able to win this struggle, we will never be able to overcome the military power that is facing us."

The woman beside him who had argued for peace talks speaks. "Yes, Manuel, it is probably true. We are better, smarter fighters, and we believe in a cause of justice, but they will always be better armed. We can never win. The Northern Empire will never let them lose and our people will continue to die."

"Unless..." The Comandante replaces his glasses and looks at the faces around the room. He points to the man who had argued for an all-out final offensive. "How long would it take you to send a word, and gather a response, to this massacre to our people in Cabañas, Morazán, San Miguel, and the others? And how soon can we speak to Santa Ana, San Vicente, and Cuscatlán?" His large hands are gripped tightly to the sides of the table. "How long before we can gather and raise up enough of our fighters, our people, for a grand and final act of justice and democracy, and—yes, *revenge*—to finally and suddenly end this murderous and evil regime?"

"We can do it soon," the man says. "Our fighters are ready. We have already discussed plans. In one week, we could quietly begin infiltrating the cities so that the army will not know that we are there until we fire on them. In ten days we could have thousands ready at every entrance and hundreds inside. We would have strength and surprise, and we could defeat them...if we decide to do this."

The Comandante smiles, but it is a bitter, vengeful smile. He looks at the wall beside the gathering, where there is hanging a tourist calendar of El Salvador with cartoon drawings of dancing coffee beans and ears of corn. "Call them all," he says. "Tell them that we have decided. Tell them what we need to do. Call, too, the people still at FENASTRAS, if indeed there are people still there. And then those at UNTS, and Radio *Venceremos,* and the other *Tendencias*. Give all this message."

He leans forward with his hands, palms down, on the table and looks at the others. "Inform them that we are now aware of the brutal, evil slaughter perpetrated by the enemy government of El Salvador and their US allies. We know that many people are hurt, and many have died and that one of them is our faithful colleague and comrade, Febe Elizabeth Velásquez. And tell them that with that act, the truce has been broken and that therefore the peace talks have ended. And that we will strike back." The woman who had spoken for restraint closes her eyes and looks down. "And tell them this—and I tell all of you—that we will end this war this month. We will gather such a force that the enemy and its ally have never seen before, for an offensive that before now, they could only have known in their nightmares. It will be a military offensive on all the cities of the nation at once. It will be a *Final* Offensive, and we will call it..." his voice rises in excitement, the "*Febe Elizabeth Velásquez Vive*," because in it she will in fact 'live.' She will be with us in this fight." He leans forward again, looking at all of them, smiling. "Comrades, brothers, sisters...today we commemorate the 'Day of the Dead,' but this year we will make it a day of 'death.' We will end the rule of tyranny and desecration of life in this country forever. We are going to war."

CHAPTER THIRTY-EIGHT
BUS

Early the next morning, minutes before four o'clock and a full hour before the sun would appear over the mountains in the distance, Beatriz and Alf pulled their car into the parking lot in front of the *Terminal de Oriente* near San Salvador center. Beatriz was driving and Alf was in the passenger seat, clutching the one bag that he had allowed himself to bring, and trying hard not to appear nervous. Beatriz was nervous too, but it was because she was not happy with anything about this trip. Too far, too long, too dangerous, and too few phones in the area in case he needed to get in touch with her. But Alf had been insistent. His argument was that he was the only one of the three who knew something about the area. David only knew what he'd read, and that kid from the Embassy was just stupid. That was true, she had admitted, but those points were good reasons for them not going at all, not for why he should go with them. "*No te preocupes,*" he had told her. They'd be fine. They'll be gone just three days, and it's only a few hours up north, and they would look up people whom Alf both knew and trusted. Also true, she thought, but that also still didn't mean they would be safe—or at least not as safe as Alf claimed they would be—but she dropped the argument. She knew it wouldn't do any good. Her husband could be the most wonderful, loving man she had ever known, but he was also one of the most stubborn. And if he had made up his mind to travel into a war zone accompanied only by David and Robbie, then no amount of logic or pleading or arguing from her would change it. And no amount of explaining from his side could make her believe she was wrong.

He leaned over and kissed her goodbye. "You take care of yourself," he said.

"Me?" she said, laughing without smiling. "*You* are the one who is going into one of the most dangerous zones on the planet."

He acted as though he hadn't heard her and started to get out of the seat, but before he could do it, she grabbed his shirt and pulled him in again, and gave him another kiss, longer this time, and on the lips. When she finally let him go, he spread the biggest smile he had across the front of his face. "Do you know how much I love you?" He asked. "And I will do nothing that would keep me from being able to love you for the rest of my life."

"I love you too, but don't do something stupid that would make that 'rest of your life' event happen sometime tomorrow afternoon. I don't want to have to miss a day of work just because I have to take a box of pictures of you over to the 'Victim Identification Office.'"

"I'll try to do the best I can," he said. "Survival is always at the very top of my job list." He closed the door, and she began backing the car out towards the exit, leaving him standing in the dim light, smiling, waving, and trying hard not to look as frightened as he felt. From behind him, he heard a voice in

English. "Good mornin', handsome. Wanna go for a ride?" He turned and saw David in front of a cab, waiving, and next to him was Sara. Alf pointed at her and said, "Hey man, I thought we said we wouldn't take on any extra luggage."

"Don't worry," said Sara. "I'm just the sendoff party. Go load your bags and leave us alone. We've got more goodbyes to say."

David gestured to the terminal office. "I already got our tickets. Just give me a few more minutes and I'll join you." Alf looked at them one last time and smiled. They looked good together. "Okay boss I got it. Any sign of that Embassy boy yet?"

"He got here just before you, he went inside to get some coffee and use the bathroom."

"I hope he doesn't do them in that order," Alf said walking towards the bus.

David turned to Sara and took her hands and held them tightly together. "Thank you for coming out here with me this morning," he said.

"I had to. I could not let you go without a real goodbye." She pulled her right hand out of his and lifted it to his face and touched his cheek. He felt a slight shiver when she did that. Her hand had a familiar warm scent to it that he recognized and liked.

"I wanted to come," she said. "And more than anything I wanted to thank you."

"Why?"

"Because, before we met, I was so hurt and lonely that I was afraid I would never be able to love again. And you helped me through that. And I thank you for that."

He took her hand from his cheek and kissed it. "And I was afraid of never *wanting* to love again. Love, to me, meant so much pain and guilt that I didn't want to ever put myself or anyone else through that again. I didn't think I *deserved* to love again."

"Maybe we were what each of us needed? Maybe we were good for each other?" She pulled his face down to hers and kissed him lightly on the cheek. "There. Once that meant that we were friends. But now it means that we are more than that."

He returned the kiss but on her lips. "Yes, and I want us to be 'more than that' for a very long time." He turned and glanced at the taxi next to them and saw the cabbie waiting impatiently inside. "But now I've got to go. I've got a father figure and a spoiled kid to take care of."

"I am going to worry about you," she said. "Yes, I know you are going to be careful. And you are going to do good for the people. But I am still going to worry about you because... because I really like you. I am in love with you."

He kissed her hand again and took a deep breath. "I am too," he said, "and let's talk more about that when I get home. And maybe make some plans. But for now, I need to be on the bus, and you need to get the boys up and make them some of your *huevos picados* for breakfast. I'll try to call when we settle in this evening. And I want you to throw me a big 'welcome home' party when I get back. I'm looking forward to it."

"I will. I promise."

They shared one last hug, and he turned towards the bus. Behind Sara, the cab driver beeped his horn. "*Bueno, novia,*" he yelled up at her with a sarcastic tone and pointed sternly at his meter which was still running.

The bus they were taking was one of several lined up in bays to be cleaned and refueled and boarded. It was bright yellow, with "Ruta 37" lit up on the front. The back had a door and two ladders going up to a luggage rack on top that ran the width and most of the length of the bus. It was overloaded with bags, boxes, plants, a carpenter's sawhorse, a wooden chair, and three small wire chicken coops, two with chickens and one without. About halfway up one of the ladders hung the driver, who looked too old for this task, whipping and pulling at a long rope trying to get it to cover a tarp over the luggage in front of him.

When David reached the back of the bus he yelled up at the driver. "*¡Buenos días mi amigo!*"

"*¡Buenos!*" the man said back, not looking down.

"*¿Puedo subir mi maleta al autobús?*" "May I put my bag on the bus?" He paused for a moment waiting to see if the man understood him. "*Para el viaje a Chalate*" "For the trip to Chalate."

The man, still not looking at David, wiped his hands on a cloth on his belt and stiffly stepped down from the ladder. Then, in a large gesture of frustration and weariness, he jerked open the door, lifted David's bag, and threw it into the bus. Then he slammed the door shut and climbed back up the ladder to finish roping the other bags. I guess this means no baggage check, thought David, and he went around to enter the side door.

When he got on, he saw Alf waving at him from the rear of the bus. "Back here," he shouted. "Any sign of Robbie out there?"

"Not that I saw, but I was storing my bag, so I wasn't looking for him."

A loudspeaker over the terminal entrance made a popping and rattling noise and then announced the upcoming departure: "*El autobús número 37 con destino a Chalatenango.*" The man loading luggage appeared at the door and stood next to the driver's seat and began counting the passengers and tickets for the trip.

"*¡Espera!*" David said to him. "*Tenemos un amigo más.*" "We have one more friend."

He stopped in the aisle and yelled down to Alf. "Think I should go back and look for him?"

"Not sure. We probably have a few more minutes."

The driver finished his counting, sat down in his seat, and turned on the ignition. The engine began a low rumble.

David turned around. "I'm going back."

But before he could get back to the front of the bus, Alf pointed at the side window and yelled, "*Look!*" In the distance Robbie was stumbling awkwardly through the side door of the terminal, one hand holding up his pants and the other balancing a tray of coffee and donuts. The driver cranked the door closed and put the bus in gear. David yelled to him, "*¡Espera! ¡Espera!*"

The driver waved his index finger back and forth signaling, "Not my problem." David grabbed the driver's shoulder and pointed out the front window. "*Otra persona, ¡Allí!*" pointing at Robbie stumbling towards them, but the driver continued backing up. David grabbed the handle for the door himself and cranked it back open while the bus continued moving. "Robbie," he yelled. "Hold your pants but drop the damn donuts and run. We're leaving." For a brief moment, Robbie looked down at his pants and his donuts trying to decide but then dropped the tray and started running. "You can make it," David called to him, "I've got the door."

Just as the bus approached the end of the parking lot, Robbie reached the door and David, standing in the opening, grabbed his shoulder and pulled him in. He had managed to get his pants up so that he could run faster, but he couldn't do that and fasten his belt at the same time, so both the belt and his shirttail waved behind him when he fell inside the doorway. "Oh, thank you. Gosh, thank you," he repeated, breathing heavily. "I don't know what would have happened if you hadn't gotten the door open for me."

David gave him a long laugh. "Well, you probably would have just gone back to bed and slept until the sun came up. And probably would have gained a much bigger chance of living a longer life."

David pushed him down the aisle towards the back where Alf was saving a seat for them. "Just a little black humor. But I was looking forward to the coffee."

"What?"

"Never mind, just kidding. Go on back. We'll all be fine... just thirsty."

CHAPTER THIRTY-NINE
REPORT

REPORT

REPORT OF COMMUNITY INTERVIEW:
EL BATALLÓN TIGRE
(English Translation by
Dr. Manuel Lopez-Levenson, Lic.)

Location, San José de Los Morros
From: El Capitán Matías López, special inves-
tigator in FMLN Terrorist Zones
To: Gen. Alfredo Benevides
Date: November 10, 1989.
Re: Report of Reconnaissance Mission in
<u>Chalatenango</u> <u>Department</u>, lower Guazapa
Valley.

Saludos, Gen. Benevides:
Following your receipt of our reports of
investigations on previous communities, we

have today brought to you an important development from a neighboring indigenous community, San José de Los Morros.

The community had been reported to us many
times for its support of terrorists and that
some of their men from the town have left to
join the fighting in the mountains.

In addition, it had been recently reported to
us that the terrorist, Subcomandante
Hernández y Pérez, had come from this community and we uncovered an indigenous woman who
also has that same surname. We interrogated
her following strict rules of the government's "Normas del Ejército." But we were
unable to get actionable information
from her.

We introduced to her the importance of our
investigation as formally and fairly as we
could, but she resisted our questions. So, we
persisted.

After some talking, she did admit that her
son (of the same surname) had left the
village some years earlier to go into the
mountains and fight against our homeland, but
she denied (without evidence) that he was the
Subcomandante. It was our conclusion that she
was lying.

Her report was that she did not know anything

about her son, that he had been away for many
years, and that she has had only small meetings with him since. It is our conclusion
that that was impossible, so we demanded many
times without doing harm to her that she tell
us about her son and the Subcomandante, whom
we judge to be the same. She continued to
resist.

She continued that she did not know where the
son was and reported only that she
missed him.

After much time spent in this line of questioning, while treating her fairly and
legally, and doing her no harm, our men voted
that, due to the time constraints and seri-
ousness of our call, we had no choice but to
force her to confess to us. We demanded again
that she tell us where is her son, and she
again refused the official, legal, government
command that she comply. The investigating
men then had her take off her dress.

Then to help her, they also helped her take
off a cloth constraining her breasts that
she used as a brassiere. One of our men,
acting as our official government representative, came forward to her and asked her once
again, without anger, to tell us where he
was and how we might find him, but once
again she violated the law and the constitution and refused to cooperate with the offi-

cial government representative. She said
nothing.

Another of our men, one who is more experienced concerning combatants, then lifted her
left breast in his hand and asked again about
her son. And she again denied having recent
knowledge of him. Another took his machete,
and while reminding her of her silence and
the governmental
legality of our inquiry, brought it down over
her breast and cut through the flesh. It
bled, and then she fell to her knees. But it
is the conclusion of our men that her
response was deliberately larger than necessary and intended to move us emotionally to
stop the interrogation. While in this condition, we asked her once again.

But again, she disobeyed our request and
would not confess. So, once again, our man
brought the machete down on her second
breast. This time she screamed more loudly
than before and fell onto her side. She lay
there making loud noises for a large amount
of time, but eventually she stopped. And she
also stopped moving. And breathing.

Our conclusion about this investigation is
not yet final. It is, however, our opinion
that it was the mother's decision to lie and
to protect a lawbreaker, not ours to take her
life. Her death was not forced upon her. She

did know the location of her son in the mountains, but she was practiced at lying and was
in fact a sympathizer for the lawless terrorists and was protecting them and him.

However, it is now impossible for us to
continue the investigation with her to establish this with complete certitude.

It is nonetheless our conclusion that we
dealt with the person with high respect for
her gender and her class (indigenous) and the
rule of law. In anticipation of your agreement, we respectfully submit this report.

Respectfully presented,

El Capitán Antonio Matías López

El Capitán Antonio Matías López

CHAPTER FORTY
EL CAMPO

The route from the Terminal to the edge of San Salvador and then up to Chalatenango was straight and direct, and David had taken a portion of it many times going home to Colonia Zacamil. Left, out of the station, then north for about five miles. Normally he would get off there and walk the extra blocks to his apartment or take a second bus if he was tired. But today they would go straight through the city out to the countryside and then another hundred miles up to Lake Suchitoto and finally to their first stop, Los Morros.

They passed scores of familiar shops and small businesses, many closed with sheet metal over their windows and concrete walls covered with graffiti, scared and abandoned from the stresses of poverty and war. Some now populated by birds, animals or homeless citizens who were too poor even to leave the country. Lining the streets were broken sidewalks, painted trees, and dozens of small carts selling all manner of clothing and other—sometimes stolen—consumer items. Food stands with bread, fruit, sodas, and spits of smoking meat, watched over by women with weathered faces staring at the heat and turning a pig or a chicken, and cutting off servings for sandwiches to sell to passersby.

They passed the *Guardia Nacional* compound, a major center for education, training, and troop deployment throughout the country. From the compound, and others like it, came an abundance of patriotism and war, valor and killing. It was the largest and most pervasive sector of the country. And with seemingly limitless funding from the US, it also had become the wealthiest. Past the compound, the bus finally entered the neighborhood of Zacamil, the area that David knew best. Though they were blocks away from Los Cañones, he still looked hard into the city horizon from his window and imagined, with some difficulty, that he was able to see a few of its television antennas and Sara's apartment on a fourth floor. She was somewhere out there, he thought, making breakfast, getting the boys ready for school, and probably wondering if she would ever see David again. And to himself, and no one else, he wondered the same thing about her.

When at last they left the city limits of San Salvador, they quickly entered the smaller city of Apopa, where Dr. Morales had the clinic that David had visited just a few weeks earlier, a clinic that served mainly war victims and fighters. To David, it had felt like a sacred place of pain and faithfulness, darkness and dedication, and he realized that it had been one of the early motivators of his desire to journey north to the war zone. It was led by good people who worked tirelessly to treat and heal, and sometimes bury, others who had been brought in to them. If he had been traveling alone that morning, he would have considered getting off the bus for one last visit, but he knew that even if he could, they would probably be just as busy today as before. Instead, the bus simply stopped briefly to take on and let off passengers and then move on. Several local laborers, farm workers, household cooks, and construction workers got off, but no one got on.

Then, finally leaving Apopa, and the last scenes of the city, they entered the countryside of rural El Salvador. Immediately the immensity of air and fields and grass surrounded them and a light from an emerging sun poured over them. It spilled color and brilliance everywhere, over millet fields on the right and maize on the left and away from the dense smells and stains of the city. It was the wild and beautiful expanse of the *campo* that he had seen far too seldom since moving here. It was breathtaking and David struggled to take it all in. Behind and to their left, he could still see the beautiful but ominous peak of Quezaltepeque Volcano that had attracted and destroyed countless humans, animals, and plant life for thousands of years. And in front was the wide and ravaged face of Guazapa, also beautiful and also once a live volcano, but now too worn and aged to be of danger. He took in a deep and grateful breath. It felt good and he wished that he had decided to do this much earlier. And now that it was becoming more likely that he would be staying longer in El Salvador—perhaps forever—he made a vow to himself to come back to the mountains and rural countryside again, perhaps next time as a family.

He fell back into his seat, exhausted. It was still only about six-thirty. He'd had little sleep the night before and they had at least two, maybe three hours to go on the journey. He began to relax into the seat. In these last few weeks he had, for the first time, felt the beginnings of something that resembled peace residing within him. And today he was off on a great adventure with his best friend and a well-intentioned young volunteer, and, despite the dangers, it would be something to remember forever. Perhaps more importantly, back in the city, there was also a wonderful woman and her dear sweet boys who all seemed to love him, and he was feeling the same about them.

He thought excitedly about getting back to Sara and talking more about the possibilities of creating a new life for all of them. He also had a very interesting job that did good in the world and paid a middle-class salary by Salvadoran standards.

He had pleasant thoughts of moving in with them and sharing expenses, making life even easier for both of them—in more ways than one. The thought made him smile. And he felt good. And he was happy. And he fell asleep.

CHAPTER FORTY-ONE

CHECK POINTS

First there was gunfire, then shouts, then loud banging on the sides of the bus. David woke up, startled. He looked out the window and saw a long line of young Salvadoran army soldiers standing stiffly, propping their rifles up straight on their left hips in a way that forced them to lean awkwardly to their left. The driver cranked open the door, and two soldiers came in and began shouting at the passengers. One of them raised his pistol and waved it menacingly as he shouted his orders. "*Todos deben bajar del autobús, ¡Ahora!*" he said. "Everyone must get off the bus. Now!" "*Empezando por los hombres.*" "Beginning with the men."

David looked around, thinking that something bad had happened, but the other passengers were calm, gathering their things and moving quietly to the front, beginning with the men. He saw Alf calmly reach into his pocket and remove a small leather bag that was roughly shaped like a pistol. He slid it discretely into the space between his seat and the window. Then he reached over the aisle and tapped Robbie on his arm, waking him, and gesturing with his chin that they should follow the others to the door. "Oh...sure...right," he said. He started looking around his seat. "Do I need anything?"

"Do you have your passport?" Alf asked. "They want to search the bus, and they'll ask for some ID."

"Okay," said Robbie, and anxiously pulled it out of his suitcase and stood up. David carried his passport in a small traveler's packet looped around his neck and down his shirt. As he waited for Robbie to start down the aisle, he self- consciously tapped his chest to see if it was still there. It was. He wondered if perhaps he should have put the new USAID ID that Doug Grantham had given him into the packet too, but it was too late to worry about that now. He stood up and got in line with the rest.

Within minutes, all the passengers had been led off the bus and were lined up by gender outside. They stood quietly with a look of ordinariness that seemed to David to be surreal. Two of the soldiers, carrying surplus US M16 A1 rifles, stood by the door, ushering passengers. Men were ordered to face the side of the bus, with their hands against the glass. Women were placed further away facing outward. The small division leader, a *Teniente,* who was older than the others and in control of the operation, walked with a formal kick in his steps down the line of passengers demanding to see what proof each of them had for being on this trip. Some had work visas, some ID cards, and one had a simple picture of his family at home and the address of the *Propietario de la plantación* in Chalate where he would be working. The Teniente took it and looked at it suspiciously for several seconds but then let him go. When it came to his turn, David reached inside his shirt and took out the bag and passport and gave it to the soldier. He opened it and then looked up at David and said in English, "Purpose?"

David was startled to hear the question in English but said

back to him in Spanish that he worked for a university doing economic development research.

The soldier turned through the pages of the passport. "Which?"

"Universidad de El Salvador."

He studied David's face for several seconds and then handed back the passport. "*Universidad del Socialismo,*" he said, with a smile, more to himself than to David, and moved to the next in line. David didn't respond but carefully put his passport back into his shirt.

Next to him was a young man in his early twenties who looked as though he had been drinking, which struck David as odd, since it was still morning. He waved and stumbled and laughed frequently as the group was being forced into lines. When he was asked for his papers, he smiled agreeably but said that he'd forgotten and left them on the bus. The Teniente demanded to know why he had done such a thing if, in fact, he was not a spy or confidante of the terrorists. The young man laughed and swung and pointed up at the window saying that he'd even forgotten where they were in his bags. Without speaking, the Teniente took his rifle and shoved the butt end of it into the young man's back causing him to smash his face into the side of the bus hitting the glass. "*Lo siento,*" the young man said. "I'm sorry." But before he could finish, the second soldier kicked at the back of his knees, forcing him to fall backward onto the pavement, his head landing sharply on the asphalt with a loud clap. David started to lean down to help him, but another soldier yelled, "*¡No te muevas!*" "Don't Move!" and pushed him back. The man on the concrete appeared unconscious and blood gathered around his head. The soldier who hit him looked up at the Teniente, smiling. "*Es joven.*" "He is young," he said and asked the Teniente if they could take him as a recruit.

The Teniente was by that time studying the papers of the next man in line who was even younger but sober. He looked up from the papers and down at the bleeding, unconscious body on the ground and said, "*No, él es un borracho y un cobarde,*" "He is a drunk and a coward." "*Querrá servir a su madre más que a su país.*" "And he will want to serve his mother more than his country." The soldiers took the young man's arms and began to drag him towards the bus, but the Teniente stopped him and said, "*¡Para! Déjenlo morir. Les enseñará a los otros una lección.*" "Let him die here. It will teach the others a lesson." Then he turned back to the papers in his hand and the next young man who was standing before him. The Teniente looked at this one coldly and asked him how old he was, where he lived, and where he was now going. He replied that he was seventeen, he lived in Soyapango, a colonia in northern San Salvador, and that he was going north to La Palma, in Chalate, where there was a newly established coffee plantation looking for workers. The Teniente asked if he had a job already, and the young man replied that he did not.

The Teniente turned to his assisting soldiers and said, "*Conozca a nuestro más reciente recluta. Llévalo al campo.*" "Meet our newest recruit. Take him into the camp."

The "recruit" began to scream, "*¡No, no! No puedo ir. Tengo una familia. Tengo una madre.*" "No, no, I can't go. I have a family. I have a mother."

The Teniente had by then already moved on and was asking the next in line for his credentials. But he looked back with a bored look and said, "*Puedes escribirle una carta.*" "So, write her a letter." "*Estará muy orgullosa de tu patriotismo.*" "She will be proud of your patriotism." The soldiers took the young man away and the Teniente returned to reviewing the next person's identification.

When he had finished with the last man in the line, he

waved to the other soldiers, and they began allowing the passengers to return to the bus. When David and Robbie were about to enter, he looked at them with an angry smile, *Hola Gringos,* he said. "*¡Bienvenidos a El Salvador!*" Welcome to El Salvador."

CHAPTER FORTY-TWO

BABY

The whole village of San José de Los Morros is hiding. Some are hiding under beds in houses, some are under pews in the church. And some are gathered in small groups along an enclosed ravine behind a stand of trees in dense foliage, more than three hundred yards from the village. They are hopefully so far from the paths, hills, and troops who are still in the village, that they will be safe. Relatively safe. Several families are there, parents hiding with their children. A father has a hat that is too white, so he takes it off and buries it in the leaves. A young boy is holding a stick as though it is a rifle and stares with it out into the darkness. His father tells him to lay it down because it could be seen at a distance. A mother and baby are with them, and the baby is crying, and she is soothing it to make it stop. She cradles it and speaks to it, but it cries. She comforts it, but still it cries. Army troops, crisscrossing the forest surrounding Los Morros, are drawing nearer. They are tossing stones into the thick bushes and then pausing to listen for sounds of people who might be hiding there and get hit by one. The baby continues to cry. Its mother holds it and rocks it and rubs it gently, but it cries. The others look at her, their eyes wide with fear. They will all die if they are discovered. She rocks the baby and hums softly to it, but it has been terrified by the sounds of bombs and shots and explosions, and it cries. The mother looks around at the others. Sometimes quietly, sometimes loudly, the baby still cries. The mother's eyes are filled with despair. If they are captured, it will be death. For all of them.

They hear the sounds of men drawing closer, searching in the bushes, and waving the butts of their rifles in the branches above their heads, and the baby cries. The dark colors and shapes of some of the soldiers become visible at the edges of their ravine and they can see them. One of them looks in their direction and tilts his head listening. The mother holds the baby. The soldier motions to the others and points in their direction. The baby makes a faint cry again. The men stop and listen. The mother holds her baby up next to her breast and closes her eyes. She wraps her arms tightly around it and puts her hand over its mouth, and holds it there, silently, for seconds, ten, then twenty, then thirty. One of the soldiers yells into the trees. "*¿Estás ahí?*" "Are you there?" He pauses and looks in their direction "*¿Te escondes?*" "Are you hiding?" The baby jerks and twists and pushes at her arms. One of the soldiers throws a stone into the dense brush and listens for a response, but under the mother's hands, the baby is silent. Forty, fifty, sixty seconds she holds it and holds it while the soldiers discuss if they should stay or go. She wraps her arms more tightly around the baby and its mouth as it struggles, sixty seconds, seventy, eighty, until finally she feels it slowing, and loosening, then stopping. The soldiers shake their heads and wave back at their leader. "*No es nada,*" they say, "It is nothing." "*Sigamos Adelante,*" "let's move on." They look hard into the thick brush and then turn to rejoin the detachment.

The mother opens her eyes and looks down at her lap, stricken with unimaginable horror, her eyes burn hollow in shame and grief. They all are safe. She has saved them. The soldiers did not hear the baby and have now gone on. Their group will survive. And the mother is crying, and crying, and crying.

CHAPTER FORTY-THREE

ARRIVAL

David was troubled by the incident at the checkpoint but tried to hold it in. In truth, all three of them were agitated, but Robbie showed it the most. He was breathing rapidly and heavily and rubbing his chest. He reached down in his bag and pulled out an inhaler and pumped it with his thumb to spray it into his mouth. *My God*, thought David, *he has asthma.*

David leaned back in his seat and tried to relax. The next official stop was Aguilares, the unofficial entrance into the rebel-held zone. By his estimate, it was only a few more minutes ahead, so not enough time to try to get back to sleep again. Across the aisle, Alf was in an intense conversation with Robbie, evidently trying to reassure him. After a moment, he looked up at David. "And how are you doing over there, big guy?"

"A little shaken, but not bad. Just hope we don't see many more of those again."

"*En realidad,*" "Actually," he said, pointing up through the front window, "I think we have another one coming up in just a few minutes."

As he spoke, the bus began to slow and pull to the right of the road. In front and to the side were a number of young men waving rifles and yelling at the driver to stop. *Here we go again*, thought David, but this time it was the guerrillas. The driver stopped the bus and turned the crank for the door, but unlike the previous stop, only one person came on board, and no one was ordered out. Instead, a small man in a green shirt and camouflage pants got on and he greeted the driver as though they knew each other. They spoke for a moment and then the driver opened the glove box and handed him the bundle of tickets he'd put there. Together they counted the tickets and then turned and counted the passengers. When they had finished, the man turned to the passengers and said, "*Buenos días a todos*," he said to them. "Good morning to all of you." Well, that's different, thought David. "*Siento retrasar su viaje*," the man said again, "Sorry to delay your trip." "*Que tengan un buen día*." "You have a good day." He stepped back off the bus, the door closed, and they were again on their way. David looked over at Alf who was grinning broadly. "So, that's the way the guerrillas do it? I didn't expect that."

"I am not an expert," said Alf, "but I would say that it is because the army is trying to find enemies and the rebels are trying to find friends."

For the next hour, the trip was much less eventful. They stopped briefly as they approached Aguilares to let off and take on a few passengers, and again as they left it on the other side of the town, and then a third time at the bridge that crossed the Rio Lempa, the southern border of Chalatenango. There they were forced to wait for nearly half an hour as a herd of sheep crossed over the highway, coming from the other side of the river. The bridge was long, narrow, and metal, not wide enough for both sheep and a bus.

"Look at that," said Alf, pointing out of the window. "Pelibuey."

"What's that?"

"It's a type of sheep. They are originally in Trinidad and the Bahamas, but recently they were introduced up here in Chalate because they are cheap, easy to raise, and very fertile. Add it to our list. They were sent here by one of those religious development organizations you'll talk to. I think Mennonites or someone."

"I'll do that." David stood up to assess the number of sheep in front of them but then saw, out the side window, the view of the river in the distance. A golden sun was rising in the distance, blocked by black streaks of morning clouds still clinging to the water below. "I'm going out for a second," he said.

"*Seguro,*" said Alf. "We have a few minutes."

He got off the bus and walked to the edge of the bridge and stood there for a long moment by himself looking and not speaking. The sun had just begun to show itself through the clouds in the distance, causing the water below to ripple with rows of red and gold. Long, thin blue herons, barely spots in the distance, circled the colors. Some silently dipping into the waters searching for a meal.

Along the shores of the river, were several women standing in the water, some were doing their laundry, and some were bathing. Further up the banks, a smaller group of young men in khaki rebel uniforms sat and ate breakfast...and occasionally watched the women.

What am I doing here, he thought, looking at the sun and the morning, both rising together. But he was laughing when he thought it because he knew exactly why he was there and had not been so certain of anything in many months, maybe years. "And I'm glad I'm here," he added out loud. "*This* is the bridge. El Salvador has been the bridge for me all along, and I'm finally seeing it. I'm finally crossing it. I think I'm going to make it." He felt frightened and exhilarated at the same time.

When the last sheep had passed, the bus driver opened the door and waved at David, then stepped back in. Slowly, deliberately, David went back to the door and got in. It moved slowly forward across the bridge and then up the northern shore of Lake Suchitoto, looking down at it from a high ridge. The lake was deep blue and shining in the sunlight. Rich green forests surrounded it, announcing life and freedom. Watching it pass, David thought that if someone could visit just this one place in all of El Salvador, they would never believe that this scene of peace and beauty was in a country so stricken with blood and war.

"Not much further," said Alf, pointing out the window. "In just a few minutes we'll be passing through San José de Los Morros which is that first village on our list. Héctor said he'd called ahead for us to meet the new mayor in town when we get there and she would take us around and show us the town.

"A lady mayor," Robbie said. "That's got to be a first."

Barely five minutes had passed, and the bus began to slow again. This time, however, the driver did not stop decisively to pull into a market or check point. Instead, he simply began to drive more and more slowly, past a high wall that separated the village from the highway, and a large arch at its entrance.

"What's going on?" Robbie asked.

Alf was on his feet and looking out the front window. "I don't know. Looks like something has happened and the driver doesn't want to go through the entrance."

By that time, many others were also concerned and were talking to one another about what might be wrong. The driver peered out the front window for some time and then turned to the passengers. "*Lo siento,*" he said. "I'm sorry." He shook his head and then looked back at the wall and the gate into the town. "*No sé qué ha pasado, pero...no hay nadie aquí.*" "I don't know what has happened but...there's nobody here." He pointed at an empty parking area, empty food carts, and the wall. "*Nadie,*" he said, shaking his head. "Nobody."

At that, several passengers rose from their seats and moved towards the door. Some were curious, but others who lived in Los Morros seemed frightened. The driver opened it, and they pushed through, stumbling and falling off the step in their eagerness to get out. When David, Alf, and Robbie managed to get off they saw the driver and others standing silently looking through the tall open entrance into the village. They were talking among themselves, but it was unclear what they were saying. Alf ran first to join them and then stopped suddenly at the gate, looking at a long rough-stone road that sloped down through a string of small adobe block homes, ending with a tall white church at its end. When David joined them at the entrance, he heard Alf say quietly to himself, "*Dios mío*"

CHAPTER FORTY-FOUR
LOS MORROS

They both stood there for several minutes not speaking. David tried, but he couldn't. They heard Robbie's voice coming behind them. "Hey guys, wait up." Neither responded, and seconds later Robbie's face appeared next to them. "Sorry, I thought I'd lost you guys." Then he followed their gaze down into the village and he let out a long whistle. "What happened here?"

"I think you know what happened," Alf said, not taking his eyes off the scene below. The town below them was in ruins. Walls, buildings, and houses were collapsed, roofs missing, and smoke rising from many of those still standing. A few yards before them was a crater several feet deep in the middle of the street. There were no humans visible, but there were two horses, one standing by the crater and the other probably dead, laying sprawled on its side at the edge of the street, a large tear in its stomach and surrounded by a dark pool of dried blood.

By then, several of the other passengers had begun stepping through the entrance and were walking cautiously and fearfully down into the ghostly village. Alf, David, and Robbie joined them. They walked in silence, unable to speak, looking intently at the devastation and trying to comprehend what they were seeing.

The street was paved with flat irregular stones with patches of green showing through the spaces between them. On either side were rows of modest adobe houses, most damaged or burned with roofs missing and clay walls scattered in pieces. None seemed to be on fire at present, but some still had smoke rising from them. Some looked as though they had been bombed, but others were untouched. "I don't understand," said David. "Was this from planes overhead? Or grenades thrown into the houses? This doesn't look like gunfire."

"I'm guessing grenades, but there's no reason why it couldn't have been both. That would explain why some houses look damaged and others are gone altogether." Alf pointed to an empty space between two houses, now filled with layers of mud and bricks. "What you would call 'aerial bombardment' usually means around here pushing barrel bombs out of helicopters, not dropping old fashioned bombs out of a B-17, like in World War II."

"What's a barrel bomb?"

"Just what it sounds like. They get a barrel and fill it full of gasoline and chunks of steel, like nails or metal shavings. Then just throw it out of a helicopter. Sometimes they shoot at it, but usually it just blows up on its own and kills everything in sight. It can sometimes take out two homes at once like these unless you're flying at an extremely low level."

The street was littered with bricks, mud, clothes, glass, and broken branches. But other than the two horses at the entrance, there was no other sign of life, dead or alive, anywhere. If there had been bodies from the destruction, their families and companions had probably taken them. It was eerie in its silence and emptiness. The other passengers spoke to one another in quiet, hesitant voices. One of them recognized one of the shattered houses, and rushed into it, calling out names. Then after a brief pause, they heard a loud shriek of horror coming from inside. As the group grew closer to the church at the center of the village, they heard muffled voices coming from inside it. The church had also been hit and much of the left side and all of its large front doors were missing, and a mound of bricks and broken glass lay in their place. Robbie's eyes began to tear. "This is awful," he said. "Awful." David and Alf reached the opening first and stood looking through the jagged wall into the sanctuary and were startled to see what resembled a military field hospital. Many of the pews had been pushed to one side and in their place were bed cots, floor mats, stretchers, and a number of hammocks hanging from beams in the corners. Each held people in various levels of pain and consciousness, some looking like they were there for recovery, others appeared to have died. Three young women, were moving quietly about in the room, caring for those on the beds.

Soon, a handful of the other passengers, apparently those who lived in Los Morros and were on the bus coming home from work in the city, began pouring through the opening. When they realized what was inside, they rushed over the rubble and began excitedly searching the cots and beds for faces they might recognize.

At the front of the church stood a woman with long black hair, wearing a black coat and carrying a black folder in her hand. She seemed to be in charge. When the newcomers began stumbling into the room looking through the beds, she raised her hand and told them to stay back and enter more slowly. This was a hospital now, she told them, and they needed to be careful and respectful. Each of the wounded who had been identified had a white tag tied to their arm or leg. She said that if the searchers found a loved one, they should greet them, let one of the attendants know, and then go back outside to wait. There was nothing more that they could do for them right now.

Most of the searchers slowed their rush into the sanctuary but still moved nervously from patient to patient looking for faces that were familiar. One screamed in relief at finding a family member or friend and gave them a thankful—but gentle—embrace. Others, after several minutes of searching in every cot and bed but failing to find the ones they were seeking, went to the woman to ask for more information. She said she would try to be helpful, but that they didn't have a complete list of all the survivors. She opened her notebook and took out two sheets of paper with handwritten names on them. One was a list of all the people who they knew had been wounded and who had been brought to the church. The other was a list of those they knew—so far—who had not survived. She said that neither list was complete, but it was the best that they could do so soon after the attack. Some were still out in the woods hiding, she told them, and hadn't yet returned. Others had been so damaged in the bombings that they could not be recognized. She handed the lists to the eager searchers who anxiously looked through them. Seconds later, one of them smiled and pointed to a name he recognized on the survivors' list and the woman led him to a second room behind the sacristy where others were being treated for more serious wounds. The rest continued poring over the names, again and again, looking for a wife or parent or child or friend. Even after searching the list two, three, and four times, some of them, often in tears, would not give up trying one more time.

David, Alf, and Robbie stood silently in the back of the church, watching the scene of sorrow in front of them. "What a homecoming," said Alf at last. "I never want to have to go through that with Beatriz."

"Me neither," said Robbie.

While those at the front were looking intently at the lists, the woman who was helping them looked up at David, Robbie, and Alf standing at the hole in the back of the church. She cupped her hands around her mouth and yelled, "*¿Doctor Patterson? ¿Es usted el Doctor Patterson?*" David was startled, but yelled back, "*Sí.*"

"*Un momento, por favor.*" She went back into the sacristy again. When she returned, she was accompanied by a large older man with long gray hair, wearing a ragged black shirt torn open at the neck. It looked like a priest's shirt with no collar. She pointed up at the three of them at the back of the church. He put his hand over his eyes to see them more clearly with the sun behind them, then called out to them, "*¡vengan, vengan, bajen al coro!*" "Come down to the chancel."

They made their way down through the sea of beds and patients. David realized, as they got closer to the patients, that this room was mainly for those who had wounds still waiting to be addressed. People who had already been treated were somewhere else—probably in that back room—and were now just waiting. The people around them in the sanctuary were often just feeding or comforting them. It would be a long time before many of them would be able to go home—and there probably wouldn't be much to return to when they could.

When the three of them reached the front of the sanctuary, the woman greeted them in slow, halting English. She said, "We are glad you here. I am Rosalina Estrada. I am *Alcalde.*" She stopped for a moment searching for a word. "I am mayor—of town, Los Morros." She put out her hand to shake David's. He shook it and she gave him a strong, forceful grip. "And this, my friend...Father Raul. He...good English."

"Just 'Raul,'" The man said, extending his own hand. "Too many people dead here for titles."

"Okay, Raul," said David. "I don't know what to say. This is such an awful, horrible time."

Alf put out his hand. "You evidently already know who Dr. Patterson is. We are both from the University in San Salvador. I teach there and this is Robert..."

"I'm Robert Sweeney," said Robbie, also reaching out his hand. "And I am representing the United States Embassy. And I am authorized to help you in any way that we can."

Raul stared at him, not smiling.

"I'm sorry," said Robbie. "That's what I'm supposed to say when I meet someone."

"I let you know when I need a visa." He turned back at the others, all wondering how to proceed. "This is not a good time to talk."

"I know that, and I am sorry," said David. "Listen, we can go away, or stay and help, or do whatever else you think is best. We had no idea that this had happened."

"No one does. The government does not send out announcement cards."

"I am priest here and also in Los Flores. Señor Héctor said you will visit there tomorrow. I came to Los Morros when I heard of the attack. They called me to come anoint the wounded and administer last rites, but when I arrived and saw what had happened, I took off my robe and now help wrap cloths on wounds."

"Is there anything we can do?"

He gestured out to the cots before him. "Do any of you have medical training? Are you young and strong enough to dig out homes and rebuild walls?"

David and Alf looked at each other and shook their heads

but Robbie burst out, "I can! I used to do construction work in high school with my father. We built houses. I can help."

"Good. We have heard the recent terrible news in the city and know you will probably want to return home soon, but if one of you is able to stay for even a short time, I am certain that there are ways you can help. Today many who hid on the mountain will be returning home. And many of them will maybe be needing help digging out walls of their houses."

"Raul," David said, "I'm uncomfortable even being here at all, in the middle of all this slaughter. We can just leave now if you need to get back to your people. I think a lot of what we would do here would be just getting in the way."

"Yes, we need to work, but it is also good for us for you to learn of the army's murders and then go back and tell your people of our village."

David took a deep breath. He had received this same request from Sra. Martínez and had no idea if it would do any good. "Certainly," he said. "We'll do whatever we can."

"We need to speak to you quickly, but not here. These need to rest." He nodded at the rows or wounded people in the sanctuary. "Come with us. We have office for conversation." Rosalina opened the door by the chancel, which led through the small sacristy and into a large function room that was filled with a smaller number of patients. In this room, a handful of people were actively dressing critical wounds and cutting into bodies. There were occasional gasps and screams and the air smelled of disinfectant and blood. Just inside the door, on a simple, brown, metal folding chair, sitting against the wall, were portions of a person's leg and an arm. The first was cut just above the knee, red with blood but no longer bleeding, and the other just below the elbow. Robbie was the first to see them and he choked. "Holy Mary, Mother of God…"

Rosalina pushed open a door on the side of the room and

waved David and the others into it. "Come," she said, "Here we talk."

It was a small room, with a desk, bookcase, and four metal folding chairs. It was enough for only four of the five of them to sit. Rosalina stood behind the chair at the desk, looking clearly in control, even though she understood only portions of what was being said. Connected to the side of the bookshelf was a wooden table holding a small metal box with an engraved cross on its top. David wondered if it was a traveling eucharist set for this pastor of many parishes. The priest saw him looking at it and said, "This day I use mainly the oil, not for Eucharist, but for anointing the dead."

"*¡Siéntese!*" "Sit!" said Rosalina, waving at the chairs. "We talk now."

David pulled out one of the metal chairs and sat in it. It wobbled under his weight. One of the rubber caps on the end of a leg was missing. "I guess, first, thank you Rosalina and Father for talking with us at all in the middle of..."

"Raul!" he said.

"Sorry. *Raul.*"

"What was it that you needed from us?"

"Well, it's probably irrelevant now, but I study local economic development programs, and we came because we had heard that communities like Los Morros and Los Flores and others are—or were—wonderful examples to look at. Your self-governance, sharing, equality and self-reliance...and all with very little help from the government."

"With *no* help from government," Raul said with a growl. "They never help any of our villages until we agree to let the military rule our people. They do not want our democracy. They do not like any democracy. That is why your US government supports them. And, yes, until two days ago, I would have said, yes, Los Morros is good example of the self- governance and equality." He began counting on his fingers. "We have better food, better education, better equality, and better health than in any time in history. And they did it with democratic voting, sharing food, small donations, and good leaders." He looked up at Rosalina over his shoulder and pointed at her with his thumb. "This is a smart woman. Good leader and good example for our young women and totally accepted by the men as their leader." She turned her head and looked embarrassed but didn't speak.

"I think they are probably lucky to have both of you here," said Alf.

"Thank you, but today it is maybe all lost."

David shook his head. "I'm sorry. I hope you are wrong."

"This morning, I anointed forty wounded people. Yesterday I did Mass for forty dead. *Forty*, all at one time. Our little cemetery is not large enough for the numbers that your American gifts have killed. We bury some in fields just beyond the cemetery because we have no more room here." He paused to make sure that they had heard him. "The government of this country wants to make sure that the wealthy live like kings, and the poor live like dogs. The majority of our country lives in areas with no electricity or clean water. We go without water, and the wealthy use it to wash their cars. And when we protest this, they shoot us, or they 'disappear' us. Do you know of this?"

"Yes," said David and Alf.

"No," said Robbie. "I thought they just beat people up." Raul gave him a disapproving look. "Do you think that, because we had an election recently, with red, white, and blue banners and a handsome young man with a nice smile and clean shirt became president, that we are a democracy? I pastor five *aldeas* in Chalate, and not one of them has a voting booth in it. Not one. And only three have mail."

"How do you vote?" asked Robbie.

"Much of the time we cannot. Our ballots arrive here almost always late. Then when we mail our votes back to the city, it takes a week for them to arrive, and then we are told that they arrived too late. And by then another member of the ruling oligarchy has already won. And if we complain about this 'democracy' then they call us communists or socialists, and raid through our towns and kill us. This is not the first *aldea* to be destroyed, and it will not be the last."

"I'm so sorry," said David.

Raul studied their faces, frowning. "In our Bible, there are *six* stories of Jesus feeding the poor and homeless. And *no* stories of his killing disciples to make them loyal. He told parables praising hated foreigners who did good deeds. He talked to women who were shunned by the authorities. He taught poor people, he healed them, and he criticized his government who did nothing to help them. So, do you know what his government did to him?"

No one spoke because all of them knew where this was going.

"They killed him," his voice rising. "Their *Guardia Nacional* caught him, beat him, and murdered him, and would have thrown his body in a trash yard until someone offered a cave to put him in." He glared at them. "So, can you see why the people in El Salvador want to follow *that* Jesus and not the plastic, white, pretty one on the walls of the office buildings back in the capital?"

Rosalina, standing behind him, touched him lightly on his shoulder. "Raul..." she said softly.

"I am sorry," he said, lowering his voice. "Our town has been destroyed, and I am very angry. I pray to God today to control my anger, but it is hard."

There was a long silence, and then David said, "We are so

sorry. Really. We have no way of understanding—I mean *really* understanding—what all of you are going through. This little village is lucky to have you with them right now."

"Padre Raul is best *líder espiritual*," said Rosalina.

Raul reached up and patted Rosalina's hand that was still on his shoulder. "We help each other," he said. She smiled. "We are not first town for this," she said, "or second town. We are many towns they kill. They kill many towns in *el campo*."

Raul, still holding her hand, said, "Nine hundred people were killed in El Mozote. Six hundred shot while running from the army and trying to cross the Rio Sumpul into Honduras. Three hundred women and children massacred in Suchitoto. This is how they choose to fight their war."

Robbie's eyes widened. "All of this must really make you question your faith."

Raul turned and looked at Robbie, his eyes widened in anger. "No!" he shouted. "God did not do this. God did not kill these people."

"I was just saying..."

"God is not in this war. God did not drop exploding barrels of nails on our people. God does not shoot us in the streets when we run from them. God is there!" He waved his arm in the direction of the sanctuary where lay nurses were treating wounded bodies. His voice grew tense. "God is not in the killing. That is what humans do. God in the healing. God is in the *médicos* treating people who may be dying. God heals. *People kill!*"

Rosalina paced her hand on his shoulder again and he stopped. "I am sorry," he said, breathing heavily. "I say too much. I should not go further because of the Embassy person with you."

"No, no," said Robbie. "Please, I want to hear. I'm not reporting back to anybody. I won't tell anyone what you say."

David slumped back in his chair. "Raul, what can *we* do? Anything?"

"I tell this to every gringo who comes here. I tell you too, you must go home and tell our story. Leave us your address and Rosalina will mail you pictures of our town before and after. Talk on the TV. Talk to the Senators. Tell them what you see. There are people in your country who want what we have here—smiling wealthy people, ruling by force and corruption, holding elections that do not count, lying to the world about how happy we are, lying about how free our press has become. Go home and tell them instead what you have seen. Your country is a democracy now, but you also will be here too someday, unless you go home and warn them what you could become."

Alf took out a pen and piece of paper and began writing down the address of his office at the University. He handed it up to Rosalina who smiled and put it into her pocket. "But now," said Raul, "you probably want to leave soon to get back to your families."

"Why is that?" said David. "You keep saying that we need to leave soon, but we don't have any timetable. "We had planned on being in the area for a couple more days."

A look of alarm grew on Raul's face. "Do you not hear of what is happening in the capital?" The three looked at him silently. They hadn't. "Today," he said, "maybe as we speak, fighters of the FMLN launched a major *ofensiva* on the big cities of the country. And there is talk that the government will go into the city neighborhoods that support them and destroy them, maybe one where you live. We thought you did know this."

"No," they all said almost in unison.

"Are you sure? How do you know about this?" asked Alf.

"It has been on FMLN Radio, *Venceremos*. You have not heard it?"

"No," said David, "I'm afraid not. We left early this morning and haven't heard any news of anything since yesterday. Is it going to be just on the Guardia Nacional? I mean, is it going to be local or the whole city?"

Raul rubbed his beard and looked at each of them solemnly. "I am sorry. This is not told to public, but the underground that we hear is that the *muchachos* have a presence in every colonia of the city, especially in the north, Zacamil and Soyapango, where there are strongest supporters. There will be fighting everywhere. They have been saying this in code, but even I was able to know it. So, it will be very large. It is very dangerous."

David turned from the others for a moment and felt suddenly weak. Racing through his mind was his conversation with Sara before they left and him assuring her that he would avoid danger but now the danger was coming to her. They had to do something to get back there, and quickly.

"And army..." began Rosalina, "they leave Los Morros yesterday only for go to capital. They move people there and they remove here..." She waved her hands around indicating the church and town. "They drop bombs...*todos los barrios*."

David leaned forward. "Raul, do you have a phone here that I—or we—could borrow?"

"Yes, of course." Raul slid open a drawer in the side of the desk and took out an aged, black rotary phone. "Here," he said. "And it still works. Some in Los Morros do not." David took it and dialed Sara's number. No one answered. He told himself that he shouldn't automatically be worried. She could be shopping, he thought. She could be at the University, translating. She could be at the school. She could be anywhere, so it didn't necessarily mean he should worry...but he did. Then he called

Carlos at the apartments. No one answered there, either. He put the phone back down, a look of fear growing in his face.

Alf picked up the phone, "Raul, may I also...?"

"*Seguro.*"

He dialed first his home and then the university. No one answered at either place.

"Anything?" David asked him.

"I don't know. Beatriz could be out and the children away. But why is no one answering at the University? Someone is always there; classes are going on." He dialed again, but still no one.

"Mister Embassy," said Raul, "would you like to call?"

Robbie picked up the phone and held it in his hand for some time looking at it and then at the others and then put it back down. "I don't think so," he said.

"Are you sure?" asked David. "Don't you have family in San Salvador who would be looking for you?"

"The only person there would be my uncle at the Embassy, and he doesn't like me. The only thing calling him would do is to bother him and make him mad about my coming here. I don't want to do that anymore." He stood up and turned to Raul and Rosalina with a solemn and official look. He took a breath. "Are you serious about needing help with some of the digging out and rebuilding? I really am pretty good at that stuff. And I'm also pretty strong. And I really would like to do something that would help your people here. I have the time, and I've had some experience, and I'm also younger and stronger than some of these old guys." He smiled and pointed to Alf and David.

Alf looked at David. "What do you think?"

"Well, I don't know how I feel about the 'agism' comment, but he's an adult and we can't stop him."

Alf nodded at Robbie. "If you really want to stay here for a while, and if Raul and Rosalina really can use you, you're free to do that, you don't need our permission. But we can't do anything to protect you if you stay."

"I know that. And I'm getting a little tired of people protecting me. I think I'd like to do something to protect someone else."

"Right now, since the soldiers have pulled out, he might actually be safer up here than down in the city," said David to Alf.

"Thanks, but that's not why I'm volunteering. I just feel like finally doing something that was worthwhile. I haven't done anything like that in...in *forever*." He looked back at Raul and Rosalina, "I could do simple things like helping dig out the homes, and I also know things like how to line up walls and frame doors. It's probably not quite like you do it down here, but I think I could adapt and do some of that for you."

Raul reached over and put his hand on Robbie's arm. "You are a good young man. And you are right. There is much here to do. But are you certain that you want to do this thing?"

"Yes, I'm certain. I'm more sure about this than anything else in my life."

"Then we will let you stay, and we will take care of you. We will find you a place to sleep and give you food and work you harder than at any other time in your life. It will be good for all of us."

"Father—*Raul*," said David. "Do you know of any way that we can get back to the city?"

Raul turned to him with a look of sudden realization. "We do not receive new buses again until tomorrow, in *la tarde*.

"Oh my God," said David. "Is there any other way? Is there a car we could borrow? Or walk to another town?"

"Probably not walk," said Alf. "It would take a long time to walk anywhere, and I'll bet there aren't more than one or two cars in the entire town."

"This is true," said Raul, smiling. "But the parish has one of them." He turned to Rosalina and asked "*¿Qué hora es ahora mismo?*" "What time is it?" She looked at her watch. "*Son las dos y media.*" "Two-thirty." To the others, he said, "Suchitoto is bigger town. It has buses twice times each day. There is a bus leaving from there in about..." He looked away, trying to remember, and then looked again at Rosalina. "I think, about one half hour?" She nodded.

"And how long would it take to get there?"

"About one half hour."

"Can we make it?"

"How fast can you run?"

CHAPTER FORTY-FIVE

ASSIGNMENT

Jerienda wasn't happy. He had been unhappy for several weeks already because he was not allowed to sleep in the barracks like most of the other recruits and he felt cheated. He was left out simply because he and his little brother, Jorge, lived close enough to the military compound that they could—and was told that they had to—go home in the evenings. He realized that the military had expanded rapidly during the war, and that there was a shortage of on-base housing, but it still made him mad. Couldn't there have been even a small place, somewhere, where they could have slept? Some of his comrades were also his friends and he felt as if he was being treated like a child when they sent him home while the others went on to bed in the Army quarters.

But he was especially not happy today, because his mother woke the two of them up early this morning for a call from the office of the *Capitán General,* saying that there had been an incident, and they needed to go in. He had already heard a little about the incident. It had been announced the night before that a band of communists were sighted coming down from

Guazapa mountain and would be entering the city sometime in the morning. But they were also told that the invaders were all weak stupid socialists and that there was nothing to be concerned about. But now, the office had called to say that the Capitán was wrong. Actually, it didn't say he was wrong. The office would never say such a thing. But it did say that there had been a larger number of communists entering than they had first realized, and from more directions than they had expected, so they decided to call up a larger number of soldiers, just to be safe.

That surprised Jerienda. He hadn't been in the military very long and didn't have much experience or training. So, unless they simply wanted to frighten the enemy with a large number of soldiers in military uniforms, and it didn't really matter how old or inexperienced they were, he wouldn't have thought they would call him up. But there he was, with his brother, out of bed, dressed in fatigues, and standing in a long line of soldiers, all in their teens and twenties, outside of the barracks gate, being briefed. Jorge was next to him, limp and dozing, while the *Capitán* was boring them with a long list of soon-to-be- forgotten orders. And that made Jerienda even more mad because Jorge was younger than he was and had even less experience and was probably dangerous. He'll kill us all someday, he thought because he's so little and doesn't know what he's doing.

The *Capitán* had a clipboard in his hand, and he was shouting at them. "We learn that the terrorists have been hiding in the *colonias* around San Salvador, especially in Zacamil and Soyapango, waiting for a time to come out and attack and kill our people and capture our city. We must stop them. They are devils. They want to destroy our freedoms and create a communist state. They will kidnap and rape our women and kill their children." Jorge was awakened by the thought and looked frightened. "There is no end to their sins. We need to protect those *Colonias* and save them for the fatherland." The man stared into the sky. "Soon we will have powerful Huey Helicopters surrounding the city, running reconnaissance. On the ground, we will have good men, with 105mm howitzers, firing at targets they have discovered. And then, after the communists have been terrified and weakened, we will send troops into those neighborhoods to kill them and capture them and fortify our city." He slapped his hand loudly down on the clipboard, applauding the strength of the plan.

He stopped at the end of the line and studied his clipboard. Then one by one he began pulling young men out: this one will go do *one* task; that one will do *another* task, this one *another*, and so on, until he got to the very end where Jerienda and Jorge were standing. "And the rest of you...." He lifted a page, searching for something. He looked at them and silently counted the number of young bodies left. Six were still there. He ran his finger down a list of tasks remaining. "And for the rest of you men," he paused, still searching, "we need volunteers for a very important mission in..." His face lit up and he ripped the page from the board. "This is it!" he shouted, waving it at them. "These will be your orders, men. Pay attention." He looked at them sternly.

"We need to send three armored, motorized, vehicles into the streets of the Soyapango, San Pedro, and Santa Lucia communities, and have them send back to us first-hand information about where the enemy is and what it is doing." He stood straight and hard as he spoke, staring down the line, with his chin pointing forward. "We have intelligence that they will be hiding in the houses, apartments, and churches of sympathizers to receive food and medicines and protection for their advancements. With your help, these military vehicles will perform an important mission of scouting and screening the area looking for the terrorists and will be the first to attack their defenses and the buildings where they are hiding. Each one of the tanks will contain two brave men who have volunteered to come forward for the good of the *patria* to kill the communists, clear the streets, and prepare the way for our fighting forces to come in."

Jerienda looked down the line at the remaining recruits left to volunteer. There were three tanks, each requiring two people, and there were six of them left in the row. Jorge, standing next to him, was now very much awake. He noticed it too. He looked up at Jerienda and mouthed the words "Six volunteers?"

"And we are the six left?" Jerienda mouthed back.

"And you will all be made very safe," the *Capitán* continued. "Your fighting vehicles will each be equipped with weapons, ammunition, and the best built-in, forty channel CB radio in the world, and through them, you will be able to communicate all your findings to the gunships above and to the office below in the brigade. You will be outfitted with bulletproof vests, powerful MP5s, should you need to do face-to-face fighting, and a shoulder belt bandolier for extra cartridges." He paused, eyeing them, waiting for the climax. "And you will be doing all of that by driving the finest, strongest, thickest, fighting vehicle in the world: the M5A1 Stuart Light Military Tank!"

The *Stuart*? Jerienda looked again at Jorge next to him. He stared in disbelief. The M5A Stuart was *ancient*, he thought. It was an old WWII tank made in England that the Salvadoran army used only for practice. Yes, he and Jorge and others had once been through a training exercise for them, but it was only one day, and it was weeks ago, and they were told this was temporary until they had the newer, stronger, armored Cashuat trucks, that would be their *real* fighting vehicles. The

Stuart was clumsy, slow, weak, and still ran on treads instead of tires. Its gun was a recoiling cannon that went off like a blunderbuss rocket destroying everything in its path. They laughed at it when they first rode in it.

Jerienda felt Jorge slowly back away from the line while the *Capitán* was facing the other recent recruits, still describing the task. Jerienda reached back and grabbed him by the arm. "No," he whispered. "If you leave, I will tell Papa. And it will be worse for you than to be killed in combat." Jorge returned to the line, his eyes were red, and he was sniffing.

The *Capitán* finished his speech, and he opened his arms wide and smiled at them all. "So, soldiers, it is up to you. We need six of you strong fighting patriots to step forward and man these vehicles." All six of them stood still, trying to take in the unreality of his words. "So, which ones of you will be the first to volunteer for the defense of your country?" No one spoke. All six glanced nervously at each other, afraid to speak or move. Finally, the *Capitán* broke the silence and clapped his hands together. "*Entonces bueno!*" he said. "Congratulations! Therefore, I commend all of you for your courage and bravery in stepping forward. All of us will be with you...in spirit. And you will be remembered for your courage for years to come. Now come, follow me and I will take you to your vehicles." Jorge was openly crying now.

CHAPTER FORTY-SIX

MARKET

It was chilly outside, and Sara regretted that she had come to the *Mercado* without wearing a jacket. Normally El Salvador didn't get cold until spring when the rains came. But occasionally, in November, a cold wind could flow down the slopes of the volcano, Quezaltepeque, just west of the city, and then the neighborhoods beneath it, like Mexicanos and Zacamil, would feel chilled and uncomfortable. That's what Sara was feeling today, for the first time in a long time, and she didn't like it.

She also wondered about the boys at school. They were lucky to be enrolled in the private school close to them, because of the government service of her deceased husband, but that benefit didn't do anything special to protect them from normal crises like playground accidents or common colds. They hadn't worn coats that morning either, and the sky around them was beginning to grow ominously gray, as though they might even get some unseasonal rain before the day was over. Little Tomás, in particular, was very sensitive and she often worried about him. She knew she shouldn't, but she did. He woke up not feeling well that morning and she almost kept him at home. But he cried and wanted to go, so she relented. He'll be fine, she thought. They have a school nurse, and if he gets worse, they'll have her look at him.

She looked up at the mountain, Quezaltepeque, and the volcanic crater of Boquerón inside it, and it was majestic and overwhelming. It stared gravely at the city, and clouds gathered around its slopes, but for now it didn't look too serious. Probably fine, she thought. Even if it does rain, it shouldn't be a hard one, it seldom is this time of the year, and she'd still have time to buy the frijoles, tomatoes, corn, and cheese for their meal that night. She also bought some *refrescos* for the boys, because they loved them, and secretly, she did too.

While pointing to a big block of goat cheese and measuring with her fingers to show how much she wanted the woman behind the table to cut off, she also thought about David and the others up in Chalate. She had been worrying, and she wondered if perhaps she should have gone with him, because it could be dangerous, and they had grown very close these past few months. But she shook her head at the thought. No, that would have just put both of them in the same danger if something happened, and also where would she have left the boys? Their *abuelos*, the grandparents, love them, but really couldn't take care of them for what could become a whole week. She did the right thing by staying behind.

She smiled inwardly for a moment. It gave her quiet, private pleasure to think of David and the boys at the same time. They seemed to really like him, and he liked them too. The four of them have felt almost like a family for the last few weeks. She hoped she wasn't projecting, but it felt like he would be a part of their family from now on, though he had been much slower in realizing that than she had. She picked up an avocado from the bin and considered it in her hand. It felt too soft and dark, and perhaps old, so she put it back and looked through some of the others. It had been a long time since she had felt truly happy. She felt like she was acting like a lovesick teenage girl, but she also knew that inwardly the feeling was very pleasant.

She picked up four other avocados and studied them, they looked fine. She put them in her basket and counted out coins to give to the woman by the bin. She heard a popping sound and looked up but didn't see anything. Probably nothing. There were dozens of people around her at all angles and none of them seemed concerned. The woman across from her took her money and dropped the four avocados into a plastic bag and then tied the top. Anything could have made a sound like that.

When she heard it again, she looked up, towards the east, towards the air force base in Ilopango, and heard another pop. The sky was clear and blue in that direction, unlike the clouds around the mountain to the west, but in it were four tiny dots. Maybe birds, she thought. They were black, so perhaps buzzards were circling around some fresh meat below them. But as she watched more closely, she saw that they were further away than she had first supposed, and much larger, and they were not circling. And they were moving towards the city.

As they came closer, she feared they might be the US helicopter gunships used by the Salvadoran Air Force at the base, but she had seldom seen them except for that time when they had hovered over, taking photos, of a demonstration she had joined in the Central Plaza. She felt tense as she watched them, first in the direction of the city and the market but then banking north and disappearing behind the buildings and trees.

Where could they be going, she wondered. North and east

of the capital was Guazapa Mountain and beyond that Chalatenango, where David and the others were doing their interviews. Nothing there but corn, small villages, and rebel strongholds—the resistance villages. And then she heard another pop and then another, and the sounds were growing louder, almost like something cracking. *Oh my God!* she thought. Something *is* happening. She quickly thanked the woman, took up her bags, and ran back to the street to get to the boys' school.

CHAPTER FORTY-SEVEN
SAN SALVADOR

When the bus reached the edge of the city and tiendas and buildings began to appear, David felt the beginnings of a sense of relief. Almost there. But then he remembered that Zacamil was at the northern edge of the city and *Terminal de Oriente* was in the center, nearly an hour out of the way going south. Alf tapped him on the shoulder and pointed at the street signs passing. He had realized the same thing.

"Stay here," Alf said, pulling himself up from his seat and making his way down through the standing passengers to the driver. David could see the two of them talking heatedly for several seconds. When he returned, he said, "How much money do you have on you? Do you have any gringo money?" David was puzzled at the request, but he reached in his pockets. "The driver says this is a cross-country bus and there's no stopping before the terminal. And he legally can't budge. So, we're going to help him find the courage to commit a felony. Give me what you've got."

David's wallet had a US twenty in it and a wad of *colones*.

"Here, take what you need, but leave me a little for a taxi when we get off."

Alf took it, parceled off an estimate of what a bribe and later cab fare would cost, and pushed the rest down into his front jeans pocket. "Follow me," he said. The two of them then weaved in and out of the crowded aisle to the front and Alf showed the driver what he had. The man looked at him in disbelief. "*¿Está usted seguro?*" "Are you sure?"

"*Si, muy seguro. ¡Sí y rápido! ¡Muy rápido!*"

The driver looked up the street for a moment and then pointed at a corner. "*¿Aquí? ¿Esta bien?*" "Is this good?" Alf nodded, pointed at it, and the driver began pulling the bus to the side. When it stopped the driver turned a crank and the door opened. Alf got off but stopped suddenly.

"What's wrong?" asked David.

"Wait a minute," Alf said, and he took off his backpack and set it on the ground. He reached inside and took out the leather bag he had put in it earlier. He tied its draw string to his belt and slid it into his pocket.

"Alf, what have you got?" yelled David from the front of the bus.

"Don't ask," he said. "We live in a dangerous neighborhood."

The driver yelled down at them, "*Ten mucho cuidado,*" "be very careful," and cranked the door closed.

Alf turned back to the door. "*Gracias,*" he said to the driver, "*Muchas gracias.*"

David looked around. "Do you know where we are?"

"Yes, but that doesn't make it much easier." He was looking to the west. It had begun to rain by now and the skyline was gray and smoky, lit up in at least four, maybe five, places with lights or flames. "What the hell?" he said. Sounds of gunfire and explosions split the air.

"How far do you think we are?"

"Well, you're better off than I am, we live about a mile further in than you do. Let's see if we can get a taxi that will take us to the university and then split up from there. He can take you on up to Zacamil, and I'll get a truck from the university to take me home to Beatriz and the kids. At least where I hope they'll be."

"Are you going to be alright?"

"No, I'm going to be shot as soon as I get home, and birds are going to eat my body."

"That's not very funny."

Alf shook his head. "Sorry, sometimes I'm better at this than others." He stepped out into the intersection and started looking up and down for a taxi. Normally there would be many in the streets at this time of the evening, but not today. Nor were there local buses. The few cars that they could see seemed to be heading outwards away from the city center. "Let's walk. It is better if we are not just standing here."

After they had gone about a block, they heard a yell behind them and turned to see a man panting and running as fast as he could toward them, and a black Jeep Cherokee with its lights off was following slowly not far behind. They jumped to get out of his way, but as they did, they heard the hammering sound of an assault rifle firing from the Jeep, and the man fell to the ground screaming, blood pulsed from his leg.

"Don't stop," Alf said, looking straight ahead. "And don't look at them." David felt panicked. He didn't want to continue walking when someone so near was bleeding on the ground, jerking and crying, but he also realized that there was nothing they could do, and they could easily join the person on the ground if they quit walking.

The Jeep stopped just behind them, its doors opened and two tall men in military fatigues got out. "Keep walking, my friends," one said to them in American English. "This shouldn't have happened, but don't get involved or it will only get worse." The other man kneeled over the twitching body and said, "It's not bad," also in English. "He won't die."

"Let's get him into the back," said the first one. "And tell that 'José Trigger Finger' in there to put that gun down. We'll all get in trouble if this happens again." The two of them crouched down and lifted the still-screaming young man off the ground, walked to the side of the car, and placed him in the back seat. They both seemed twice his size, and they tossed him in like they would throw a bedroll.

After the Cherokee pulled away and they were walking again, David and Alf finally saw a taxi making its way in their direction, away from the noise and chaos ahead. Alf stepped out into the street, almost in front of it, and waved his arms wildly. It stopped. He went to the window and asked the driver about taking them to the university. David could see a small silhouette of someone in the front seat speaking rapidly and not enjoying the conversation. The driver had just come out of the center of horrific fighting in Zacamil and was not wanting to take them back into it again. After they argued for a few minutes, the driver finally agreed, but begrudgingly and not for the normal fare. Alf pulled out their remaining money and handed half of it through the window but said he would hold the rest until they had gotten to the university. Alf looked up and waved at David to join him. They both got in and the car turned around and headed back into the nearly abandoned streets.

CHAPTER FORTY-EIGHT

SCHOOL

Sara paused only for a moment, thinking about what she should do. It was still nearly three blocks back to the boys' school and the noises around her were getting louder, and her bags were feeling heavy. She decided to drop them on the sidewalk so she could run. Normally the distance to the school seemed short and convenient, but today it felt miles away. All she could think of was their possible danger. She ran the first block down a long sidewalk and then crossed in the middle of the street, passing barking dogs and cars that swerved around her, honking. She continued to the next corner and across a parking lot. She had to get to the school.

When she finally reached the school's corner, she was surprised to see that its gate had been left open and the guard who checked cars coming through it was gone. She was even more surprised to see that the playground beyond it was filled with people gathering around the fronts of the classrooms and administrative buildings. Parents were searching for their children. Tomás' classes were in the *Tercer de ciclo* to her right and Dani's were in the building just beyond it. There was a large crowd of mothers and children around the closer one, fighting to get in, so she ran instead to the second. It was smaller, only one floor, and the door was open, so she ran through it without stopping and then down the hall. Rushing up and down were students, teachers, administrators, and a growing number of parents who had suspected the same thing she had and were looking for their children. She managed her way past them and around a corner down to the last classroom on the right which was Dani's, and there she saw him in a line with other boys standing in front of their door. Their teacher had lined them up against the wall anticipating their parents coming for them. Dani saw her in the distance and ran to her, and she hugged him tightly in relief. His grown-up demeanor was gone, and he was frightened. "*Mi pequeño hombre*," she said, holding him tightly, "My little man." And asked if he had seen his brother. He hadn't, so they pushed back through the crowds to the schoolyard and back to the front door of the *Tercer de ciclo* where many of the other mothers were still trying to get in.

"*¡Quédate aquí!*" she said, "Stay here," and ran to the door. She worked her way around the crush of anxious bodies, and found her way in. She saw that once again teachers had lined students up in front of their classrooms waiting for parents to claim them. She hurried past several doorways searching for Tomás' class. The teacher for this room had not yet lined his students up outside the door and the class aide was attempting to keep the parents from rushing in before it was done. Then they came. One by one, a line of twenty little boys, seven and eight years old, came through the door and lined up militarily just outside of it. The aide stood next to them, ushering them out, and urging them all to stay quiet and in line while looking around anxiously at the worried parents in the hall. "Your children are all here," she said to them cheerfully in Spanish. "Do not worry." Some of them came out and

Sara recognized them as friends of Tomás. More came. "Do not worry," the young woman repeated. "They are all here." The line outside began to fill up and Sara jumped up to look over the heads of the other parents. "See," the aide said at last, as she welcomed the last little boy into the hallway. "They are all here. They are all safe." She smiled and waved her arm down the line of them. But Sara was watching, and they were *not* all there. Tomás was not in the line.

She was frantic. "Where is my Tomás?" she yelled.

The aide at first looked annoyed at the question, and then with a quick look of recognition said, Tomás? *Oh, Tomás!* I am sorry, I forgot. He is in the infirmary." She pointed back up the hall towards the main offices. "He wasn't feeling well, so we sent him to the nurse."

Sara thanked her and tried hard to do it calmly without hitting the young woman in the face and then she ran back up the hall to the school offices. Over the first door in the building center was the word, "*Enfermería.*" Inside, a woman in a white uniform sat quietly at her desk, reading and making notes. Sara screamed at her, demanding to know if Tomás De León was there. The woman was at first startled at Sara's outburst but looked through some cards on her desk and then smiled and said calmly that Tomás was not there. He had simply gotten ill, so they sent him home.

Sara couldn't believe it. In another life and time, she would have stayed there and yelled at the incompetence and nonchalance of this woman who was supposed to be a professional and then demanded her resignation. But now she simply turned and ran out, as furiously as she ran in, towards the front of the building and out the door and into the field where Dani was still standing, stiff and frightened, waiting for her to return. She rushed to him, took up his hand, and continued running out to the street. "Come, we're going home."

CHAPTER FORTY-NINE
TRUCK

After what felt like an endlessly long drive, the taxi arrived at the main gate of the university. On one side of the street was ANDA, the city water utility plant, on the other were the massive orange columns of the entrance to the campus. Sounds of explosions and rapidly-firing machine guns were happening more and more frequently now. Much of it seemed to be coming from inside the campus. Alf rolled down the window and looked hard at the gate. One side was standing open, wide enough for a car or truck to enter. "That's good for us." There was another explosion, this time clearly from within the campus and the car shook. Smoke and a piercing sound of screaming, followed by cheers, came from inside.

Alf spoke quietly, without taking his eyes off the gate. "David, you and our friend here should probably go ahead and leave. The university maintenance vehicles are just inside the gate, and I know where the keys are. So, I'll be fine."

"No," David said, "I'm going with you. You may need some help."

"That's an honorable decision, and you may be right, but just to let you know, it is also stupid."

"I've made worse. Befriending you was probably one of them."

He cocked his head at David. "What a funny guy. Keep it up and you'll probably die young." He turned and told the tiny, silent driver to wait outside for them while they went inside. He turned back to David. "Okay, let's go."

They got out of the car and ran to the gate. Inside it, they watched in horror the chaos of guns firing and hand-to-hand fighting. The entire front of the School of Physics and Mathematics had been blasted open, evidently by some kind of mortar fire. Smoke and flames were pouring from its upstairs windows. The street in front was scattered with bodies, some dead, some nearly so. Just beyond them was the shell of a large blue and white news van with the words "Canal 12 TV" on its side, with its hood twisted and burning, and next to it a long, thin dog writhing, whimpering, and surrounded by blood.

The two of them stood staring silently at the scene for some time. Finally, Alf took out the leather bag he had tied to his belt and removed a Browning sub-compact pistol. He rubbed it for a moment with the sides of the leather bag, as though polishing it, then carefully checked the chambers. He walked towards the burning van and whimpering dog and stood for several seconds looking at the dog while rubbing his gun. At last, he raised his arm and pointed it at the dog. When it yelped a painful cry, Alf fired a shot. It jerked once, then a second time, and then stopped. Alf turned back to the gate, walking faster than before. When he arrived, he said, more to himself than to David, "Sometimes you have to do something evil to do something good."

To the right of the gate was a large gravel field, protected by a tall chain-link fence. And behind it were several rows of cars and trucks. David looked down at them and said, "How do we get in it?"

"I know a way."

When they reached the fence, Alf turned to the left, where the fence met the campus wall, and kicked at the grass until he uncovered a small metal plate on the ground. He kneeled down and pried it open and underneath was a box containing several groups of keys on rings. After looking at several and turning them over in his hand, he took out three. "One of these should work," he said back to David.

At the fence gate, he tried each key on the padlock holding the fence. The first two didn't fit, but the third did and when they pushed on the gate it opened with a loud squealing noise. Once inside Alf began looking up and down the rows of vehicles.

"What are you looking for?" David asked. "Just grab one."

"I want one in particular," he said, scanning the rows. "There's a *Camión gigante* in here that will be just what I need." Then he saw it. Deep in the lines of trucks was a strange- looking, giant green truck with double tires, and a long flatbed in back that looked like it could be used for hauling mountain timber or small houses. "There it is," he yelled. "That's the one."

"That's a monster, alright," said David. "What is it?"

"It's called a 'Shackman VFJ,' made in India as a fighter." He opened the driver's door and pulled himself up into the seat. "It's just what we need. Built originally for their army to transport troops, but we used it for building and construction work. It was made to withstand machine gun fire. It's almost a tank but with a flatbed. I'll be safe in this thing if I have to drive straight through the wall to get back to the street. "*¡Vámonos!* Get in!"

David got into the passenger seat and just as he did so, he

heard the whistle of a bullet flying over their heads. He pulled the door shut and then heard another. "Put your head down," said Alf, and then leaned his own lanky body down as low as he could and still see ahead. "It's probably just random shooting, so there shouldn't be more like it soon." He sorted through the other keys in his hand, put one into the ignition and this time the first one worked, and the engine started. "*¡Precisamente!*" he yelled, and the truck moved forward. He eased it through the line of trucks, and back to the chain link gate that had swung closed.

"I'll open it," David said.

"No, don't get out," Alf said, looking intently at the fence ahead of them. "It's not safe." The whizzing noise of more bullets flew over them. "I've got this." He stamped his foot down on the gas and drove forward, straight into the fence rolling through it as though it was plastic. Metal, fence, and concrete burst away from them in all directions. "Ain't she a beaut?" he yelled in delight. It lunged again towards the pavement and campus entrance gate.

David looked back at the grounds inside and by that time hand-to-hand war had broken out in all the open spaces. He saw fighters running from building to building firing weapons and tossing grenades in windows. Each hit shook the air even hundreds of yards away. He couldn't tell who was winning and who was losing but it was ferocious, and the sound was deafening. One side—he wasn't sure which, but he thought it was the Salvadoran Army—was firing something that looked like a hand-held rocket launcher from behind the Humanities building to the right of the university entrance. Fire streaked out when it went off and the ground shuddered when it landed.

When the truck pulled through the outside gate, Alf looked at David and said, "You need to get out now. It's been fun, but we're both kind of in a hurry." He reached down in his pocket and took out the last of their combined money. "This is what I've got left. The cab driver promised to get you home for this. So, be firm in case there's some disagreement about that."

David wasn't sure that they should split up. He said, "Are you sure you're going to be alright?"

"Of course. Remember, you'll be in a 1970 Ford Falcon, and I'm in a tank. So, don't talk to me about being safe."

David laughed. He knew Alf was right. "Okay," he said. "But if you make it home and everyone is safe—or if they aren't safe—you call me tomorrow. And I'll do the same with you. You've been too good of a friend to me through all of this. I don't want to lose you."

Alf reached an arm over to David and gave him a hug. "I'll do it, *Amigo*. And you do the same. You're crazy as a Guatemalan cane toad, but I love you." He grinned widely. "You go take care of Sara. The only thing that could hurt me is if they dragged one of those bazookas out here and hit me dead on in the face."

David wrote down his address on a small piece of paper for the driver and got out of the truck. "Be safe," he yelled back, and both of them laughed at the unlikely odds. He walked to the taxi, got in the back, and handed the driver his address. The driver studied the paper for a moment and looked up. She turned and put her arm over the back seat and looked at him. "Sr. Patterson?"

David's eyes grew wide, shocked at the recognition. "Lessi? Is that you?"

CHAPTER FIFTY

TANK

The British M5A Stuart "Light" tank rolled forward. It slowed and started and slowed again, as though thinking of what it might do next. What *was* it supposed to do? Where was it supposed to go? Jerienda wasn't sure. He knew he had to find the communists and keep them from stealing his country and swaying the stupid people into following them, but he didn't know how this tank would do that. He knew that they were supposed to go first to Soyapango and then Zacamil but he didn't know where either one of them was, so he didn't know if he could do that. He stopped again and looked around inside the mysterious tank for a clue as to how to proceed and then slowly drove forward. Jorge yelled down at him from the hull above. "What are you doing? We need to find rebels." That made Jerienda mad. Jorge was a child, what did he know about rebels? He called back up at his brother, "Which ones are the rebels?"

"They're *all* rebels!" Jorge's voice rose with excitement and patriotism. "They have all joined forces against the country, and they are all now the enemy. Shoot them. Stop them. The nation depends on it!" With that, Jorge reached into a large green duffle bag in the left hull of the sponson and pulled out a grenade and put his fingers over the fuse plug. "If you aren't going to do your duty, I will do it for you." He turned the wheel to the top of the tank and slid it open.

Jerienda was not sure what to do. He couldn't *not* obey their orders. He would be imprisoned for life. He would be gone, and little Jorge would be a decorated hero. He looked out of the small slit in his cockpit and tried to see into the neighborhood. It was nothing but houses and apartments and small *tiendas*. Jorge was above him now, watching the scene from the opening at the top, and holding a bag full of grenades.

"Jorge!" Jerienda yelled, "Give me cover." He looked back through the opening. There was a two-story adobe house in front of them, with a small stairway on the outside that connected the two floors. It had a narrow lawn in front, a driveway, and a small car. Jerienda thought the car looked European. He wondered where it was from. He pulled the trigger. The tank shook and a massive sound of cannon fire roared in front of him. The car and the left side of the house exploded into a rage of light and fire.

"*Maravilloso,*" yelled Jorge. "*Otra vez, otra vez.*" "Do it again, do it again." Jerienda heard the sound of a grenade explosion on his left and then a second. He pulled the tank cannon around to see Jorge's work. Two small cottages had their windows blackened and the front of their roofs torn open. A third grenade was in the air. It exploded and bricks, windows, and curtains blew out of the smoke and blackness.

"Stay on your side," yelled Jorge. "We'll work together." Jerienda turned the cannon back to the right. The tank had better aim than Jorge's arm, but it was less agile.

"*Todos ellos son rebeldes,*" he yelled again. "They're all rebels."

CHAPTER FIFTY-ONE
SARA

In normal times, the boys' school had seemed close to home. The boys could walk to it alone, and she felt safe letting them do that. But not this time. On this day she was anguished at the distance she had to run back to the entrance, out to Calle Zacamil, around to her street, and down the long wall and parking lot to Los Cañones. Especially so with dark wet clouds gathering overhead and Dani still crying in fear beside her. The length felt like miles not yards. And hundreds of people were everywhere, rushing in all directions, all seemingly intent on slowing her down and blocking her way. When they reached the lot, she heard a voice call out to her. "*¡Sara!*" A large woman carrying bags and wearing a brown scarf around her head was rushing the opposite direction. "*¡Vas por el camino equivocado!*" "You're going the wrong way."

Sara recognized her as a neighbor. "*¿Por qué?*"

"The fighting is coming," the woman said in Spanish, "and we need to leave the city."

"I must find Tomás," she shouted back, but the woman had

already disappeared into the tangle of bodies. For a moment she felt a swelling of some of the sharp fear she had experienced years ago when she first learned that Daniel had died. It hadn't been a fear of physical harm for herself, but of the possibility of being totally without a constant companion forever. And now she was close to feeling that fear about her children. But she forced herself not to think that now. Right now, she needed to stay focused and keep moving and get home. Finally, they rounded the high wall of the school, and she got a shiver of excitement. Maybe we will make it, she thought.

"*Mami, Mami,*" Dani said, pulling at her hand. "I cannot go any further."

"Oh *Amorcito,*" she said. "We must keep going. Maybe we can just walk very fast now? Instead of running? But we have to find Tomí. We *have* to." He continued but was tired and pulled at her hand as they hurried walking. When they reached the corner of the complex, she looked down the row at David's apartment and wished that he was there with them. Probably David would carry Dani on his back, and they could still run. But, she thought, he is still high up in the mountains, past Lake Suchitoto, enjoying his work and probably not knowing anything about what she and the boys were going through.

The air was wet with rain, and the sky was shaking with thunder when they reached their apartments at the end of the seven rows of "canyons." The gate was open, and a frightened crowd of her neighbors was struggling to get inside a basement door in the middle of the row. But when she turned to the stairs to go up to her own apartment, she heard a voice from the crowd at the door calling to her. "He is not there," it said in Spanish, "we have him." She turned to the crowd expecting an explosion within her of more loss and fear but saw instead Isabel standing in front of them. "He is fine,"

Isabel called out. "When I got home today, I saw him sitting in front of your door, waiting for you. He didn't feel well, so I kept him in my apartment, and he is here now."

"Here? Where?" Still frantic, she looked through the crowd trying to find his little face.

"He is inside, in the basement. We were one of the first to go in. I also brought him some baby aspirin and a pillow and some *dulce*, and he is feeling better." She smiled, "He liked the *dulces* best."

"Oh my God," Sara said. "Thank you, Isabel, thank you." She came back down the stairs and followed Isabel through the crowd and through the door. The basements in Los Cañones ran the entire underground footprint of their apartment buildings and were surrounded by walls of concrete. This one was full of boxes, tables, lamps, tools, lawnmowers, and dozens of metal folding chairs. A start-up Baptist church had met there a few years earlier, and when they finally moved to their own building, they left chairs and wooden pews behind. And there, against the front wall, on one of the pews, holding Isabel's pillow, alongside two other children, drinking a bottle of sweet fruit *refresca*, she saw him. "*Tomás!*" She cried to him. He looked up and squealed back. "*Mami, Mami!*"

She and Dani ran to him and the three of them held each other tight for a long and tearful hug. "*Ahora estamos a salvo, estamos a salvo,*" she said to him. "We are safe. We are safe."

CHAPTER FIFTY-TWO

DAVID

"Lessi? Is that you?"

The sky was growing darker with gathering rain and thunder, and the radio in the taxi was filled with a voice that was screaming the news, but so loud and fast that David could only understand parts of it. The driver looked back at him with shock in her eyes. She was smiling, but her voice was very serious. "Señor Patterson," she said. "It is you too?"

"Lessi, it's good to see you. It is so good to be driven by someone I know."

"Señor Patterson, it is good to see you too, though it is also sad because I believe tonight you will probably die."

David smiled at the grim assessment. "Well, you may be right, but I'll worry about that later. Right now, I need to get back home to Los Cañones. Can you do that for me again?"

"That area is *cerrado*, it is closed. I can no go into it."

"Why not?"

She gestured at the radio. "It is there that they fight the most. The *muchachos* fight the Army there and the radio says it is *mui peligroso*."

David was growing more frightened, but he asked "Can you take me even part of the way? I need to get home."

"Five blocks, they say, maybe six into Zacamil and then they say cars can no more go in. But it is only not many blocks after that to your home if you do not die."

Actually, when the taxi began moving forward, they weren't able to get even that close. They drove for only four blocks and then Lessi slowed and pulled to the side. In the street ahead was a wall of tires blocking any further passage. On one side was rapid gunfire from behind the tires, and on the other, Salvadoran army soldiers firing back from the eaves of businesses and houses. Even at this distance, David recognized the eerie sound of a bullet buzzing overhead. In the center of the street was the shell of a black Jeep Cherokee, like the one with the Americans that he and Alf had encountered earlier. The windshield and roof were missing, and smoke was coming out of the driver's side.

Lessi put her elbow over the seat again and looked at David. "I not charge you for this driving," she said. "But you should not go more into Zacamil. It is *muy peligroso*. You will maybe die. If you stop now, I will take you back to where is no more fighting." Her eyes were wide with fear. "You are now my friend, and I do not want you to die."

He knew it was true, but he had to go on. Part of his feelings were caused by the irrational need that Alf and Héctor had pointed to, about atoning for a sin in his past that still emotionally condemned him. But he also realized that today most of it was seriously about Sara and her boys, all of whom he had grown to love and couldn't imagine losing. They gave him something to live for, for the first time in a very long time. And maybe even something to die for. He could not allow himself to let something happen a second time to another life that he cared so much about.

"No," he said. "Keep the money. You deserve it, but I need to go home," and he got out.

Lessi looked at him silently for a long time. Finally, she said, "You are a very good man. Your family is very lucky to have you. *Buen suerte.*" She waved goodbye, turned the car around, and drove it back the way that they had just come.

The rain was pouring now, and he couldn't see far. He knew that the street they were on was Don Bosco, but he'd never been on any of the side streets that he would need to take to avoid the fighting. He also didn't want to go back the direction he had just come from to find a street he recognized that could take him around the battle. That would cause him to lose time, with no guarantee he wouldn't meet up with fighting somewhere else. To his left was a private school with what appeared to be a long, unnamed, alley next to it. He didn't know where it would come out, but at least it was pointing in the right direction. He knew that north and west of the school was a wooded, undeveloped area that stretched for several blocks, then opened to more apartments like his. Perhaps if he could get in there, he could wind his way through or around them, avoiding the fighting, and come out safely at Los Cañones, just a few blocks further. He decided to take the chance.

He started running down the alley in the rain and dark and then, when he passed the buildings and came to an opening in the woods, he turned right to go north. The terrain wasn't rough, but it was muddy and slippery. The trees and bushes were dense, ingrown, and now wet, and for a while he was unsure where he was going and where he would eventually come out. But after running and stumbling for several minutes through the dark and the woods, he saw buildings and concrete emerging up ahead of him. When he came out into the opening, he was in front of a large sign that said, "*Los*

Ranchos," a string of apartments he recognized that were just a few blocks south of his own. He heard rapid gunshots ahead and they seemed to be coming from the direction of Los Ranchos. He was right. The long wide street in front of the buildings was filled with violent fighting. At the right end of the row, doorways and alleys were filled with army and rebel fighters firing at each other and residents running from the complex into the woods to get away. Smoke swirled up from many windows in the apartments. Further down was a Green Cross truck used to bring the wounded to the hospital. But it was empty. The front window was crushed inward, and flames billowed up from the hood. A dark Huey gunship appeared above and swooped down over the apartment roof firing at people running away. Two houses on the left had large holes blown in their walls and windows. In front of one, a man lay on the grass, screaming. His coat and shirt were on fire around his neck. David ran to him and saw that his face was burned and blackened. Two eyes seemed freed from their sockets and looked crazily up at him. David rolled him back and forth on the grass until the fire was put out. Then he shook him to see if he was alive. But by then his face was charred and lifeless.

Behind David a little boy stood in the middle of the street, crying and looking helplessly for his parents. For a moment memories of little Gil at the border flashed in his mind. About the same size and age and very possibly about to face the same fate. David ran to him and picked him up and took him back to the woods. He was not hurt but was terrified. "*Espera aquí*" David said. "*Mami y papi vendrán pronto.*" "Stay here. Mommy and Daddy will come soon." He had no idea whether that was true, but he didn't have anything else to offer. He turned back to the apartments and saw a wall of shattered glass, ruined fruit stalls, and destroyed homes. The little boy would at least be safer here in the trees than out where the devastation was happening. *"Espera aquí,"* he said again quietly.

He heard a scream from behind him and turned to see a man in front of an apartment that was on fire, trying to pull a woman out of the front door. The door was a jagged, blackened hole. A shell from a bazooka or grenade launcher must have hit it head-on. The woman appeared to be unconscious, and the man was looking helpless and crying. *"Ayudame,"* he was shouting. "Help me." David ran to them and with his boot kicked out pieces of the damaged door, then the two of them managed to pull her the rest of the way out of the wreckage. She wasn't conscious but appeared to be still breathing. Her face was gray with ash and smoke, and blood streaked across her face and down to a pool of red on her dress. A small crucifix was tangled in a leather cord around her neck. *"¿Tiene usted coche?"* he asked the man. "Do you have a car?"

"Sí, sí, tenemos un coche," he answered, and pointed to a small blue Toyota Corolla in the parking lot a few hundred feet away.

"I'll help you," he said in English, and then repeated in Spanish, *"Yo te ayudaré."* The man nodded and the two of them lifted her carefully and took her to the car and laid her in the back seat.

"Espera aquí," he said to the man. "Wait here." He left them and ran back into the woods where he found the little boy still crying but waiting for his parents. *"Ven conmigo,"* he said. "Come with me," and lifted the boy in his arms and took him back to the Corolla. When the man saw the two of them approaching, he cried out, *"Mateo!"*

"¿Es tu hijo pequeño?" said David, "Is this your little boy?" *"No, es de mi amigo,"* he said. "It's the boy of my friend." He gave the boy a hug and told David that the boy's family were neighbors and that they had been killed when a shell hit their

apartments. He helped the boy get in on the other side and told him he would take them all to safety. "God...bless...you," he said to David in halting English and hugged him as he had done with the boy. "*¿Tú también?*" "Will you go too?"

David shook his head. "No, I need to find my own...my own *family*." The word felt strongly appropriate and not awkward. "*Pero cuida de tu esposa.*" "But take care of your wife."

"*Bueno, gracias,*" he said, and he pulled his car away, leaving David standing alone in the parking lot.

CHAPTER FIFTY-THREE
SARA

The long, damp basement under *fila siete Los Cañones* was nearly dark and nearly silent except for hushed comments between family members and the sound of an occasional cough or chairs being pulled together to form a group. Some were trying to rest, and some were trying to sleep, but few managed to do much of either. Sara was sitting on one of the abandoned church pews between her two boys wrapped in Isabel's blanket and holding their heads on her lap.

There were close to forty or fifty people hiding in the room altogether, some she knew and some she had never seen before. Directly across from her was Isabel, who had come in right after Sara and the boys and was now in a heated conversation with several other women who were shorter and younger and leaning in to hear what she was saying. To their right was a neighbor who Sara seldom saw in the complex, and never with his wife and family, but who were now all gathered around him holding on to one another and looking frightened. In the back against the wall and under the maintenance crew's long ladder, was Carlos, also looking frightened, but standing up straight and strong and trying his best to look brave. Standing beside him and leaning close, was Camilia, also looking strong, and mysteriously comforted. And the two of them were holding hands. Sara smiled quietly and waved at them. They lifted their joined hands and waved back. Maybe sometimes good things can work out, she thought.

Directly to her left and in front of the only window on the wall, a large wooden cross hung precariously from a wire, a remnant of the defunct church that once met in this dark and gray shelter. When a roar of thunder outside boomed into the room, the cross rippled and pulled against the wire. In front of it was the remains of a pulpit, its base was still strong, but the lectern table at the top was broken in the middle and hung to one side by what appeared to be a single nail. She smiled again. Just like my country, she thought. Strong at the bottom but broken at the top. And it didn't look like a top that could ever be totally repaired.

Beyond and above the cross and pulpit was the window, near the ceiling, that looked out on the remains of San Salvador. It was dark, and the rain was thick, but she could still see a black silhouette of the tall tower of the school in the distance and other buildings around it. Periodic streaks of light flashed down from the sky when A-37s fired white phosphorus at the neighborhoods of suspected enemies, and bursts of flames flashed upwards in response.

"Mami," Tomás said, "how much longer do we have to wait here?"

"Close your eyes, little *Amorcita*. It is going to be a long night, and we all need to rest."

Dani, much calmer now and wanting to reassert his role as the older brother, said, "Go back to sleep. We may be here for days. We may never go home."

The thought frightened Tomás even more, but Sara rubbed

his back and told them both not to worry, that it would not be *that* long, and that the fighting between the *muchachos* and the army would soon be over.

"Mami, I need to go pee."

She looked up surprised. She hadn't thought of that. There were many people there, and it was still just a basement. Soon that would be a question that everyone would be asking. "*Mi príncipe,*" she said, "how badly do you have to go? Can you wait just a little while longer?"

"I have to go *now*. I wanted to go even when Sra. Isabel brought us down here, but I didn't say anything."

At that moment, Dani looked up too. He didn't say anything, but his face showed that he was needing the same thing.

"Oh, *mi ángels.*" She looked around the room again. Soon there would be not just bathroom needs but also hunger. The sun was down and eventually people would be wondering about their evening *cena*. She saw Isabel across the room still talking with the three young women. She gently pulled herself away from the boys and wrapped the blanket around them. "Wait here and rest. I will be right back." She went to the women and asked, "Does anyone have any news? Does anyone know when we will be able to go back to our homes?"

The women looked at each other and shook their heads. They hadn't heard anything. "Do you need to go somewhere?" Isabel asked.

"No, but my little *niños* are needing the bathroom and soon they will be hungry...in fact soon all of us will."

Isabel shook her head. "You are right. One or two here have brought some food, but it is not enough for everyone, and soon all of us will be having...bathroom needs. And there is nothing down here for that."

Sara looked at the door, and then to the boys. "I think I will take them up. We will try to be quick, but we have to go. I'll also bring some food down. They can eat it here when we get back."

"I will go with you. I will need to feed my own *'Niñas'* too." She smiled at the three young women.

They went back and gathered up Tomás and Dani who were eager to go by now and left the basement. They quickly ran out and around and up the stairs. When they reached the fourth floor, Sara paused and looked out at the scene of her neighborhood below. At first, what she saw was what she always saw from that level. The buildings of her beloved city were still in place and many of the sites still looked familiar. But then there were the popping noises and beams of phosphorus streaking down from the sky. Buildings in the distance had waves of smoke and fire rising from them. Several of those black dots, which she now realized were helicopter gunships, were diving down to near ground level, and firing rockets at...at what? She didn't know. But more smoke and flames rose with each firing. Something must have exploded, she thought. And when they hit something, someone probably died.

"Come," said Isabel, "We must hurry." Sara gathered the boys and pushed them to their door, the first one on the row, at the end of the complex, on the fourth floor, facing the parking lot. "Tomi, you go use the bathroom first, and Dani and I will find some food for us."

CHAPTER FIFTY-FOUR

TANK

here were they? Jerienda and Jorge realized that they must be lost. They had been driving north through the city for over an hour looking for Soya-pango but had seen few signs of an invasion. The last report through their radio said that the tanks had arrived in Colonia Soyapango by now, and that heavy fighting was occurring. There had been gunfire and cannon shots and many of the residents were fleeing the area. In some neighborhoods the rebels and their sympathizers had torn up stones from the streets and constructed barricades to keep the soldiers out. There were casualties. The local radio station was announcing that the whole community was in danger of rebel control and that the Army was preparing a stronger force to go further in. But Jorge and Jerienda, on a street somewhere unknown, in their antique M5A Stuart tank, could hear the noises in the distance but saw nothing.

Jorge was up in the turret, belted in tightly, in case he needed to fire the 30 caliber anti-aircraft gun. But it was big in his hands, and cold. And the reaction was supposed to be strong when it was fired. He pulled the seat up, as close to it as possible, so it would catch him if the gun kicked back. Jerienda was down at the controls and dials with the radio headset on, trying to see through metal flaps in front and the tiny hole of the periscope on the cannon. It wasn't a good view either way.

They clearly had wandered far away from the targets, but he didn't know how far or even in what direction. The voice on the radio wasn't helpful. It was screeching orders to all the tanks at the same time, "Fire on them! Stop them! Track them down! Fire, fire, fire!" Jerienda could see none of this and was sure they were lost.

He reached around in the metal box containing supplies and found a San Salvador street map, and yelled up to Jorge, "Look for street signs and I'll find us. I'll get us there." There was a long pause as the giant tank lumbered on an unknown street and in an unknown direction. Finally, Jorge yelled back, "I think we are in Zacamil and not Soyapango."

"How do you know?"

"Because the sign just said 'Calle Zacamil,' and Mama and I have been on this street before."

"Good," yelled Jerienda back. "Can you tell where we are on the Calle? What direction are we going in?"

Another long pause. Finally, "I think I see the hospital on the right, where Papi was that time when he was hurt. I think we are going west."

That was terrible. Soyapango was in the east, and they were going west. How did that happen? "We need to turn around. Do you see a street corner?"

"We are at that private school for the rich children. And there is a street just past it."

"Good, tell me when we get there, and I'll look for it down here too."

"Should I be shooting at people?" Jorge said.

"Maybe...I don't know. Do you see any?"

"I think so. There are men in the streets. Some of them are running. Some, I think, have guns and they don't look like soldiers."

"Then, yes, if you are sure, fire at them."

There was silence. Jorge wasn't sure who he had seen and so for a moment he didn't fire. "There's one," he yelled, and then there was a loud burst of shots, and the turret shook with each firing. *Tat, tat, tat, tat, tat.*

Jerienda tried to look through the metal flap on the front to see what had happened, but it was too far to the right. "What did you hit?"

"I didn't hit the man with the gun, but I hit the house he was coming out of. I hit a door and a window."

"Good, that was probably a rescue house where they hide the guerrillas. You are supposed to hit those too."

"Okay," Jorge called back, nervous at the amount of firepower in his hands. "Should I shoot another one?"

"Do you see another guerrilla? If you do, then shoot him. You don't need to ask." He heard another round of shots being fired and this time he saw the target. In the street ahead of them was a car and, at the sound of the firing, its hood and top exploded and flew into the air. He couldn't see if there were people in it. Hopefully, there were, because that meant that they had finally killed a communist. He heard Jorge cheering from above.

"How far until we get to the corner?"

"*Lo siento,*" "I'm sorry, it is right *here!* Turn now to the left. Turn left!"

Jerienda couldn't make a sudden turn, but he pulled all the way back on the left lever and pushed forward on the right one and managed a slow wide bend that crossed the curb and sidewalk of the next street before straightening out. "What is this street?"

"Calle Las Margaritas, and then turn, turn again, very fast. It is the next corner."

"And *this* street. What is it?"

"I don't know, it looks like an alley."

Jerienda slowed the tank. "Then why are we on it?"

"Because it is pointing us to the east. If we continue on it, I think it will take us out to Santa Rosa and Santa Barbara, and then Soyapango."

"That is good. And if we get there soon, we can still be heroes. And we will let them know that we were a part of the fighting too, defending the city."

"Yes! We are defending our country!"

"Are there more targets?"

"I think so.

"Then fire on them, but let me get behind the cannon first, so that I can fire too." He shifted a gear and pushed down on the heavy foot feed in front of him and the tank moved forward. He sat with one hand on the drive levers and his head pressed against the eyepiece of the long cannon, prepared to see the enemies that Jorge spotted. Through the lens, he could see far down the long street, with the wall of a school on the left and houses on the right, and at the end, he could just make out the outline of several rows of long narrow apartments, each with gates and fences between them. Then he saw that the road had a sharp forced turn to the left. "*¡Maldita!*" he said, pounding on the steering bar. "Where are we?"

"I do not know," yelled Jorge from above. "But maybe if we turn again, we will come out again at Calle Zacamil? And then if we turn right, we can be going west to Soyapango?"

"*¡Mierda!*" He shouted back. "I am mad. We are still lost and trapped in this place, and we are going to be in trouble when we find the others. I am *very* mad, and we are not doing anything to fight for our country."

Screaming in anger, he turned the cannon to the left, at the great outside wall surrounding the school, and fired. Rock, stone, and concrete flew in the air, and he could see the playground in the distance through the hole he had made.

"*¡Maravilloso!*" Jorge cried excitedly.

CHAPTER FIFTY-FIVE
LOS CAÑONES

David ran as fast as he could, winding his way through several more streets, some inflamed in battle and some eerily quiet, until he finally emerged onto the long parking lot that led to his apartment. All the lights in his row were strangely dark, except for the one in the ice cream shop on the first level. It appeared to be completely empty, as though the owners had left quickly and didn't bother with the lights. I think I made it, he thought. Exhausted as he was, he felt a sense of hope for the first time in hours.

Then he heard a noise that was different from the guns and explosives he had just left behind, and he saw what appeared to be a giant military tank coming toward him. Its sides glistened in the rain, reflecting light from the streetlamp above. He had never seen one of these before. It was moving slowly and hesitantly. In the wide drive between the school on one side and houses on the other, it looked like a gray, moving mountain. It had a narrow black cannon in front that was moving from side to side, like a long dark eye, firing almost casually, first at the wall on the left and then at one of the houses on the right. Above, in the turret, was a 75mm Howitzer and sitting behind it was a small head of someone wearing an oversized Army helmet, holding up two round objects in his hands, and leaning forward, apparently studying the neighborhood. What were those, David wondered. Rocks? Grenades? *Oh my God*, he thought and slowly stepped back, off the pavement and behind the shrubbery of a house on the side. As he watched, it crept closer, grinding and scraping the concrete drive. Whatever its cause or purpose, or whoever it was looking for, it kept coming.

Hiding in the dark next to the house, he let it pass him by. The sounds of gunshots were behind him, and the tank was moving forward in front of him. He slid from the shrubs of the first house to behind a large amate tree in the next, quietly moving closer to his row of apartments. They didn't see him. The tank had a World War II look about it. Not a modern military vehicle on high wheels that could lift it over debris strewn in front of it. This had treads along its sides, and it rolled over bottles and boxes and rubble, crushing everything it hit. It moved with painful, deliberate speed as it approached the corner of the alley. Then for a moment, it stopped. A long moment? A short moment? Time was strange and indecipherable in the dark and smoke and rain, and David couldn't tell. What he did know was that if it made the turn to the left, it would be parallel to his apartment and traveling directly towards the one that Sara lived in.

CHAPTER FIFTY-SIX

TANK

Jerienda slowed the tank, pleased with the destruction that it had caused. Then he turned the cannon to the left and fired a second round at the school walls. There was another explosion and more rock and concrete fell to the ground. That felt good, he thought. He fired again and the entire wall fell backwards onto the lawn behind it. He jumped with pleasure. When they reached the end of the parking lot, they were facing the first of the several long rows of apartments. "What are these buildings?" he yelled up at Jorge. "They look like empty apartments."

Jorge from his perch above was wondering about them also. "The *Capitán* said that the guerrillas hide in these places, tunneling between the rooms and connecting them and stealing their food to prepare for the bigger attack later. And maybe here are some of them." Jerienda didn't remember the *Capitán* saying that. He was worried that Jorge was just making this up.

"But how do you know that these are the ones that are hiding the guerrillas?"

"It is easy. They're empty. All the people have left. See, there are no lights in many of them. So, if we hit a wall, and nothing happens, it means no rebels are inside. If we hit it and men in camouflage run out the front and bodies fall out of the top, we know we got them."

Jerienda fired at the front wall of the ice cream shop. The wall looked like a bomb was detonated in it, glass and stone sprayed everywhere, but nothing else happened. Nobody ran out.

"Try it again."

Then he fired a second time and there was an explosion. "¡Dios mío! cried Jorge. "What did you do?"

"Hit a stove, I think. Maybe there is gas in this apartment." He shot again at the same area at an apartment in the next row. Another explosion. They both screamed with delight. "Look what we just did. Did you see that?"

"Go to the next building," said Jorge. "Hit another one."

CHAPTER FIFTY-SEVEN

SARA

Sara heard a flushing sound from the bathroom and that was good. "Tomas, don't forget to wash your hands when you are finished."

"I am doing it now, Mami, can you hear it?"

"Yes, that is good, and hurry. Dani wants in next." Actually, Dani was wanting in the bathroom very badly, and wanting to go in *now*, and as soon as Tomas had announced that he was washing up, he rushed in with him. Sara was in the kitchen filling two canvas bags with food they could eat in the basement. She wished that she hadn't dropped her bags at the market earlier, but she found enough other things—cheese, milk, bread—to tide them over if they had to stay.

"Hurry *niños*, we must go back down as soon as we can." She heard a second flushing noise. She put the two bags down on the floor for them to take to the basement and looked at the clock in the kitchen. It was nine o'clock. Normally the boys would be in bed by now. A momentary fear went through her about what they were going through and whether she would be able to keep her boys safe. But she pushed it aside and called out to them again. Then she heard another noise. It was a dull vibration noise, like a large motor, larger than a car. It came from down below in the parking lot in front of the apartments. She went to the window, pulled up the blinds, and looked out into the darkness. At first, she didn't see anything but when she looked off to the left, she saw a large black, metal object slowly moving down the rows. What is that? She wondered. What could it be? And then she saw a bright streak of light shooting from the object at something out of her sight to the left and she heard a tremendous explosion. "*¡Dios mío!*" She shrieked. "Boys, hurry. Hurry! We must go." At the explosion, all the apartments began to shake.

CHAPTER FIFTY-EIGHT
TANK

Jerienda steered the tank slowly down past each of the rows of Apartamentos Los Cañones, firing at one and then another, carefully aiming for the spot on the walls where he had found the gas lines in the first building. Jorge gleefully joined in, throwing grenades into the openings of the exploding walls, expanding the damage even further. Finally, they reached the last row at the very end of the complex. This one exploded also, but before he fired a second time at it, the apartment just above it exploded also. "*¡maravilloso!*" Fire burst out of the windows. The ground shook and the wall bent outward.

"Do it again," cried Jorge, "but fire higher up. See if you can make it explode an entire wall.

Jerienda slowly and carefully aimed the cannon higher and higher until it was pointing directly at the explosive gas line spot on the third floor.

"Wait," called down Jorge. "Let me come down first. This could be dangerous."

He closed the turret door and dropped down next to Jerienda in the cabin. "Okay, now do it."

Jerienda looked at him with excitement. "Are you ready?"

"Yes, very ready. Fire at it. The buildings are empty, so you won't hurt anything. If you kill anyone it will be communists hiding in the building."

CHAPTER FIFTY-NINE
DAVID AND SARA

David watched in horror as the huge tank made its way down the rows of apartments, destroying first one and then another as it moved closer and closer to the end, and to the apartment of Sara and the boys. Most of the windows were dark, but in the distance, he could see one apartment row with a light in a window. It was the last in the row on the fourth floor, and it was Sara's. In panic, he ran towards the tank. When he caught up with it, he screamed, "Stop, stop!" He banged with his fists on the proudly thick, mortar-proof walls, but nothing stopped it. They don't even know I'm here, he thought. When it reached the end, it stopped and turned its cannon to the first-floor wall. Fire came out of the cannon and the wall burst into flames. The explosion of bricks blew a wave of dust in his face, and for a moment he could barely see. The tank turned its cannon upward to the third floor.

He picked up two of the bricks that had fallen around them and began banging them on the slits in the walls of the tank. This time they heard him.

"Who is that?" Jerienda said.

"I don't know.

"Well, shoot him, he may be a terrorist."

"I don't have a gun. All I had were the grenades, and I left them up in the turret."

"Well, close the window and we will ignore him. If he doesn't have a gun, he can't stop us anyway."

Sara finished in the kitchen and took the bags into the living room near the front door. When the boys came out of the bathroom and were ready to go, she thought of something. "Wait here," she said and went back to the bedroom. On the nightstand, she had a photo that was taken of her and David one day when they visited the Cathedral. She put it in her jeans pocket and then went out to the boys standing by the front door in the living room. "Ready?" she asked.

Jerienda fired again, one last time at the last floor of the last building. High up at the special spot in the center of the wall, the one where the gas and power lines converged, and where a mother and her children had gathered food and toys and a photo, and were trying to make their way to the door. And with this final explosion, the entire five floors of wall roared and shook and burst into flames and then slowly crumbled forward, walls and floors and fire and people, covering the tank and the ground in bricks and ash and horror. And a young man standing next to it watched and screamed, and screamed, and screamed.

EPILOGUE

Welcome to San Salvador. The current time is eight twenty-three, and the temperature is eighty-seven degrees. You may now turn on your cellular devices. Please keep your seatbelt fastened until we arrive at the gate..." David was asleep. He heard very little of this. "... and the aircraft has come to a complete stop and the fasten seatbelt sign is off."

Something in him began to be roused at the words. It pulled him back to a state that was not quite awake but slightly more conscious.

"For passengers who will continue to another destination, please proceed to the transfer desk at the arrival terminal."

He pulled one eye open and looked slowly up. They had landed. They would be disembarking soon.

"Check the airline website or see an agent for information on connecting flights. Thank you for flying Avianca Airlines. We know that you have a choice in airlines, and we hope to see you again soon!" Then the voice changed to Spanish and repeated the announcement.

His companion sitting next to him was sleeping too. He nudged her arm gently, and she began to moan and look around. "I think we're here," he said.

"Oh no," she said, "I just finally got barely to sleep." She looked glum and a little annoyed, but David looked at her and smiled. Even asleep she looked nice.

"You slept for over an hour," he said, still smiling.

She gave him a groggy look and managed a weak smile. "Did I really? It must have been the scotches that you ordered for us back there."

"Ya think?" he laughed. "How are you feeling?"

She nodded an "okay." He stood up and opened the luggage bin over their heads. They were in the back of the plane with few people around them. They had matching Swiss Gear bags. His was navy blue. Hers was white. He pulled them both out of the bins and down to the floor. His in front, hers in back. And then they waited for the line to begin moving forward.

"I'm fine," she said. "I probably needed the sleep anyway, so I'm good." The line began to move, and they made their way toward the exit.

"Is someone meeting us here?" she asked. "Or do we need to get a taxi?"

"No, there'll be someone there from the university."

"Someone you know?"

"Possibly. I won't know too many people this time at the conference, so it may be just someone from the Institute that they hire to drive around the participants. Maybe a student."

An attractive young woman in uniform, and of unclear nationality, greeted them at the door. "Bye-bye," she said. "Have a nice evening." The two nodded appropriately and dragged their bags through the door, down the ramp, and across the tarmac to the gate. And then down a long corridor toward waiting areas, escalators, customs, passports, and finally the last gate before the exit, visitors on one side, residents on the other. The two of them stood with the visitors to purchase temporary tourist visas. Her line moved rapidly, and she passed through with little conflict. But somehow his line got hung up. The clerk's visa-processing machine was frozen and wouldn't take credit cards and he didn't have the money to change the fifty-dollar bill that David was offering him instead. David was anxious to get moving, but thought, oh well, these things happen.

Beyond the tables, a wall of glass and doors spanned the entire width of the corridor and looked out onto a walkway and a street lined with buses, vans, cars, and dozens of smiling faces looking excitedly for exiting travelers. David saw a round elderly man wearing a big smile, a dark business suit, and a bow tie standing in front of one of the cars holding a cardboard sign with the name "PATTERSON" hand-written on it. David laughed and pointed her toward him. "That's Héctor," he told her. He waved and smiled, and the man waved back. "Go on out and tell him I'm on my way. Give him your bag and he'll probably offer to give you a hug and a kiss."

She raised one eyebrow. "I think I'll just give him my bag." She walked toward the door. When she got to Héctor's car the two of them spoke for a moment and then he did in fact give her a hug, but no kiss. He put her Swiss Gear in the trunk and then the two of them stood talking together while waiting for David. The man at David's table was negotiating with someone at another table to find change. Two of the people behind him had grown restless at this delay and moved on to one of the other tables.

Three tables in front of David, another family was checking through and also having problems getting processed. Two teen girls were in front, followed by a woman of what appeared to be of grandmother age in back. She was small, with short, cropped hair and large brown eyes. And she looked familiar.

While she waited, she looked up at David and he looked at her, and for a long uncomfortable moment, they stared at one another. Finally, he glanced away, not wanting to look like a stalking stranger, but when he looked back, she had also turned to look at him again. He had been to El Salvador several times over the years, as the work of the Institute had grown in size and programs, and this woman looked familiar. Possibly someone he had met during some of the meetings at the Institute. But also, possibly, someone else, someone who lived in a far more distant place in his memory. Someone he might have encountered and loved and even been healed by, decades ago in a now ancient world, but who was now older, distinguished —and still beautiful?

He looked at the glass door and saw Héctor waving at him from outside. He was making a circling motion with his hand and pointing at the car. Evidently, the guards had told him to move, and he was going to "circle" around the airport to give David more time. David nodded that he understood.

One of the young teens with the woman across from him was anxious to get away. She was saying, in clear American English, "Nana, what's wrong? We need to go." The woman was tied up with some kind of delay like David's at her table. "I'm coming," she called back in clear, but accented, English. Then she looked at David again.

The two teens ran out through the glass doors and waved at a van waiting in the driveway in back of where Héctor's car had been. Soon after, the woman managed to free herself from whatever problem had held her up and began walking toward the doors to join them. But she stopped for a moment and turned back at David. She frowned, as though trying to recall something. David's agent was still at the nearby office arguing with a supervisor about the failed machine, so he started walking towards her. And in a slight moment of fear, he wondered if this was a woman he had once loved, or a stranger who would be surprised and angered if he greeted her. All he could say was "Hello."

"Hello," she said in return. Was it recognition or puzzlement? At first he couldn't tell. She took a breath as though about to speak but one of the teens outside the door knocked on the glass and called for her to come. She looked back at David, but now with a look of sadness. Without turning she spoke to the voice outside. "Tell them I will be right there." The girl ran back to the van with the message.

They stood silently for some time just looking at each other. He wanted to say something appropriate that would show recognition but without embarrassment if he was wrong. Finally, he said, "Do we know each other?"

She smiled, with a look that seemed slightly embarrassed. She lifted her hand to David's cheek and touched him. It was a warm touch with a scent that he recognized and remembered once loving. His whole body quivered. "Sara?" he asked.

She lowered her hand and spoke quietly, so quiet that he should not have been able to understand what she said, but he did. "David?" she said, "Are you David?"

He smiled and nodded. "It's good to see you."

She closed her eyes and took a deep breath. "I thought you had died."

"I was in the hospital for a few days," he said, "but I was fine."

"So were we. Perhaps the same?" She laughed at the unlikely possibility.

He looked down and realized that they were holding each other's hands. "I'm married now," he said.

She nodded. "And I."

"That's good. I'm happy for you." He paused for an awkward moment and then started, "Sara, I just want to say…" But then a hand hit the glass behind her. Several times. The two young teens were back, anxiously pleading with her to join them.

She reached up and took his head in her hands and gave him a brief kiss on his cheek. "Now perhaps we are friends again."

Days and lives and memories and tears swirled inside of him and pounded in his chest. "Sara," he said at last, "thank you." He took her hands again and held them close to his chest. "Just…thank you."

She nodded. "And you."

He let go of her hands and stepped back. "Now, you need to go. Your family is waiting for you."

Smiling and still looking at him, she backed through the door. The young girls outside quickly took hold of her and draped her arms around their shoulders like they were welcoming home a champion athlete. They got into the van at the curb. The door slid closed. The engine started, and they drove away.